CORA FOERSTNER

LEAGUE OF THE DARING
FINDING PEDRO

Sorrel Leaf Press Redmond, WA

League of the Daring: Finding Pedro

Copyright © 2020 by Cora Foerstner

Cover Design: Deranged Doctor Design at https://www.derangeddoctordesign.com/

Published by Sorrel Leaf Press, an imprint of Wood Sorrel Studios LLC: 7345 164th Ave NE Ste 145-1218, Redmond, WA 98052 info@woodsorrelstudios.com

Hardback ISBN: 978-1-949945-08-9

Paperback ISBN: 978-1-949945-03-4

eBook ISBN: 978-1-949945-04-1

Library of Congress Control Number: 2020922742

For everyone who loves adventures, alternate histories, and mysteries, and for Diane, who treasures stories as much as I do, and Rachel, who is awesome and makes everything happen.

CHAPTER 1: PEDRO

THE INVESTIGATION

July 18, 1890
11:35 p.m.

Pedro Hernandez hid in the alley about a hundred paces from the building he planned to search. Across the road, a gas streetlight cast an eerie circle, illuminating the wooden sidewalk. On the opposite wall, he placed a small mirror atop two nails and slanted it to reflect the building on his side of the street. Except for one light from a dirty window, the rest of the businesses were dark.

The night's graveyard silence gave him the jitters.

Taking his pocket watch out, he tilted it so he could see. Two hours. He'd been waiting two hours, and the man hadn't gone home. He had no way of knowing how much longer he'd have to wait. Perhaps he should leave? If his mother discovered he'd sneaked out, she would thrash his backside.

A few feet away, a brown rat weaved through the trash-littered alley. Stopping to examine and smell pieces of food and other unidentifiable discards, the rodent ignored Pedro, who scooted away from the rat and situated himself a little closer to the street.

From somewhere down the alley, a cat yowled. The echo sounded like a child screeching in terror. After several minutes, the noise stopped. A few seconds later, hissing and wailing filled the silence.

Someone yelled, "Shut up."

The clanging and clattering noises followed. The cat screamed in pain, and the night grew quiet again.

Pedro took a deep breath, and the stench of rotting garbage assaulted his senses. Pinching his nose, he groaned. This was his first experience of Los Angeles in the middle of the night. He hated it.

The only thing keeping him from rushing home was his determination to find out what was in the basement of this building. Something was hidden there. It could be nothing or goods being smuggled to Canada or something unknown. If he stayed and searched the place, he might discover who was running the smuggling ring. That was the best-case scenario. The worst-case he didn't want to think about.

The mirror reflected the only light within the area. The City Hall clock chimed twelve times, peaceful sounds echoing in the darkness like the musical equivalent of a town crier calling out, "All is well."

With a feeling of relief, he decided to give up his vigil, but he promised himself that he'd return with one of his friends. He stepped from the shadows and took two steps toward the street when the lights in the shop went off, plunging the walkway into shadows.

Springing back into the alley, he pressed his back against the wall and waited. He crossed himself and sent up a quick prayer.

He heard the office door open and close, followed by the clanking of keys. The mirror showed a man, his face hidden by the brim of his hat. He straightened and walked toward Pedro's hiding place.

Holding his breath, Pedro used the mirror to watch the man approach. The footfalls fell on the wooden planks, pounding out a steady beat like a warning. If he were discovered, he'd sprint down the alley. Slowly he pulled the navy blue hood from his pocket and slipped it over his head. Except for the two slits for eyes, his head was covered. He'd left his gloves with his bicycle, so he thrust his hands into his pockets.

The thud of footsteps grew closer.

If he had to, he'd run to New High Street where he'd hidden his bicycle. He'd ride so fast the wind couldn't catch him. If he were lucky, he'd get home without disturbing his mother.

An elongated shadow preceded the man and blended with the night. He walked past and strolled away. The seconds passed, and the sounds of his footsteps grew more distant and faded.

Pedro rested his head against the wall and looked up at the stars. After a few seconds, his heartbeats slowed and faded into a natural rhythm. Still he waited, making sure the man was gone. Several minutes later, he took off his hood and snatched the mirror off the wall.

In the distance, the whispering sound of turning gears moved closer. Staying in the shadows, he peered down the street. A horse-shaped automaton trotted down the center of the road, pulling a brown carriage. The Clydesdale-sized horse gleamed a bronze color in the diffused light of the streetlamp. The beast's mechanics hummed like a mother's lullaby. The driver hunched forward like a tired old man.

Pedro grinned and stepped closer to the street to watch the carriage vanish from sight. When it turned the corner, he sprinted down the walkway and fitted the skeleton key into the lock. He slipped inside. Waiting a few seconds for his eyes to adjust, he inched forward like a blind man.

The echo of footsteps sounded on the walkway.

He froze.

Someone fumbled with the key. The door opened. Light from the streetlamp fell across Pedro's face.

So much for stealth, he thought.

Fear pounded in his head and chest while his brain screamed *run*. But his feet were glued to the floor.

For the hundredth time, he wished he were home safe in bed like a good son.

CHAPTER 2: ALROY

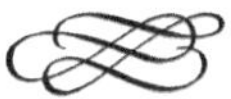

THE TIME MACHINE

July 19, 1890
8:00 a.m.

Balancing the china cup and saucer with both hands, Alroy Franklin Doyle made his way to the parlor. He watched the brown liquid and slowed when the tiny tea waves threatened to slosh over the cup's edge. At the doorway, he paused, took a breath, and exhaled. He forced a smile and stepped into the room.

Beth Anne Doyle sat in the armchair facing the window. With her hands folded on her lap, she appeared as delicate and lifeless as the lace curtains on the window. Her hair was swept up in a bun that puffed out, circling her face like a halo or a crown.

"I brought your tea, Mama," Alroy said.

She continued staring at the window, lost in her silent world.

He placed the teacup on the mahogany table next to her and sat in the other high-backed chair. Reaching out, he touched her hand and gave it a gentle squeeze. Despite the morning sunlight, shadows and gloom bathed the room. He hated the parlor with its faded memories and echoes of laughter and joy.

"It's your favorite cup with the little red birds. Look," he said, fingering the sleeve of her cotton day dress. "These red roses match the cup."

For a moment, Alroy thought she was going to turn her head and look. He thought he saw an ever-so-slight movement. A wild flutter danced in his chest. His heartbeats slowed when he realized she sat as still as a statue. Every day his hope tricked him into thinking she moved.

He knew she wasn't beautiful to the world, but to him she was lovely and kind. This person sitting before him was a mirage. His mother had deserted her body and left this shell behind. Right now, her mouth didn't curve up or down. He remembered her smile, how she filled every room with her laughter. He wondered how her vibrancy could vanish. How could someone so full of life grow quiet and still?

Like Papa she was dead, except she wasn't buried in the ground. Mama and Papa, it was his fault.

"The other day, Doc said I was tall for a fifteen-year-old. Maybe I'll be tall like Papa." He didn't say like Wyatt, his half-brother, who was taller than his father.

The word *papa* always made his stomach tighten. He didn't like saying it, but he tried to work it into his one-way conversations with her.

"I'm off to Doctor Grimes' workshop. Zella says she can't come." He shrugged. "It's okay. Pedro will be there, and Toby's coming over this afternoon."

He leaned closer.

"I'll tell you a secret. Doc is testing his time machine this morning. I've crossed my fingers."

Holding his crossed fingers up, he grinned.

He watched her face. Even a slight flinch or an almost nod

would make him happy. Zella said he was a fool for trying, but he had to try. He'd never give up. Someday something would wake her up.

"If Papa were here, he'd go with me to see the time machine."

When he said *papa*, her eyes moved in his direction. A thin film of liquid covered her eyes.

Alroy jumped up and stood in front of her.

"I miss him, too. Mama. Mama."

The words came too late. She stared past him. In an instant, the life vanished from her eyes.

He took her face in his hands and didn't care if everyone thought he was crazy. A promise was a promise, and he'd promised himself he'd bring her back, even if it took the rest of his life.

"I wish you'd drink your tea while it's still hot."

He said this every morning, even though he knew that Liza would come in when he left and somehow get her to drink her tea and take a few bites of her biscuit.

Sighing, he kissed her forehead and walked out of the room. She'd definitely moved her eyes and looked at him. The look only lasted a moment, but for the first time, something happened. That was good. He smiled.

* * *

Once he was outside, the morning sun invigorated him. Before getting on his bicycle, he rolled his brown jacket like a blanket and tied it to the handlebars. He headed toward downtown Los Angeles, riding as if a demon were chasing him away from his tranquil neighborhood. The swish of his bicycle was the only noise on this lazy summer morning. The more distance he put between himself and his home the more alive and free he felt.

A few minutes later, he turned onto Spring Street, slowed,

and mingled with morning traffic. Trolley 36 rolled toward him, clanging its bell to warn traffic out of its path. He cut across the street and skirted around a horse-drawn delivery wagon. He pedaled a little faster, glancing back to make sure the trolley wasn't too close.

Downtown bustled with life and energy that made him feel alive. He relished the warm air tousling his unruly red hair. As his white shirt billowed out around his red suspenders, he imagined he could become a balloon and float into the sky.

A copy of H. G. Wells' *The Time Machine* peeked out of his back pocket. His bicycle wheels kicked up dust and left a cloudy trail behind him. In the distance, the church clock chimed the half hour.

Doc's time machine experiment pushed all other thoughts from his mind. Today, he and Pedro would help Doctor Grimes test his redesigned time machine. Last week, he'd told them the new design was superior in every way to the old version. Alroy hoped today was the day the machine worked.

Ahead, a delivery wagon slowed. He darted around it but misjudged the distance and cut too close. The horse neighed and reared up. Alroy pumped his pedals harder, shooting away from the danger. He glanced over his shoulder.

The driver stood, pulling up on the reins as people scurried out of the way.

"Whoa, girl. Whoa, girl."

Alroy kept riding.

Behind him, a man shouted.

"I know that's you, Alroy Doyle. Your brother will hear about this."

Without looking back, he waved. He didn't care if everyone in Los Angeles told his half-brother. He didn't give a fig for Wyatt's good or bad opinion of him.

He arrived at Doc's street hot and sweaty. The only traffic on the quiet street was an ancient buggy pulled by an old-fashioned automaton horse, and he rode beside the machine long enough to get a closer look. It was Benson's old-fashioned design. Old man Benson had died four years ago. He'd been good in his day, but his automatons were dated and quaint. They didn't trot smoothly, and their gears clanked.

When Alroy reached his destination, he pulled up on his handlebars and jumped onto the walkway. A few feet from the door, he hopped off and leaned his bicycle against the brick wall.

Old Elijah stood a few feet away, mumbling to himself and scratching his head. Alroy felt sorry for the man. He didn't have a family and drank too much. Elijah glanced at him.

"I think I'm lost."

"Where you going?" Alroy asked.

"Jake's Cafe. I think. Mr. Lee gave me some money for sweeping his sidewalk."

"Go back to the corner," Alroy said, pointing back down the street. "Take a right. It's three blocks that way."

"Thank you." He stepped closer to Alroy and whispered, "This is a bad neighborhood. You shouldn't be here. Be careful."

Alroy grinned.

"Thanks for the advice, Mr. Elijah. I'll be careful."

The old man shuffled away.

Alroy dusted off his brown pants and white cotton shirt. Doc liked his protégés to dress properly. He slipped into his jacket. For his finishing touch, he ran his fingers through his auburn hair, brushing it back. He rushed inside. His shoulder bumped Doc's black ulster coat, knocking it off its hook.

His friend sat at his desk and glanced up from his writing. He pushed his glasses up, making his bushy eyebrows fan out above the frames. The large mahogany desk where he sat was the only nice piece of furniture in the place. Everything else was utilitarian and rough-hewn.

Doc was the greatest man Alroy knew. The best thing about

him was his facial hair. His magnificent sandy-blond mustache grew down past his mouth, but it didn't come to a point like the men who waxed their mustaches. Someday he'd have a mustache exactly like Doc's.

Alroy scooped up the long black coat and hung it on the second hook rather than the first. However, as soon as he dropped the ulster into place, it brushed against the table, sending pamphlets, papers, and books flying onto the plank floor. He stooped to pick up the mess.

"That's why I use the first hook," Doc said, chuckling softly.

A copy of *The Time Machine* lay amid the papers. Alroy reached back to check his pocket. His copy was still there.

While gathering up the fallen items, he asked, "You reading *The Time Machine?*"

"Of course not. I'll leave that fantasy and philosophy to Wells and you boys."

"Zella and Lavinia, too." Alroy stacked everything neatly on the rustic table. "We're all reading it."

"Suitable reading material for girls and philosophers, not future scientists."

Alroy picked up a pamphlet titled *Eugenics for a Better Future.*

"Eu . . . gen . . .ics? What's that?"

"Are you here for a lecture or an experiment?"

"Experiment. Can I take this?" Alroy asked, stuffing the pamphlet in his back pocket.

"Of course." Doc closed his leather notebook, stood, and straightened his waistcoat.

"Toby can't come. He's taking his parents to the air station." Alroy glanced around. "Where's Pedro?"

"Umm." Doc furrowed his brow.

"He's supposed to be here," Alroy said.

Doc moved to his desk and looked at his calendar.

"He was here yesterday to sweep." He glanced around the room and nodded as if satisfied with Pedro's work.

"Where do you think he is?" Alroy asked.

"Don't know. His mother's ill. Perhaps he's home with her."

"Well, he should have informed you." His words sounded like Wyatt, and he never wanted to sound like his brother, so he clamped his mouth shut.

"He's responsible." Doc shook his head. "It's a pity he's missing the experiment. Maybe he's just late."

"Sure," Alroy said. "Sometimes he does lose track of time."

Doc pressed his lips together the way he did when he was thinking about something.

Alroy hoped he wasn't going to postpone the experiment.

"Don't look so glum. Since the others aren't here, I wanted to give you something." He opened the top drawer of his desk. "I'm not good at sentimental exchanges."

Alroy suppressed a grin. Doc wasn't very good at anything that had to do with social exchanges among people.

His friend held out an envelope and cleared his throat.

"Umm, your father sent me this." He looked at the floor. "Before his unfortunate, umm, his demise. Well, I thought you might value it. You don't need to read it now. Private is good. You may keep it."

Alroy took the envelope and stared at it. His father's distinct handwriting addressed the letter to Doctor Finch Grimes. He stared a little longer than he should have, but he couldn't help it. His throat had suddenly gone dry. Holding the letter was like squeezing the head of a rattlesnake so it wouldn't strike and bite. The problem was how to let go.

"Thanks, Doc."

He placed the letter between the pages of *The Time Machine* and shoved it back into his pocket.

Doc looked relieved and waved Alroy over to the long wooden table against the south wall. He wasn't a medical doctor but a scientist from Chicago, which to Alroy sounded as foreign and as exotic as Cairo or Peking.

Today was the day. They had tested the time machine before, but today Alroy felt sure the test would work. Of course, there was always the possibility of another bloody experiment.

CHAPTER 3: ALROY

THE EXPERIMENT

July 19, 1890
8:45 a.m.

Alroy glanced around Doc's office, which was more like a huge workshop than an office. He walked around the room, looking at things he'd already studied. He was waiting for Doc to prepare everything. Near the table where Pedro had his latest experiment, he caught a whiff of a rank smell.

"Something stinks in here," he said.

"What?"

"Bad smell," Alroy said and pinched his nose.

Doc smiled. "Dead rat. I found it this morning and threw it out. The smell will fade."

Alroy guessed dead rats were part of having a scientific laboratory. He preferred the rustic place to a real office because Doc had hundreds of gadgets, machines, and plenty of room to experiment. Sketches, charts, and designs hung on the otherwise bare walls. When Doc finished a project, he'd pull down the designs, roll them up, and store them in a large cabinet on the other side of the room. He encouraged Alroy and his friends to bring in their plans and ideas to his shop, and if they were having problems, he helped them find solutions. Doc made him feel important.

The girls in The League of the Daring didn't come often. They didn't like Doc because he thought girls and women should be at home engaged in appropriate girl occupations. Zella and Lavinia were suffragettes and had strong opinions about women's rights and men who oppressed women. Sometimes Alroy thought Zella might punch Doc for some of the things he said. So far she hadn't resorted to violence.

One nice thing about Doc's place was no one tried to make things look pretty. Doc smoked his pipe and laid it about wherever he wanted. He dressed however he wanted, did whatever he wanted, and smoked whenever and wherever he wanted. Doc had the kind of life Alroy admired—no rules, no one telling him what to do, or what to wear, or when to clean up. Freedom and life without rules would be perfect.

Of course, sometimes Alroy got bored because Doc sat at his desk lost in his thoughts and making notes. He didn't have time for chitchat. Alroy thought being ignored felt as if the other person wasn't in the room, and he was an in-the-room kind of person. Today, Doc would be in the room, explaining the experiment and making observations. He wished Toby and Pedro were here. Toby would entertain him when Doc grew quiet or wrote in his journal, and Pedro would explain the things he didn't understand.

Finally, the scientist strolled to the table in the center of the room. A large gray blanket draped the time machine, which sat in the middle of the table. Alroy was curious about the new design and tried to imagine what might be under the blanket.

He bounced up and down on his toes. He looked from Doc to the covered time machine.

Come on. Why are we waiting?

"Maybe today it'll work," he offered.

Doc rubbed his hands together and grinned.

"I'm hopeful."

He nodded to Alroy and grabbed the blanket. With the dramatic flair of a magician, Doc pulled the blanket off and watched Alroy's face.

"Corker," Alroy said, grinning at Doc.

The machine on the table was bigger and better than any of the past prototypes.

"Corker, indeed. Almost full size," Doc said, reaching out and touching the smooth brass tubes.

A leather seat, big enough for a toddler, looked like a miniature chair. It was bolted to the center of the machine and only needed wheels to make it look like a carriage. Two long leather belts hung on either side of the seat.

"What are the belts for?"

"Good question. Since I'm close to the final version, I thought I should protect the time traveler from falling off the machine. A safety precaution." Doc's eyes twinkled.

"So the traveler doesn't get bumped off at the wrong time."

Doc pushed his glasses up.

"Exactly. If he gets dislodged and the machine goes on, the poor fellow would be stuck forever in the wrong era, and the machine would come back empty."

"So time is linear?"

"Yes, I believe it is."

"When you time travel, you'll leave this time and be deposited in this exact spot in another time," Alroy said.

"Yes. And I believe a traveler could go backward and forward in time. But that's a discussion for another day."

Doc sounded pleased, and Alroy felt rather proud of himself. For a brief moment, he thought of telling Doc that the time traveler in H. G. Wells' book also believed time was linear. But he decided he didn't want to take the chance of changing Doc's mood. He smiled instead.

Alroy inspected the machine. In the back, enough gears and cogs to motorize ten automatons waited to be turned on. In front of the seat, three large gauges stood out because of their size and shape. The center gauge appeared to be four concentric timepieces. The two on either side were also concentric circles with symbols Alroy didn't recognize. Below those, bronze settings held three large stones in place. They gleamed in the sunlight coming through the window.

The gems fascinated Alroy. He reached out and ran his fingers over each one. They felt cool and smooth. If he didn't know better, he'd think the center one was a diamond. The two others looked like a ruby and a sapphire. Alroy didn't think Doc was a wealthy man and wondered how he could afford real gems.

"Have you tested it?"

Doc shook his head. "I was waiting for you boys. But, alas, I can't wait another day. My anticipation has reached its limits." He rubbed his hands together and grinned. "We will proceed without Toby and Pedro. Bring a rat over."

Alroy hurried across the room, making his way around three other worktables that sat parallel to each other. Near the back door, Doc kept the rats in birdcages. Today four cages with gray rats lined the worktable. Alroy studied each rat. The one at the far end scurried up to the wooden bars and wiggled his nose. He chose that rat.

"This one," he said.

Doc took the rat and pointed to the end of the table.

"Goggles."

Alroy grabbed a pair and slipped them on while Doc used binder twine to tie the rat cage to the seat and buckled the leather straps across the rat's enclosure. Once it was secure, he turned the middle gauge.

"I've devised a new system," he said. "The one in the center sets the month, day, year, as well as hours and minutes."

Doc got a far-away thoughtful look as if he could see into the future.

"It would take considerable time for a full explanation. Let's just say the other gauges make it possible to bring the machine back at a specific time. The gems stabilize the machine. I tested a smaller version earlier. This design is definitely superior. I'm setting it to leave now and return in . . ." Doc glanced at Alroy. "Eighteen minutes?"

Alroy nodded.

Doc set the gauges and then plunged into a lecture about the new design, the formulas, and the science. He pointed to various aspects of the drawings hanging on the wall beside his desk. Since Alroy didn't have an interest in details, he only half listened and smiled a lot.

When he finished, Doc put on his goggles.

"Do you want to do the honors?"

"How do I start it?" Alroy asked, trying not to sound too eager.

"I designed what I call a starter-switch system." Doc pointed to the two switches on the side of the chair. "I've already wound up both mechanisms." He indicated the two small cranks on the right side of the machine. "One will take the machine forward in time, and the other will bring it back. Mr. Rat will go forward one year, and then immediately return to this time in eighteen minutes."

Doc chuckled and slapped Alroy on the back.

"Imagine, if we are here in this room in one year, a machine with the rat in it will appear and then vanish."

"Corker. Let's do it. Let's be here in a year," Alroy said. "What about when you use the machine? Will it go forward and come right back?"

"No, I'll crank the machine up when I'm ready to return. Now, flip the switch nearest the back of the seat first. Once you hear the gears turn, count to five and flip the switch in the front."

Alroy leaned over and flipped the switch. He waited. After several seconds, the gears moved and turned. He counted aloud. When he reached five, he flipped the other switch.

"Remove your hand. Quickly," Doc said.

Alroy pulled his arm back. Like dammed up water being released, all the gears moved faster. They clanked as they turned, the machine shook, and a high-pitched whining filled the room.

Doc grabbed the collar of Alroy's jacket and pulled him back.

"Safety, young man."

The floor vibrated. The shaking pulsed through Alroy's body. An odd sensation settled over him. He watched the scene and the time machine as an observer rather than a participant. He felt almost as if time caught him up and separated him from the present moment.

If someone asked him, he'd never be able to explain what happened, but something strange and slightly off-kilter seemed to yank him out of reality. Time slowed. Something seized his wrist for about five seconds. Then the pressure loosened. Almost immediately, he felt as if a firm hand gripped his other wrist and let go.

The sensations were so startling that he glanced around and saw Doc standing next to him with his mouth opened as if about to speak, but he didn't move or say anything. The experience felt as if Alroy were inside a photograph that captured a moment in time, but he lived and moved.

He wasn't sure how much time passed, but when the sensation vanished, he was back in the room and everything seemed normal. The experience made him nauseous. He stood still, waiting for the feeling to pass.

Beside him, Doc held his pocket watch and stared first at the time machine and then at his watch.

Whatever happened to him, it didn't appear to affect Doc.

The clicking of gears grew louder. The time machine shook violently. The rat squealed and raced around the cage. The diamond lit up, then the ruby, and finally the sapphire. The light in the gems pulsed. The time gauge remained stationary, but the circles on the other two devices swung in one direction and then the other, turning as if an invisible hand moved them. The screeching sound grew louder.

Alroy and Doc covered their ears.

The light emanating from the gems mixed into one mass of bright white. The light pulsed faster and faster. The machine became translucent. It pulsed and vanished. At the next pulse, it reappeared. The appearing and disappearing continued for about ten seconds. The time machine vanished. Silence replaced the machine's clamor.

It happened so quickly Alroy blinked to make sure he wasn't seeing things. Then he jumped into the air and whooped.

"Leaping lizards. That was corker."

Doc rocked back and forth on his heels and grinned. It was the happiest Alroy had ever seen him.

"How long until it comes back?"

Doc glanced at his pocket watch and said, "Sixteen minutes and twenty-three seconds. Now, young man, occupy yourself while I make notes."

Sitting at his desk, Doc wrote furiously while Alroy alternated between pacing and going back to the table. He leaned over the worktable and swiped his arm where the time machine had been. He ran his hand across the pitted boards of the table.

Alroy wanted to run outside and shout to anyone who would listen. Instead, he moved to the table nearest the window. Alroy and Toby were working on an automaton doll that could play the piano. It was a surprise for Zella. Pedro had helped them with the design. He and Toby were collecting and making the gears and other parts they needed. At some point, they would need Pedro's help to finish it.

He looked through the gears and the list of parts they needed, but he couldn't concentrate. All he could think about was the time machine and the strange experience he'd had. Somehow he felt changed. If Toby were here, he'd say time altered him. Of course, Toby had about a bazillion crazy ideas every day and nearly all of them were figments of his imagination.

"Well, what do you think about the experiment?" Doc finally asked.

"The best one yet." He grinned at Doc and leaned against the table. Doc's glasses had slipped down his nose again. "If this works, will you travel all through time? Past and future? And go everywhere?"

The older man shook his head.

"I just want to go into the future and bring back technology. Something amazing. I'll make a name for myself."

"You know what I'd do?" Alroy asked. "I'd travel everywhere. Be a time explorer. I'd go back and see dinosaurs, Egyptian pyramids, the Aztecs. Grace Camero told me about the pyramids. I'd see King Arthur and . . ." Alroy made a sweeping gesture with his arms. "Everything. I'd see everything."

In that moment, all his imaginings seemed possible.

"My dear boy, I don't think you have a scientist's heart. You have an adventurer's heart."

"Can't I be both?"

"I fear you would be divided," Doc said. "Some people think you can do both, but I say at a cost. A true scientist commits his entire life to science."

"What about Darwin? He had adventures."

Doc gazed behind Alroy for a moment and his lips twitched upward.

"I see your meaning. However, you talk about seeing things.

Darwin studied nature, to learn how it works. Science for knowledge, not thrills." Doc chuckled. "But scientists do find adventures. Yes, indeed."

Alroy moved to the desk and sat on the edge.

"Grace has seen everything. She's traveled almost everywhere, and she's a scientist."

Doc wrinkled his brow. He didn't like Grace, and she didn't care for Doc. Pedro thought they disliked each other because they were rivals, but Toby guessed they disagreed on the morality of scientific investigation.

Alroy leaned forward.

"This afternoon, I'm going for a ride in her airship. She's built a family-sized dirigible."

"You're a busy lad." Doc glanced at his watch and stood. "But you prove my point. Miss Camero is an inventor, not a scientist. She is a woman. One can't expect . . ." He glanced at his watch. "Come. Put your goggles back on. It's time. Let's find out if it worked."

As Alroy slipped his goggles over his eyes, he made a wish. He crossed his fingers and hoped the rat wouldn't come back a bloody mess like the last one.

CHAPTER 4: ALROY

FAILURE OR SUCCESS?

July 19, 1890
9:00 a.m.

Alroy sent up a silent prayer that the machine would return, but he quickly added a postscript. If it's as bad as last time, don't let it come back.

Beside him, Doc held his pocket watch and glanced from his timepiece to the table.

Outside a dog barked, and a wagon rumbled past. Inside the workroom, neither spoke. Seconds sped away one after the other. Then a humming sound filled the quiet. A low, distant vibration surrounded them.

The muscles in Alroy's back tensed. He cocked his head, listening.

Like a far-off train whistle, the noise grew louder. The volume increased to a pulsing rhythm.

Loud. Soft.

Loud. Soft.

Loud. Soft.

A high-pitched screech shook the room. The bottles and

supplies on the shelves vibrated and clanked as if a steam passenger train chugged right into the room.

Doc pressed his lips together. Alroy divided his attention between watching the scientist and staring at the table.

The whine increased until the man and the boy covered their ears. The outline of the machine, a translucent phantom, appeared. On the next pulse, it vanished.

Another pulse, it appeared.

Another pulse, it was gone.

With each appearance, the device looked more solid. Abruptly the noise stopped. In the next instant, the time machine sat on the table, solid, still, and whole.

Doc glanced at his watch. "Eighteen minutes on the nose."

"Corker."

Alroy's stomach tightened as he stepped closer. His glance went to the rat.

He'd watched similar experiments, six to be exact. The first two machines exploded. The next two had vanished but didn't return. The fourth had returned, but the rat was dead, body parts and blood coated its cage. In the last experiment, rat bones covered in blood were all that remained. When Alroy saw that rat's skeleton, his stomach turned sour, and even Toby grimaced and looked away. The question of what had happened to the rats gave Alroy nightmares.

Alroy exhaled and sighed. The rat lay in its cage, still and lifeless but intact.

"Sorry, Doc. But it's got its body. That's good."

His friend shook his head. "And the machine appears unharmed." Doc sounded relieved. "That's progress."

They stepped closer.

The rat's body jerked.

Alroy jumped back.

The rat convulsed for several seconds then lay limp and still. But the rat breathed. Its little chest moved up and down. After a bit, it opened its eyes. Alroy bent down to study the rodent. The little black eyes seemed to look right at him. Finally, it stretched, got to its feet, wobbled, and sank back down. After several tries, it stood. Stepping forward, it swayed and stumbled forward a few more inches. It plopped down and got back up. Staggering forward, it sniffed the air.

"Doc, you did it."

Doc studied the rat as it moved about the birdcage. It stopped for an instant to look up toward them. Alroy rushed to the rat table and grabbed some feed and a small cup of water. Back at the time machine, he poured water into the rat's bowl and dropped the pellets in the cage. The rat went for the food. Sitting on its back legs, it ate with gusto. Then it went to the water.

The experiment worked, and the rat lived. Alroy grinned. Unable to contain his enthusiasm, he whooped again.

Even his shouting didn't budge Doc, who hadn't moved since the rat stood up. The scientist could have been a statue, frozen in time, a life-like automaton.

"It's corker," Alroy shouted.

He nudged his friend and glanced at the rat to confirm time hadn't stopped. The rat scurried around the cage, nibbled his food, and raced around again.

"Doc," Alroy said, nudging him.

As if in a daze, Doc shook his head and staggered to a nearby stool. He took a handkerchief from his trouser pocket, mopped his forehead, and pushed his glasses up.

"I did it," he whispered. "I did it. This will show him."

"Who? Show who?" Alroy asked.

Doc jumped up and grabbed Alroy's hand and pumped vigorously. Then he moved closer to the time machine and examined the rat. He ran his hand through his sandy-blond hair and grinned at Alroy.

At that moment, he seemed young. Doc was about his half-brother's age, but because his speech was formal and his only topic science, he always seemed older, like a distant father.

"Not a word of this to anyone." Doc shook his finger at Alroy. "You understand? Not a word to Pedro, or Toby, or Zella, or Lavinia."

Alroy nodded.

"I need a verbal confirmation. This is important. I don't want anyone stealing my work. You vow to keep this secret?"

"Can't we tell Pedro and Toby? They will keep it secret. They should have been here."

"Absolutely not. This is your vow. When it's time, we'll tell them, agreed?"

It didn't seem fair. His friends would have been here. They were part of all the other experiments, and they should know.

"I see your hesitation, but look at this from my point of view. As a scientist, this is my life's work. We have to keep it secret until we perfect the process. Many people would steal from me, take credit for my work. Bring Pedro and Toby back, and we'll do another experiment. I'll make the same contract with them. Not the girls. They've taken no interest in this. There are more experiments and tests to do. This is just the beginning. We have to know the process is safe. You understand?"

Everything Doc said made sense. Alroy would get Toby and Pedro here as soon as he could. He was terrible at keeping secrets.

"Doc, what about Zella?"

"What about her?"

"I tell her everything. She's my twin. She's like part of me."

"Young man, when we are certain, we'll announce it to the world. Before we make the announcement, we'll tell Zella and Lavinia. They'll understand. The League of the Daring will know first. Besides, I'm sure there are things Zella doesn't tell you."

Alroy doubted very much that his twin would understand or that she had her own secrets.

"Yes," he said. "I agree."

While Doc made notes in his journal, Alroy examined the machine. In the quiet workshop, he thought about the touch he'd felt. Now it seemed silly to think that some invisible person touched him. He decided the sensation had been a result of static electricity.

Dismissing the experience, he allowed his imagination to race through future possibilities. Would Doc let him travel through time? How long would it take before they'd test the time machine again? Where could they go?

More than anything, he wanted to find his friends and tell them about the experiment. Only he couldn't because he'd promised. There was one positive—he knew about Doc's success before anyone else. Once they found out, Toby and Pedro would be jealous.

"What's the rat doing?" Doc asked. "Describe its behavior."

Alroy leaned closer.

"He's moving. He finished the food. He's sniffing around the edge of the birdcage. He still seems a little drunk, staggers a little but not like when he first stood up. Other than being off-balance, I don't see anything out of the ordinary."

"Good. But I'll have to watch him over the next few days."

Doc finished scribbling his notes. He chuckled and rubbed his hands together.

"I have some elderberry wine set aside. Do you think your mother would permit a small toast to our victory?"

Alroy didn't hesitate.

"I'm sure she wouldn't mind."

From the shelf behind his desk, Doc grabbed two speckled tin cups. He poured a little wine in each.

Giving one cup to Alroy and lifting the other in the air, he said, "To science and its advancement."

The cups touched, making a hollow tinny sound. They drank.

The wine wasn't as good as the elderberry wine his mother made for Christmas, but he didn't care. He was part of scientific history. He had flipped the switch that sent the time machine into the future, and the rat came back alive. Little shivers raced throughout his body.

"Doc, how do you know time travel is linear?"

"Um, well . . . since there's not much research in this area, it's an educated guess. Most scientists dismiss time travel as impossible. Why do you ask?"

"Because of one of Toby's books. You know he writes penny dreadfuls."

His friend frowned but nodded for him to continue.

"The scientists in one of his books speculated about time and space being factors in time travel. If space could be bent, you could travel to a different place as well as a different time."

"Toby came up with this idea?"

Alroy nodded.

"It's an interesting theory. Does he say how space could bend?"

"No, but he wants to talk to Grace Camero about it." Alroy wasn't about to tell him that Toby thought Grace was a time traveler because that was one of his craziest ideas.

"Miss Camero." The man shrugged, and a sour expression replaced his cheerful countenance. "He'd be better off discussing this with me."

"I'll tell him that," Alroy said, wanting to be diplomatic, but he couldn't contain his curiosity. "Doc, why don't you and Grace Camero get along? It seems like you should be good friends."

Taking another sip of wine, Doc pressed his lips together and puckered them.

"I admire Miss Camero, but we disagree about the basic precept of science."

"What exactly?"

He wanted to know Doc's position. Mostly he wanted an opinion of his own, and he didn't have one yet.

"Well, Miss Camero believes that science and progress should be examined from a moral stance with an eye to future consequences. I believe science and discoveries should be pursued and developed without regard to moral or future consequences. Scientists discover how the world works. We don't make judgments about its workings."

"Give me an example."

"Well, let's consider something I have little interest in . . . the combustion engine. You know the basic principle, right?"

Alroy nodded and wondered if he'd asked the wrong question. He hoped this wasn't going to turn into a boring lecture.

"The technology has been around since last century, but lately inventors have made startling progress. The discovery of more crude oil expands the possibilities for the combustion engine. Some claim this engine could replace steam. I say that's all well and good. Science should move forward as should progress and exploration. To me, the combustion engine is nothing more than a scientific discovery, which might improve commerce and improve living conditions."

Doc emptied his glass of wine and took up his pipe. He struck a match on the corner of his desk and touched it to the tobacco. When it flamed, he took several drags and exhaled. He tossed the expired match on the floor and continued his lecture.

"I've heard Miss Camero caution people in a very public and vulgar way for a woman. She says this engine could bring about pollution, which in turn could contaminate air and water and create unhealthy conditions."

"I'm sure she's not against progress or new and better technology," Alroy said.

He didn't like the idea of saying negative things about Grace, who was also his friend.

"You're right, but she worries about the morality and possibility of harm. She insists science should consider what future problems technology might cause. In this example, she claims we shouldn't embrace the combustion engine, but we should find other options that don't have the same potential for harm."

Alroy squirmed on his stool. He really wanted to have an opinion, but he didn't have one. He saw Doc's point and Grace's, which only made drawing a conclusion more difficult.

"Her point sounds good to me," he said.

"Yes, if you care about such things. But morality or future consequences shouldn't influence a scientist. He should be concerned with discovery and knowledge. Others can sort the morality out. Let people like Miss Camero worry about the use of scientific discoveries. Some people might object to using rats to test the time machine."

Alroy laughed.

"What could be wrong in using rats?"

"An argument could be that using rats harms the rats and is inhumane. Also, such practices might lead to using cats or dogs or even humans, which would indeed be inhumane."

"Well, that's a whole different matter. We couldn't use humans for experiments."

"Indeed," Doc said and puffed on his pipe.

"But when you perfect the machine for the rats, how will you know if it works on humans?"

Doc grinned.

"At that point, I will test the machine myself."

Alroy leaned forward and whistled.

"That's corker. Brave. Yeah, it's brave."

Doc nodded. "Indeed."

Alroy realized it was getting late, and he had another adventure to pursue. He finished the elderberry wine and set his cup on Doc's desk. Looking at the desktop, he noticed an envelope addressed to Doc from Sara Hernandez.

"This is from Pedro's mother," he said, pointing to the letter. "Maybe you should open it?"

"Oh, I forgot about this," Doc said. "A young girl brought it in just before you arrived."

He opened the message, furrowed his brow, and looked up at Alroy.

"It says Pedro left home last night and hasn't returned. Have you seen him?"

Alroy shook his head.

"This doesn't sound good." Doc frowned. "It's probably a silly prank. You boys and your jokes." He glanced at the note again.

Alroy wanted to tell Doc that Pedro didn't do pranks. Pulling pranks was Toby's style, but even Toby wouldn't stay out all night.

"Do me a favor and check on Pedro. Let me know what you find out," Doc said.

"Sure. It's probably a mistake. I bet Pedro got an early start. He has about four odd jobs. He'll be at Grace's for the airship ride. I'll tell him to stop by and talk to you. You can tell him about the experiment."

"You're probably right," Doc said, as he slipped the note back into the envelope.

As Alroy left Doc's workshop, his thoughts turned to his father's letter safely tucked into the book in his back pocket. He gripped his handlebars so tight his knuckles turned white, and his nails dug into the soft skin of his palms. He tried to reignite his excitement over the time machine but failed. He needed to read his father's letter, but he was hesitant.

What if the letter made him cry? He missed his father so much almost anything made him cry. What if there wasn't anything important in the letter? Would Doc give him a letter that wasn't important? What if the letter was really important?

CHAPTER 5: ALROY

THE LETTER

July 19, 1890
10:15 a.m.

Alroy rode his bicycle to the Plaza, where he found an empty bench under the shade of a palo verde tree. For many years, the Plaza, the church, and the old government buildings were the center of all activity. Los Angeles grew and expanded from this one spot, and the center of activity shifted to downtown.

But this was one of Alroy's favorite spots. A wide sidewalk outlined the perimeter. The well-placed benches provided comfort and privacy, which he needed right now. On his left, two older gentlemen conversed and laughed. On his right, a woman watched two boys play.

Alroy held his father's letter in his hand and stared at the writing. He dug his white handkerchief out of his pocket before he opened the envelope and carefully unfolded the pages. There were no flourished lines. His father's penmanship was simple and easy to read, but Alroy's eyes didn't focus. The letters ran together. Without warning the memory of his father, dressed in his best suit, lying in a coffin, popped into his mind. Gone were his father's warmth and enthusiasm for life. His face looked pasty and stiff.

People kept saying, "He looks so peaceful."

But he didn't. He lay there with a blank, annoyed face as if he weren't ready to leave and wanted to pick a fight with someone.

Alroy closed his eyes. He took several deep breaths.

"I'm sorry, Papa. I'm sorry," he whispered.

He'd killed his father. He hadn't meant to, but he had. They'd argued. It was the first time he'd seen his father so angry. They'd both yelled.

"Why are you being so mean?" Alroy shouted. "Why?"

Then he watched his father grab his chest. Choking and making gurgling sounds, he reached toward his son. Alroy froze and watched his father's face turn white and grayish. He was so scared he couldn't move. Now all he could think of was that he should have rushed to his father. His outstretched hands begged Alroy to help him.

He stared like a fool as he watched his papa crumple to the carpet in the parlor. Then he shouted for help, but it was too late.

His mother ran into the room, fell to her knees, and cradled his father. She rocked him back and forth.

"No, no. Don't leave me," she pleaded.

When she looked up at Alroy, her eyes stared, unfocused and far away. He didn't tell her what had happened. He tucked the secret far back in his mind.

Until the funeral, his mother talked and moved and did things, but part of her had already left. Her blank eyes looked but didn't see. At the wake, Doctor Stone took him aside and told him his father had a heart attack.

"His heart was bad. He'd known for a while." Doctor Stone touched his shoulder and looked him in the eye. "It wasn't your fault, Alroy. It wasn't your fault."

It didn't matter how many times Doctor Stone repeated those words. Alroy knew it was his fault. If he'd been a better son, it wouldn't have happened.

They had argued about Wyatt, his stupid half-brother, who left as soon as the funeral was over and disappeared for four months. He left right when they needed him most. Then, one day, he just walked into the house and took over as if he could replace their father. He deserted them when his mother needed someone. When Alroy thought about it, he felt like punching Wyatt in his skinny nose.

He opened the letter and read.

Dear Finch,

I cannot fully express my gratitude and thanks to you. You have taken Alroy, Zella, and their friends under your wings. Your tutelage has been good for them.

My friend, I am proud of you. I'm sure you find teaching high school students challenging. I know you wanted to teach at the university alongside your father. Keep in mind that these young people are only a step away from the university. Your teaching and encouragement means the world to them and to me.

I don't know if I ever told you that I came to America as a young lad. I left Ireland with my uncle. He died on the voyage over, and I was left to my own devices. I hated New York City and worked my way to California. I came to Los Angeles when it was little more than a village. Señor Ruiz owned a large ranchero. He took me in and welcomed me as part of his family. His daughter Isabella and I grew up together. You know Isabella as Grace and Ernest Camero's mother.

I tell you this story because Señor Ruiz's compassion, understanding, and generosity helped me become part of this great city. I have always tried to welcome others as he welcomed me. Like me, you came here without friends or family and have proven once again that Los Angeles welcomes all.

My friend Doctor Stone has recently informed me my bad heart is getting worse. My shortness of breath and tiredness are due to my heart becoming too weary for this world. I know my time here is short, and I wanted to tell you something about your charges while I can.

Zella is the moon and the stars all rolled into one. She has an uncanny ability to see the false, the weak, and the anomaly. It's true she leans toward journalism and not science, but her mind is sharp. When the others are stumped, they turn to her for analysis. She can spot and understand problems quicker than Mr. Edison. She will run you a merry chase, for she will not back down or quit once she has decided to pursue something.

Alroy burns as bright as the sun, and his love of the world is as deep as the ocean. He is a renaissance man in an era moving toward specialty. You are a specialist, and I believe you may find my son challenging to understand. He is like his mother. I understand Zella's focused passion better than I do Alroy's curiosity about the world.

Oddly, he and my son Wyatt have much in common. However, I was a young man when I raised Wyatt. At every turn, I tried to shape and mold him into my image. That was a mistake. I should have cultivated his desire for knowledge and experience. With Alroy, I have tried to nurture him to make up for my poor parenting of his brother. His brilliance is different from the others. He will embrace the world and will gather knowledge and disperse it. His understanding can only grow and mature.

As I'm sure you have discovered, Pedro is gifted and multitalented. He will succeed in any endeavor he sets out to accomplish. His mind is marvelous, and he is a good lad in the best sense. However, he lacks confidence, which might be his downfall and hold him back. Take care to expand his vision of himself. If you must admonish him, do so gently, for he will take it to heart.

Toby is a talented writer, more capable than he realizes. He sees the world through a storyteller's eyes, but do not let that fool you. His mind is quick, and his understanding of the world and people cannot be matched. He is curious about science, and, one day, I imagine that he will be a patron of the sciences. He has a head for business and will probably become an influential part of this great city.

Lavinia has an intuitive gift for the sciences and one day will outshine them all. She is also a great manager of people. She could put Buffalo Bill in his place. Because of her mixed race, she has a deep-seated need to fight for justice. She occasionally pretends to be silly and shallow. Those are her tricks to fool people into ignoring her. Do not be deceived. She is perceptive and wise beyond her years.

Be gentle with them all, especially the girls. I suspect you are not in sympathy with the suffragettes, but my wife and I are. We wish the girls to have the same education and opportunities as the boys. These young people are our gift to the future. We must value them for who they are.

I am indebted to you and your kindness.

Your friend,

Liam Doyle

Alroy stared at the pages. The letter amazed him. He hadn't known his father encouraged Doc or that he had thought so deeply about the kind of people he, Zella, and their friends were. He'd called Alroy *as bright as the sun* and *as deep as the ocean.* He didn't feel bright or deep, but the letter gave him a desire to become the person his father saw. He made a silent oath to try. Alroy Franklin Doyle would become his father's legacy.

He folded the letter and slipped it into the pages of his book. He'd show it to Zella later.

His mood changed the moment he slipped the book into his back pocket. His determination to live up to his father's image didn't vanish, but he didn't think he could ever forget that he caused his father's death. How could that kind of son ever be as bright as the sun?

He grabbed his father's pocket watch and ran his finger

across the ornate design before pushing the latch to open it. He needed to start home.

The League of the Daring was meeting Grace for a ride in her airship. This would be his first ride in a small dirigible. Would the trip be the same as riding in a commercial flight? Or would it feel more open or more dangerous? He hoped for exciting, like a ride in a balloon.

CHAPTER 6: ZELLA

A NEW LOOK

July 19, 1890
8:30 a.m.

Having the body of a little girl was the bane of Zella's fifteen-year-old life. Her friends blossomed into young women while she watched with angst and jealousy. Most vexing of all, her chest remained flat. Standing sideways and looking in the mirror, she saw the concave torso of an undernourished boy.

The girls at school made jokes about her body and teased her that she'd never have a boyfriend, as if she would want one. Well, she'd never admit such a thing to those girls, but a boyfriend would be fun. She knew some cute boys, but none of the boys would give her a second glance, especially with Mary Beth flaunting her blond curls and female curves.

Last summer, Zella grew three inches taller, but, so far this summer, her body refused to change. She looked like a baby. School would start in a month, and she had no hope of any change.

She paced in her bedroom, trying to avoid the looking glass

on her dressing table. But each time she turned, she caught sight of her reflection. Not only did her reflection mock her, but the yellow daisies painted around the mirror's frame seemed entirely too cheerful. Today, of all days, she had to look mature.

Most of the time her child's body didn't hinder her. After all, looking like a kid was handy for snooping around unnoticed. There wasn't anything Zella liked more than snooping around.

Since she'd read Nellie Bly's newspaper story, "Ten Days in a Mad-House," all she could think of was becoming an investigative reporter. Nellie shook people out of their apathy by exposing the vile treatment and shocking conditions of patients in mental institutions.

Zella wanted to do the same kind of reporting. Her father said reporting could bring problems and issues to the public's attention. Once a problem is exposed and defined, those with authority and power are forced to work toward solving the problem. Of course, Zella knew that making people take notice wasn't an easy task. She liked a challenge and was going to be just like Nellie Bly, a strong, bold woman.

When she'd told her father her plans, he'd frowned, but, almost immediately, he rallied with a smile and encouraging words. Now that he was gone, she was more determined than ever to be a successful reporter. She didn't know much about heaven, but she hoped her father could watch her and Alroy, or know what they were doing, or at least be able to read newspapers.

When he was alive, he read the newspaper every morning, and if there were newspapers in heaven, he'd read them. She was determined to see her stories in *The Daily Herald*, and she would imagine her father reading her byline and smiling.

She plopped on her bed and lay looking at the ceiling. She pushed thoughts of her father away. She didn't want to think about him. Instead, she reminded herself of the benefits of looking young. She could disguise herself as a boy. She liked to dress in Alroy's clothes, pin her hair into a hat, and go on boy adventures. Those experiences liberated her and helped her understand Toby. Sometimes she'd sneak out and go exploring alone, but usually, she went with Alroy, Toby, and Pedro. The boys didn't mind her and Lavinia tagging along.

But today she would look like a woman.

Jumping up, she went to the window and pushed the lace curtains aside. She saw nothing interesting, so she grabbed the telescope Pedro had made for her. He had made one for everyone in The League of the Daring. Each one folded and could easily slip into a pocket. Zella made hers unique by painting yellow daisies on it. She scanned the neighbor's yard and across the street.

"Boring."

Her neighborhood was agonizingly middle class and quiet. The most exciting thing she saw was the neighbor's dog, jumping up and grabbing a white shirt from his owner's clothesline. A few paces away, an automaton cat wagged its tail and stared at the dog. Little wisps of steam floated from its ears. She smiled. The cat wasn't useful, but she loved it.

She tossed the telescope on her bed. Liza should have finished her dress an hour ago. For the hundredth time, she glanced at her pocket watch.

A knock on the door startled her.

"Who is it?"

"Liza."

She threw open the door. Liza Sutton stood in the hall, glaring at Zella. The lines and shape of her angular face presented a disapproving gaze to the world and belied her good nature. She was Zella's mother's best friend and their live-in housekeeper. They really couldn't afford a house-keeper, but when Papa married Mama, Liza was part of the deal. Zella guessed Liza's frowns and sour expressions hard-ened on her face when she was an orphan. She frightened people, but Zella was used to her angry looks and the harsh color of her words.

Liza held a green dress in her large, bony hands. Zella wanted to grab it, but she knew better.

"Exactly who'd you think was knocking at your door, Missy?"

"It might have been Alroy," Zella said.

"Well, it ain't." She chuckled as she scooted into the room and closed the door. "Too bad it wasn't him. You'd have given him the vapors standing there in your unders."

"Has he left?"

"Naw, he's with your ma, giving her one of his daily monologues. Poor thing."

Zella wasn't sure if she meant her mother or Alroy was a poor thing, but she wasn't about to ask. She didn't want to draw the conversation out. She wanted to see the dress, to put it on, and to find out if it worked.

"I can see you're chomping at the bit," Liza said, handing Zella the garment.

She shook the dress out and held it up to her body. Looking in the mirror, she sucked in her breath. It was beautiful. Liza had taken one of her mother's old dresses and redesigned it into a modern style. Now it had puffed sleeves and yellow lace, which started at the shoulders and went down the front to form a V at the waist. The slightly gathered skirt was trimmed at the hem with the same lace as the bodice. It looked like a dress right out of *Harper's Bazaar*. Most important of all, the breast area was full, sticking out as if a female ghost wore it.

"Quit gaping. It ain't going to bite you. Hold up your arms."

Zella raised her arms as Liza slipped the dress over her head. She put her arms into the sleeves and let the dress slide down her body. Liza straightened the waist, tugging at the fabric and adjusting it to fit.

Zella stared down at her fake breasts.

"Holy corsets, they're so . . . big," she whispered.

"Speaking of corsets," Liza said.

"We aren't speaking of corsets. They're barbaric. I will not, now or ever, wear one. I don't intend to bruise my ribs and distort my body for anyone."

Liza chuckled. "If some boy takes a fancy to you, you might change your mind."

"No, I won't. He'd better like me for me."

"Now, don't start spouting suffragette nonsense. Are you having second thoughts about the dress?" Liza tugged at the waist and straightened the breasts. Then she moved around to the back of the dress. She pulled the straps that attached the padding.

"These pieces of cloth have buttons. I'm going to pull them. Tell me when it feels good and tight."

"Now."

Liza tugged a little harder and buttoned the padding before fastening the back of the dress. She turned Zella around and pointed her toward the looking glass.

Staring at her reflection, she thought she looked like a girl playing dress up. Maybe she should go to the interview as herself? She turned one way then the other until Liza pushed her down onto the dressing table's chair.

She watched Liza comb her long auburn hair. The brushing and arranging weren't gentle, but staring in the mirror gave Zella time to adjust to her looks. Even Mary Beth would be jealous if she could see her.

Zella the little girl transformed into Zella the woman. Her hair was swept up in an elegant style. She wore one of her mother's summer hats, refashioned with clusters of yellow flowers fastened by loops of ribbon on the brim. She'd borrowed a pair of her mother's shoes. The hat and heels added a few inches to her height. She pushed down the feeling of being a phony and took one last look in the mirror.

"Get out there and conquer the world," Liza said.

Those words sounded like something her father would have said to her.

Zella hugged her and whispered, "Thank you."

Downstairs, she hesitated at the parlor door. Her mother sat alone in the dark parlor. Zella wondered what her mother would do if she went into the room and pulled back all the curtains? Maybe she would wake up or get angry or do something.

Alroy wasn't around. Thankfully, she wouldn't have to explain her appearance or where she was going.

CHAPTER 7: ZELLA

RESEARCH

July 19, 1890
9:45 a.m.

A half hour later, Zella stood in the County Clerk's office. The bare wooden floors and the austere furnishings should have put her at ease, but the pedestrian atmosphere seemed too foreign. By the window, a square oak table and two matching chairs looked as out of place as she felt. She'd expected something more official and modern. The room reminded her of a large closet thrown together haphazardly.

Straight ahead was a long wooden counter, which served as a barrier and prevented anyone from getting into the backroom. The door stood open, and she could see rows of shelves littered with boxes and books. On the countertop, a rock held a stack of papers in place. The hot, stuffy air felt oppressively heavy, billowing around the room like an invisible campfire. She'd write to the mayor about the unfit conditions.

She took a breath and gathered up her courage. She dismissed the idea that she might soil her new dress and marched forward. Among the papers on the counter, a neatly printed sign read, "For assistance, ring the bell."

The clerk, an older gentleman, shuffled in from the other room and glanced at her. His dark hair and graying beard were neatly trimmed. He wasn't wearing his jacket. She couldn't fault him, the room had no ventilation.

She smiled.

"May I help you, Miss?"

"Yes, I want to look up some deeds and land sales for several properties."

He didn't call her a child and shoo her out of the building. Looking over the list she'd handed him, he disappeared into the backroom. She released the breath she'd been holding and waited for her heart to stop pounding against her fake breasts.

The realization she'd fooled one person into thinking she was an adult boosted her self-confidence. Returning, he led her to the table by the window, where he placed the oversized leather-bound record books. He gallantly dusted off a chair and motioned her to sit. Although she had some qualms about her deception, she enjoyed the attention.

As a girl, she was generally ignored and overlooked. Being treated like a young woman gave her a strange feeling of power. She sat up straight and hoped she appeared as ladylike as she felt.

"These aren't in alphabetic order," the clerk said. "The transactions are recorded as they come in. So if you're looking in the Ks, just run down this list until you find the name you're searching for. If you need anything else, ring the bell."

She placed her new valise, a gift from Wyatt, on the table and glanced at her pocket watch. She had plenty of time before she had to meet Mr. Widney, the editor of *The Herald*.

She had given the clerk five names and five properties, but she was only looking for two. A reporter needed to use her wits.

She found Hornsby first. Her hands shook a little as they

lingered over the entry. Pedro believed this man was the leader of the smuggling ring they were investigating. Gathering research and facts would help her write a story. She paused for a moment to imagine the headline: Smuggling Ring in Los Angeles Exposed, and under the title, her byline, Zella Louise Doyle. Such a story would be a significant triumph and establish her as a real investigative reporter.

Getting back to business, she made quick notes. Zachariah William Hornsby purchased the land and building belonging to Samuel Wong. The purchase took place on September 3, 1883. She couldn't find a purchase price, which was odd. There was a detailed description of the land, and a map detailed the property. Some of the notations were illegible.

The Wong information was in the second book. He purchased his lot in 1873. She studied the building's plans and the permits for the laundry, noting that most of the other buildings didn't require permits. In several different handwritings, people made notes of Wong's race, Chinaman, Chinese, from China via San Francisco. One person noted: Despite all obstacles we place in his path, Mr. Wong seems determined to finish this building.

These notations annoyed her. Her father had told her stories of the hardships he'd faced when he came to the United States from Ireland. People judged him by his origins. He'd always used those tales as a moral lesson to judge people for their character. Just as she admired her father, she found admiration for Mr. Wong, who persevered in the face of opposition.

Continuing to read, she discovered Wong only held the land for ten years. Pedro said the laundry was successful.

Zella wondered why he'd sell a successful business, especially since he worked so hard to establish it. According to Pedro, Mr. and Mrs. Hornsby were unpleasant, which she interpreted as downright mean and hateful because Pedro rarely said anything negative about people.

She wasn't sure how this information fit into the smuggling ring, but she'd get the back-story and piece things together. Plus, Pedro thought there was something odd about Hornsby's acquisition of the property. If he had cheated to get the property, that would make for a juicy, titillating story.

When she finished, she packed up her notes and returned to the counter. The clerk was in the back. As she rang the bell on the countertop, she couldn't stop a smile from spreading across her face.

"Thank you for your help," she said as the clerk stepped through the door. "I wanted to let you know I finished so you could return the books to their proper place."

He beamed at her.

"Thank you, Miss, very thoughtful. Have a good day."

She stepped into the fresh air, holding her head high. She'd fooled the clerk. She knew deceiving the editor of *The Los Angeles Daily Herald* wouldn't be so easy. He had a reputation for sniffing out stories and seeing through politicians who twisted the truth. Plus, she had heard that he was gruff and demanding.

She tried to ignore the flutters in her stomach and the perspiration on her palms. Unexpectedly, she wished she'd dressed as herself. Would the editor see through her disguise?

* * *

Outside the County Clerk's office, she headed toward Broadway. She held her head high and smiled at the people she passed. Almost everyone smiled back at her. As she moved closer to the center of town, she walked faster.

Broadway was her favorite street. She was sure everyone felt the same. She loved the throngs of people, the trolleys, the carts, the cheerful greetings of shop owners, even the presence of a police officer strolling down the street. Broadway bustled with a sense the unexpected was within reach.

A block before the newspaper office, she stopped to admire a child-sized automaton in a store window. The porcelain-faced girl wore a frilly dress. Her head turned one way and then the other as if she were watching the crowd walk past. Then she raised her arm, waved, and motioned toward a sign. "New Children's Clothes from New York, London, and Paris."

Zella crossed the street. The sight of the newspaper offices always brought a sense of anticipation. The large ground-floor windows spanned the front of the building and held everyone's attention. She stopped and stared at the steam printing press inside. At the moment, it stood motionless and silent. Inside, the printers prepared for the afternoon edition.

She was eight the first time she saw the printing press. Her father and mother brought her and Alroy to see the new machine. They watched the steam rising upward and heard the gears turning as the printing press spat out newspapers. The noise of the crowd on the streets paled in comparison to the excitement Zella felt as she watched the printers and reporters. Their faces were animated and the activity endless. Once a day, when the enormous printing press started up, a crowd gathered around the window and watched.

A man stepped up next to Zella and spoke. A few seconds passed before she realized he spoke directly to her.

She looked up at him. "Pardon?"

"Are you interested in newspapers?"

"Yes. I'm a writer."

"Really?"

His reaction annoyed her, and although she had no intention of bragging, she couldn't seem to stop herself.

"You don't need to look so surprised. I have an appointment in an hour with Mr. Widney."

She'd expected to impress him, but instead of responding with awe and fascination, he chuckled. She automatically frowned and had a response for him, but he spoke first.

"Delightful. Perhaps we'll one day be colleagues. I'm William St. James, but please don't stand on formality. Call me Ike."

If she had wanted to, she wouldn't have been able to suppress the grin that spread across her face.

"Mr. St. James, I'm pleased to meet you. I'm Zella Doyle. I do admire your work, and Mrs. St. James' as well. I have a collection of your articles."

"Excellent. Perhaps ink is in your blood. Are you by chance related to Wyatt Doyle, the detective?"

"He's my brother."

"I went to Berkeley with him and Ernest Camero. Two fine scholars. What are your plans for the next hour?"

Now Zella knew what girls meant when they said their hearts were all aflutter. Until this moment, she'd thought the saying was ridiculous. Now one of her newspaper heroes stood before her, chatting easily and telling her he went to school with her brother and Ernest. She took a deep breath.

"I'm going to the archives. I have some research to do before my meeting."

"Then, with your permission, I'll show you the way." He offered his arm and led her inside the building.

The immense room smelled of ink and paper. Workers rushed to and fro, getting the press ready. They walked by the men and through a door that separated the public from the newspapers offices.

"The exciting stuff happens upstairs," he said. "Here is where we warehouse paper, ink, and other supplies. Accounting is there," he said, pointing to one of the closed doors. Nodding toward the back of the long hall, he said, "When you're ready for your appointment, use the elevator."

A few more steps led to a wide staircase. A brass sign to the right of the door proclaimed Archives Downstairs.

"Unfortunately, the archives are in the basement. However, there's plenty of light, and Derek only looks like he'll bite your head off. He's harmless, and if you smile, he can be friendly.

Downstairs was well lit and expansive. Three large oak tables with plenty of chairs filled the first few feet. Ike lead her to the large desk, where a tall, angular man with glasses and a very pointed nose nodded to them.

Behind him were row after row of bookcases filled and neatly organized. More current editions of the paper hung on wooden stands, draped over dowels.

"Derek, this is Miss Doyle. She's here to do some research. Give her all the help she needs."

"Miss Doyle," Derek said, in a low voice that sounded bored and uninterested.

"Nice to meet you," Zella said.

"Of course. I assume you have permission to be here," he said.

"What part of help her did you not understand, old boy?" Ike asked.

Derek only raised an eyebrow in answer.

Zella smiled at him and looked him directly in the eyes. She wasn't sure if that would help her, but it couldn't hurt.

"I'll tell my wife to keep an eye out for you," Ike said. "Mr. Widney's a good man. He'll hire a female who can write, but he doesn't like female wiles. Be all business, and don't be afraid to speak your mind. You'll do fine."

"You're a reporter?" Derek asked as Ike took the stairs two at a time.

"Yes," Zella said without hesitation.

Derek nodded, and his face softened slightly before saying, "Don't let the men give you any guff."

He gave her a quick tour of the archives and explained his organizing system.

"If you need specific help, let me know," he said and disappeared into the cavernous stacks.

Happy to be left alone, she quickly searched for the back editions she needed. One thing she could say for Derek—she admired his organization system.

Before the hour was up, her note pages were full, and she'd learned Wong's Laundry was a very successful business. One newspaper article told of Liam Doyle and Roberto Hernandez's support for Samuel Wong and his business efforts. She felt pride as she read of her father's efforts to help Wong establish his business. By all accounts, Mr. Wong worked hard to be a model citizen.

On the other hand, Zachariah Hornsby didn't seem to be anything close to a model citizen. He worked for Wong, and, in 1883, he bought the business.

Over the next several weeks, there was a series of articles questioning the Wong family's disappearance. Several letters to the editor implied Hornsby had run the family off. Others accused him of seizing the business without paying for it. There were more accusations and hints of wrongdoing, which led to an investigation that exonerated Hornsby.

The story boiled down to the strange disappearance of the Wong family, and the unlikelihood Wong would sell a thriving business to a man of dubious character. Hornsby insisted he purchased the land and claimed the Wong family left to return to China. The Wongs abandoned their home, which seemed odd to Zella. They did not book passage back to China or anyplace else. Hornsby insisted he bought their tickets to San Francisco. One anonymous letter writer was excessively emotional as well as angry and accusatory.

Zella knew this had the makings of a great story. Even if she couldn't prove there was a smuggling ring, this search might lead to a story of its own. A few things were clear. Mr. Wong had established a good reputation in the community, a surprising accomplishment considering the time and his race.

On the other hand, Hornsby had a bad reputation and wasn't

liked yet was able to secure Wong's business. She wanted to clear up the mystery surrounding the Wong family's departure.

She wouldn't be surprised if there were more to this story than the newspapers let on. She cautioned herself not to jump to conclusions before gathering all the information, and she briefly wondered if she could solve a past mystery.

Did Pedro know about the controversy surrounding the laundry business? He had mentioned the laundry, but he'd been adamant that she shouldn't go there or try to talk to Hornsby because he was unpredictable.

Maybe unpredictable was Pedro's code for dangerous. Whatever Pedro meant, Zella was pretty sure the man wasn't honest. Her instinct told her to be cautious, but if she had to, she'd follow these leads and throw caution over the cliff.

CHAPTER 8: ZELLA

THE INTERVIEW

July 19, 1890
10:00 a.m.

Upstairs in the newsroom, Zella glanced around and took in the sight.

Cigarette smoke billowed over the room like a wispy cloud. Old desks of every shape and size filled the room in haphazard arrangement, leaving little space for walking. In the vast sea of men, she saw two women. For a brief moment, she imagined herself at one of the desks, typing furiously to meet a deadline.

Many reporters banged the keys on their typewriters. While some talked, others shouted across the room. A few sat at their desks, ignoring the chaos.

A pretty, dark-haired woman with ink smudges on her cheek left her desk and came to greet Zella.

"Miss Doyle? I'm Kate St. James. My husband told me you'd be up."

"Mrs. St. James. I'm delighted to meet you, and, please, call me Zella." She thought her little speech sounded very grownup.

"And call me Kate." She chuckled. "We women must stick together."

Kate nodded toward a man who stood in a doorway a few feet away. He stared at Zella with narrowed eyes.

"Miss Doyle?"

"Yes."

"Well, I haven't got all day. I'm a busy man." He spun around and marched into an office.

Zella scurried after him, her sense of being grown up diminishing as she raced forward like a puppy chasing a horse and carriage. He sat behind a desk covered with papers. Rocks served as paperweights. Newspapers and journals filled a shelf within arm's reach of his desk. He motioned her to take a seat.

The room smelled of cigar smoke, paper, and ham sandwich.

Kate sat in the chair beside her. The woman's presence gave Zella a sense of relief and support. She wanted to make a good impression, but, at the moment, she couldn't seem to breathe properly. Her hands shook, and she gripped her valise tighter to hide the trembling. She stared with unforgivable rudeness and couldn't think of one thing to say.

Her moment had arrived, and her vocal cords strained as tight as an old woman's corset.

Mr. Robert Widney shuffled through some papers and grabbed several pages, which Zella recognized as her article. He looked up at her. His squared-off beard reminded her of pictures she'd seen of Egyptian pharaohs. His brown eyes stared at her as she imagined a pharaoh might examine one of his subjects.

As he cleared his throat, he said, "So you want to write for the newspaper?"

Her mouth had gone dry. She remembered what Wyatt had told her, "When you're scared, imagine yourself brave."

"Yes, I do."

"Your writing is passable."

"Robert, quit scaring the poor girl. Her writing is more than passable, and with a little editing, her article will be better than most."

He frowned and leaned back in his chair and glared at Kate.

"You do manage to ruin all my fun. Now, Miss Doyle, your writing might be up to snuff, but is your spirit up to the task? That's the primary question. Being a reporter takes more than stringing words together. "

"Sir, I assure you I have what it takes."

"Nonsense. Let me see your hands."

As Zella pulled off her gloves, Kate glared at him and frowned. Proud of her ink-stained hands, Zella held them out for him to see.

"No ring, I see." He grinned.

"Ring?"

"I don't want to hire someone who is going to run off and get married."

She stood up and saw his eyes grow wide.

"Have I offended you? Are you going to leave?"

"No, I'm not. Mr. Widney, single or married doesn't change my writing abilities. Mrs. St James is married."

"Sit down. I don't like women standing over me.

"I intend to be an investigative reporter, and my private life is of no concern."

He burst out laughing and slapped his desk.

"Well said. I admire spirit and boldness, both qualities you'll need. Now, sit down. I intend to buy this story. I'll look at anything else you wish to send me, but you'll not become a staff member. Someday . . . maybe. You must prove yourself. And you must finish school. I'd like to see you go off to college as well. Nothing beats a good education."

When he mentioned school, her elation turned sour.

"Don't look so crestfallen. We did investigate you. Can't have just anyone writing for *The Herald*. Can you come by in the morning? Kate will show you around and will go over our policies and procedures."

"Of course," Zella said.

"Off with you. Paper's going to press soon, and I have work to do."

"Thank you," she said.

Kate walked her to the elevator.

"Are you all right?" Kate asked as the elevator clanged its way up to their floor.

"I'm not sure. He's a rather strange man."

"He is indeed," Kate said. "He was testing you, and you gave an admirable performance."

"I feel rather silly. I was trying so hard to deceive him into thinking I was an adult."

Kate's chuckle was musical and light. Hearing her laugh should have raised Zella's spirits. Instead it accented the wide chasm that separated them. The metal cage stopped, and Kate pulled open the decorative iron door and motioned her inside.

"You'll be fine. Disguises can be useful to an investigative reporter. Things will be different in the morning. I'll give you the tour, and soon everything will be familiar. Give Wyatt hearty greetings from me and Ike."

"Hold," someone called.

Kate held the cage door open as a young man rushed forward and stepped inside.

Zella smiled halfheartedly as the elevator moved downward. She leaned against the iron bars of the cage and stared at the printing press below. The realization that her dress with its large breasts made her look ridiculous and childish stung. For several long moments, she allowed her embarrassment full rein.

"Zella?" the young man said.

She turned to look at him.

"Hi, um . . ."

"Charlie," he said.

"Hi, Charlie."

She knew what his name was because she'd had a little crush on him for about two years. He stared at her, his almond eyes growing a little wider. His Adam's apple bobbed as he swallowed.

Usually, she stuttered because any boy she liked made her nervous. Right now, he was far more nervous than she was. He probably wanted to ask her how she grew giant breasts in two months. Of course, he wouldn't ask. She decided to shock him.

"They aren't real," she said.

"Uh, what's not real?"

"These," she said, pointing to her breasts.

He stared at her with a wide silly grin on his face.

She burst out laughing, and he followed suit. There was something companionable about their laughter, and her embarrassment vanished in an instant. The iron cage bounced once as it came to a stop. He opened the door and held it for her.

"You fooled me," he said, following her. "I like the real Zella best."

She wasn't sure how to respond, but he saved her the effort.

"I'm the errand boy," he said, opening the outside door for her. "I'm off to pick up sandwiches."

She watched him rush away and grinned. Her self-pity vanished, she headed for home pleased with herself and thinking of the handsome Chinese boy who said he liked the real Zella best. They'd never spoken before because she'd only had enough courage to admire him from afar.

She strolled down Broadway, humming to herself. Despite her disappointment, this was turning out to be a good day.

Maybe looking like Mary Beth wasn't all it was cracked up to be. She'd take her chances as Zella Doyle. Of course, she wasn't about to give up wearing disguises.

CHAPTER 9: ALROY

TOBY

July 19, 1890
11:30 a.m.

When Alroy left the Plaza, he cycled home via Broadway. After the time machine's success, the usual high energy and bustle of the crowded streets held little interest for him. He rode fast because his thoughts traveled at light speed. One second he thought about his father's letter, the next he wondered if Pedro would be at Grace's, and then the excitement of the airship ride kicked aside all other thoughts.

He felt like roaring and shouting. His thoughts were crazy and mixed up. It wasn't until he spotted a carriage pulled by a bronze horse-shaped automaton that his attention focused.

He couldn't take his eyes off the horse's design. He darted ahead until he rode next to the carriage. The automaton looked so life-like Alroy wouldn't have been surprised if it whinnied. He could hear the gears turning, but they hummed rather than clanked. Steam flowed from the mouth. The metal horse was a work of art. Whoever crafted it wasn't from Los Angeles. Alroy knew all the designers. The craftsmanship was exquisite and the quality superior. Either a new inventor was in town, or the horse was imported. Etched into the left side of the horse's flank one word stood out, Prospero.

A broad-shouldered, dark-skinned man drove the automaton. Alroy pedaled faster and tried to ride alongside the driver, who smiled at him and nodded.

"The horse is amazing," Alroy shouted.

"Yes, young man, it is. It rides smoother than an airship."

"Who's the designer?"

The man turned his head and pointed his chin toward the two passengers in the carriage.

Alroy glanced in the carriage. A young woman with a heart-shaped face smiled at him, and he thought her as pretty as a summer sunrise. The man sitting beside her had the look of someone who rarely smiled. He frowned as he read *The Herald* newspaper.

"The horse is a beauty," he said, slowing a little to ride along-side the carriage. He could feel his cheeks flush. He wanted to say the horse was corker, but he didn't want the girl to hear him use slang.

"Thank you. I'll tell my father you admire his work." She pointed to the man. "He's preoccupied and doesn't hear a word we're saying."

"I'm Alroy Doyle." He grinned and made a decision that he'd find a way to meet this man and perhaps get to know his daughter.

"Pleased to meet you. I'm Miranda, and my father is Thomas Stanbury."

"I'm very pleased to meet you." He had a name, which was all he needed. "Perhaps, we'll meet again?"

She giggled. "I hope so."

Upon hearing her giggle, his first thought was Zella wouldn't like her, but his second thought was a wish. He wished he were wearing a hat so he could tip it, but he nodded to her and pedaled forward. The girl and her father weren't in his social circle, but he wouldn't let that detail stop him.

On the crowded sidewalk ahead, he spotted Zella. She marched toward home with her head held high. For a second she went out of view amid the throng of people. Then the crowd parted, and he found her again, striding forward like a girl with a purpose. Hopping off his bicycle, Alroy pushed it onto the sidewalk and weaved through the crowd toward her.

"Excuse me, ma'am," he said as he brushed past an older, well-dressed woman.

"Those contraptions shouldn't be on the walkway," she said as he hurried on.

Zella's red hair was pinned up and off her neck. She wore a wide-brimmed shade hat with a cluster of yellow flowers fastened by loops of yellow ribbon. Alroy pushed his bicycle faster.

She was probably rushing home for their meeting with Grace. He'd never seen the green tailored dress she wore, which was odd. There was some sort of yellow lace around the hem. He stared at her back. The unfamiliar dress made him wonder if he were chasing a stranger. Taking longer strides, he pushed forward, skirting around a gentleman and a lady who moseyed along the sidewalk arm in arm. Finally, he was beside her and almost running to keep up.

"What are you doing downtown alone?" he asked.

She didn't slacken her pace. "Hello to you, too, dear brother."

There was a nasty bite in her voice when she said *dear brother.*

"Well?"

She sighed.

"If you must know, I was at *The Herald*. They are going to buy one of my stories." As if she were practicing piano scales, her inflection ascended from annoyance to elation.

The full meaning of her words took a few seconds to make their impact.

"That's great. Great." He stopped, but she kept walking. "Slow down. It's hard to push this and keep up with you."

Turning, she grinned at him and her blue-green eyes shone with excitement. "They are paying me."

He couldn't speak. He could only stare.

"Close your mouth, Alroy."

He swallowed.

"What happened to your . . . your front? They're so big."

"Could you say that a little louder? They didn't hear you in Whittier."

"Hop on. I'll give you a ride."

He suddenly wanted to get Zella and her large breasts home.

"No, not in this dress. I don't want to soil it."

They blocked foot traffic, and people stepped around them. Some glanced at them as if annoyed by the inconvenience. The couple he'd passed earlier walked by and grinned.

"Get on the handlebar. I'll be careful. We're going to be late. You don't want to keep Grace waiting, do you?"

She grimaced but lifted her skirt and climbed on. Alroy pushed off hard with his right foot and let the bicycle bounce off the sidewalk. He stood up and pedaled hard until they were clipping along.

"You shouldn't be in town alone," he said and immediately regretted his words.

He wished he hadn't admonished her. She could take care of herself, and he wanted her to be independent, but he also worried. He worried about practically everything, especially about bad things happening to Zella.

"You're not my keeper. I'm perfectly capable of . . . you sound like Wyatt."

He pressed his lips together and looked straight ahead. He whipped around a wagon and heard the horse whinny as they whizzed past. Pedaling faster, he came up along the right side of the noon trolley and grabbed the metal side rail, which stuck out just enough for him to grab and hold on for a faster ride.

He didn't say anything. The sun was high in the sky, and the hot breeze flowing over his face cooled his anger.

After two blocks, he released his grip on the trolley, made a sharp right turn, and sped up. The street was empty, so he continued at his breakneck speed.

Zella squealed and put her hands into the air.

"Yahoo," she yelled.

As they got closer to home, he slowed. Liza might see them, and she wouldn't approve.

He stared at the back of Zella's neck. He didn't like her saying he sounded like Wyatt. She was angry at his bossiness and probably said it to get back at him.

"I'm not Wyatt," he finally said. "And I don't sound like him." The devil part of him added, "and you shouldn't be downtown. Not alone."

"Don't be a fuddy-duddy. I was and am perfectly safe. I wasn't exactly alone. There were hundreds of people. I couldn't very well walk into the newspaper office with you or Toby. Maybe Pedro. At least he acts like a gentleman."

He swerved around a cat that darted in front of them. The bicycle swayed to the left, and Zella squealed. He righted the cycle and continued toward home.

"Just how old do they think you are? Is that why you padded your breasts? And where did you get that dress?"

"Why are you being so . . . so old-fashioned?" She sighed. "Liza made the dress and padded it."

Mister Thompson, their neighbor four houses down, waved to them as they drove past. Zella waved back.

"Does mother know about this? Does Wyatt?"

"Does mother know anything? And does Wyatt know you

were off in the bad part of town experimenting with a time machine?"

"Good grief. I'm responsible for you."

"You are not responsible for me. And if you were, just how responsible were you when you latched onto the trolley?"

He hated it when she was right and hated it even more when she sounded unhappy because the world was out of kilter when Zella had a sour face. She was mostly cheerful and smiled so much he guessed her cheek muscles must be strong. Her smile was something he could count on. But mostly he was angry with himself. He knew he was being stupid, and he didn't want to nag but couldn't stop himself.

"Well, you just need to be careful." He tried to sound apologetic without actually apologizing.

"If you weren't driving this, I'd bonk you on the head."

He turned into the driveway which led to their carriage house. Liza stood on the large wrap-around porch.

Before they'd come to a stop, she called out, "How'd it go?"

"I sold it," Zella shouted.

Liza clapped her hands together and grinned. Alroy stopped by the brick chimney. He let Zella get off and leaned the bicycle up against the side of the house.

"I'm going to change. I'll meet you at Grace's," Zella said. She unpinned her hat and took it off. Her red hair shimmered like gold in the sunlight. "Unless you don't think I can walk two blocks by myself."

He stuck out his tongue, but she'd turned toward the house and was shouting something to Liza.

"Alroy, you ready?" Toby shouted from above him.

Toby sat on the ledge of his bedroom window, which was on the second floor of the house next door.

Alroy glanced up for a moment before looking toward the porch. He watched his sister climb the worn steps. She looked older, too grown up. He didn't like her padded breasts or the and he didn't think she'd put herself in danger, but just a few years back Los Angeles had more murders than any other city in the United States. Everyone said things were different now. But he wasn't so sure.

He didn't know why she couldn't be like other girls and get all giggly over boys and dances. No, she wanted to be a reporter like Nellie Bly. Alroy imagined Miss Bly put herself in danger every minute of every day.

To make matters worse, Liza encouraged Zella. Just about everyone encouraged her. He wanted to shout from the rooftops that investigative reporting was dangerous. One of these days, his sister was going to rush off on one of her mad adventures and find herself in danger.

He worried about his mother and Zella. Now, he had to add Pedro to his list. If it turned out Pedro wasn't missing, he just might challenge him to a fight. Why was he out at night? And why didn't he come home? And, most of all, why was he doing something without telling his friends?

CHAPTER 10: PEDRO

THE ABYSS

July 19, 1890

Somewhere between sleep and consciousness, Pedro floated as if bobbing up and down on a sea of gray fog. His forehead and eyes hurt with a kind of pulsing insistence. A cloth filled his mouth, soaking up his saliva and drying his mouth.

He tried to swallow but couldn't. He was sick. Yes? Maybe? He didn't know.

Wherever he was, it smelled like an old outhouse.

He couldn't open his eyes. They felt glued shut and heavy. He lay on his right side. He moved and immediately regretted it as tiny pinpricks of pain ran the length of his arms to his hands.

His hands and feet were tied.

Somewhere nearby, people whispered. He didn't recognize the voices. Maybe because they were too soft, like the wind hissing through trees, shaking the leaves, and begging for attention.

Someone shook his shoulder.

He tried again to open his eyes. He managed to squint. Then his eyelids fluttered and closed.

woman. Ernest's family was from Spain, and he had inherited an aristocratic bearing. Zella said his green eyes made women swoon. She also said, "Tall, dark, and handsome was invented to describe Ernest." Alroy wondered what it would be like to be good-looking, intelligent, and charming all rolled into one.

He didn't get why Zella had a crush on the man. He was old. Wyatt's age. But there were many things he didn't understand about girls.

Alroy and Toby admired the ship. They took in everything—its shape, size, and design.

"It's a beauty," Toby said, grinning so wide anyone would have thought he'd designed it.

"Corker," Alroy agreed.

"You boys feel free to look around. I'll be in the workshop," Ernest said.

After Ernest had stepped back inside, Alroy whispered, "Do you think we should be going up in the airship? Shouldn't we be looking for Pedro?"

Toby pinched his lips together and scrunched his eyebrows together.

"We'll only be gone a couple hours, at most. He's probably already home. Two hours can't make any difference."

Alroy's gut told him two hours could make a difference. He considered arguing. Even though he was more worried than he wanted to admit, he decided to go along with Toby. Since his father's death, he worried about everyone close to him. He'd feel pretty dumb if Pedro were home, and he stopped their ride when Grace had gone out of her way to plan this trip for them. Plus, they'd all been looking forward to this ride for weeks.

Staring up at the cigar-shaped balloon, he compared its size to the commercial airships. Compared to the lumbering airships that traveled up and down the California coast, Grace's was compact and perfect for a small group.

"Look," Toby said, motioning him inside the gondola.

Before stepping inside the ladybug-shaped passenger section, he ran his hand over the red metal. It felt warm. For good luck, he tapped one of the round black circles on the ladybug's shell. The ship seemed playful and fun, like a child's toy. Even the flat observation platform blended with the control cabin to form a bug face.

Up close, it wasn't so small. The passenger compartment could fit six people, and two more if he counted the pilot's station, which was forward from and above the passenger seats. It overlooked the observation deck and had a sweeping view as windows spanned the entire cockpit.

He climbed up the ladder to check out the control panel. Toby followed.

There were enough gadgets to satisfy his love of machinery. The ship's wheel, just like on a sea ship, was mounted in front of the pilot's seat. A compass sat in the center of the control panel. Other gauges lined the metal wall above the window. He didn't know what they were all for. The largest gauge held a prominent position by the pilot's seat. That one he knew measured the helium pressure.

As he sat in the pilot's seat, he imagined flying up and drinking in the vista. In that moment, he decided two things. He'd learn to pilot an airship, and he'd build one. The League of the Daring could have grand adventures.

After a complete inspection of the cabin and the deck, the boys rejoined Ernest.

"Grace will be up in a moment," he said. "She's changing into inappropriate attire. Thankfully, we'll be in the air, and society won't be shocked."

Alroy could never tell if Ernest was joking or being serious, so he asked the obvious question.

"You don't approve?"

"Of course, he doesn't approve."

Grace stood in the doorway, and the light from the porch

windows illuminated her, making her seem taller. She walked into the room and bestowed a warm smile upon her brother.

"He only pretends to be a progressive man. Like you boys, he's a product of his culture."

Ernest rolled his eyes.

"She thinks she knows all."

Alroy sometimes wished Wyatt were as congenial as Ernest. The two men were best friends, but none of Ernest's personality rubbed off on Wyatt. Ernest was playful, sometimes flippant, and never seemed concerned about anything. As far as Alroy knew, Ernest did little work. He was a lawyer, but he always seemed to be home or off on an adventure. He was his own man and lived the way he wanted. Of course, his family did own an obscene amount of farmland.

Grace patted Ernest's cheek and laughed. She was the only woman Alroy knew who didn't always pin her hair up. Her light-brown hair hung down to her shoulders and framed her face in riotous curls, which was slightly scandalous. But her attire, long trousers, a white shirt, and a jacket that no man, even at gunpoint, would wear, didn't shock Alroy. He was used to her unusual wardrobe. Ernest was all about propriety. Grace didn't care what other people thought.

"Nice riding costume," Toby said.

"Are you poking fun at me, Tobias Bailey?"

"No, ma'am. If anyone does, let me know, and I'll write him into a story and turn him into a vampire."

"Someday women everywhere will wear trousers."

Grace said things like that all the time and sounded so sure that Alroy often believed her. She talked about the future as if it were the present.

"Where's Zella?" Grace asked.

The stairs creaked.

"Ah, there she is," Grace said without turning to confirm her assumption. "Grab goggles. It'll be windy and cool up there." Grace pointed to the wall where her extra goggles hung.

Zella walked into the room. When she spotted Ernest, her cheeks flushed.

"Um, are you going with us?" she stammered.

"I'm your pilot," Ernest said.

Zella's smile faded.

"You will survive," Toby whispered. "Maybe you can think of an excuse to sit in the copilot's seat.

Zella punched his arm and grabbed a pair of goggles.

Inside the airship, Grace and Ernest sat in the pilot's and copilot's seats. Alroy, Zella, and Toby settled into the leather seats in the passenger area.

Alroy's anticipation increased as he heard gears turn and watched the propellers sputter into action. He watched out the window as the airship lifted and slowly rose above the houses. As they ascended, the ladybug didn't jerk but rose smoothly upward and forward. They climbed until they were above the city, but not so high that they couldn't see the buildings and the people moving below them.

After they leveled off, Grace gave the controls to Ernest and came down the ladder to join them.

"We can go to the observation deck. It's a better view than the windows. Ernest is going to fly over the city, circle back, and then head out toward the ocean." She glanced at Toby. "Let's not do anything dangerous. Any questions?"

"No," Zella said, but she glanced up at Ernest, whose attention was focused on piloting the ship.

"I have a question." Toby grinned. "What do you consider dangerous?"

"Do you plan on causing trouble? I can always tie you to your seat," Grace said.

Toby winked.

"No, I'm not planning trouble, but I wouldn't mind having a little fun."

"Non-dangerous fun." Grace's eyes sparkled as she spoke.

Alroy guessed she'd like to have a little fun, too.

"If you get cold, I brought extra jackets, or you can come back inside," Grace said.

On the deck, Alroy was glad for the goggles and the high railing. He experienced vertigo for a few seconds as he looked down. The wind blew stronger and colder than he expected. For a second, he wondered how it could be so hot below them when it was chilly up here.

The city spread out like a map with small moving parts. New High Street, Main Street, and Broadway ran parallel for a while. Then they met and formed a triangle. Alroy knew the streets, but seeing them from above gave him a snapshot image of the whole.

He'd flown on commercial flights, but those were crowded, and he was never close enough to windows to have a good view of what lay below them. Standing on Grace's observation deck was like walking in the clouds.

Compared to the sweeping vista below, he was small and insignificant. Then he considered all the cities in the world. He was smaller than a dot or one of the black circles Grace had painted on the airship. In such a vast world, what was one person?

Zella leaned forward.

"Look. The Plaza. The church. From here, the center of the Plaza looks perfectly round."

Alroy glanced at Grace. She stood tall, her blue-gray eyes looking off into the distance. Alroy knew she saw the future, and he wanted to see what she saw.

"Look, City Hall, the new high school, and the YMCA." Zella's voice sounded excited.

"The Women's Temperance League building," Toby said. "What's that building?"

"I think it's the orphanage," Zella said. "I wish we had a map."

"Naw, it's Saint Paul's. The orphanage is over there," Alroy said, pointing in the other direction.

He turned his attention to the Los Angeles River, which snaked toward the ocean. A few small boats floated in the water. Probably people were fishing, hoping to catch something for supper. Now, as they moved south, the city slid behind them. Alroy glanced back for one last look. The afternoon sun bathed the streets and buildings in white light.

He loved the city and felt part of it. His father used to say, "I'm one with the land. It's in my blood." Alroy didn't feel connected to the land. He was connected to the city. Los Angeles thrived on excitement and had become the center of science and invention. Every day new inventors and scientists arrived. It was a city for the young and for those who fed off excitement and imagination.

Of course, it was also a city imbued with shadows, darkness, and the possibility of evil. Alroy didn't like to think about the seedy side. Yet the light and dark couldn't be separated. Los Angeles was at once an edifice of progress and a gray mirage. Alroy loved the good and hated the barbarous, but he had to accept the inevitable mixing of the two. Where the light was brightest, the shadows were deeper.

The turning of the airship's gears and the swishing of the propellers pounded out a beat of impending adventure. The sounds sent Alroy's blood pumping. He dreamed of traveling the world and discovering everything.

Below there were fewer houses and more fields, which looked like organized, geometric shapes. The ship turned toward San Pedro Bay.

In the distance, the ocean shimmered in the sunlight. Alroy tasted salt in the air and breathed in the smell of fish. For a brief moment, he wondered how the smell reached into the sky. Then he spotted four ships in the distance.

"Look."

The ships bobbed in the water like balsa wood boats in a bathtub.

Ernest flew over the water and circled each ship. Below, some of the crew waved. Toby took his jacket off and let it billow like a sail. Zella laughed and waved.

"I think my next story will be about pirates, ghost pirates, or invisible pirates," Toby said. "No, ghost pirates. And their ship flies, and it's invisible."

Alroy chuckled at Toby's exuberance, which made him think of Pedro, who should be with them. It seemed wrong to be having fun when his friend might be in trouble. Then the worst possible thought popped into his mind.

What if, while they were having fun, Pedro was hurt or dead?

His words punched him in the stomach, and his muscles tightened. He wished he could take back his thoughts.

Without warning, the airship jerked, lurched forward, and plummeted twenty feet. Zella screamed, and Alroy stumbled.

CHAPTER 12: ALROY

TURBULENCE

July 19, 1890
2:30 p.m.

The airship plummeted again. The front of the ship rose upward, regaining altitude. Alroy tried to reach for the rails as he slid toward the passenger's doorway. Zella slid sideways and screamed. Toby grabbed her hand. Slipping and sliding, they ran toward the passenger compartment.

Alroy couldn't move. Grace shouted something, but he couldn't hear her. A gray whirlwind surrounded him.

Howling like a wounded coyote, the wind held him in its grip.

"Help," he shouted.

The swirling funnel jerked upward, lifting him off the deck, and flinging him toward the rail.

Grace caught his leg. Her grip was surprisingly strong. She shouted, but the wind swept the words away.

"What?"

Glancing around, he could see beyond the haze of the gray

funnel. Everything around him looked calm. There wasn't a cloud in the sky. The airship flew as if nothing were happening on its deck. He punched the wind with his fists and tried to move toward Grace, but the whirlwind held him prisoner. Its force grew stronger and pulled him higher.

He realized he might be ripped off the airship.

Grace's hold on him tightened, and she yanked his leg, trying to pull him down. He watched her feet lift off the deck. The whirlwind spun faster, throwing them near the airship's cabin door. Alroy spotted the tubes and wires that ran from the deck floor to the top of the pilot's cabin. If he could get a hold on one of the pipes, he might be able to break free. He made a wild swimming motion, pushing against the funnel and reaching for something to grab.

His fingers brushed against the metal tubing but slid away. Frantically, he flung himself forward.

Desperate, he shouted, "Help. Help me."

Then his hand slammed into metal. Pain shot up his arm, and he screamed.

Ignoring the fiery stinging in his knuckles, he grabbed the cold metal, clutching it with both hands. Feeling safer, he closed his eyes and waited for the pounding in his chest to quiet.

Grace still held his leg. Her touch grounded him and kept him from complete panic.

The whirlwind roared around him. It smashed them both in the corner as if angry or trying to compel him to let go. The strength of the current pulled at his fingers, but he held on tighter. He focused on moving downward. Inch by inch, he slid his hands down the tubing. While the gale tugged and lashed around him, he worked his way downward. When he felt his fingers slipping away, he tightened his grip.

When he'd lowered himself enough, Grace grabbed him by his waist and jerked him downward. Now she was inside the whirlwind. Together they moved toward the cabin door. Toby held the door frame with one hand and reached out toward them with his other hand.

Alroy and Grace made incremental progress toward the door. Time slowed, seconds felt like minutes as they moved toward Toby's outstretched hand. Alroy felt his fingers slipping off the tube. He couldn't hold on.

Toby grabbed Grace's wrist.

"Let go," Grace yelled.

Alroy released his grip.

Toby jerked them toward the door.

The funnel tugged harder almost wrenching Alroy away from Grace. But she held him fast.

Toby pulled harder, straining against the force that surrounded them.

Wind whipped Alroy against the metal siding. Darkness spread inside the funnel, and he couldn't see Toby or Grace, who still held him. Then he saw the door frame and Toby, who screamed soundless words.

Grace tightened her hand around his and yanked him forward. He grabbed the door frame pushing Grace into the airship and propelling himself forward. His forward motion freed him from the whirlwind. He tumbled into the cabin.

Zella slammed the door.

The whirlwind roared and butted the door, pounding it again and again. The airship rocked back and forth.

Alroy crumpled onto the wooden floor, taking deep breaths. The gulps of air burned his lungs, and his body shook. He couldn't stop the tremors.

His inner voice repeated, "I'm alive. I'm alive."

"What happened?" Zella sat beside Alroy, holding his hand.

"There's a blanket under each seat and water's over there. Wrap him up and get him a drink." Grace glanced up at Ernest. "What's happening?"

"Nothing, except the damn funnel banging against the ship. It's calm outside." Ernest sounded frustrated.

The ship rocked again as the funnel hit the door.

Grace glanced at Alroy.

"You okay?"

He was far from okay, but he nodded anyway.

Grace raced up the ladder.

She and Ernest had their heads close together, talking about something. Grace glanced at gauges and pointed outside. The airship shot up into the air. Tossing Alroy against a seat, which stopped his slide. The ship straightened, flying parallel to the ground.

Toby lifted Alroy to his feet and helped him to the nearest seat. Zella threw a blanket around his shoulders, hovering over him and fussing. When Toby brought him water, he drank, thankful for its soothing effect on his throat. He took several deep breaths and pulled the blanket around him. His body relaxed, and his tremors lessened.

He couldn't take his eyes off of Grace. She'd saved him from flying off the ship. He watched her siting next to Ernest, talking and shaking her head.

Then she vanished.

One second she was there, and the next he couldn't see her. Alroy blinked several times and pointed to the copilot's seat. Before Zella and Toby turned to look, Grace reappeared. He rubbed his eyes and glanced at the observation deck. The whirlwind was gone.

"What happened?" Alroy asked.

"We were standing there, and you had a funny look on your face. Then . . ." Zella glanced at Toby.

"Then the whirlwind hit the ship and wrapped around you," he added.

Grace descended the ladder and motioned Zella out of the

seat next to Alroy. Taking his hand in both hers, she pushed up his jacket sleeve and rubbed his wrist. After a few seconds, she did the same with his other hand. Her hands were cool and soft. When she touched him, a calm feeling spread through this body. His tense muscles relaxed, and his anxiety receded.

"What's wrong?" Toby said. "You think we're going to crash and die?"

"Nothing so melodramatic," she said, her soft blue-gray eyes watching Alroy.

"That wasn't normal." Toby plopped down on the floor in front of them.

"No, it wasn't normal." Her voice sounded even, calm.

Her touch had the strangest effect on Alroy. Before, he'd felt weak and drained, but her massage gave him strength. She examined each of his wrists. She stared as if she were expecting to find something.

"What were you thinking about when the airship started to rock?" Grace asked.

"Well," Toby said. "I was thinking that Zella needed a ribbon to keep her hair in place."

Grace glared at Toby.

"Alroy, what were *you* thinking?"

The muscles in his chest tightened. He glanced at Zella, who looked anxious.

"He's upset," Zella said. "I don't see how his thoughts had anything to do with what happened."

"Trust me," Grace said and gazed at Alroy, and her look demanded an answer.

He took a deep breath.

"I haven't had a chance to tell you," he said to Zella. "But Pedro might be missing. He didn't come home last night, and his mother is worried."

Zella stared at him as if she didn't understand.

"I was thinking about Pedro," he said to Grace. "I was worried that . . . something might be wrong."

"I don't see—"

"Not now, Toby." Grace still held Alroy's hand. "This airship is different from other ships. It's more advanced. Your thoughts have upset . . ."

"The ship?" Toby raised his eyebrows. "Do you know how stupid that sounds?"

Before Grace could answer, Ernest's voice boomed out. "Tobias Bailey, apologize to my sister. Now."

Ernest stood at the edge of the pilot's station. A fierce, thunderous look replaced his devil-may-care expression.

Toby lifted his hands, palms up.

"Did you hear what she said?"

Ernest raised one eyebrow ever so slightly.

Toby sighed.

"Miss Camero, please forgive my rudeness."

Grace nodded to Toby, and Ernest returned to the pilot seat.

"I know what I said sounds crazy, but the ship may have been reacting to Alroy's thoughts." She scrunched her lips together. "Or something else. Let's hope it was his thoughts."

"Are you saying the ship is alive? It can read minds? Or something else?" Alroy asked, thinking Toby was right. She sounded crazy.

"It's a bit more complex than that. It's not as hocus-pocus as it sounds. And none of you can speak of this to anyone. I don't like to be dishonest, but it's best. I'll figure this out, and I'll talk with Wyatt."

Alroy was getting tired of people telling him to keep secrets. He didn't mind keeping his own secrets, but not everyone else's, too.

"I don't think Wyatt would understand," Toby said. "My imagination dreams up all sorts of crazy stuff, and I don't understand."

Grace didn't exactly frown, but her lips went tight.

"You don't have to understand. Ernest is flying us home, and you three need to check on Pedro. See if he's missing or if he's home."

Zella covered her face and sobbed. Alroy tried to jump up to comfort her, but he felt weak. He couldn't help sinking back down into the seat like a helpless ninny.

"It's my fault," she said.

"Naw," Toby said.

She glanced at Toby. Her face scrunched up as if she were in pain.

"Yes, it is. Pedro is helping me investigate a smuggling ring. We have four suspects, maybe five. Pedro works for some of them."

She sobbed again, but immediately straightened up, standing tall as if bracing for their reaction.

"Don't you see? These people are criminals. He was checking things at work. What if one of them caught him? What if--"

"Let's leave the speculation for later," Grace said. "Right now, we need to find out if Pedro is or isn't missing."

"We are landing in about two minutes," Ernest called out.

Alroy took Zella's hand. "We'll find him."

He thought he should be angry with her for keeping her investigation a secret. But he wasn't. He was too exhausted to be worried. He knew why Zella didn't ask for his or Toby's help. Toby was a blabbermouth, and he would have lectured her as he did this morning. Maybe if he didn't nag so much, she would have asked for help.

A smuggling ring? What was she thinking? And, Pedro, why'd he let her? It was dangerous, beyond dangerous.

Alroy kept his thoughts to himself. He didn't want to make Zella feel worse. Plus, Pedro could be in serious trouble. He hoped he was wrong.

On top of all that, the airship might be something right out of one of Toby's crazy stories. Grace sounded like a loony bird. What if the ship had heard his thoughts? Why would it grab him? To punish him for having evil thoughts?

But one thing was crystal clear. They had to find out if Pedro was missing or safe at home.

CHAPTER 13: ALROY

SONORA TOWN

July 19, 1890
3:30 p.m.

Alroy, Zella, and Toby left Grace and Ernest as soon as the airship landed. They took a trolley to the edge of Sonora Town. After the excitement of the time machine's success and the crazy whirlwind attack, Alroy felt drained and lethargic, but he kept going. He had to know if Pedro was home.

They entered Sonora Town, which wasn't a town but a neighborhood in Los Angeles.

To Alroy, this part of town was like another world. They'd left behind the modern Los Angeles they knew and stepped into this old, poor, rundown area. He knew this was where people without resources settled. His papa used to say going to Sonora Town was like taking a culinary world tour. Mostly Mexican families lived here, but there were also Italians, Chinese, Negroes, and a few Indians.

This wasn't a tree-lined neighborhood with two-story houses. Here, the houses and businesses were crammed together adobes in need of repair. The plaster on some buildings had holes and missing chunks. He'd heard about this section of town, but he didn't expect it to be so dreary.

The atmosphere felt oppressive.

The neighborhood had a reputation for being wild and dangerous. The Women's Temperance League called it a sin-filled place, but Alroy didn't see those things. Sonora Town was run-down and impoverished. But in the light of day, it was quiet and sleepy.

The savory smell of beans, potatoes, and something else he couldn't place filled the air. The odors reminded Alroy he was hungry. Half a block later, he breathed deeply and discovered the wall beside him reeked of urine and stale tobacco. He grabbed Zella's arm and pulled her closer. She didn't protest, so he assumed she'd inhaled the olfactory mixture too.

Ahead of them, two boys chased a lone donkey up and down the street, trying to catch it as it brayed and ran from them. An older man with a wooden bucket balanced on his head ambled toward them. Atop the bucket, a neatly folded, heavy cloth made a lid. The man held a basket filled with small glass cups and spoons.

"*Helado. Helado,*" he called.

Alroy didn't know much Spanish, but he knew that *helado* was ice cream. His mouth watered, and the thought of eating something cold in this heat appealed to him, but he He tried to convince himself that Pedro was home and safe. He imagined heckling him for giving them a fright. They'd all laugh and tell him about the airship ride. Pedro would have a good laugh when he heard Grace's crazy claim that the ship could read thoughts. He'd pretend he hadn't been frightened out of his mind. Toby would make the story sound funnier than it was.

"Where's his house?" he asked Toby.

"Not far. I think there." He pointed to a narrow street.

Halfway down the block, they entered what looked like someone's yard. Slipping through the unpainted gate, they found a dirt courtyard surrounded by a large horseshoe-shaped adobe. In the far corner, a small California sycamore made a valiant effort to survive in the hard-packed soil. When they entered the courtyard, two children playing under the sycamore stopped and stared. Alroy wondered if this was what it felt like to visit a foreign land, or to fly to the moon, or to fall down a rabbit hole the way Alice did in *Through the Looking Glass*?

Toby knocked on the second door.

"What is this?" Alroy whispered.

"Pedro's house. Well, his room. They live in a room."

"A room?" Zella glanced around at the other doors.

Toby knocked again.

Someone pulled back the window curtain and peeked outside. A few seconds later, the door opened. A short, pretty girl, who looked oddly like a female Pedro, opened the door and smiled. Alroy hadn't seen Maria in a while. She'd grown taller.

"I'm so glad you came. Come in."

They stepped inside a dimly lit room. A candle on the table and one on a wooden cupboard gave off the only light. The room smelled stuffy. A patched blanket sectioned off the room from whatever lay beyond. In the corner opposite the table, a bed made of planks and a lumpy mattress hugged the wall. Next to the bed, a homemade bookcase overflowed with books— Pedro's books. The bed was neatly made with a quilt Grace had given Pedro for Christmas.

Unable to keep still, Alroy tapped his fingers on the side of his leg. Zella casually swatted his hand. A fish riding an elephant would be more at home than he was. He flashed Maria an unenthusiastic smile. In his wildest imagination, he couldn't believe anyone lived like this, especially not Pedro, who was optimistic, intelligent, and clean. He was meticulous in his dress, and he never once complained about his new home. His other house had been a few blocks from Alroy's home.

For the first time, Alroy wondered why they'd moved.

Pedro's mother had run a boarding house that always had renters. Some of them had lived there for years. This didn't seem right.

"Is Pedro here?" Alroy asked.

Maria pressed her lips together and shook her head. She glanced at the makeshift curtain.

"He's missing. He didn't come home last night," she whispered.

Alroy's earlier hopes vanished. The dim, oppressive room added to his disappointment, and his exhaustion returned.

Maria tried to smile, but her mouth looked thin and stretched. The droop of her shoulders echoed his wretchedness. His earlier hope that his friend was safe vanished.

Zella immediately hugged Maria and gazed over the girl's shoulder at Alroy. In her eyes, he saw fear. When the girls parted, Zella stiffened her back. Alroy knew she'd decided to fight with all the ferocity she possessed. Beside him, Toby hung his head and sighed.

Knowing the truth didn't set Alroy free, but knowing Pedro was missing gave him a clear objective. He promised himself he'd do whatever it took to find his friend.

"*Mija*, are Pedro's friends here?"

"Yes, Mama."

"I'll come out."

Behind the makeshift curtain, a bed creaked. A few seconds later, Sara Hernandez shuffled into the room. Under normal circumstances, she was a pretty, vivacious woman, but today she looked frail and pale. The white lace shawl wrapped around her shoulders couldn't hide her bony frame. She shuffled forward in her worn slippers and carefully lowered herself onto one of the wooden chairs. She leaned her elbows on the table as if she needed the support to stay upright.

Alroy sucked in his breath. His instinct was to rush forward and help her, but he didn't want to embarrass her. Mrs.

Hernandez didn't have a summer cold as he'd imagined. She was ill.

"Do you know where Pedro is?" Her voice sounded breathless.

"No, we don't. But we will find him." Alroy hoped he sounded convincing, if for no other reason than to convince himself.

"I'm worried."

Maria placed a hand on her mother's shoulder.

"Our brother is a detective. He'll help," Zella said.

Mrs. Hernandez patted her daughter's hand.

"She told Officer Henderson. He did nothing."

"My brother will help," Zella insisted.

She sounded so confident Alroy almost believed her. Almost was the key word because he didn't think Wyatt would care about Pedro. If Alroy went missing, Wyatt wouldn't bother looking for him. Heck, his brother would probably celebrate.

A coughing fit shook Mrs. Hernandez. She put her handkerchief to her mouth and doubled over. When the coughing passed, she gasped for breath. Each time she inhaled, her chest rattled with a wheezing sound.

"Mama, you need to get back to bed." She put her hand on her mother's elbow and helped her up. They disappeared behind the curtain.

Toby moved to Pedro's bookcase and rummaged through their friend's belongings.

"Stop that," Zella hissed.

Toby waved her back as if dismissing her. He knelt down. On the bottom shelf in the back, he pulled out a notebook and flipped through the pages.

"A journal."

"So what?" Alroy shrugged.

"Pedro writes everything down. Did he give you notes?" Toby asked Zella.

"He didn't have time."

"I'm sure this will help." Toby handed the journal to Zella.

"Some of it's in code," she said as she glanced over the pages.

Behind them, Maria cleared her throat.

"Take it. If it will help, take it."

Maria glanced back at the curtain and motioned them forward.

"Pedro acted nervous yesterday," she whispered. "I heard him leave. He waited until he thought we were asleep."

Zella put her arm around Maria.

"Don't worry." She guided the frightened girl back to the table. "Is it okay if they look through Pedro's things?"

Maria nodded.

Alroy couldn't remember how old Maria was. He guessed ten or eleven, but her face carried a burden. When he looked at her, he saw darkness and sadness. She was a little girl. For a moment, he was angry with Pedro for being gone. Almost as soon as he had the thought, guilt accused him of disloyalty.

Alroy watched Toby search the bookcase. He wanted to act, but his feet were planted in one place, and all he could do was stare. This moment was a trial or a test of his character. He'd failed. Zella and Toby took action. He froze. They were helpful. He inactive. In a frenzy of desperation, he glanced around, searching for some way to redeem himself.

Pedro knew how ill his mother was. He wouldn't leave her. Which could only mean one thing, he was in trouble. If he were here, he'd get a doctor, and he'd take care of his mother.

"Look." Toby rummaged through a cigar box filled with newspaper clippings. "The shanghai trade is lucrative," Toby read. He grabbed another clipping. "Listen. 'There are unsubstantiated rumors of smuggling and slave trade in Los Angeles.'"

Alroy whistled and sat down next to Toby.

"We need these. He was collecting evidence," Alroy said, picking up the article on smuggling.

"Think she'd mind if we took them?"

"She offered the journal. I don't see a problem."

"We gotta go. We gotta get Wyatt's help," Toby said.

"What about his ma? She looks real sick."

"We can't do anything about that."

"What would Pedro do if he were here?" Alroy ran his hand through his hair. "You got any money? Maria could get some food, some kerosene." He pointed to the empty lanterns on the other side of the room.

Toby rummaged in his pockets. He pulled out some change. After a fast count, he said, "Sixty-three cents."

"I've got seventy-five, no wait, eighty-five," Alroy said.

Zella marched across the room with her hand outstretched for the money. She put it on the table in front of Maria, who stared at the coins.

"I don't know how to thank you."

"We're going to send a doctor to look at your mother." Zella glanced at Alroy, "Right?"

He nodded. For about the millionth time, Alroy wondered if Zella had read his mind. More often than not, she knew what he was thinking.

"We can't pay for a doctor," Maria whispered.

"Take care of your mother. Don't worry about the doctor." Alroy patted her shoulder. He felt awkward, but he hoped his words comforted her.

When they left and stepped outside, Alroy expected the world to be different. At the very least, he wanted the sky to be black and littered with thunderclouds. Instead, the heat and bright sunlight mocked him.

At least, now they knew Pedro was missing, and they had a plan. Go to Doctor Stone's for help, talk to Wyatt, and decode the journal. Positive steps helped him focus. He could push his worry away and take action.

At the trolley stop, Toby threw his arms up.

"Well, Sir Lancelot, we're broke."

"A good Samaritan doesn't give all his money away." Zella held her coin purse and shook it.

At First Street, they got off the trolley and headed to Doctor Stone's office. Zella marched ahead like a soldier going to battle. A closed sign didn't stop her from pushing the door open. Doctor Stone stood in his empty waiting room and frowned when he saw them.

"Going home," he said.

"Pedro's mother is very ill. You must go see her immediately."

"Young lady, you can't barge in here and make demands."

"Yes, I can. A woman's life is in danger. She needs medical attention."

Dr. Stone grabbed his jacket and slipped it on.

"Listen here, Zella, I brought you into this world, and I know for a fact that you know next to nothing about being a doctor."

"I know enough. She's weak, looks like a sack of bones, and has a hacking cough. She's wheezing."

"Girl, you remind me of your father, stubborn like a mule. I'm going home. It's roast beef night. I'll see her later."

Zella blocked his way.

He glanced at Alroy.

"Is it as bad as she says?"

"Yes, sir. Maybe worse. You got time before dinner," Alroy added.

"My observations aren't as good as his?" Zella crossed her arms as if challenging him.

"Unknot your knickers." Dr. Stone grabbed his hat, plopped it on his head, and grabbed his bag. "I don't know why you didn't turn out like your mother. She's a quiet, gentle soul."

"And look where that got her." Zella sounded angry.

"She's worried." Alroy stepped between his sister and the doctor. "We came here from Pedro's. His ma's bad, real bad."

Alroy couldn't tell if his words pacified the doctor, who glared at Zella as if he were going to give her a piece of his mind. As much as he loved his sister, there were times when he wished she didn't rush at things like she was going into battle with Satan himself.

"Maria is the daughter, and Sara Hernandez is the mother," Zella said, ignoring Doctor Stone's sour expression. "Here's the address." She shoved a piece of paper into his hand.

"This is in Sonora Town. Have you kids been there?"

"Yes, we have," Zella said. "Wyatt will pay your fee and for any medicine she needs."

Alroy couldn't stop himself from grinning. How could he stay annoyed with Zella when she just put Wyatt's pocketbook on tap. His brother would be madder than a vampire without blood.

The doctor studied the address.

"Why are they in Sonora Town?"

"That's where they live," Toby said.

"Tobias Bailey. You know that's not what I mean."

"They moved. We don't know why." Toby looked to Alroy, who nodded.

Dr. Stone slipped the paper into his bag.

"I'll get to the bottom of this."

"Bottom of what?" Alroy asked. "His ma's sick. There's no bottom to get to."

"A lady like Mrs. Hernandez doesn't own a nice home, run a boardinghouse, and suddenly move to Sonora Town. I'm going home first, no arguing."

He frowned at Zella.

"I'll have my missus pack up some food for them. Now, get out of here. I gotta lock up."

He made a shooing motion with his hands.

"You won't forget?" Zella looked very much like someone who regretted her words as soon as she spoke.

"How's your mother?"

"The same," Zella said.

"Have I ever forgot about her?"

"No, sir."

Doctor Stone looked at Zella, and the hardness around his mouth softened.

"Think before you speak. Passion can be a good thing, but you have to control it. Or it will control you. I'll see Mrs. Hernandez, and you'll show some respect."

"Yes, sir," Zella said. "Since you're going home first, they could use some kerosene. It's pretty dark inside their room."

"Hmph," Doctor Stone grunted.

Zella nodded. Alroy took his sister's hand and squeezed it. Toby had the good sense to keep quiet until the doctor was out of hearing distance.

"What was that about Pedro's house? He made their move sound fishy," Toby said, staring after the doctor.

Adults were about as cooperative as a litter of cats. They said things to make you curious, and then they ran off without explaining. He and Zella were fifteen, and Toby was sixteen. He thought it was about time people started treating them like adults.

When Alroy was grown, he was going to tell kids everything. He wouldn't keep anyone in the dark. Even though the doctor's insinuations about Pedro's house worried him, he wasn't going to get sidetracked. Right now, his motto was "stick to the plan," even when that plan meant asking his self-righteous brother for help.

CHAPTER 14: ALROY

WYATT

July 19, 1890
5:30 p.m.

Wyatt was the last person Alroy would choose to help find Pedro, but he knew Toby and Zella were right. His half-brother was a detective with the Los Angeles Police Department, which didn't mean Alroy liked asking for his help, but it was the practical thing to do. He grudgingly agreed.

Pedro was part of the League, and the League was family. His father's motto was loyalty to friends and family, and Alroy clung to his father's values. He, Zella, and Toby would find Pedro with or without the police, but they might as well try the police first.

The police anchored their dirigible on the roof, which made it visible from blocks away. Large black letters on the white balloon proclaimed L.A. Police Dept. It amused Alroy that criminals could see the coppers coming from miles away. Once he asked Wyatt for a tour of the airship, but his half-brother ignored his request. Since then, every time he saw the dirigible, a small cloud of annoyance gathered over him. He shrugged the feeling aside.

Outside the police station, two automatons flanked the doorway. Among business owners and some wealthy home-owners, the current fashion was to post automatons to guard against thievery. The irony was blatant. At best, the automatons sent an ambiguous message. Everyone knew Bracken's Automatons paid the department to display their product. If he wanted to annoy his brother, he could always ask him if the police were taking bribes. Not today, he'd save that barb for another time.

The downtown streets were nearly empty. When Alroy, Toby, and Zella stepped inside the police station, they left the quiet behind. The noise from the station echoed in the entryway.

Alroy loved the diverse people that assembled in the police station. Polite society worked hard to distance criminals and unsavory elements from everyday life. Here all spectrums of society paraded and pranced.

Old Elijah turned away from the police officer he'd been talking to. As he walked toward them, he grinned and took his hat off when he noticed Zella.

"Boys, Miss Zella," the old man said.

He grabbed Toby's arm.

"I told them about the vampire," he whispered. "No one will listen. Told me to go get some food. Fools."

Toby patted the man's back.

"It's okay. You got food?"

The man grinned and patted his pocket.

"Yeah, half a sandwich from this morning."

Elijah shuffled past them.

"I think he's getting worse," Alroy said. "He was lost this morning."

They walked to the front desk where they had a clear view of the main room with its arched doorways, lofty mahogany ceilings, and worn pedestrian furnishings. Two coppers, deep in conversation, stood by a tall window. Alroy reminded himself not to say *copper* aloud. His father always insisted he eschew slang words. He tried, but, more often than not, he forgot.

A few feet away, a tall, lanky man shouted at two big-bosomed women, who looked like painted dolls dressed in shabby clothes. An officer stood between the man and the two women.

"Sit down and shut up. Now," the officer shouted, pointing to the bench by his desk.

Sergeant Matthews, a round man with squinty eyes, sat at the wooden counter that separated the public from the inside of the police station. He did his best to smile, but his mouth only managed a smirk.

"Here to see Detective Doyle?" the sergeant asked.

"Yes, sir," Alroy said, poking Toby, who was staring at the women.

Toby nodded toward the telephone. They'd read about Thomas Edison's patent litigation and wanted a closer look at the candlestick telephone. He knew Wyatt had one in his office. Maybe they'd get a chance to examine it.

The sergeant picked up the receiver, clicked the switch hook twice, and spoke into the carbon microphone. He knew all this because he, Toby, and Pedro had read everything they could get their hands on about the new telephone.

"Your brother and sister are here," the sergeant said.

Matthews placed the receiver back in its cradle.

"Go on back."

As they trooped toward the back of the building, Toby glanced around the room. Alroy had been here several times, so he didn't see much to gawk at, except the women's bosoms, and he wasn't inclined to do that with Zella at their side. Toby had a habit of examining places and people because he was a writer. He'd probably put the police station in one of his books.

Maybe some monster would kill the police. Alroy smiled at the idea.

Maybe a werewolf could eat Wyatt.

His half-brother's office was in the back of the station. There were three small offices. Two detectives shared an office. Detective Doyle and Detective Jackson's names were painted in neat black letters on the windowed door. Half the office wall was glass, so they could see Wyatt, sitting alone and reading. When he noticed them, he stood and motioned them inside.

Alroy's stomach tightened, and he stood up straighter. He decided to be calm and aloof.

Wyatt was thirteen years older than Alroy and Zella, but he still looked boyish and deceptively earnest. He stacked the papers he'd been reading into a pile and pushed them aside. His long black duster and black Stetson hung on hooks behind his desk and his rifle above them. When he walked around town in his duster and hat, he looked like a cowboy from Tombstone and acted like Los Angeles was still the wild town of the past. Other detectives dressed in street clothes and felt hats so they could blend in with everyone. The idea that they thought they could blend with ordinary citizens amused Alroy. Since there were only six detectives in the city, and their pictures were in the newspaper all the time, everyone knew them by sight.

Their father always bragged about his oldest son's height. Wyatt stood a little more than six feet tall, but he was too slender to be intimidating. Alroy guessed that in Ireland, where his father came from, most men were short. He didn't see anything special about how tall a person was. It wasn't like Wyatt did something to get taller.

"Well, this is a nice surprise," Wyatt said as he sat down. "Have a seat."

Wyatt's voice was the other thing that annoyed Alroy. It was deep and sort of raspy, which normally would be a good thing, but Wyatt was soft-spoken and wasted the benefit of a manly voice.

Toby wandered over to the small table in the corner while Alroy and Zella took the chairs facing the desk. Wyatt puckered his lips as he watched Toby, who moved closer to the equipment. Running his hand over the microscope, he bent down, examined the metal handcuffs and the wooden baton before glancing at the papers on the table.

"Finger impressions?" Toby glanced at Wyatt.

"Yes. Dactyloscopy. I'm creating a catalog."

"Catching criminals with science." Toby grinned. "I like it. I read they are calling them fingerprints."

Wyatt grimaced and squinted his eyes. He ignored Toby's comment.

Alroy wanted to get up and look at the fingerprints, but doing that wouldn't exactly be acting calm and aloof. So he frowned instead.

Zella cleared her throat.

"We're here about something important," she said.

Toby plopped on the edge of Wyatt's desk. For a second, Alroy thought his half-brother might say something about Toby's seating choice, but Wyatt leaned back in his swivel chair and raised his auburn eyebrows.

"So, what can I do for you?"

Alroy waited for Toby or Zella to speak. They were the ones who insisted on coming here. They should start the conversation. *He* certainly wasn't going to tell Wyatt anything. He stared at the brass contraption that looked like Grace's automatic tea-making machine and realized the invention was a twin to hers. Grace probably made it for Wyatt. Alroy frowned. The aroma of coffee permeated the small room.

He wasn't sure how many seconds passed, but the silence seemed extensive. Then, as if someone said, "One, two, three, go," Zella and Toby talked at once.

"One at a time, please." Wyatt pointed toward Zella.

"We have a serious problem. Pedro is missing. He's been gone since yesterday. His mother is sick . . . very sick. We think something has happened to him. He and I have been checking on . . ." She licked her lips and glanced at Alroy.

"Yes?" Wyatt asked.

"A smuggling ring. We're investigating a smuggling ring."

As she spoke, Wyatt squinted his eyes until only a sliver of blue eye showed.

"Smuggling? What in the Sam Hill are you kids doing?"

"First, we aren't kids. We're almost adults." Zella smoothed her skirt and folded her hands in her lap. "We, Pedro and I, are investigating. Pedro was gathering information, and he and I were going to write about it."

Wyatt wasn't just frowning. His face grew redder as Zella spoke, and his cheeks looked as if they would catch fire and explode.

"Have you lost your mind?" He turned his fiery gaze on Alroy. "And, you. You allowed this?"

Alroy shrugged.

"I'm not my sister's keeper."

"Don't be flippant with me, young man," Wyatt said, as he stood and leaned toward Alroy.

"I think we should all calm down." Toby stood and stepped away from Wyatt.

Wyatt glared at Toby.

"Shut up."

Toby didn't flinch.

"With all due respect, we came here to ask for your help," Toby said. "Our friend is missing, perhaps in trouble."

"Maria, Pedro's sister, told a police officer he was missing, and the officer didn't do anything about it," Zella added.

Toby and Zella sounded about a zillion times calmer than

Wyatt, whose veins popped out on his neck. He took a deep breath and exhaled before sitting down.

"Which officer did Pedro's sister speak to? And when?"

Zella glanced at her notes and ran her index finger down the page until she found his name.

"Officer Gunter Henderson. This morning." She looked up at him with a challenging glare.

"This morning. That's only a few hours ago," Wyatt said.

"Did he put in a report? Did he look for Pedro? If I'd been gone since last night, would you sit around saying we'll give it more time?"

Her voice sounded fierce.

"Hold on," Wyatt said.

He marched out of the office and slammed the door, which rattled the glass windows. In the main room, he spoke to an officer, who pointed to another man. Wyatt stomped over to a portly police officer with a straggly mustache and beard. When he saw Wyatt, the man straightened up. His half-brother did most of the talking, but from time to time, the officer frowned and glanced at them.

"That conversation went well," Toby said.

Zella punched Alroy in the arm.

"I'm not my sister's keeper."

"Hey, I'm trying not to nag," Alroy said.

"I don't know why he's so angry. He always encourages me," Zella said, ignoring Alroy's response.

"I think he imagined you investigating something less dangerous. Like why doesn't the marching band have new uniforms?" Toby picked up the large piece of quartz crystal on the desk and set it back down.

When Wyatt returned, Toby smiled, Alroy sat still, and Zella challenged him with her best "don't give me any guff" look.

"Officer Henderson doesn't know anything about Pedro. The sister never reported a missing person."

"He's lying." The words popped out of Alroy's mouth before he had time to think.

Zella nodded.

"You can't make accusations about an officer. Am I supposed to take the word of this little girl?"

"Yes," Zella said. "She's scared. She didn't have a reason to lie. The person who was supposed to help her didn't."

Wyatt sighed.

"You, too, Zella?"

She looked at him with wide eyes. "Yes."

Toby stepped toward the office window and stared at Officer Henderson, who was talking to another officer.

"Suppose he is lying," Toby said. "Would it be the first time an officer lied? Why would Maria lie? She wants to find her brother."

Wyatt rapped his fingers on his desk, "Sometimes—"

"I know, sometimes you want to slap me. I get that a lot," Toby said.

"That's true, but what I was going to say is sometimes you ask the right questions."

"Yeah." Toby grinned. "Well, the next question is . . . why's he lying?"

"First of all, I'm not going to jump to that conclusion. Officer Mason also patrols Sonora Town. Maybe Pedro's sister got the two mixed up."

"I don't think she was mistaken. She said Henderson doesn't like Pedro because he snoops around Sonora Town." Zella tapped her notes as if they were proof of Maria's truthfulness.

"You all have a habit of snooping around." Wyatt hammered the words as if he were trying to control his anger. "Officer Henderson thinks Pedro ran away."

Wyatt held his hand up.

"Before you start, listen to me. Officer Henderson says a lot of boys in Sonora Town have too many responsibilities. Eventually, the burdens wear them down. They can't take the pressure and run off. In this case, he said Pedro's father ran off, and Pedro probably did the same thing."

"That theory stinks more than old lady McMacken's outhouse," Zella said.

Alroy suppressed a grin.

"Look, I'm going to get to the bottom of this, but I'm not jumping to conclusions. I'll talk to Pedro's mother and Officer Mason. What did Pedro's mother tell you?"

When Zella finished reading her notes, Wyatt asked for them. She ripped the page from her notebook and passed it to him.

"The address is in the corner."

She reached into her bag. When Alroy saw her grab Pedro's journal, he held his breath. Toby stepped behind her and placed his hands on her shoulder and squeezed.

"That's all we know," Toby said. "We'll leave, and let you get to work."

Zella released Pedro's notebook, and it slipped back into her bag.

Wyatt shook his finger at Zella.

"I'm not done discussing this smuggling business. I want to speak to Alroy for a moment. He'll meet you two outside. Then go directly home."

Zella paused in the doorway.

"By the way, we sent Dr. Stone to check on Pedro's mother. I told him to send the bill to you."

Wyatt looked constipated.

"Perhaps you should--"

"I know." Zella gave him a coy, innocent grin. "There wasn't time. She's very ill, as you'll see."

Alroy wanted to block Toby and Zella from leaving, but he didn't. He sat alone and stared at his brother, who rubbed his chin before running his fingers through his auburn hair. He figured that Wyatt would blame him, and he'd say all the things he wouldn't say in front of Toby.

"I'll do what I can," Wyatt said. "But you have to keep Zella out of trouble."

Alroy shrugged.

"Goddamn." Wyatt shook his head. "I'm disappointed in you."

Clenching his jaws, Alroy waited.

"Say something."

He struggled to keep his voice calm. "There's really nothing to say."

"Quit being a mule."

Wyatt sat higher than Alroy, making him feel small and childish. So he stood and glared down at Wyatt. His courage and determination seemed to grow stronger.

"Zella doesn't need your help or my help to stay out of trouble. She's smart. She can take care of herself."

Wyatt pointed at him.

"And that's the problem. You two are out of control, running around town, doing whatever you want. It's gotta stop. No more going to Sonora Town. No more investigating."

Alroy couldn't calm his breathing. He sounded like a bull ready to charge. In fact, he wanted to lower his head and ram into Wyatt.

"You're not my father." The words sounded high-pitched and juvenile, like some whiny eight-year-old. The last thing he wanted was to act like a kid.

"I'm not trying to be your father." Wyatt rubbed the back of his neck.

"My father taught us to follow our dreams. He told Zella being a girl only kept her from her dreams if she let it. Every morning at the breakfast table, he told us, 'Take a chance. Do something brave. Don't let fear hold you back.' You'll have to step over my dead body before you cage Zella."

"You got the doddering old fool for a father. *My* father taught me to keep my mouth shut, work hard, and follow the rules. That keeps you out of trouble."

Alroy didn't trust himself to speak. He imagined jumping Wyatt and punching him in the face.

"Being an investigative reporter is foolish and dangerous," Wyatt continued. "She's a girl and needs to be protected."

Alroy straightened and looked Wyatt in the eye.

"I wish Grace had heard that. I've heard you tell her that women should be able to vote, hold jobs, own property, and be equal to men. I guess you're just a goddamn liar."

Wyatt's eyes grew wide. Alroy knew his words had punched his half-brother in his hypocritical face.

"I'm not sure why I bother with you."

"It would suit me just fine if you didn't bother with me or Zella."

"One more thing," Wyatt said. "I'm okay with Toby staying with us, but it's time he sleeps somewhere besides your room."

"What exactly does that mean?"

"It means it's not appropriate for him to be in your room."

Alroy stared, trying to find something witty and smart to say, but anger made him fume.

"Don't glare at me. We can pretend Toby's a boy, but we know he's not."

"If I were a little older and bigger, I'd punch you in the face."

"Leave."

Alroy took several steps forward.

"No. Toby's a boy. He might have the body of a girl, but he's a boy. The only people in all of L.A. who know that are his family and our family. You aren't going to start acting weird around him. And you aren't going to say one single word about this to anyone. You're not going to talk to Toby either."

"I will if I feel it's necessary."

"No, Wyatt, you won't. Is this the way you treat Ernest?"

"We aren't talking about Ernest."

"Why not? You think I'm stupid. Ernest likes—"

"Don't you say it," Wyatt said, standing up and glaring.

"Why? You afraid I might think you're like Ernest?"

Alroy stepped closer. He and Wyatt stared at each other across his desk.

"My father, the doddering old fool, taught me to accept and respect my friend. Toby is a boy even if his body says something different. I'm not going to let anyone hurt him."

He walked to the door and, before opening it, he looked back at Wyatt.

"I bet your father told you something similar about Ernest."

Wyatt's face had gone whiter than usual. He lowered his eyes. Alroy left.

Toby stood in the center of the police station waiting for Alroy.

"Where's Zella?"

"Waiting at the help desk," Toby said. "Thanks for sticking up for me."

"You were reading Wyatt's lips?"

Toby nodded.

"Well, he's a jackass."

"*Mule*, I think he'd want you to say *mule*," Toby said.

They both laughed.

"Let's get home so we can start searching Pedro's journal," Alroy said. He wanted to forget his stupid brother and get busy finding Pedro. "Do you think Wyatt's going to help?"

Toby shrugged.

"Maybe. Zella said she doubted he'd do much, and you know how she thinks Wyatt's the bestest brother."

"We're on our own."

"Yeah, what could possibly go wrong." Toby grinned like a prophet predicting the end of the world.

CHAPTER 15: TOBY

TOBY'S LETTER

July 19, 1890
6:30 p.m.

As they walked away from the police station, Toby's mind played one message over and over. *Wyatt is going to make my life miserable this week.*

When he was a kid, he imagined being part of the Doyle family because Mr. and Mrs. Doyle made him feel safe, which rarely happened at his home.

Wyatt obviously didn't share their views. He saw life in blacks and whites and ignored all the gray areas where people really lived. Right now, he didn't want Toby sleeping in the same room as Alroy. What would be next? Telling him he was a freak, crazy, and a sinner? What did Wyatt think was going to happen? Did he think he'd attack his best friend?

Adults were dumb.

This was the first time he worried about things going wrong for him in the Doyle family. He imagined Wyatt's next request would be for Alroy and Zella not to be his friends.

Alroy jabbed him in the side.

"Ignore Wyatt," Alroy said.

"It's hard to ignore him. He's more or less the head of your family."

"Less," Alroy said.

"Alroy Doyle." A man waved at them and darted across the street, rushing toward them.

"Great," Alroy whispered.

Toby recognized the man but couldn't recall his name. He delivered for the General Store. He didn't exactly look happy to see Alroy. Zella glared at her brother and frowned. They stopped and waited.

"What have you done?" Zella whispered.

The man's brown jacket was open, displaying a potbelly and brown suspenders holding up his brown pants. By the time he reached their side of the street, he was breathing hard.

"I'm sorry about this morning. I was in a hurry and didn't see you," Alroy said.

"That's no excuse. My horse is fine, by the way."

"I expected," Alroy said.

"The little boy on the sidewalk isn't doing so well."

"What boy?" Alroy asked.

"The one who was standing next to my horse. He has a broken arm, and his mother wants my horse killed. Without my horse, I can't make a living."

"What is going on?" Zella said.

"Shhhh," Alroy said.

"Don't you shhh me."

"I was a boy once, and there's a big world out there to explore, but you can't hurt people in your rush."

Alroy hung his head and stared at the man's shoes.

"I didn't mean any harm. I'm sorry about your horse and the boy. What can I do to help?"

The man shook his head and sighed.

"Not much you can do. Be more careful. I talked to your

brother, and he got things squared with the lady. She's not pressing charges and has decided that I can keep my horse. I want you to think about things before your brother gets a hold of you."

"Thank you, sir," Alroy said.

The man crossed the street at a more leisurely pace.

"Well," Zella said. She tapped her foot up and down. The toe of her shoe made her skirt bounce.

"I was riding my bike to Doc's, and I rode too close to his wagon." Alroy shrugged. "The horse got spooked. I didn't see a boy. I kept on riding. I didn't know anyone got hurt."

Zella's face looked less like a storm ready to cut loose and more like a sister who understood. She had this soft look she got when she felt sorry for someone. Toby saw that look a lot. Now she bestowed it on Alroy, who didn't seem to appreciate it.

"Is that what Wyatt was talking to you about?" she asked.

"Obviously not. I didn't know about the boy or the horse. I guess I'm going to get his fury tonight."

"Maybe he's trying to be nice because he knows we're worried about Pedro?" Toby said.

"That would be a miracle." Alroy grinned at him.

"Don't be an ass," Zella snapped. "Let's get home before one of you causes more trouble."

Their walk to the Doyles' house was pretty quiet. Alroy hurried ahead, walking with his shoulders slumped and staring at the ground as if something mighty important was transpiring in front of him. Zella was lost in her thoughts, and Toby gnawed over the idea of losing his best friends.

For about ten seconds, he thought about having a man-to-man talk with Wyatt. He dismissed the idea because the only person he'd ever had a man-to-man talk with was Mr. Doyle, who knew exactly how to talk about things without making Toby feel like a freak. He doubted Wyatt had the same skills.

The front door to Alroy's house opened before they reached

the porch. Dr. Stone stepped onto the wrap-around porch and waited for them.

"Your mother's doing fine," he said. "Liza says she's eating better. That's a good sign."

"Good," Alroy said, sounding as enthusiastic as a tuna fish, if a fish could talk.

"And," Dr. Stone added, "this morning I set a young man's arm. He was in a lot of pain."

"I heard," Alroy said. "I didn't know anyone got hurt. I'm about as sorry as I can be."

"Yeah, I guessed as much. I recommend thinking. Works for me."

"Yes, sir."

"How's Pedro's mother?" Toby asked.

"Well, Zella was right. She's mighty sick. My wife sent some food." Doctor Stone nodded to Zella. "I brought kerosene and left medicine. I'll check on her in the morning."

"Thank you," Zella said.

All that sounded good to Toby, but he was starting to feel sorry for Alroy. He imagined Liza would give him what for when they got inside, and Wyatt was probably saving the big talk for later so he could pace and yell.

They found Liza in the kitchen preparing dinner. There was a peach pie cooling on the counter. Toby stepped forward to get a better smell. Before he knew what was happening, Liza shook her wooden spoon in his face.

"That's for dessert."

He lifted his hands and stepped back.

"I was only looking."

"You got a letter on the table in the hall," she said. "Looks like it's from your mother."

"Really?" Toby said.

"Yeah, she left it here with me and told me to give it to you tonight. It's almost night, and I'm curious about it."

Toby started for the hall table. Behind him, he heard Liza say, "Go with him, Alroy. That letter's been sitting like a bad omen on my mind."

In two shakes, Alroy was at his side. Toby grinned at him.

"She's so superstitious that I gotta put her in a book."

"For your sake, disguise her good. If she recognizes herself, she'll nag you forever and beyond."

The letter with his mother's flowery handwriting sat next to a vase of red and pink roses. It stood out against the polished mahogany of the oval table. Something about his mother leaving a letter for him unsettled his stomach. Why didn't she just tell him what she wanted to say?

He glanced back toward the kitchen. Liza stood in the doorway, drying her hands on a dish towel. Her face contorted with worry, but then her face usually looked that way.

"Let's go out to the porch," he said.

Alroy sat next to him on the steps and waited as he opened the letter.

Dear Toby,

I have to write this fast. I do not have much time. Your father has forbidden me to speak of this, but he said nothing about writing. Technically I am not disobeying him.

I cannot leave without explaining what is happening.

And now that I have paper and pen, I am at a loss for words. There is no easy way to tell you this, so I will write as best as I can.

We are not returning. Your father has arranged for the people who have been renting our old home in San Francisco to move out. There is no other way to say this. We are deserting you.

The words seem so brutal and barbarous. I am sorry I cannot think of a way to lessen the blow.

You will not be allowed to return to us. Your father has told everyone you died in a boating accident.

I have wept and begged him not to do this. But my words and pleas did not move him.

He will tell your sister once we arrive in San Francisco.

I hope that someday you will find a way to forgive us. You will always be in my heart and on my mind.

Regards,

Mother

It wasn't until he got to the end of the letter that he realized he was crying. Not aloud, but the silent kind of tears that slide down the cheeks. The warm breeze cooled his face and dried the tears.

He handed the pages to Alroy, who read the first page and said, "This can't be true."

Toby wiped his face with the back of his jacket sleeve.

"It's true."

"He can't desert his son. That has to be against the law."

"He doesn't consider me his son. I'm a mistake."

"We'll talk to Wyatt when he gets home," Alroy said.

"No. Don't tell anyone. I'll take care of this."

"How?"

"Don't know. I'll figure it out. Go inside. Don't say anything."

"I think I should stay with you."

"No. I'm going over to my house to pound holes in the wall."

"Holes?"

"Maybe I'll just go into the basement and yell until I feel better."

Alroy stood up.

"I'll tell them that your ma left instructions for you to water the plants and dust all the furniture. I'll tell them if they hear someone pounding holes in the wall that it ain't you."

"Don't embellish too much. You're not good at it."

Toby counted each step as he strolled to his house. When he got to the edge of the house where the roof overhang created shade, he stopped. He stared at the small bed of daisies his mother planted every year because they were his father's favorite flowers. He deliberately stepped in the center of the patch. Then he jumped up and down until daisy petals were flattened and ground into the dirt.

He glanced at Alroy, who stood on the porch watching him. He waved and grinned. His friend saluted him and walked back into his house.

Inside what used to be his home, Toby sank down on the hardwood floor and cried aloud. Occasionally he screamed. When fatigue calmed him, he curled up into a ball and closed his eyes. He wasn't sure how long he lay there, but it was long enough for him to realize he could survive without his father.

He would miss his sister, and he'd find a way to see her. He could read between the lines of his mother's letter. She loved him in her own complicated way, but not enough to take care of him. She loved him just enough so people wouldn't be shocked by her coldheartedness. She showed affection when it was socially expedient. At other times, she distanced herself from him in a million little ways like writing, *Regards, Mother.*

He went to the bathroom, washed his face, and proceeded to his mother's sewing room. There he found a large pair of scissors. In his father's library, he studied the leather-bound books. He considered putting them all in a pile and setting them on fire.

Sanity took over.

Instead, he decided to box up the ones he wanted and give the rest to the public library. The librarian would be delighted. His father detested public libraries. He believed that important, intellectual people should have access to books, everyone else should be excluded. Knowledge corrupted the masses.

Toby grinned when he thought about giving the librarian their San Francisco address so she could write and thank Mr. Bailey for his generous donation.

From the library, he went upstairs to his parents' bedroom. He pulled his father's clothes out of the closet and flung them into two piles. One pile for the poor. He found clothes his fat father couldn't wear anymore. He thought a few of them would fit Old Elijah. The other pile was for his father's favorite suits, shoes, and ties. The clothes he wore to meet important people. Of course, they weren't all in the closet. He'd probably taken the best ones with him.

He lifted his father's Sunday suit from the pile. He laid it on the bed as if his mother had set it out for her husband to wear. Holding his mother's scissors, he snipped off the jacket cuffs, then the entire arms. He grinned before cutting the rest of the jacket into narrow strips of fabric. The remains he scattered across the bed. They looked like black streamers on the blue quilt.

The fourth stair from the top of the staircase creaked.

"That you, Alroy?" he called.

His friend stepped into the doorway.

"Yeah, it's me."

"And me," Zella said, poking her head around the corner.

Toby glared at Alroy.

"Don't look at me like that. You know what she's like. She badgered it out of me."

"I'm not going to tell anyone if that's what you're worried about," Zella said.

"Stop staring at me with that doe-eyed look you give me when you think I'm hurting."

"I don't have a doe-eyed look."

"Yes, you do," Toby and Alroy said at the same time.

Toby laughed.

"I could help you cut up those fancy clothes," Zella said.

"Yeah, but dinner's ready, and Liza isn't in a waiting kind of mood," Alroy said. "Plus, Wyatt's home."

"He tear into you yet?" Toby tossed the scissors on the bed.

"Not yet."

"Let's go. I'm hungry," Toby said.

As they walked down the stairs, Toby began to whistle.

"I've got about a million ideas to get back at him."

"As soon as we find Pedro, we'll help you," Zella said and put her arm through Toby's.

They marched across the yard, and Toby imagined they were going to face Wyatt's wrath and Liza's questions.

He still had his best friends, which was much better than being stuck with his coldhearted family. He hurt more than he should have. His family had always viewed him as a burden. He never dreamed they'd desert him. His friends were better than having parents. They cared about him and wouldn't abandon him. Well, that might be true unless Wyatt's influence changed that.

CHAPTER 16: ALROY

PEDRO'S JOURNAL

July 19, 1890
7:45 p.m.

In the short time Alroy and Zella were at Toby's house, Wyatt left again, telling Liza he had work to do and would be home late. Alroy relaxed when he heard the news. At least, he wouldn't have to deal with his brother's unwanted lecture or suffer through an uncomfortable dinner.

It turned out they ate the evening meal in hurried quiet. Alroy's mother stared at her plate. Liza watched Alroy, Zella, and Toby sprint through their meals. When they turned down dessert, she grunted.

"I'll be reading to your ma and getting her settled for the night," Liza said. "You three go do your investigating. I ain't likely to tell Wyatt anything."

Zella grabbed her bag and started up the stairs.

"Thank you, Liza, for the nice meal," Toby said. "I can help you with the dishes if you'd like."

"No need. I'm just fine. I'd rather you help find Pedro," Liza said.

Alroy kissed his mother's cheek and nodded to Liza before hurrying upstairs.

Most people think of an attic as a dark, dusty room filled with discarded items, but to Alroy, the attic was a sanctuary. Like no other place in the house, happy memories of his father lingered in the attic and comforted him. Sometimes Alroy thought he could hear his father's voice. He wished he'd paid closer attention to his lectures.

When Alroy put his foot on the third step from the top of the staircase, Hyde, their Janus faced automaton, moved. His gears clanked, and his metal arms moved outward until his palms pointed toward them as if signaling them to stop. His eyes, several mismatched marbles melted together, opened, and in a low, menacing voice, which sounded remarkably like Toby, he said, "Stop. Password."

The automaton was Hyde when he guarded the door and Jekyll when he stepped away from the door. Grace had given them pointers on the automaton's construction and design. Toby constructed Hyde's face, which was as gruesome and loathsome as the monsters in his stories. Zella fashioned Jekyll's face, which had a striking resemblance to Ernest Camero. To make Jekyll/Hyde look more human, Toby smeared brown paint over his body, making him look like a metal-man who had taken a roll in the mud. In the end, the mishap appealed to them, and they left their automaton looking like a disheveled machine-man.

His head reached the top of the door frame, and his body covered the width of the door. He provided a formidable obstacle for anyone wanting to come into the room.

Alroy opened the hinged door on Hyde's belly and pressed the correct series of buttons.

"Welcome to The League of the Daring. You may enter," Hyde said.

As he finished speaking, Hyde stepped sideways, allowing

them access. When he stopped and stood back from the doorway, his head began its slow turn, and Jekyll stared straight ahead.

The attic was the League's workshop and their private space. They experimented, designed, and built gadgets and prototypes. The room was also Alroy's retreat from the tension that often filled the house since his father's death.

After a visit to Grace's workshop when he was nine, his father gave him and Zella the attic space. He built two large wooden worktables and allowed them to rummage through the attic for old furniture. Liam and Beth Doyle had encouraged their curiosity and their experiments. At first, most of their imagination was devoted to drawing and discussing books, but over the years, their interests took flight and their inventions became more complex.

Toby, never willing to be left out, joined them. He insisted the group had to have a name. The League of the Daring was born, and their father encouraged them to find intelligent, trustworthy friends to join them. Pedro was the smartest person they knew. Lavinia, a close friend of Zella's, completed the group.

Although the other parents thought Liam Doyle was eccentric and complained that he encouraged eccentricity in their children, Alroy believed they were secretly proud of their children's accomplishments.

Pedro and Toby built two cable systems. One went from Toby's bedroom to the Doyle attic and back, and the other to Lavinia's house, which was directly behind the Doyles' house. They used baskets to move things like parts, plans, gadgets, books, and found items from one place to another. Most of their projects made their way to the attic.

Lavinia had a talent for discovering useful items other people discarded. They had collected a shed of spare parts, metals, and sundry items. Zella with Lavinia's help designed an elevator system that took them from the backyard to the attic window and back down. Everyone preferred to arrive at the workshop via the elevator. Even Zella and Alroy used it more often than necessary.

However, the system was noisy. If they wanted to come and go without notice, they sneaked out, using the trellis, which was as strong as a ladder and connected to a three foot wide ledge that circled the attic area. Toby used the highway, as he called it, the most because he liked slipping in unannounced.

Alroy and Zella's father insisted the walkway was designed for easy access to the roof and to paint the upper part of the house. That explanation was far too practical for Toby, who pretended he was a cat burglar. Anyone with a sense of balance could traverse it without difficulty. Even so as an extra precaution, they'd put a handrail along the outside wall. Even Lavinia, who was a little squeamish, found the trip easy.

When they read *The Three Musketeers*, they took *one for all and all for one* as their motto. They created and followed their motto and their pledge, the Four Commitments.

"As a member of The League of the Daring, I am committed to Trustworthiness: I will always be honest, reliable, and loyal. I am committed to Respect: I will always act with civility, courtesy, dignity, tolerance, and acceptance. I am committed to Responsibility: I will always be accountable, pursue excellence, and demonstrate self-restraint. I am committed to Fairness: I will always act fairly, with impartiality, equity, and caring to all. All for one and one for all."

Zella rushed into the attic and sat at the closest worktable. She opened Pedro's notebook and began reading.

"Let's find Pedro," Toby said, rubbing his hands together..

Zella glanced at him. "You okay?"

"Definitely."

"Good," Zella said. "I need butcher paper."

Toby hurried across the room and grabbed the large scissors.

He pulled out the roll of butcher paper hanging on the wall. He cut a generous piece and spread it across the table in front of Zella. Alroy grabbed several pencils, while Toby searched through their map collection and brought a Los Angeles city map to the table.

Alroy didn't like ignoring Toby's problem, but finding Pedro was urgent. They'd help Toby later. For the millionth time, he wished his father were alive. If he were, he'd help them find Pedro, and he'd find a way to help Toby.

"Okay, where exactly were his odd jobs, and who did he work for?" she asked.

"He worked for Mr. Lee, who owns the Chinese herbal shop." Alroy pointed to Broadway and tracked his finger several blocks south to Sonora Town.

Toby stuck a pin on the spot.

Zella added, "Mr. Lee (Chinese herbal shop)" in neatly printed letters.

"Then there's Mr. Clyde Garcia," Toby said. "He sells to farmers and people in Sonora Town. You know, things like feed, horse gear, and farming tools."

Alroy used a stickpin to marked the store on the map, while Zella made notes beside the pin.

"And Doc. He sweeps and puts things away." Alroy stuck another pin on the map as Zella made notes.

"Mrs. and Mr. Hornsby, they own Wong's Laundry. Pedro's mother works there, too," Toby said, pointing to a spot closer to the river. "I think it's here."

"Actually, it's here," Zella said as she moved the pin. "I was doing background research this morning." Her voice sounded quiet and thoughtful.

"I haven't done research, but the Hornsbys live here." Alroy placed a pin six blocks from their own house. "Josh Roswell lives next door to them. He doesn't like the man. Says he's meaner than a coyote."

There was a moment of silence as they studied the map.

"How can Pedro do so much work?" Alroy counted the names. "That's one, two, three, four jobs."

"Hey, I think we're missing one." Toby snapped his fingers. "Rosa's Cantina. Once a week, he runs errands for . . . can't think of his name."

Zella wrote Rosa's Cantina.

"Some fancy-pants, rich guy owns it, but old Francisco Narez runs it." Toby grimaced. "His face is creepy. He has a glass eye and burn scars."

Alroy frowned. "Maybe we should start with him?"

Toby shook his head.

"His face is creepy, but he's nice. Got hurt in the Civil War. His face is messed up, but that doesn't mean he did something to Pedro. Plus, he keeps out of sight, probably because of his face. He hired a manager, Juan, who's there all the time. We'll talk to him. I know him pretty well. "

Zella nodded and made notes about the cantina.

Toby tapped the paper.

"Put down Copper Henderson. He looked real nervous when Wyatt was talking to him."

Alroy stared at the map. There were too many suspects. He wasn't sure how to sort through them all, but they had to eliminate people as fast as possible.

"Zella, how were you and Pedro investigating? Were you asking these people questions? Did any of them get angry?"

She sighed.

"One evening at the laundry, Hornsby and his wife got into a fight. Pedro noticed that she was always coming to work with bruises. She said she bruised easily, but he didn't believe her. When his wife left the laundry, Hornsby waited a few minutes and left. He was so angry Pedro thought he might hurt his wife, so he followed him."

"What's that got to do with smuggling?" Alroy asked.

"Let her finish," Toby said.

"Thanks," Zella said. "When Pedro followed him, he didn't go home. He met two men, who were waiting for him by the river. They had a big wagon loaded with crates and boxes. Pedro hid and watched."

"Who were the men?" Toby asked.

"He couldn't make out who they were. But a few minutes later, Officer Henderson joined them. The men gave him money, and he left. Pedro thought the money was a bribe. The three men got in the wagon and drove away."

"So a bribe to look the other way." Toby pointed to the map. "Where?"

"Here," she pointed to the map, "in Sonora Town, by the river."

"So, they put their cargo on a boat and row to the ocean where a ship waits for them." Alroy studied the map. "You think that's what happened?"

"Wait," Toby said, as he grabbed the newspaper articles they took from Pedro's house. "Ah ah. Look. There are three articles. Two from *The Los Angeles Herald* and one from *The San Francisco Chronicle*."

Toby handed each of them a clipping.

Alroy scanned his quickly and said, "Smugglers take goods to Canada. The ships make stops along the coast on their way to Canada. Things start here."

"Yeah," Toby said.

"What did Pedro find out?" Alroy asked.

"It was dark and he couldn't see the other men." Zella shrugged. "I bet at least one is on our list. He followed the wagon as best he could. He caught up to them at the river. They loaded the boxes on a barge. He was close enough to hear them talking about meeting a ship and getting paid. He heard them say Canada."

"We should tell Wyatt," Toby said.

"I agree," Zella said. "But let's do a little investigating first. If the police start snooping around, people won't talk to us. We can say we are looking for our friend, and no one will think twice about us."

Alroy glanced at Toby, who nodded.

"Okay, let's go through Pedro's notebook, and see if we can cross any of these people off the list," Alroy suggested.

"Who were you and Pedro investigating?" Alroy asked.

"All of them." Zella frowned.

"Even Doc?"

She nodded. "Most of them have locked basements to prevent anyone from going down. We weren't thinking Doc was smuggling. He's probably hiding his dumb time machine. To be safe, we kept him on the list."

Alroy knew the time machine wasn't dumb. It worked, but he couldn't tell them that. Doc was smart to guard it. He rubbed the back of his neck and moved his head back and forth. His shoulders felt stiff, and he wanted to do something to distract himself from spilling his guts about the time machine.

"Locked basement. I don't think that means anything, but let's leave Doc on our list," Alroy said, hoping to pacify Zella.

"We all know it's his time machine in the basement," Toby said.

Zella rolled her eyes.

"Don't do that thing you do," Toby said. "Someday the machine is going to work. Then, we'll go someplace crazy."

"In the meantime, let's find Pedro," Zella said.

Alroy kept his mouth shut.

"When is Lavinia coming back?" Toby asked as he hurried over to the supply cabinet. "We could use her help."

"She's on vacation for another week. We're on our own," Zella said. "But with Wyatt's expertise, we'll find him."

"Right," Alroy said and regretted the remark because Zella

looked at him as if she had laser eyes that were going to melt him. "I hope he's as good as you think he is."

"Knock it off," Toby said as he selected red, blue, and yellow glass squares from the cupboard.

He placed them beside Pedro's notebook. The boys stood on either side of Zella. On the top of the first page in Pedro's neat handwriting were the letters "CG aka AK?"

Alroy tapped on the butcher paper. He pointed to Garcia. "Clyde Garcia. CG."

"AK?" Zella looked at him.

He shook his head and shrugged.

"Me neither," Toby said.

The rest of the page was covered with colored drawings that looked liked various angles and shapes. Toby placed the red glass over the page, a paragraph of writing appeared.

Investigating C G: he's married to Laura, has two kids, Jaime and Juan. Seems like a nice man, but he has a phobia about having his picture taken. He allowed me to take photos inside and outside his shop, but when I went to take a photograph of him, he forbade it. Got upset. Does he think photos steal the soul? Or is he hiding something? I'll search old newspaper articles. Maybe he's hiding something.

P. S. Research complete. It is a good story, but not one the League would want to publicize. Garcia's a good man. AK vanished. Let the past lie.

"Not helpful. Try the blue," Alroy said.

With the blue glass over the page, another entry appeared:

Goggles and gears, I think someone's blackmailing CG. It's gotta be CH. Must bring up at League. Dangerous for CG and his family, nice wife and good kids. Maybe dangerous for me if CH finds out I know.

Toby immediately removed the blue glass and replaced it with the yellow, but nothing appeared.

"He didn't finish," Toby said.

Zella spoke as she made notes under Garcia's name.

"Garcia's hiding something. Pedro found out what it was but

didn't think we should expose him." She paused in her writing. "Agree?"

Toby and Alroy nodded.

"But the blackmail thing could be dangerous. Not just to Garcia and his family but Pedro, too. Maybe that's what got him into trouble. If he was snooping and asking questions, maybe this CH found out." Alroy put the blue glass back on the page and stared at the words, thinking. "CH . . . CH," he said aloud.

Toby pointed to Henderson. "I told you. Copper Henderson. The man's shady."

"Let's go tell Wyatt," Zella said.

"No," Toby and Alroy spoke at once.

"Why?"

"Because Pedro thinks Garcia is a good guy. If we tell Wyatt, we'll get Garcia in trouble."

"Alroy's right on this one. We need to trust Pedro's judgment. That's part of the League." Toby stared at Zella as if he were willing her to agree with him or at least understand.

"We don't need to tell him about Garcia. Tell him he saw Hornsby and two other men paying Henderson. Police aren't supposed to take bribes." Zella glanced at Toby.

"Maybe." Toby tapped his fingers on the table. "Alroy?"

"Pedro isn't just missing. He might be in danger or hurt," he said. "And this could be an important clue. We should tell Wyatt something."

Toby scrunched up his face and paced the room, marching back and forth with his head down. Alroy touched Zella's arm when she looked as if she were going to speak. When Toby paced, he did his best thinking. After a couple of long minutes, he stopped.

"I think we should tell Wyatt that Henderson took a bribe, but not about Pedro's journal. Tell him Pedro told you that. We need to keep the journal for now. Plus, they can't read it without the glass squares. We don't want to give away our code. Right?"

Alroy and Zella nodded.

"So, first thing in the morning, before breakfast, Alroy and I will ride over and talk to Garcia. We'll find out what's up and be back before Wyatt leaves. Then we can tell him . . . something."

"Okay." Zella sounded hesitant and reluctant. She reread the page, looking intent as if she were trying to find something else there.

Alroy liked Toby's idea, but he had second thoughts, too torn between accepting Pedro's analysis that Garcia shouldn't be exposed and letting Wyatt know. If Henderson was involved, then waiting could be dangerous. Wyatt hadn't come home yet, which might mean he was out looking for Pedro, which Henderson would know.

"We need to do this fast, or I'm telling Wyatt," Zella said. "I don't want to wait until morning. I don't want to get Garcia in trouble, but I want to find Pedro more than I want to protect a man I don't know."

Zella nailed it. They all probably felt the tug-of-war between protecting someone Pedro thought needed protecting and exposing a family man to find Pedro.

"She's right," Alroy said, grabbing Toby by the arm. "Let's go talk to Garcia right now."

"We don't know where he lives."

Alroy stared at the map.

"His business is here, on the edge of Sonora Town. He sells to farmers and *rancheros*. Old Man Lance has the main hardware and farm supplies store near downtown." He tapped the map again. "Garcia has to live in Sonora Town."

"And somebody will know where he lives," Toby said.

"Exactly. We can cycle there and be back before anyone knows we're gone."

"You want to go back there? You know the vampires come out at night." Toby grinned.

"Shut up, freckle face."

Even if it was his idea, it was a good one. They could act fast and let Wyatt know whatever they found out. Zella could stay here and keep reading Pedro's journal. The plan was smart and efficient.

Zella stood and put her hands on her hips.

"Get back here as fast as you can. If Wyatt comes home, what will I tell him?"

"Tell him or Liza--"

"Tell them, we went to my house to get something," Toby said.

Toby pulled Alroy toward the window.

"Be careful," Zella said. "Don't go missing, or I'll kill both of you."

Alroy and Toby slipped quietly onto the roof's ledge. The smell of jasmine and a cool breeze greeted them as they walked along the ledge toward the trellis. In the distance, gas street-lights dotted the city like earthbound stars. Alroy stared into the distant darkness and hoped that Pedro was safe. The last time he felt this afraid was when his father lay on the floor, pale and gaunt. He pushed that memory aside and told himself they'd find Pedro, and he'd be safe and healthy.

They took the short ramp they'd built to the second-floor overhang. Toby climbed down first. He was a more experienced and agile trellis climber than Alroy, who took cautious steps on the trellis rungs until he touched the ground and relaxed. The boys raced to their bicycles and rode away, pedaling into the gray shadows of night.

Although he tried to shrug off Zella's warning to be careful, his mind began to recount all the horror stories he'd heard about Sonora Town at night. He pedaled faster, making sure he rode as close to Toby as he could. *Safety in numbers*, his mind whispered.

CHAPTER 17: PEDRO

THE PLAN

July 19, 1890

Pedro had three problems—day and time of day and how to escape.

Jaime and Elijah didn't know what day it was or what time of day. Basically, they sat day and night, day after day, in a dark basement, and neither knew how long they'd been there. Nor did they create a system for keeping track. They didn't have a plan for escaping because they'd given up.

He wasn't about to give up. Since he'd woken up, he'd inspected the cage and stared out at the basement, searching for something that might help them. Boxes were stacked all around them, so there wasn't much to see. What lay beyond the boxes was obscured from his view. There wasn't anything he could use to pick or break the lock on the cage door. To get out, they'd have to make something happen.

If they were going to escape, they'd have to do it at night when the place was empty. He needed to estimate the time of day or night.

"Try to estimate how long you think I was unconscious," Pedro said.

"We can't," Jaime said, sounding annoyed.

"Try," Pedro begged.

"Can't, 'cause he gives us something in our food. When we woke up, you was here," Elijah said.

"That's something," Pedro said. "Does that happen often? I mean, does he drug you at specific times?"

Elijah glanced at Jaime, who shrugged.

"Yes, we think so. Jaime has to eat, or he gets sick. So we think that at night we get the drug?"

"Shut up you fool."

"No," Pedro said. "This is good information."

"That I'm addicted to something," Jaime's voice raised.

"I didn't mean no harm," Elijah said. "He's been here the longest." He glanced at Jaime. "He says that after a while, we'll all be addicted. He's right."

"What I mean," Pedro said, trying to defuse the tension and smooth Jaime's ego, "is that I got here in the middle of the night. So unless you slept all day, this is July 19th. Probably afternoon. So we can start tracking time."

"Why? What's the point?" Jaime glared at him.

"If he drugs you at night so you won't make noise, then we won't eat. We can get out of here."

"Yeah, that makes sense, but I have to eat, or I get sick. It's bad," Jaime said.

"Eat a little bite or two. Enough so you don't fall asleep. When we get out of here, Doctor Stone will help you."

"See, I told you he's smart," Elijah said.

Jaime laughed and shook his head. "How we getting out of here, Mr. Smart?"

Pedro couldn't help but grin.

"I do have a plan. When he comes down here, I'm going to tell him that Elijah's real sick. He'll act sick. Then I'll tell him the latrine needs to be cleaned because it's dangerous to have our waste right next to us. Eventually, we'll all get sick. He'll bring a bucket and something to scoop with, hopefully, something metal—"

"Hold on. That's the dumbest thing I ever heard. He ain't gonna care if Elijah's sick or about cleaning up our outhouse."

There wasn't an outhouse. There was the dirt floor in the far corner of the cage. Open, smelly, and foul. They stayed as far away from it as they could.

"Yes," Pedro said, "he will care because I'll point out that Elijah could get really sick. We could all get sick. I think he wants us alive."

Jaime pushed his hair out of his face.

"Until he doesn't," Jaime said, "but go on. So far, I ain't heard a plan."

Pedro stood and shuffled closer to Jaime and Elijah. He pointed to the chain attached to his ankle.

"Look at the third link."

"There's a gap," Elijah said.

"It's small, but if I can get something in the gap and force the gap a little wider, I can break the chain. Then we can file the link until it fits in the lock—"

"And he's not going to notice you doing all that?" Jaime asked, smirking as if he'd told a joke.

"When he brings a bucket, you two keep him busy talking or whatever. If he brings something to scoop with, it'll probably be metal. With any luck, I can use it to widen the gap. All I need is a little distraction, so he doesn't notice what I'm doing. We'll do the rest after he leaves and thinks we're sleeping."

"You're a dreamer. It won't work," Jaime said.

"It might," Elijah said. "We could try it."

"Or," Pedro said, sitting down and leaning against the bars, "we could give up."

Jaime sat quietly, staring off into space. Elijah walked over and sat next to Pedro.

"He's thinking," Elijah whispered.

Pedro nodded.

"I got a better plan," Jaime finally said. "We get our food and pretend to sleep like you said. When he comes in here to get the bowls, we jump him. Bet you didn't think of that because you make things too complicated."

Pedro had thought about that but dismissed it as too risky. He'd let Jaime believe what he wanted.

"Good idea," Pedro said. "But let's try my plan first. If that doesn't work, we'll try your plan."

"Why not go for it?"

"If your plan fails, he's going to be suspicious of everything we say and do. He's not going to make concessions to keep us happy. He'll analyze every move we make. He'll watch us eat. We won't have a chance to try it my way if your way fails."

Jaime reached his hand out to Pedro and said, "Deal. Plan A first, then my plan B."

They shook hands, and each reached out toward Elijah, who grinned and took their hands in turn.

Pedro knew both plans had a high possibility of failure, but he wasn't about to share that view. The lone candle outside the cage flickered twice and sputtered out.

CHAPTER 18: TOBY

CLYDE GARCIA

July 19, 1890
9:30 p.m.

Toby loved contrasts. The difference between Sonora Town in the light of day and in the dark of night delighted him. He couldn't wait to see Alroy's reaction to the transformation.

Once they left the dark and deserted downtown area and moved toward Sonora Town, the change was fast and striking. Live music filled the night. Lanterns and gaslights lit the streets and buildings, creating a festive atmosphere. Laughter echoed around them.

He pedaled forward unaffected by the familiar transformation. Alroy rode beside him, glancing around staring.

People crowded into the open bars. The music grew louder and faded as they rode past various establishments. Men and women roamed the streets, laughing and calling out to one another. Ahead a small crowd gathered around two men.

When they got closer, Alroy stopped and balanced on his pedals, trying to peer over the crowd. Toby didn't have to look.

He knew people gathered to see a fight. Even if the men didn't want to fight, the group would egg them on. Toby backtracked to Alroy.

The larger man took a wild swing at the slimmer man. He missed and stumbled, falling into a woman. Both men were drunk, and blood splattered their faces and clothes. Toby had seen plenty of fights among his peers, but two grown men slugging it out looked pathetic and humiliating. The crowd watched with eager faces, shouting and cheering encouragement.

For a moment, Toby made eye contact with one of the three women who watched the fight. She was well dressed, but her contorted face looked more like a gruesome mask than a real woman. Her eyes gleamed with unveiled enjoyment.

"Hit him," she shouted.

A chill swept over Toby. He turned away, sickened and repulsed.

"Keep moving," he shouted at Alroy and didn't wait to see if his friend followed.

He tried to dismiss the image of the two men and the woman, but the unforgettable picture was embedded in his mind. Someday he'd have to write about it. Behind him, Alroy pedaled hard to catch up.

A block later, they reached the *cantina*. *Mariachi* music filled the street but abruptly stopped as they drew nearer. The bar had a large patio on the left side that circled around to the back of the building. Men and women seated at tables talked and laughed. Ornate iron lanterns held candles that gave off diffused light.

They rode to the front of the *cantina*, where a hulking man with long black hair stood outside the door. Although the man didn't smile, he didn't look dangerous. He stood like someone who was slightly bored, doing a tedious job, and counting the passing minutes until closing time.

"Where you boys think you're going?"

"We need to see Juan," Toby said.

The man shook his head and grinned at Toby, who shrugged. He dug into his pocket and pulled out several coins. He opened his hand and slipped them to Sam, who pointed into the *cantina*.

"I'll keep an eye on your bikes."

"Yeah, don't mess with the lights. They're my invention," Toby said.

"If I do you this favor, you'll put one of those lights on my wagon?"

Toby stepped closer to the man.

"I'm looking for my friend, Pedro Hernandez. You help me when I'm in Sonora Town, and I'll put lights on your wagon."

The man's lips widened into a grin.

"I don't know where Pedro is, but I'll ask around."

They propped their bicycles up against the wall and stepped into the smoke-filled room.

Alroy grabbed Toby's arm.

"Is it safe here? That fight was --"

"It's safe. The *cantina* is the nicest place in Sonora Town. That fight and other stuff are why Wyatt doesn't want you down here."

Alroy glanced back at the man who guarded the door.

Toby had never told Alroy he came to Sonora Town at night. This is where he got his inspiration for his books. He tried to fill his stories with grown-up insights and monsters that could live right here. It didn't take much of an imagination to fill these spaces with vampires, werewolves, ghosts, and demons. In one way or another, those types were already here. He only had to look behind their masks.

Inside, two large wooden bars took up most of the space. Men stood drinking, talking, and laughing. The tables scattered around the room were filled mostly with men and a few women. In the far corner, he spotted Mr. Jackson, who owned the barbershop on Main Street. He tapped Alroy's shoulder and nodded toward the barber, hoping the sight of someone familiar would reassure him. No one in this crowd looked as if they'd be happy to see two men beating each other silly.

The *mariachi* band started playing again. One of the men playing the guitar began singing in Spanish. Toby knew enough Spanish to get most of the words. He liked the sound of the language. The simplest, everyday things sounded musical. Hardly anyone there listened in to or watched the band. He almost wished he and Alroy could sit down and listen. If Pedro weren't missing, all three of them could listen, and Pedro could translate the lyrics. He promised himself he'd come back after Pedro was safe and do that.

Toby crossed the room with Alroy at his side.

"Try not to look like a tourist," he whispered to Alroy, who glanced around like someone walking through a museum.

"You boys get out of here. You wanna get me in trouble? Out." A short Mexican man was waving his arms in the air as if to shoo them away.

Toby ignored him and motioned Alroy to follow.

The man shouted, and Toby outshouted him. "I wanna talk to Juan. Where's Juan?"

"*Madre de Dios*, get out before the police see you."

"We'll get out when we talk to Juan."

The man started shouting in Spanish and talking so fast Toby couldn't understand him.

"*Jóvenes*, you looking for me?" The voice came from behind them.

The short man who had been telling them to leave shrugged and returned to his place behind the bar.

Juan waved them over. He wore a bright blue shirt, and Toby wondered how he missed him in the crowd. The man loved colorful clothes.

When they got closer, Juan stepped between them and slung his heavy arms around their shoulders, pulling them close. They were all about the same height. Juan leaned even closer, pushing their heads together.

"You two trying to get me in trouble?"

"No, sir," Toby said. "Our friend is missing, and we're looking for him."

"Listen, boys, I got a legit place here. Alcohol and *musica*. No prostitutes, no shanghai, no opium. Just good clean fun. Don't know nothin' about your friend."

"Pedro," Toby said, wishing Juan would take his arm off his shoulder.

"Pedro Hernandez, Sara's boy?" Juan asked, the smile leaving his face.

"Yes."

"Ay, not good."

He turned the boys around so they faced him.

"You check with the Good Time Saloon behind Mr. Lee's shop? And you, you're the detective's brother?"

Alroy nodded.

"Your brother's been down here all evening asking questions. You tell him to ask his *amigo* Henderson some questions about that bar and about men and boys that go missing on ships. Ships are in port right now. We don't hurt our own in this part of town."

Juan mentioned Lee, who was on their list. Toby knew Henderson was up to no good. He guessed the copper probably knew where Pedro was.

"We'll do that," Toby shouted.

"We're looking for Clyde Garcia," Alroy said, loud enough to be heard over the music. "We don't know where he lives, but he might know something that would help us. You know him? Where he lives?"

Juan studied Alroy. His brown eyes assessed him as if he were deciding for or against an answer.

"Clyde's a good man. Home with his family." He looked around the *cantina* and waved to a girl. "Margarita, come here."

A pretty girl with flawless skin and a pouting mouth made her way across the crowded, smoke-filled room. She was probably a few years older than they were, but she looked at them as if they were children beneath her notice.

"Show them where Señor Clyde Garcia's house is and get right back here. You got work."

Margarita nodded and walked toward the door. Outside, they grabbed their bicycles, pushing them as they followed her through the dirt streets. Two men ambled along, moving like sleepwalkers, staring off into the distance. Alroy stared. Toby guessed he couldn't blame him.

"Zombies?" Alroy whispered.

"Yes. Opium," Toby said.

Many of the people on the street were simply drunks who smelled of beer and cigarette smoke. Others were opium addicts.

Ahead of them, Margarita strutted, her hips swaying like a slow, hypnotic pendulum. Toby couldn't take his eyes off her. He pushed his bicycle faster until he caught up with her.

"Is it far?" he asked.

Staring straight ahead, she continued walking.

"I'm Toby. And he's Alroy."

She glanced at him with fiery red-brown eyes that swept past him.

"Do you go to the high school? I haven't seen you," Toby said.

She stopped and glared at him. A feeling of impending doom settled over him. She had the same kind of look Liza had when she was about to give him a lecture on manners and behavior. She leaned closer, and his entire body buzzed in anticipation.

"*Cállate!*"

She walked forward at a faster pace.

Alroy chuckled.

"Even I know what that means, Romeo. She told you to shut up."

"Yeah, she did. I'm putting her in my next book, and it won't be flattering."

They followed her at a discreet distance. A few blocks later, she turned right onto an empty, quiet street. They took two more turns, moving deeper into the residential neighborhood. They could still hear the music, but it wasn't as loud. The girl stopped and pointed.

"There. The house with the blue door."

She left without a glance in their direction.

"Thanks," Toby called out, but she didn't look back.

"Wow," Alroy whispered, staring after her.

"She's just a silly girl. Come on."

"I like the way the silly girl walks," Alroy said.

They stood in front of the door and looked at each other.

"What are we going to say?" Toby asked.

"Don't know. Let's just see what happens."

Alroy knocked, and they waited a few seconds before the door opened. A short, squat man squinted at them.

"What are you boys doing here?"

"Um, . . ." Alroy stared at the man as if he'd lost his voice.

Toby understood why he was staring. The man's face had deep wrinkles, and he frowned in a mean way as if he were going to punch them. He looked about as angry as someone could look.

"Sir," Toby said. "Our friend Pedro is missing, and we were hoping you might be able to help us."

Alroy shot Toby a look that said, "If he doesn't kill us, I'm going to kill you."

"Missing? What does that mean, missing?"

"He left home last night and hasn't come back. No one knows where he is."

Alroy nodded in agreement.

Garcia's face softened.

"Come in. And bring your bicycles."

Toby expected this house to be as shabby as Pedro's, but it wasn't. They walked into a large living area with furniture and lace curtains on the windows. Two boys played on the floor, and a voluptuous lady with a pleasant face and long black hair smiled at them.

In the light, Mr. Garcia didn't look as angry or as mean. Toby tried not to stare at his big nose, which spread over most of his round face. Garcia pointed to the wall by the door, and they leaned their bicycles against it.

"Sit down." Garcia nodded to two overstuffed chairs as he sat down next to his wife.

Toby wasn't exactly sure how to ask this man if he were hiding something or if Officer Henderson were blackmailing him. Now that they were face to face with their suspect, he thought this was the worst idea of all the bad ideas they'd ever had. Much to his distress, Alroy stared at Garcia. Toby poked him, but he remained mute.

Clearing his throat, Toby said, "Mr. Garcia, I'm not sure how to ask you this, but . . . well, you see, our friend Pedro, who works for you, is missing."

Mrs. Garcia put her hand on her husband's arm.

"No, this is terrible. Clyde?"

Garcia nodded.

"I heard today. I don't know how I can help you."

"We were wondering if you'd seen him or knew where he might be?"

"No, I don't know anything. I can't help you."

"*Cariño*, you should—"

The younger boy looked at his father. "Pedro? He gave me a book."

Garcia smiled at his son. "Pedro's a nice boy."

"Big boy," his son corrected.

"Laura, take the boys and put them to bed."

She glared at her husband, but she called to the boys, who followed their mother out of the room.

"We came here because Pedro thinks you're a good man. He thought maybe Officer Henderson was . . ."

Toby glanced at Alroy, pleading for help. He didn't know what else to say, short of accusing Garcia of being a criminal and a kidnapper.

Garcia rubbed the back of his neck and turned his head from side to side. He stared at the floor thoughtfully.

"Pedro's a good boy," he said. "But I can't help you. I can't talk to the police or get involved."

"Can you at least tell us about Officer Henderson?"

"No, I can't. Did Pedro tell you about me?"

Toby shook his head.

"No, we were just hoping . . ."

"Well, that's something. I have a family. I like it here. I don't want to have to leave."

"Our friend could be hurt or injured," Alroy finally said. "He's got a sick mother and a little sister. He takes care of them. He's got a family, too."

Garcia did the neck-rubbing thing again, and his wife came back into the room without the boys. She looked at him with brown eyes that seemed to communicate something.

"*Querido, por favor.*"

Garcia sighed.

"Woman, you'll be the death of me."

He frowned at them, his brow wrinkled. He stared at the far wall as if thinking.

His wife sat down and took his hand in hers.

"*Por favor, ayúdanlos.*"

"She wants me to help you, and I can't resist her pleas." He shook his head, still scowling. "I don't know much. I know that Officer Henderson makes money from the neighborhood. Ask around. People don't like or trust him. They'll confirm his behavior. There's a bar. It's behind Mr. Lee's shop."

"The Good Time Saloon," his wife said.

Garcia nodded.

"They sometimes get men and boys drunk. Put something in the drinks. When they pass out, the owner sells the drunks to the ship captains. Sometimes the captains need new crew members. For a price, Officer Henderson looks the other way there and at the opium den. You don't need me to give you this information. Many people will confirm this."

"Are you saying Pedro could be on one of those ships?"

"I don't know. Pedro wouldn't go into that bar. I'm telling you about Henderson. Pedro knows these things. He warns men to stay away from the saloon. Henderson hates Pedro. He is the law in this part of town. Pedro asks too many questions, and he warns people about the kidnapping business. These are dangerous things. I've told Pedro to stop, but he is young and doesn't listen."

Garcia shook his head and made a chuckling sound that sounded like a desperate sigh.

"He told me the only thing necessary for evil to triumph is for good men to do nothing."

Toby swallowed and nodded. Edmund Burke said those words. Pedro painted the words over the top of the attic door, adding them to the motto for The League of the Daring. The muscles in his chest tightened, and he breathed deeply. Pedro was trying to be a good man.

"Edmund Burke said that. He was a great Irish statesman."

"Well, he was a damn fool." Garcia stood up. "Those words are fine for a white man with money and position, but for someone like Pedro, they are a death sentence. How many men die following this Burke person?"

"You're wrong," Alroy said. "Pedro's not dead, and good people have to do what's right, or they aren't good people."

Garcia stared at Alroy and then looked at Toby.

"When you live here, it's better not to ask questions or make trouble." Garcia's voice was soft and thoughtful.

"Does Henderson get money from you?" Toby asked.

"Did you hear what I said about asking questions?" The angry looked returned to Garcia's face.

"Are you threatening us?" Toby stood.

He wasn't trying to be confrontational, but he wasn't going to let Garcia bully them. He remembered the two men who had been fighting and hung his head.

"I'm sorry. I'm worried about my friend."

Garcia nodded.

Toby grabbed Alroy's arm.

"Thanks for your help."

Garcia looked at this wife.

"I wasn't threatening you. I'm telling you what it's like for your friend. Do not be naive about his life. Please, don't use my name in this, please."

Toby nodded at Alroy.

"We won't," he said.

Garcia put his hand out.

"You'll shake on this? A man's agreement."

Toby took Garcia's hand and shook it. Alroy did the same.

"Before you leave," Mrs. Garcia said. "In the basement, below the bar, that's where they keep the men and boys. If it's empty, they have already gone to the ships."

Garcia glared at his wife.

She put her hands on her hips and said, "You don't look at me like that. If our boys were missing, these boys would help us." She faced Alroy and Toby. "You said Pedro's mother is sick, yes?"

"She's very sick."

"I will check on her first thing in the morning."

"Thank you, Mrs. Garcia."

Outside, Toby put his index finger to his lips and pressed his ear to Garcia's door. A couple minutes passed, and Toby signaled Alroy they should leave. They rode their bicycles a few blocks from the house and stopped.

"What did you hear?" Alroy asked.

"He told her to pack a bag for him and to take care of the store. She told him not to leave. She asked him why he didn't trust us. He said he trusted us, but we live in a world among bad people who don't keep their word, and they would force us to give him away. She cried. I stopped listening."

"What do you think? Do you think he knows something about Pedro?" Alroy asked.

"No. I think he was trying to help us, and he's scared about something. Whatever he did before could get him into a lot of trouble now. He's afraid."

"You think Garcia's right?"

"Yeah. We don't live in a perfect world," Toby said, "but we made a promise. We won't drag Garcia into this. You make sure Zella understands."

Alroy nodded. "Our word is our bond."

As they neared the center of Sonora Town, the noise grew louder, until they were once again surrounded by the chaos of the night. They talked to a few people on the street. Some were too drunk and preoccupied to tell them anything, but others were tipsy enough to give them more information than they would have gotten otherwise. People were more than willing to tell them about Henderson. Several people confirmed Henderson forced businesses into paying for protection. They also learned that three ships had come into San Pedro port in the last few days, and none of them had left yet. If Pedro were shanghaied, he might still be on the ship.

In a short time, they'd confirmed Garcia's story and would be able to tell Wyatt about Henderson without mentioning Garcia.

Toby couldn't wait to get back to Alroy's house. The lights, the music, the drunks, and the feeling of frenzied fun left him exhausted. As they left the noise behind, he took a deep breath and listened to the silence. The light from their bicycles cut a narrow path as they rode. When they heard the sound of gears turning and the hiss of steam being released, they stopped to look around but saw nothing.

Alroy pointed up. Above them, a metal man with propellers flew past and vanished as it moved toward San Pedro Harbor.

"What was that? What's out that way?"

"Don't know what it is," Toby said. "There are only farms and ocean out there. That's something we should tell Wyatt about. What if these shanghai bastards fly men to ships in that thing? It came from Sonora Town."

The night wrapped Toby in a cocoon of thoughts. If Pedro were on a ship bound for some unknown destination, how would they ever find him? A determination like nothing he'd ever known pushed his fear away. He was scared Pedro was in serious trouble.

What if his friend were worse off than they realized? What if they were too late? What if they couldn't find him?

He wasn't going to believe those thoughts.

He knew one thing. He would act like a good man, no matter how dark the shadows got or how desperate the situation seemed.

They arrived back at the house in record time. They parked their bikes in the back.

Toby headed for the trellis and started climbing. Alroy was close behind. At the attic window, Toby stepped inside. Wyatt sat beside Zella at the worktable and watched him step through the window. He stopped. Alroy bumped into him and knocked him sideways.

Wyatt grinned like the Cheshire cat in *Alice's Adventures in Wonderland.* They'd walked into a well-set-up trap.

CHAPTER 19: ALROY

CAUGHT

July 19, 1890
11:45 p.m.

After their trip to Sonora Town, the last thing Alroy expected was to find his half-brother waiting for them in the attic. But Wyatt sat at the workbench beside Zella, calmly grinning. Startled wasn't the right word to describe how he felt. Every fiber of his being panicked.

Wyatt never came to the attic. For some reason, he hated that they had this space to themselves. The last time he'd been there was when their father was converting the space into their workshop. Wyatt had told his father he was coddling and spoiling the group and that no good would come from his weak parenting. They needed a strong disciplinary hand.

Now, Wyatt seemed to think he was the disciplinary hand.

His half-brother folded his arms across his chest, cocked his head sideways, and waited.

Alroy tried to survey the room without being obvious. On the far workbench, Pedro's model monorail was covered and hidden. The design and plans for the monorail were clearly displayed on the wall. He doubted Wyatt would be interested in examining them. The mechanical walnut cracker and the sundry pieces he'd assembled to complete the task were an arm's length from Wyatt. Alroy had an odd desire to rush over and push his brother away from his project.

Zella puckered her lips and stared at him with wide unblinking eyes.

It wasn't her fault they'd been caught. However, in that instant, Alroy decided the League needed a warning system. While they were investigating, Hyde should guard the door and keep intruders out.

Wyatt looked like a cat ready to pounce on his victim. He knew they had been in Sonora Town. Alroy didn't know how, but it was evident in his stupid grin that he thought he had them in his clutches.

Toby plopped down into the nearest chair.

"Hi, boys. Where've you been?" Wyatt finally said.

"We're coming back from my house," Toby said.

Alroy collapsed onto the overstuffed chair next to Toby.

Wyatt's grin grew wider.

Tapping his fingers on his thigh, Alroy tried desperately to think of a way out of this predicament. Neither a solution nor a strategic lie presented itself. As the seconds marched forward, he realized the tap, tap of his fingers hurt. For some reason, both his wrists burned as if someone had set them on fire. He couldn't breathe properly.

On the other hand, Toby had a way of shifting into a casual attitude when under duress. His friend's body language said, "You got nothing on me, and I can outwit you at every turn."

"We were over at my house for a while." Toby studied his fingernails as if he were considering a trip to the barbershop for a manicure.

"That's what Zella was telling me."

Zella stared at them, and her eyes nearly bulged out of their sockets as she moved her eyes from them to Wyatt.

She mouthed, "Be careful."

Alroy tensed. Toby thought he was in control of the conversation, but Wyatt had set a trap for them. His friend was poised to steal the cheese and spring the lever that would catch them. He edged his foot closer to Toby's until he tapped his friend's shoe as hard as he could without catching Wyatt's eye.

"Umm, we were--"

"Yeah, that's right." Toby grinned stupidly.

Alroy poked him again.

"What?" Wyatt asked.

"Uh, we went over to my room and lost track of time."

"That's interesting because I received a telephone call from Officer Mason. He's working in Sonora Town tonight. He said that several people saw you boys in the *cantina*. Mason said you talked to a couple people, but you took off on your bicycles before he could stop you."

Toby grinned as if being caught in a lie were as natural as breathing.

"We've got information. *Helpful* information."

Wyatt crossed the room and sat in the chair nearest Toby and leaned forward. Wyatt's eyebrows were bushy up close and sort of looked like an old man who scowled all the time.

"What part of 'don't go back to Sonora Town' did you two not understand?"

Wyatt's controlled voice scared Alroy more than his angry voice. Alroy wiggled in his chair and cleared his throat.

"Here's the thing," Toby said. "We had to investigate. Pedro's our friend. We were helping you out."

"We aren't going to stop looking for Pedro." Alroy was surprised his voice sounded even and normal because the pulse in his neck pounded out *Polly Wolly Doodle*.

Oh, I went down South, for to see my Sal, singin' Polly wolly doodle all the day.

"Look, boys. I want to yell at you and shake you, but I think I'd be wasting my time."

Zella made a sound as if she were going to speak but changed her mind. Instead, she came to the group and sat on the arm of Alroy's chair.

"I understand you're worried about your friend, and I commend you for that, but I need a promise. No more night trips."

"We can't promise. You weren't here when we left. We couldn't have told you," Alroy said. "Plus, we learned some important stuff tonight. Your Officer Henderson isn't such a great guy."

Toby nodded in agreement.

With crossed arms and unblinking eyes, Wyatt waited. Toby spoke first, rattling off all the things people said about Henderson.

Alroy chimed in, occasionally adding to what Toby said. Like the Los Angeles River when it flooded, Alroy and Toby spilled all the things they'd learned. They told him about the Good Time Saloon, about people shanghaiing men and boys and taking them to the boats. They interrupted each other and backtracked. The only thing they didn't mention was Clyde Garcia. Wyatt didn't look surprised or angry at anything they said. He asked a few questions and scrunched his lips. He stared out the window so long that the silence became uncomfortable.

As much as Alroy tried to concentrate, he couldn't focus. The burning sensation in his wrists got so hot he couldn't ignore it any longer. A fiery red rash blazed across both his wrists. He rubbed them with the palm of his hand so he wouldn't scratch his skin and cause bleeding.

After a few seconds, Zella grabbed his arm and shook her head.

He stopped scratching and studied his skin. He thought he could see black lines under the red. He blinked several times, certain he was imagining the lines, but they didn't vanish. Finally, he decided his blood vessels were popping out.

Wyatt interrupted his contemplation.

"How were you able to get this information?"

Toby shrugged.

Alroy crossed his arms to hide his wrists.

"We aren't coppers," Alroy said. "We were just looking for our friend. People weren't afraid to tell us stuff."

"I need to take care of this. I'm going to the station. You two write all this down. Give specific names, if you know them. When you finish, put it on my bed. I'll get it when I come back. If all this checks out, I'll board those ships at first light."

Wyatt pointed toward the worktable.

"Tomorrow, you three are going to explain that list. And where you got the names and information. And, by the way, why did you ask people about Henderson?"

"Because we'd already heard rumors, and he was acting weird at the police station," Toby said.

"We didn't have to ask," Alroy added. "People told us. They're afraid of him."

Wyatt headed for the door.

"One more thing," Toby said.

Wyatt squinted at him and frowned.

"I'm waiting."

Toby glanced at Alroy before speaking.

"We are trying to help. And don't forget the Good Time Saloon."

Wyatt sighed, a long extended sigh as if he were a bad actor and couldn't wait to get off stage.

"The police aren't dumb. We raid that place every few weeks. We've heard the rumors too. Nothing's going on there."

"You wouldn't find anything if they are paying Henderson to look the other way." Toby stared at Wyatt.

"I don't know if you are trying to goad me into yelling at you, but I'm seriously considering throwing you into a jail cell."

"I'm not trying to make you angry. I'm trying to find my friend. If you were my age and Ernest was missing, would you sit back and wait for the police?"

Wyatt took two steps toward the door before Toby spoke again.

"I read lips," he said.

Alroy groaned and wished he could stop his friend from saying anything else. He should have known Toby would try to confront Wyatt about the argument at the police station. The thing was his half-brother wasn't the kind of person who talked about things rationally.

Without turning toward them, Wyatt spoke each word deliberately, "What exactly does that mean?"

"At the police station, when you were yelling at Alroy, I read every word you said about me."

Wyatt slowly turned his head and shoulders until he could see Toby. He squinted at him for several seconds.

He walked over to the bookcase where the League kept all Toby's penny dreadful books. He grabbed one.

"I'm borrowing this. I want to see what goes on in that devious head of yours."

Wyatt left without a backward glance.

"Werewolves," Toby called out, "good choice."

Alroy couldn't believe Toby could be such an idiot. Now, Wyatt would watch them even closer. Liza was right. Toby knew how to stir the pot and get everything mixed together. What kind of mess would this cause?

CHAPTER 20: ALROY

STRANGE APPEARANCES

July 20, 1890
12:15 a.m.

Zella waited until Wyatt's footsteps faded. She put her index finger to her lips, tiptoed to the top of the landing, looked down the staircase, and closed the door.

"He's gone," she whispered, then whirled around and shouted, "What was that, Toby?"

"He annoyed me."

"So, you decided to make him angry?"

Alroy walked to the door and rotated Dr. Jekyll to the Mr. Hyde setting. He watched as Mr. Hyde stepped into place to guard the door.

"He told me Toby couldn't sleep in my room because it wasn't proper," Alroy said. "We had a disagreement. I'm going to ignore him."

"Oh," Zella said. Looking at Toby, she continued, "he was wrong. Sometimes he's a jerk."

Zella sat beside Toby and put her arm around his shoulder.

"Sometimes I'm a jerk," Toby said.

Zella laughed. "Yes. Making Wyatt angry isn't exactly a great strategy."

"Sorry," Toby said. "It's been gnawing at me all evening."

"Let's get to work," Zella said.

Toby and Zella returned to the workbench. Zella reached under the butcher paper and scooped up Pedro's newspaper clippings.

"I heard Wyatt on the staircase, but I didn't have time to hide everything," she said as she placed the clippings back into the box.

"Let's keep Hyde guarding the door at all times," Alroy said.

They mumbled their agreement. Alroy returned to his favorite chair and poured a glass of water and grabbed a cookie. When everything was safely hidden, Toby and Zella joined him.

Before Toby's outburst, the conversation with Wyatt could be described as strange and atypical. Liza was always saying, "The world's full of surprises." This was one of those times. Wyatt didn't yell at them, which was one of the biggest surprises he'd ever had. He doubted they'd get so lucky again.

"Do you think Pedro's on one of those ships?" Zella asked.

Her face looked expectant and hopeful, as if she really wanted him to be on a ship.

"I don't know," Alroy said. "It wouldn't be good, but if that's what happened to him, it's better than some of the things I've been imagining."

"Yeah," Zella agreed.

She grabbed a cookie and offered the plate to Alroy. His stomach felt queasy, so he shook his head and stared at his wrists. They were redder and felt as if someone were holding them over a fire.

"I found some more stuff in Pedro's journal and in the newspaper clippings."

"What?" Toby asked, leaning forward.

Alroy rubbed first one wrist and then the other. The burning sensation had transformed into a deep itch.

"Stop that. It's annoying," Zella said. "Garcia is wanted for murder."

Toby whistled.

Alroy forgot about his wrist and glanced at Zella.

"His real name is the Arizona Kid, well, not his real name. That's what people call him because they can't pronounce his Apache name. He was accused of murder, tried, and convicted. He always claimed he didn't do it. When they were transporting him and some other prisoners to jail, he and the other prisoners escaped. One of the guards said the Arizona Kid saved him from being killed by the others."

"Pedro thinks he was innocent," she added. "After the Arizona Kid escaped, he was never heard of again."

"He has a nice family," Alroy said. "At first, I thought he was mean-looking, but after his wife nagged him, he helped us get the information we gave Wyatt."

"I think he was scared of getting caught. We promised we wouldn't use his name," Toby explained to Zella.

"Well, for now, I'll go along with you," Zella said. "If Pedro's on one of those ships, Wyatt will find him, and we'll talk to Pedro about him. I think you two should write out the information for Wyatt."

"But what are we going to tell Wyatt about our list?" Toby shook his head. "We can't tell him about Pedro's journal. He'll take it."

"I agree," Alroy said.

"I don't like lying to him," Zella said.

"Then, let's figure out a way to tell him about the list without lying."

"I got it," Toby said. "We'll tell him it's a list of all the people Pedro worked for, and Henderson's on the list because we were suspicious about him. And they aren't suspects. Just people we wanted to talk to because they might have noticed something."

That was a simple explanation and was more or less the truth.

Alroy grabbed a cookie and took a bite. He hoped eating something would calm his stomach. It didn't work. He tossed the cookie on the table, lay back in his chair, and closed his eyes. He'd started feeling strange before they'd left for Sonora Town. Now he just wanted to sleep.

Zella's voice seemed to hum in the background as he felt himself drifting into sleep. He wanted to slip into a deep sleep, but Toby poked him in the side.

"Pedro didn't share details about the smuggling ring because he wanted to check some things out before I got involved," Zella said. "The only names Pedro gave me were Hornsby and Wong. Wong owned the laundry before Hornsby."

"What do you think?" Toby asked, shaking him.

Alroy forced his eyes open. He didn't know what he was supposed to have an opinion about.

"No more secret investigations," he said to Zella. "All for one and one for all. No one keeps secrets from the League."

"That's not what we were talking about, but you're right," Zella said. "Maybe none of this would have happened if we'd known Pedro was going out on his own."

"Does this mean I have to run all my story ideas by the group?"

"No," Zella said. "We aren't Wyatt. We don't want to know the inner workings of your mind."

"Thank heavens. I was worried." Toby winked at Alroy.

Zella grabbed Alroy's hand and stared at his wrist.

"What's that?"

Alroy glanced down expecting to see red skin. Instead, he saw what looked like a black tattoo on each wrist. On his left wrist, a snake swallowed its tail and formed a sideways number eight. On the other wrist, a snail shell with tiny numbers. He blinked and stared at the snail shape because the numbers faded and came back into focus. He stared for several seconds before looking up at Zella.

"I don't know."

Toby leaned over his hand and rubbed the marks. He spat on Alroy's wrist and tried to rub the marks off.

"They're embedded in your skin. How?" Toby asked.

"They weren't there before. My wrists started itching when we were in Sonora Town. When we came back here, they were itching and burning."

Toby whistled. "Someone must have cursed you."

"Don't be a dope," Zella said.

"Look. The snail faded, and now it's back," Alroy said as he stared at the tattoos. "The numbers are glowing."

This was the weirdest day Alroy had ever had. On top of the crazy day he'd had, he instantly developed tattoos. Of all the things that had happened, the tattoos scared him the most. No that wasn't right. Pedro's disappearance scared him the most. The tattoos made him physically ill.

He went back over the day. The time travel was scientific. Pedro's disappearance was terrible but within the realm of normal. The airship ride was probably cold air hitting hot air and producing wild air currents. But the drawings on his wrist just appeared—he couldn't think of one reasonable explanation.

Toby studied the markings.

"You've been hexed," Toby said. "Someone in Sonora Town hexed you. A *bruja*."

Alroy glared at him but refused to answer such an idiotic idea.

"Witches aren't real. We're not in one of your stupid books," Zella said.

"But I scared you for a moment," Toby grinned at Zella

before grabbing Alroy's wrist. "Seriously, you know this is the infinity sign?"

Alroy nodded.

"And that looks like a strange clock." Zella traced the snail shell, and Toby put his face close to Alroy's wrist.

"This definitely is in the realm of extraordinary." Toby glanced at Zella. "You'll have to excuse me, but in normal life, people don't just turn up with tattoos. This has no rational explanation."

"Maybe. But I'm not jumping to a supernatural cause until we find out more," Zella said.

Alroy shrugged. He was tired, didn't want to talk, and for some reason, he didn't care about the tattoo mystery. A full-blown sickness swept over him every time he looked at his wrists.

He wasn't going to tell Zella or Toby or anyone that his whole body felt dizzy and light as if the molecules in his body were expanding. He wasn't sure if expanding was the right word because when he thought about expanding, he realized he could be contracting. Either his atoms were trying to fly apart, and he'd explode, or they were shrinking, and he'd implode.

For the first time in his life, Alroy didn't want to think about anything. He didn't care. He wanted to crawl into bed and sleep forever. Maybe he'd never wake up? He made a mental note of the fact that he should be scared out of his mind. Whatever was happening to him wasn't just odd, it was terrifyingly impossible. Yet it was happening, and he couldn't muster up enough fear to stay awake.

CHAPTER 21: TOBY

ERNEST

July 20, 1890
1:30 a.m.

An uncomfortable silence filled the attic. Toby studied Alroy because his friend not only looked sick, but he couldn't keep his eyes open. Alroy's head bobbled forward as if he'd fallen asleep. A couple seconds later, he jerked his head up and looked around. Zella's lips curved downward, and her brow wrinkled.

Toby watched this with a nagging feeling that he should get help. He was positive Doctor Stone couldn't help him, but he was pretty sure who could.

"Put him to bed," Toby said.

"Where do you think you're going?" Zella demanded.

"To Grace's to ask her about Alroy's tattoos. I think those marks have something to do with what happened on her airship. Remember how Grace kept looking at his wrists. She expected something to be there."

Alroy stretched and curled up in his chair. He rested his head on the arm and closed his eyes.

"You can't wake Grace up at this hour," she whispered.

"How about this. I'll wake up lover boy, and he can wake his sister."

She slugged him in the arm.

"Aw, that hurt."

"Don't call Ernest lover boy."

"Your brother's practically in a coma, and you're worried about me calling Ernest names. Trust me, Grace will want to know about the tattoos, and she'll know what to do. "

"God, sometimes I hate you. Don't grin. You can't win me over."

"I'm going. We're wasting time."

She grabbed his arm before he could slip out the window.

"What about the notes for my brother."

"You've got a good memory. Write up everything and leave it for Wyatt."

"Please don't tell Grace you think she's a time traveler."

Toby leaned down and kissed Zella on the forehead.

"Quit worrying and take care of him."

He climbed out of the window and ran along the roof walkway. The full moon gave off enough light for him to see and move quickly. Once on the ground, he pushed his bicycle away from the house. On the street, he pedaled toward the Camero's house.

Summer nights in Lost Angeles were perfect, sometimes chilly, sometimes warm, but always beautiful and fragrant. The smell of oranges and lemons filled the warm breeze. Toby loved the night, but mostly it was the quiet that intrigued him.

However, right this second on this night, he had to decide how to wake Grace. As much as he hated to wake her, he was more worried about Alroy than anything else.

At the Camero's house, he leaned his bicycle against the porch and glanced around.

Except for a low-watt electric light on the porch, the house was dark. The yard resembled a botanical jungle. The excess of shrubbery and trees created spooky shadows and enough hiding places for animals and snakes to make even a calm person anxious.

In the day, the roses splashed color throughout the front yard. The fragrance of roses surrounded Toby. Red, orange, pink, and white bougainvilleas climbed the trellises leading to the second and third stories. Only a great fool would use the trellises as a ladder because the long sharp thorns were as painful as poisoned darts.

He took the path to the back of the house. The ladybug airship stood out in the moonlight. There weren't any lights on. He would definitely have to wake someone up. He realized he had been hoping someone would be awake.

Returning to the front door, his curiosity got the better of him, and he took a minute to examine the porch lamp. There wasn't anything special about it. He'd come to expect everything Grace did would be unique. But leaving the porch lit all night was rather extravagant, even for an eccentric.

Standing at the door, he hesitated. The housekeeper would probably answer, and she hated him. Or old Mrs. Camero would hobble to the door, and he'd feel like a cad for getting her out of bed. He was pretty sure the two older women slept downstairs. He stepped back to the middle of the yard and studied the windows. If he could figure out which one was Grace's bedroom, he could toss pebbles at the window until he got her attention. Unfortunately, all the curtains looked the same. There wasn't one that unequivocally proclaimed *this is Grace's room.*

After thirty seconds of deep thinking, he decided the doors probably weren't locked, and he could sneak into the house. Then all he had to do was check out each room. He was a master at opening and closing doors without making noise.

When he found Grace, he could wake her up, which would probably scare the hell out of her.

He grinned.

Of course, she might scream and wake everyone up. Then he'd be in a pickle. Ernest would attack him and probably beat him up. But it would make for a grand entrance.

These meandering thoughts were interrupted by the clopping of a horse's hooves and the creaking of carriage wheels. A drunk sang off-key in Spanish. The crooner's screeching grew louder. Moments later, a black carriage turned the corner and headed toward the house. Bold white letters painted on the coach door declared, "For Hire." The singer's slurred words echoed through the neighborhood and seemed excessively loud.

Ernest Camero, the dapper man-about-town, sat next to a thin, pucker-faced man, who looked as if he drove a hearse by day. Zella's crush was definitely beyond a polite tipsy. He stopped singing, stood up, and waved at Toby.

"Toby, come here, lad."

The carriage stopped in front of the house.

The driver tipped his hat to Toby.

"You know this feller?"

"Yes, sir," Toby said.

"He's more than a little gassed up and will need some help walking. You up for the job? I'd like to be getting home to my missus."

Toby grinned, thinking of how much fun it was going to be to tell Zella about this and tease her every chance he got.

"Sure."

"My good man, I don't need help," Ernest said.

He stood, stepped off the side of the carriage, and fell a good five feet. He landed on the grass face down. The driver jumped down and ran around to his passenger.

By the time Toby got to the curb, Ernest was on his feet, leaning heavily against the driver.

"Thank you, my good man," Ernest said. "Wait."

He tried to stand up straight. Swaying, he managed to fumble in his pocket. He pulled out a handful of coins and forced Toby to take them.

"Be a good lad, and find a silver dollar for the driver."

"A dollar? Are you sure?" Toby stared at the coins.

"Where are my manners. Two silver dollars should be enough."

"Sir," the driver said. "The fare is fifteen cents."

"For your trouble." Ernest leaned forward as if to whisper in the driver's ear. Instead, he almost shouted, "No doubt I've been troublesome."

The driver leaned away and glanced at Toby as if pleading for help.

Grinning, Toby handed the driver two silver dollars. This story was getting better by the second.

The driver grabbed the coins and hurriedly climbed back in his seat.

Ernest, who smelled of whiskey and tobacco, leaned heavily on Toby. Together, they struggled across the lawn. Behind them, the sounds of a clopping horse and swaying buggy faded into the night. Ernest was heavier than he looked, and several times Toby felt certain he was in danger of being dragged to the ground. Once on the porch, he leaned the drunk against the doorframe, making sure the man wasn't going to fall forward onto his face.

In the last few seconds, he'd developed an understanding of the Temperance League, but for the fact he wanted to be an adventurer, he considered joining them.

"Be a good lad," Ernest slurred. "And turn off that blasted lamp. Then help me in the house."

Toby did as he was told and contemplated all the ways he would chip away at Zella's idol. Dismantle the man and disillusion the girl. Unexpectedly, his thoughts led him to the realization that he was disappointed, too. He held Ernest in grudging admiration. Well, he had until this moment.

Inside the house, Ernest released him and tossed his hat on the rack in the entryway. The hat landed on the peg and caught. A fantastic shot for a drunk. The man peeked through the lace curtain that covered the window in the front door. He didn't sway or need help walking. He hurried into the parlor, motioning Toby to follow him.

"Look out that window," Ernest whispered and in a perfectly clear and sober voice. "Be sly, don't want anyone to see us peeking out."

"What am I looking for?"

"To ascertain if I was followed."

Toby peered out the window, staring into the night, searching in the corners where someone might hide, but there were too many shadows. He saw nothing.

Ernest signaled him to follow him into Mrs. Camero's sitting room. Again, he glanced out the side window.

In the yard next door, a shadow moved in the hedge. It could have been a breeze shaking the branch, but another shadow also shifted. Toby blinked. The outline of two men, one tall and the other average height, stood out. Their features and clothes blended into the foliage.

"Over here," Toby whispered. "They're in the bushes."

Ernest stared for a moment and shook his head. Toby pointed to the spot again.

"Ah, yes. It's too dark to make out their features," Ernest said. "In the last place I visited, there was a tall fellow drinking at the bar. Can you see anything to distinguish them?"

"Naw, but I can sneak out and take a look. I'm pretty good at sneaking."

Ernest placed a hand firmly on Toby's shoulder and smiled.

"I appreciate the offer, but I suspect they're dangerous. I

don't want to tip them off. I'm hoping they saw a harmless drunk and nothing more."

"Well, you fooled me. You gave the driver two dollars. Are you crazy?"

"If you'd kept your mouth shut, I would have given him one."

"You stink."

"Of course, I've been pretending to drink all night and spilling whiskey on my clothes. I'll probably have to discard them. And I'm pretty sure I bruised my hip and scratched my face jumping off that carriage."

After a few more minutes, the two shadowy figures disengaged from the bushes and strolled away. They stopped in the street to light cigarettes. The tall man glanced back at the house, but he was too far away for his face to be seen clearly. The men strolled away, moving in the direction of Broadway.

Ernest sighed and shrugged.

"A pity we couldn't see their faces."

"I think I've seen the tall man near the Good Time Saloon. I can't be sure, but I could point him out to you. There was a shorter man with him. Might be the same men," Toby said.

"What were you doing in Sonora Town?"

"Looking for Pedro. What were you doing there?"

"Helping Wyatt. Looking for information about Pedro," Ernest said.

Several thoughts zipped through Toby's mind. Ernest wasn't just a pretty face. He definitely had a good bit of courage, and he showed clear signs of being sneaky. For good measure, Toby added pretty good actor to the mix of Ernest, who hid his complexity like a good spy.

Once the moment of admiration passed, Toby realized that he had no idea how to ask him if Grace was a time traveler. The reality of his situation hit him full force, and he wanted to turn around and ride back to the Doyles' house. But he wasn't about to start being a coward now.

CHAPTER 22: TOBY

MAN-TO-MAN TALK

July 20, 1890
2:30 a.m.

Ernest ran his hand through his hair and studied Toby for a few long seconds.

"Follow me," Ernest said.

In the kitchen, Ernest waved and nodded toward the table. Toby took a seat.

"Tea or coffee?"

"Coffee," Toby said. "Are you going to tell me what you're doing?"

"I'm making coffee, so we can have a little chat. You first, what are you doing here? I do hope you haven't turned to a life of crime and planned to rob us."

Toby watched Ernest. The man knew his way around the kitchen. He stirred up the covered embers and added a couple small pieces of wood. In a few seconds, the wood caught, and a good blaze started up. While he waited for the heat to build up, Ernest grabbed the coffee pot, filled it with water, and added coffee.

Toby was impressed and made a note to learn how to make coffee. That skill could come in handy. Liza might teach him.

"So?" Ernest asked.

Toby's hands shook as if they had a mind of their own. He put them in his lap so Ernest couldn't see. He wasn't exactly sure how to broach the subject. Actually, he had two issues. The best strategy might be bluntness.

"I came to see you and your sister."

"At three in the morning?"

"I don't think it's quite three. It was earlier when I got here. Then there was all that drunk stuff, and the guys in the bushes."

Ernest placed two steaming cups on the table, pulled up a chair, and sat across from him.

"As someone who has perfected the art of getting information, let me give you some advice. Add some charm into your personality, or people just aren't going to like you. They'll assume you're a worthless good-for-nothing. Add a little sweet talk and a dash of mystery to your personality, and people will love you. What's so important that you'd wake us up in the middle of the night?"

"Well, I think I need a lawyer, and since you're the only one I know, I thought I'd hire you."

"At three in the morning?"

"You've got a thing about three in the morning. Anyway, yes, actually the middle of the night thing is because I need to talk to your sister. It's imperative and can't wait."

Ernest stared at him for a few seconds and then leaned back in his chair.

"First, why do you need an attorney?"

Toby took out his mother's letter and handed it to him. Ernest read and scowled and puckered his lips together. He placed the letter on the table.

"Is this your mother's handwriting?"

"Yes."

"How many people know you're a girl?"

"Until a second ago, I thought only seven people. My mother and father, the Doyles and Liza. Now you. I guess Wyatt told you."

"Your sister doesn't know?" Ernest asked.

"No."

"You want to remain a man?"

"Yes."

Toby felt this was the weirdest conversation he'd ever had. He almost felt as if he were in court or at the police station being questioned.

Ernest ran his hand through hair again and nodded.

"I'll do this pro bono."

"No," Toby said. "My father owns four houses in LA and more than that in San Francisco."

Ernest whistled.

"He wants me out of his life, and he'll pay to accomplish that," Toby said. "I only have two requests. If my sister ever wants to see me, she will be allowed to visit, and we can write to each other."

"Your mother?"

"She doesn't want me," Toby said.

"The letter was a little coldhearted, but she may care more than you think," Ernest said.

"Maybe, maybe not."

"How do you feel about all this?"

"As long as I can see my sister, if she wants to see me, I'll go along with it," Toby said.

He never really thought his parents would disown him or abandon him, but it made sense. They barely put up with him and were embarrassed to take him places. Right this second, he didn't feel much of anything. He loved his sister and didn't want them ripping her away, and he didn't want to wait until she was grown up to contact her. Thinking about her was the only thing he had to hold onto. He'd have to write and tell her that he loved her and would always be her brother.

Ernest thrust his hand toward Toby. They shook.

"A gentleman's agreement until I can get some paperwork together. Do I have your permission to contact your father and to ask Wyatt to help me?"

"Yes, on my father. Wyatt doesn't like me. I doubt he'll help."

"Wyatt's Wyatt. He'll help." He watched Toby as he took a sip of his coffee. "Can I give you some advice?"

"Sure."

"These are my observations. That letter and other things have made you angry, maybe filled your heart with a little hate, and you're sad about losing your sister."

Toby nodded.

"Over the years, you've learned to hide your emotions, bury them deep inside. I suspect that Mr. Doyle befriended you and helped you."

Toby looked at the tile floor because his eyes were filling with tears.

"You miss him, and although your friends are a comfort, your heart is still a little broken. They are hurting, too, and they don't see your pain. That's okay. They have lots of heartaches. Maybe adding yours to theirs is too much."

Ernest waited, and Toby knew he expected an answer. So he cleared his throat and looked up, not even caring that Ernest could see his tears.

"Yes."

"It's my non-expert opinion that you're at a crossroad. You need to be careful and choose wisely. You wear a devil-may-care attitude. It's not as good as mine, but your mask is pretty good. That mixed with your willingness to take dangerous chances, and you might be heading for trouble."

"Are you telling me to change?" Toby asked.

"Yes and no. I'm not telling you to take your masks off.

Everyone wears a false mask because we need them. Remember this, some need them more than others. Life is hard for everyone. For some people, it's harder."

Toby sipped his lukewarm coffee and waited for Ernest to continue.

"The anger and the hate, if you let it fester, it'll eat you from the inside and destroy you. Mr. Doyle once told me, 'Look inside your heart and ask yourself what kind of man you want to be. When you know, get rid of anything that keeps you from being that man.' I'm passing his words along because he's not here to say them."

He tried, but Toby couldn't speak the words he wanted to say. So he looked up and said, "Thank you. I will."

Ernest got up and refilled their cups. After a few seconds of silence, he cleared his throat. Toby wondered if he missed Mr. Doyle, too.

"Why did you want to see Grace?" Ernest asked.

Toby laid out the entire story, including their run-ins with Wyatt.

"You haven't told me why I should go upstairs and wake my sister."

Toby rubbed the back of his neck. Now that he was going to say what he wanted to say, it sounded crazy. Telling Ernest about Alroy's magical tattoos was different from telling Alroy and Zella, but they needed help. So he took a deep breath.

"I'm worried about Alroy. That rash I told you about, there's more. Below the rash is a tattoo-like thing."

Toby waited a couple seconds, trying to choose the right words.

"One wrist has an infinity design on it and the other a kind of snail-shaped circle with other circles and numbers. And . . ."

He didn't know any other way to say it than to say it as fast as he could.

"I think Grace is a time traveler, and those marks have

something to do with the whirlwind that happened on the airship."

Ernest didn't laugh. He studied Toby as if he were seeing him for the first time.

"You know that sounds crazy."

Toby nodded.

"Yeah, but I don't have time to sweet-talk you. I need to get to the police station and see if I can figure out what Wyatt's going to do."

"I can tell you what Wyatt's up to." He took a sip of coffee. "I was out in Sonora Town, spying for him. I think those men who followed me are involved in the shanghai trade or maybe just smuggling. Either way, they are criminals. I obviously wasn't as smooth at getting information as I thought I was. I wasn't sure about the driver. As soon as the sun comes up, Wyatt is taking the police airship out to the harbor. He's going to search all the ships in port. You want a muffin? I'm hungry."

He was up searching through the pantry before Toby could answer. He tossed Toby a lemon muffin and poured them both another cup of coffee.

"Drink up. It's going to be a long day."

"I guess this means I can't talk to Grace?"

"I haven't decided."

Toby finished chewing a large bite of muffin and took a sip of coffee to wash it down.

"While you're deciding, can I ask you something?"

Ernest cupped his hands around his coffee as if he were warming his hands.

"Sure."

"Is Wyatt your lover?"

Ernest's eyebrows shot up, and his eyes widened.

"That's a pretty direct question."

"I didn't know any other way to say it."

"No, he's not," Ernest said. "Wyatt likes women."

"That's what I thought. He's your friend, and he thinks you're okay. Why doesn't he like me? Why's he worried about me and Alroy being friends?"

"Is he worried?"

"Yes."

Ernest took a huge gulp of coffee and stared at him as if he were trying to figure out what to say.

"I think Wyatt feels guilty about leaving after his father's funeral. He didn't know his stepmother's condition. I think he feels responsible for Alroy and Zella. So, maybe he's worried that Alroy . . . I don't know. What did he say?"

"I don't feel like a girl. The only person who treats me like a girl is Wyatt. Even my parents have given up on me being a girl. They think I'm some kind of freak, but that's a different thing. I don't know what to do. Alroy's my best friend."

"I can't speak for Wyatt. He's my best friend. He accepts me. I don't know why he has a problem with you. He does believe women need to be protected, so maybe that's it. Maybe you should talk to him."

"We just butt heads."

Ernest chuckled.

"Wyatt's good at butting heads. You don't need Wyatt's approval. I don't think he'll influence Alroy. Live your life in a way that's best for you. Your life won't be easy, but that doesn't matter. Find a role model."

"Role model? How could I ever find a role model?" Toby said.

"George Sand, the French novelist. She wore men's clothes, smoked cigars, went against social expectations."

"Did people know she was a woman?"

"Yes. She married and had two children."

"You're saying I should just be a girl."

"No, I'm saying figure out how you want to live, and to hell with the rest of the world."

"I'm doing that."

"Then let Wyatt figure things out for himself. You don't have to please him or anyone else. Do Alroy and Zella care?"

"No."

Ernest shrugged.

"I should be me, whatever that is?" Toby asked.

"Yeah."

"What's going on here?" a whispered voice behind them asked.

CHAPTER 23: TOBY

THE TIME TRAVELER

July 20, 1890
3:45 a.m.

Grace, sleepy-eyed and dressed in a blue chenille robe, leaned against the doorframe and stared at Toby.

"How long have you been standing there?" Toby asked.

"Long enough. Be a dear and pour me some coffee," Grace said to Ernest, sitting in the chair on the other side of Toby.

"What are you doing here?"

Toby's palms were sweaty, and he wiped them on his pants. Now that he was face to face with Grace, everything got harder.

"Tell me about the tattoo," she said.

"How did you know?"

"I was looking for it yesterday. You were watching me. My guess is you want to know what it is. Is Alroy feeling sick?"

"Yes, sick and sleepy. There are two tattoos. One on each wrist," he said.

"Interesting, describe both," Grace commanded.

He described each one in as much detail as he could. When he finished, Grace grinned at her brother and took a sip of coffee. She pushed up her sleeve and rubbed her right wrist, causing enough friction so that her skin turned reddish. An infinity tattoo, almost an exact match to the one on Alroy's wrist, appeared.

"Holy cow," Toby said, staring at the symbol. "It's like Alroy's. What is it?"

She rubbed her left wrist and held it out for Toby to see. A tattoo of an eye appeared. A line over the eye looked like an eyebrow. Under the eye, another line slanted down and another leaned right.

"That's nothing like Alroy's second tattoo. Yours looks Egyptian. What is it?"

"The Eye of Horus. It's a protection symbol."

"His is a circle. Like this."

Toby drew a snail-shaped circle on the table with his finger.

"There are other circles inside. Some look like gears, some like planets."

He licked his lips and stared at Grace.

"Are you a time traveler?"

She grimaced and seemed both sad and serious.

"Kind of. There's no time to explain right now. I don't travel anymore. It's dangerous."

"He got these marks on your airship?"

She shook her head and held her cup out to Ernest.

"No. He got them somewhere else. I need to talk to him and see the marks."

"If you go get Alroy and Zella, we can take the airship to the harbor. We'll watch the police and see if they find Pedro," Ernest said.

"Good idea," Grace said. "You and Ernest keep Zella busy while I talk to Alroy. Don't say anything to him, let me talk to him first."

"Is this bad?"

She absently took a bite of Ernest's half-eaten muffin and sipped her coffee. Her face muscles were tight.

"It's neither good nor bad, but I need to know how he got those marks."

Toby glanced from Ernest to Grace.

"The way you're acting, I think it's bad."

"It's serious. I need information before I know how serious," Grace said.

"Does this have anything to do with Pedro?"

"I doubt it." Grace patted his hand as if she were comforting him.

"Go. Eat a good breakfast, and get back here as fast as you can. Wyatt's going to the bay at first light, which means we need to hurry," Ernest said.

"Did you hear all that stuff about me being a girl?"

Graced nodded.

"My brother's right. Figure out what you want to be. Wyatt's good at heart, but he sometimes has trouble listening to his heart. He'll come around."

Toby pedaled back to the Doyle household as fast as he could. It was bad enough that he was worried about Pedro, now something was happening to Alroy. He was almost to the house when he realized that Grace really hadn't told him much. He wondered if Alroy knew more about the tattoos than he was telling them. It seemed to Toby that if someone gave his friend tattoos, he'd know who did it.

It was one thing to have wild speculations about Grace being a time traveler. Until tonight, he'd only half believed his idea. Now, he felt pulled in so many directions it made him feel dizzy. He'd been right. The reality exhilarated and terrified.

He tried to focus on the thought that Wyatt was going out to the ships. Maybe he'd find Pedro, which would take care of one of their major problems. He'd deal with time traveling later. In a strange way, he felt jealous of his friend. Wow, time travel.

CHAPTER 24: ZELLA

HOPE

July 20, 1890
5:00 a.m.

Zella tried for several minutes to wake her brother. Usually, she felt their connection. Sometimes they didn't have to talk because they knew what the other was thinking. Right now, she needed him, and he clung to sleep like someone in a coma.

"Alroy. Alroy." She shook his shoulder, gently at first, then harder, shaking his body.

"Wake up," she said into his ear.

He opened his eyes. Her nose almost touched his face.

"I've been trying to wake you up for ages," she said.

"Go away," he mumbled.

"Don't be a goose. Wake up."

He groaned.

"It's still dark."

"It's almost five. I heard Wyatt come home, and then he left again."

He rubbed his eyes.

"You're mad," he said, turning to look at her.

He bolted up.

"What's happened? Pedro?"

"No. Nothing happened."

"You've been crying. What's wrong?" Alroy asked.

"It's just I've been thinking about Pedro. And—"

"Don't say it. It might come true."

"I know. I don't want to say it either, but I can't help thinking." She blew her nose into her handkerchief.

Alroy sat up, put an arm around her, pulling her close. He stroked her hair, and she began to relax.

"Listen," he said. "If he's been taken to one of the boats, he's okay. They aren't going to hurt someone they want to sell. That wouldn't make any sense. And the boats are still in the harbor."

"If he's not on a boat?" she whispered.

"Then we'll keep looking until we find him."

She knew what he was thinking because she was thinking the same thing. If Pedro wasn't on one of the boats, the likelihood of his being hurt increased. The longer he was gone, the more likely their worst fears might be true.

All that was true, but she couldn't help thinking this was her fault. At first, she thought those feelings were guilt, but when she took a long hard look at herself, she realized something different.

Her feeling wasn't guilt. It was a realization. She wanted so much to be an investigative reporter that she pushed everyone to help her. She'd used Pedro's good nature and sense of justice to get what she wanted, a story about smugglers, a story to make a name for herself.

It was the same smugness that made her bully Liza into making that hideous dress for her. As awful as those things were, her callousness was worse. She wanted her way, and she hadn't considered how her manipulation affected others.

The person she'd become wasn't someone she admired. She'd even shut her mother out of her life. In a way, her anger toward her mother was justified. But her cruelty and lack of compassion were unforgivable.

Glancing at her brother, she realized that she couldn't tell him all that. This was her burden. What she wanted was to be a better person, to learn to forgive and understand others. Her father taught her those things, and she'd discarded them.

Being a good person was hard.

"It's going to be all right," Alroy said.

"I know. It has to be." She sat up straighter. "I'm worried about you. About those tattoos."

Alroy pushed himself up until he was leaning against the headboard.

"Hey, don't cry. I feel a little better."

"Good. But it feels as if everything is falling apart. I thought Papa's death was the worst thing I'd ever have to experience."

"Me, too. Look, I've got something."

Alroy got up and grabbed his jacket from his desk chair. He fumbled in the pocket and pulled out a large white envelope, which he held out.

"Papa wrote this to Doc. Wait until you're alone to read it. It made me cry."

Zella nodded, staring at the handwriting and trying her best to hold back her tears.

"You let me sleep in my clothes?"

Zella shrugged. "It was hard enough getting you from the attic to here. I wasn't going to undress you, too."

"Fair enough. Do you hear that? Liza's already up and making breakfast. Why is she up so early?" Alroy asked.

The loose stair near the top of the staircase creaked.

"Toby," Alroy said, glancing around. "Where'd he go?"

Zella shoved the envelope in her robe pocket and wiped her tears.

"He's been gone a long time." She decided not to tell him that he went to talk to Grace about his tattoos.

Toby opened the door and stopped.

"Are we having a hysterical cry?" he asked.

"Go to blazes, Toby Thaddeus Bailey." Zella stuck her tongue out at him.

"Don't get your knickers bunched up." He grinned at her. "Carry on. I already did my worrying and crying."

She threw a pillow at him.

He caught it and plopped on the bed.

"While you two have been sleeping and weeping." He winked at Zella. "Did you catch the rhyming?"

"Get to the point," Alroy said.

Zella's sadness had passed, and her spirits were better. Toby had that effect on her. He could say something annoying and make a person feel better. Even if she refused to laugh, he made her smile. He could annoy her out of a bad mood.

"Okay, boys and girls," Toby said as if he were announcing a play. "I went to Grace's, found Ernest coming home drunker than a sailor on leave."

Zella scowled at him.

"Be patient, Princess, there's more. He wasn't drunk. He was pretending, so he could spy for Wyatt, who has been a busy boy. Your brother is getting ready to take the police airship to the harbor."

Zella let out the breath she'd been holding and sighed.

"Corker," Alroy said.

"Get dressed, *gooses*," Toby said. "Grace is taking us up. We can watch the entire thing and be there when they find Pedro."

"You woke Grace up?" Zella stared at Toby as if she might punch him.

"She loved it." Toby grinned at Zella. "You'll be happy to know that Ernest is very charming in the morning. Get dressed. I'll meet you downstairs in ten minutes. I got Liza up early to make us breakfast."

He left them without a backward glance.

"I'll be down before you," Zella challenged Alroy and rushed out of his room.

She dressed quickly because she wanted to go up in the airship and watch them find Pedro. Then she remembered that she was supposed to tour the newspaper. If she went there, she could give them a picture of Pedro to put in the next edition. She hated to miss being there if they found Pedro, but if he wasn't on the ship, *The Herald* could print his story and help find him.

She could tell them about Wyatt searching the ships. They'd have a second story, and maybe, the editor would see how valuable she could be to the paper.

By the time she got to the kitchen, she had everything planned.

Alroy and Toby were already sitting at the round kitchen table, munching on biscuits and sipping milk. Her brother hadn't changed his clothes and looked like a wrinkled mess.

Liza handed Zella an everyday plate with three pieces of bacon, scrambled eggs on one side, and two hot biscuits. The butter and honey were on the table.

"Eat up," she said. "You need your strength for helping Pedro."

Although she could be a big nag, Liza took care of them, especially since their mother had lost her mind. She also liked Pedro best of all their friends. Zella could tell she was worried.

"Thanks," she said.

"You three don't be takin' advantage of Miss Camero."

"We won't," Zella said.

"I'll take your ma tea and tell her all about what you three are up to. And, Alroy, put some clean clothes on. You look like a bum."

"I don't know why you bother with tea," Zella said. "She doesn't listen. She doesn't care."

"She does care," Alroy said. "And she listens. Yesterday, she looked at me when I talked about Papa."

"No more fussin'," Liza said. "We got enough to worry about without you two bickering."

They grew quiet and focused on eating.

"I'm not going with you," Zella said.

"What? You have to," Alroy said.

"No, you and Toby go. I'm going to the newspaper. I was supposed to go over there this morning."

"Pedro's more important than a dumb newspaper," Alroy said.

"I'm going to write up a short piece about Pedro being missing. I'll take his picture with me. I can talk them into putting his story in the paper. If he's not on the ship, this is a good backup plan. Someone might know something. It could help," Zella said.

"That is a good plan," Toby said.

"Yeah," Alroy agreed. "Sorry I called the newspaper dumb."

"We're all worried," Liza said. "You two, scoot."

Alroy and Toby headed to the door.

"Toby," Liza called.

She grabbed an extra biscuit and wrapped it in a white napkin.

"Here. I know you get hungry," she said, handing him the napkin.

"You spoil him," Zella said as she watched the boys rush away.

"I like spoiling all of you." She flashed Zella one of her rare smiles. "Today, could turn out to be mighty good."

"It might," Zella agreed, feeling a little optimistic and very hopeful.

CHAPTER 25: ZELLA

REPORTER'S SCOOP

July 20, 1890
6:00 a.m.

Zella finished her breakfast as quickly as Liza allowed and rushed up to the attic. She composed an article about Pedro. For an added touch, she included several of his accomplishments. If he ever read the piece, he'd be embarrassed, but she didn't care. She wanted people to be interested, and she wanted anyone with information to know to contact the police.

She found a picture of him standing by the model monorail system he'd built. It showed his face and that he was intelligent. In the kitchen, she found Liza holding a cup of steaming hot tea.

"Is that for Mama?" Zella asked.

"Yes."

"I'll take it," she said, placing her valise on the kitchen table.

"She's in the parlor."

Zella took the cup and marched into the dark parlor. Her mother sat in her usual place, staring out the window. She set the tea down, and walked across the room, raising the half-drawn blinds of each window. When sunlight streamed through all three windows, Zella glanced around the room.

Light chased away the gloom. The furniture, the bookcase, the books, the tables, the small piano, everything was covered in a thin layer of dust.

She thought filling the room with light would make her feel better, but it didn't. The layer of dust on the furniture reminded her of her father's funeral. The minister had said, "from dust to dust."

Was her mother sitting in this room waiting to die?

Zella balled her hands into fists, opening and closing them until she could force herself to unclasp them.

"Mama," she said, watching her mother's face, looking for any signal of life. "I'm tired of you sitting in this room feeling sorry for yourself. You're a bad mother. You hear me? You're a bad mother."

She took three steps closer, but her mother didn't move. Now she wasn't looking out the window because Zella's yellow dress blocked her view. Reaching down, Zella cupped her mother's chin and tilted her head up until those blank eyes gazed up at her daughter's face.

"You aren't the only one who lost Papa. We all did. We're all sad and lonely. You're worse than Papa's death. You hear me? You're worse. 'Cause we need you, and you don't care. You sit here in a dark room, like one of Toby's zombie people. You don't love us. You're not a mother. You're a thing. A dead thing. You don't love me. You don't love Alroy. 'Cause if a mother loves her children, she doesn't leave them."

Tears ran down Zella's cheeks like rain bursting from an angry cloud. She fell to her knees and put her forehead on her mother's lap.

"Pedro's missing. He might be dead. My heart is breaking. Why don't I have a mother?"

She sat, resting on her mother's lap, but the woman didn't

move, didn't speak, didn't acknowledge her pain. Leaning back with her legs tucked under her, Zella glared at her. She looked like a body without a soul. She had left them alone.

Zella took the cup of tea off the mahogany table and sipped the now tepid liquid until she emptied the cup. She placed the dainty cup back on its saucer. Standing, she shook her skirt, pressing the wrinkles until they weren't so visible.

Whatever the future held, Zella decided that she would be better. She'd be better than her mother, a better person than she was now.

She glanced up. Liza stood in the doorway, red-eyed and silent.

Zella walked to her, kissed her cheek, and said, "Thank you for being strong. I'm going to the newspaper. I'm late. Alroy and Toby are probably already at the port."

It was only yesterday that she'd interviewed at *The Daily Herald,* but it seemed like a week ago. So much had happened. She returned without feeling a sense of excitement or anticipation at getting a tour of the offices. Instead, her mind raced with ways she could ask the editor or one of the reporters about getting Pedro's story into the newspaper. The idea sounded great at breakfast. Now that she was in the elevator, riding up to the second floor, she doubted her ability to persuade anyone. Why would they listen to a high school student? She realized she didn't care if they rejected her plan. She had to try.

As the elevator clanked to a stop, she straightened her shoulders and held her head high as she stepped into the newsroom. It was early, and only a few people were at their desks. She glanced around and spotted Kate St. James. When they made eye contact, Kate waved her over.

"I'm glad you're here early," Kate said. "I just got a tip that the police are at the pier. Word is they are searching the ships docked in the bay."

"I can give you details," Zella said and recounted everything that had transpired since yesterday.

Like a good reporter, Kate took notes, asked questions, wanted Pedro's full name. The woman used shorthand to take notes.

"Now, what are you doing here with all this going on? You should have called in and rescheduled your tour."

"I'm here to get Pedro's story in the paper. I brought a photograph of him, and I wrote this short piece." She handed the photo and the article to her.

"You have the instincts of a reporter."

Kate glanced at Pedro's photo and skimmed her article.

She grabbed a green pencil and began marking Zella's article. Without explaining, Kate crossed out words, shortened a couple of sentences, and added a word here and there.

"This is good. I'm sure the editor will add it to today's paper. I'll do my best to get it placed right next to my piece. You might not get the photo back."

"I have the negative," Zella said.

"Take a look at my changes." She passed the revised copy to Zella. "Here's a good rule of thumb. When you finish a piece, let it sit for fifteen minutes. In the newspaper business, you don't have a lot of time, but fifteen minutes will give you some distance from your words. Then cut as many words as you can. Always cut at least ten percent. Then tighten up the sentences. You want crisp and to the point. Space is king in the paper. Lead with a sentence that makes people want to keep reading."

"Yes, it's better," Zella said, looking over the changes. "Thank you."

"You're a good writer. We'll get you up to speed."

The phone on Kate's desk rang.

"St. James," she said and listened to the person on the other end. Cupping the telephone receiver between her shoulder and chin, she began taking notes. "Got it. Thanks."

She glanced up at Zella.

"The editor wants me to go to the police station. The dirigible is on its way back. You want to go with me?"

"Yes," Zella said.

Kate grabbed her notepad and rushed for the elevator. Zella followed on her heels. Before the elevator started its trek down, Zella spotted Charlie across the room staring at her. Their eyes met, and he nodded. She looked away, embarrassed to have been caught watching him. But she sneaked in a quick glance back in time to see him looking her way.

"He's a nice boy," Kate said.

"But?"

"His parents wouldn't approve of a white girl," she said, grinning as if she'd made a joke. "But that's a minor detail for a woman who wants to be a reporter."

Zella laughed for the first time since she found out Pedro was missing. Charlie was the nicest boy she knew. By the time the elevator reached the ground floor, her thoughts had turned to Wyatt.

Without a doubt, he was going to be hopping mad when she arrived at the police station with a reporter. She braced herself to face his wrath. If Pedro were safe, she wouldn't care if he yelled for an hour.

CHAPTER 26: ALROY

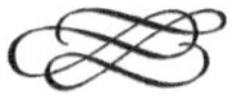

TO THE HARBOR

July 20, 1890
6:00 a.m.

Alroy and Toby rode to Grace's house. Inez Tapia opened the Camero's kitchen door, and scowled at them.

"Good morning, Miss Tapia," Toby said.

Glaring, she waved them inside.

"Always a ruckus in this house. Ain't like the old days."

Inez handed Alroy a basket that smelled like fried chicken. Without saying another word, she shooed them upstairs. In Grace's workshop, Ernest sat on a stool, drinking coffee and looking very much like a man who had been up all night.

"She's ready for us," he said and motioned toward the porch and the ladybug airship.

Without ceremony, they boarded the airship. The mysteries of the ship no longer held Alroy's attention. His thoughts bounced between finding Pedro and wondering if Grace's ship would attack him. He mentally had his fingers crossed Wyatt would find his friend and that their ride would be uneventful.

Grace climbed down from the pilot's seat. She dressed in a white blouse, a brown jacket, and a long brown skirt.

He guessed Ernest would consider her presentable. He wasn't sure why that thought amused him, except maybe watching Ernest and Grace helped him understand that brothers and sisters nitpicked each other's behaviors.

When she glanced at Alroy, he saw concern and softness in her face. No one seemed able to hide their worry.

"Here's the plan," she said. "I'll take you out to the harbor and get as low as I can. You should be able to see Wyatt's men searching the boats. If they find Pedro, I'll land the airship at the pier, and we'll wait for Pedro and Wyatt there."

"If not? If they don't find him?" Alroy could feel his eyes burning with tears that wanted to flood over. He swallowed and forced himself to dismiss all the negative possibilities.

Grace patted his shoulder.

"We'll keep looking until we find him." She pointed to the basket and said, "You can put that there."

She moved to the wall nearest the door and unlatched a metal wall-mounted table. Toby rushed over and lifted the tabletop. Looking underneath, he found the wooden triangle braces that pulled out and held the table in place. He glanced up at Grace.

"As Alroy would say, corker. I didn't notice this yesterday."

"Use the strap to secure the basket," Grace said. "Hopefully, we can share our lunch with Pedro."

"Alroy, be Grace's copilot," Ernest said.

"Sure."

He couldn't hold back a grin as he glanced at Toby before following Grace up the ladder and taking the seat next to her.

Alroy wasn't sure why Ernest gave up his seat, but he wasn't going to complain. The view would be amazing, and he could see up close how to pilot this machine. Plus, he was a little worried about going back on the deck. Toby might be jealous, but he'd get over it.

Grace nodded to him.

"Ernest checked the balloon before you arrived and unclamped the ship."

She tapped the gauge as if to make sure the reading was correct.

Alroy nodded.

She released the brake, and air hissed through the pipes. The ladybug lifted up and away from the porch. They slowly rose until all the houses were below them and the city spread out before them.

Remembering yesterday's flight, he grabbed the arms of this seat and held on tight, waiting for a mishap that didn't come. Once they were in the air, Grace checked the gauges and turned the ship west toward the harbor.

"How are you?" she asked.

He shrugged.

"As long as there's not another whirlwind, I'll be okay."

"I doubt there'll be a problem." She glanced at him and then looked out the window for a few seconds before turning back. "Toby told me about your tattoos."

"He told you?"

"He's worried about you," Grace said. "How do you feel?"

He shrugged. Anything he said would sound crazy, but Grace didn't seem surprised about the tattoos. She looked at him expectantly.

"Ah, weird," he finally said. "Can't describe it."

"Are you tired?"

He nodded.

"Your wrists burn?"

"Last night, yeah. Now they are itchy. Not as bad as they were. I feel lightheaded like I'm sick, but I'm not sick," he said.

"Would you mind showing me the tattoos?"

He pushed up his jacket until his wrist was exposed. He turned his arm so his palm faced up and showed her the one with the infinity symbol. He did the same with the other sleeve.

"They'll fade," she said.

She pushed her sleeve up and held her arm out. Then she gently rubbed her wrist.

A tattoo that looked almost exactly like his infinity symbol appeared on her wrist. She held out her other arm, which had a different design.

"The Eye of Horus?" he asked.

"Yes, protection, good health."

"The first one is like mine. How?"

A lock of brown hair fell across her forehead. She pushed it back and faced him.

"My guess, and this is only a guess, is that the whirlwind might have had a traveler in it."

She watched him as she spoke.

"Time traveler?"

She nodded.

"Corker," he said, unable to think of anything appropriate. "Are you and Toby playing a joke on me?"

"No. I'm serious."

"But that would mean you're a traveler?"

"Yes."

"Holy cow," he whispered. "I'm crazy, or you're crazy, or we're both crazy."

"Umm, I need to ask a couple questions. All right?

He nodded.

"When you were in the whirlwind, did something grab you?"

Alroy's heart pounded against his ribs. He couldn't remember anything grabbing him in the whirlwind, but he did remember the time machine experiment. Something or someone definitely grabbed him then. He couldn't tell her that because he promised Doc.

"I don't know. I was trying not to get ripped off the ship," he said.

"Okay, we'll need to explore this later. Right now, I'm going to tell you a couple of things. Can you keep this to yourself?"

"I don't know. Lately too many people are asking me to keep secrets."

"Just for a little while until I figure some things out. Then you can tell your friends. Toby's already figured out I'm a traveler. You can't go spreading this information around, or people will think you are crazy."

"I get that. Sure, I'll keep it to myself."

"Your infinity tattoo isn't exactly like mine. I've made modifications that protect me from the man who gave it to us. I'd like to change yours to match mine for your protection."

"To protect me from?"

"My father." She paused as if thinking about what she was going to say. "He's not a good man. If he could, he would use you for his own ends. This modification will protect you."

Alroy's thoughts shifted back to the idea Toby and Grace were playing a practical joke. However, the solemn expression on Grace's face dispelled that notion.

"How'd I get my tattoo? How would you modify it? I've been feeling sick, and I don't want to get sicker."

She glanced at him and waited a couple of seconds before speaking.

"My family, my father's side, are travelers. We can move between dimensions. That mark is my family mark."

"What exactly does this mean?" Alroy asked.

"It means that if you choose, you can learn to travel."

Alroy grinned. His heart pounded with excitement because, of course, he'd choose to be a traveler. He could explore time. But Grace's frown dampened his enthusiasm.

"I was about to say *corker*, but I have a feeling this isn't exactly good news."

"It's not great news, and I'm sorry this happened to you. My father is a criminal. He's been banned from this dimension. He broke the law by giving you his brand. He's trying to get back here. He could do that through you."

"If he can't come here, how could he give it to me? Why would he pick me?"

"That's what I'm trying to figure out. My suspicion is that some kind of rift happened in the dimension, and you were there. If that happened, he could grab you and leave his mark. I'm wondering how he knew where the rift was?"

Alroy knew. Doc had made it with his time machine. Maybe all the tests he did created a lot of rifts. Maybe her father was there waiting because he figured there would be more tests? He really wanted to tell Grace about Doc's experiments, but he didn't want to break his word. Maybe he should tell her? Maybe she could fix whatever happened?

"I don't understand," Alroy said.

"It's a lot to take in, and I can't tell you everything right now. My father is dangerous. On the positive side, someone is protecting you."

She glanced outside and checked the various gauges before turning back to him.

"The other tattoo is a protection symbol. I'm not familiar with it. But someone is trying to protect you. My change to your tattoo would be added protection."

"You can change it. I figure I need all the help I can get. Will it hurt more?"

She shook her head.

"No. If I have your permission, it's a painless process. You are feeling ill because you were marked without permission. Give me your wrist."

Alroy held out his arm. Grace's touch felt cool as it had yesterday, and nothing dramatic happened. She simply squeezed his wrist. After a few seconds, the burning in his arm, his headache, and the queazy feeling in his stomach disappeared. She released her hold.

Alroy studied his wrist. Here and there on the infinity symbol tiny lines curled off the original tattoo. She held out her arm, and he compared the tattoos. They were a perfect match.

"Now I'm . . . we're time travelers?"

Graced sighed.

"For now, we'll call it time traveler, but it's far more complicated than that. I'm still unsure about how you got the mark. That is something I need to know," Grace said.

"The whirlwind?"

"No. The whirlwind was more like someone trying to pull you away. If I'm right, that means you got the marks somewhere else."

"Oh."

He knew he sounded lame and pathetic. She wanted an explanation from him, but the promise he'd made Doc kept him silent.

"I'm confused," Alroy whispered.

"We'll talk more about it later. Right now, let's focus on Pedro. If you can try to remember when you might have gotten the tattoo, that will help."

Grace seemed concerned, which made Alroy anxious. He sat in an airship, talking to a woman who told him she was some kind of time traveler. He was pretty sure some invisible persons gave him the tattoos when Doc and he tested the time machine. With all his heart and mind and soul, he wanted to tell her.

He decided to focus on Pedro. They might find him. That was something good. Unless, of course, they didn't find him, which might mean something terrible had happened to his friend.

CHAPTER 27: ALROY

SEARCHING THE SHIPS

July 20, 1890
7:00 a.m.

Graces attention focused on the airship's gauges while Alroy glanced at the observation deck. He could see Toby and Ernest talking.

"Look," Grace said pointing west.

Ahead the blue-green ocean spread out before them. In the distance, the waves on shore looked darker than the ocean in the distance. White lines streaked the sand where the waves broke.

More important than the ocean were three ships in the bay. They were large ocean-going cargo ships.

Alroy listened to the propellers and engines and thought about how life had gotten crazy. He felt as if he were having one very long, very horrible, very strange dream. He wished he'd wake up, but he knew this wasn't a dream.

"Why don't you go down and join Toby. You can go out on the deck, and I'll fly over each ship Wyatt boards."

"You know Wyatt's not going to like our flying by," he said.

A giant grin spread across her face. Her eyes sparkled, and Alroy wondered if she were as mischievous as Toby.

"He'll get over it," she said.

He hurried down the ladder, not wanting to miss seeing the pier and the boats. Cautiously, he stepped outside onto the deck, glancing around to make sure there wasn't a wind funnel. Toby and Ernest stood at the bow, leaning against the rail and staring at the bay.

Alroy grabbed the pair of goggles Ernest held out for him and slipped them on. The bay and the vast water disappeared into the horizon. The ship began a slow descent.

Alroy glanced around. He knew it was silly to think the whirlwind would happen again, but he ignored his apprehension. He briefly wondered if Ernest was standing by in case the whirlwind returned.

By the time they reached the shore, they could see the police wagons and several automaton-driven carriages parked on the beach. When they reached the first ship, Toby pointed to the two boats tied to the nearest ship. Grace flew lower. They could see Wyatt and another police officer talking to someone in a uniform, probably the captain. Other officers searched the top deck.

"I'm afraid we can only observe," Ernest said, stepping closer to them.

"How are they going to find one boy in a ship that size?" Alroy asked.

"Excellent point. They could easily hide someone and get away with it, but you aren't taking Wyatt into consideration," Ernest said.

"What do you mean?" Alroy asked.

"Wyatt was the most ruthless attorney you can imagine. I'm sure he'll let each captain know he'll go easy on them if the boy is found, if not, he'll make their lives . . . difficult, very difficult."

"Look," Toby called out and pointed toward Wyatt, who was glancing up at them.

"Caught," said Ernest as he waved at his friend. "The best way to annoy Wyatt is to pretend you don't know you're annoying him."

Alroy tucked that advice away for later.

As if on cue, police officers seemed to come from all parts of the ship and gathered around Wyatt. There were at least twenty officers, but Pedro wasn't among them. Ernest handed Alroy and Toby each a set of binoculars. They watched the drama below.

"Wyatt doesn't look happy," Toby said.

"He's never happy," Alroy added.

Grace circled around the ship, the police were back in their boats and rowing toward the next ship. As Grace turned the airship, many of the crew glanced up and waved.

"Ernest, I think Grace should design a motor for the police. They could zip from boat to boat in no time," Toby said.

Ernest grinned before speaking. "Maybe you should suggest that. I bet she'd ask you to help. Might be a good way to get on Wyatt's good side."

Toby laughed, and Alroy slapped him on the back to signal his agreement.

Pedro didn't show up on the second or third ships. They all fell silent and returned to the cabin. Alroy wondered if he looked as glum and sad as Toby did. He'd placed a lot of hope on finding Pedro on one of those ships. Now they were going to have to start over.

"Ernest, do you mind if I go up and talk to Grace for a few minutes?" Alroy said.

"Not at all. I want to rummage through Inez's food basket. We can eat on the way back. I guess you two will want to look for Pedro as soon as we land."

"Yes," Toby said. "Are you going to tell Wyatt?"

"Why would I do that?"

Alroy climbed up the ladder and sat in the copilot's seat.

"I'm sorry. I was hoping they'd find him," Grace said.

"Me too. I have something to ask you, a question about ethics."

She pointed to the view. They had turned east to head back into Los Angeles. In the distance, the sun hit the buildings of Los Angeles at just the right angle, and they seemed to sparkle. On a different day, he would have enjoyed the sight. Right now, he had too many other things on his mind.

"So," he said. "I made a promise to someone that I'd keep a secret, and normally I'd keep the secret. But I have extenuating circumstances. What if keeping the secret doesn't allow me to tell you important information? And what if the man's on our suspect list? I've been keeping my promise. I haven't told Zella and Toby."

Grace looked at him for several seconds before answering. "Where'd you get this list?"

"We found Pedro's notebook. He was investigating some of his employers and kept notes. We thought maybe one of them was involved in his disappearance."

She turned in her seat and faced him.

"Have you told Wyatt?"

He shook his head.

"We gave him the list, but the notebook is in code. We're decoding it. If we give it to the police, they won't be able to make sense of it."

She nodded, encouraging him to keep talking.

"Here's the thing. Doctor Grimes is on our list. We don't know yet who Pedro was investigating, but once a week he goes to Doc's place to sweep and make things neat and tidy."

Alroy wondered if he'd already broken his word to Doc and if he should say more. The thing was that the tattoos on his wrists were worrying him. They didn't have anything to do with

Pedro's disappearance, but he wanted to tell Grace so she could help him.

He realized he'd already decided to tell her and make it right with Doc later.

"The first guy on the list proved to be okay. Doc wouldn't hurt Pedro. He's not high on our list. He's there because we want to check into every possibility."

"Alroy, you don't have to tell me anything that makes you uncomfortable."

"I know. But the thing is . . ." He scratched the back of his head. "The thing is that yesterday I was with Doc when he tested his time machine. He sent a rat forward in time. The machine with the rat disappeared and then reappeared eighteen minutes later. He's done the experiment before, and the rats died. This time the rat lived."

"Well, that's impressive," Grace said, sounding surprised.

"You'll keep Doc's secret? One scientist to another."

She nodded.

Since she agreed, Alroy took a deep breath and talked as fast as he could.

"Mostly I'm telling you because Doc has done several experiments, and maybe those experiments made the rifts you were talking about. Yesterday, when the time machine left, I felt something grab my hand. I thought I imagined the touch. Then I felt it a second time on the other arm. That's when I started feeling strange."

Grace turned back to the controls, checked the gauges, and made sure they were on the right course.

"I see your moral dilemma. Your secret is safe with me. Doctor Grimes is on the list, but that doesn't mean he's responsible for Pedro's disappearance. Innocent until proven guilty. It seems unlikely he'd hurt Pedro. He's taken a keen interest in you and the your friends. Being a suspect isn't the same as being guilty. So, unless there is some compelling reason to do otherwise, I think you are wise to keep your secret."

Alroy nodded.

"Yeah, that makes sense. I just felt strange not telling Zella and Toby."

"I understand. But I'm going to have to check for rifts. I won't talk to Doctor Grimes, but I need to know where his lab is. Tell me about the machine."

He quickly told her where Doc's workshop was, and then he described the time machine.

"I'm glad you confided in me. Let me urge you to give the police all the information you find in the notebook. Wyatt's working hard on this case, and he wants to find Pedro. Anything you can tell him will help."

"We will. But we have to translate the code first."

Now that Grace knew how he got marked, he hoped she could help him. He didn't like the idea that a criminal was trying to get to him. He looked at the second tattoo. Someone out there was trying to protect him. In a strange way, that made him feel better.

The more he thought about what she'd told him, the more questions he had. How many travelers were there? Did they just move around in time? Grace said they traveled in dimensions. What did that mean? It sounded as if there were a lot of dimensions, not just one. Most of all, he wondered if he were safe. He guessed those questions would get answered later. After they found Pedro.

Something told him they were going to have to take drastic measures to find his friend. Wyatt had to play by police rules. The League of the Daring could investigate outside those rules, which he knew they would do. He crossed his fingers they wouldn't get into too much trouble.

CHAPTER 28: ZELLA

THE POLICE STATION

July 20, 1890
10:00 a.m.

A block from the station, Zella spotted the police dirigible. She nudged Kate and pointed. If they hurried, they might be able to get to the roof in time to catch Wyatt as he disembarked.

At the information desk, Zella was a little out of breath. Sergeant Matthews squinted at her and waited for her to speak.

"I'm here to find out about my friend, Pedro Hernandez. Detective Wyatt took the dirigible to look for him. They are landing now. Can we go up and talk to Wyatt?"

"I'm not supposed to let the public up there, but since you're his sister, I guess it'll be okay. Who's this lady?" the sergeant asked.

Zella grabbed Kate's hand, pulling her closer.

"A dear, dear friend of the family. We're so worried about Pedro."

Sergeant Matthews nodded to Kate, and a broad smile spread across his round face.

"Well then, you'd better hurry. Go to the right and up—"

Zella dragged Kate along as she raced toward the stairs.

"I hope the boy is safe," Matthews called out. "Hey, aren't you that newspaper lady?"

They raced up two flights of stairs, passing several officers on the stairway. Zella charged through the door leading to the rooftop. She and Kate stopped and stared at the dirigible. Four officers were securing the lines, while others filed past them toward the stairs.

Zella held her breath, praying that Pedro would step off the airship any second.

Wyatt and two other men were the last to step onto the rooftop. Pedro wasn't with them. When Wyatt spotted her and Kate, he frowned, said something to the men he was with, and walked toward them.

"What are you doing here?" he asked, sounding more than a little annoyed.

"Well, it's nice to see you, too," Kate said.

"Sorry, Kate." Wyatt removed his hat. "My sister has an annoying habit of running around places she shouldn't be."

"Pedro?" Zella said.

"We didn't find him. It was a wild goose chase. No smuggling, no shanghaied people, nothing."

"Oh." Zella sighed.

"How did you two get up here? This roof is off limits to the public, and the *press*," he added, glaring at Kate.

"I'll have you know that I'm a dear, dear friend of the family. Does he badger you like this all the time?"

Kate grinned at Wyatt, who continued to frown.

"Wyatt, you used to be quite charming. Perhaps you should lighten up a bit." The wind whipped Kate's hair about, messing up her perfectly coiffured updo, but she merely pushed the stray strands out of her face.

"And you didn't use to be a snoopy newspaperwoman."

"Do you have a statement to make about Pedro? I'm doing a story, and we are running a short article written by your very talented sister."

Zella didn't care about their banter. All she could think about was Pedro and that he was still missing.

"No statement," Wyatt said.

"Off the record?"

"Off the record, we're still looking for the boy, and when and if I have new information, I'll give it to you. I assume Zella gave you a run down. For now, that's all I have."

"Thanks."

She glanced from Wyatt to Zella, who was trying not to cry.

"I'd like to speak with my sister," Wyatt said, breaking the silence.

"I have work to do. Zella, if you need anything, let me know. We'll reschedule your tour when this is over."

She left as Zella mumbled, "Thank you."

"Let's go to my office," Wyatt said.

They were both silent as they made their way to his office. Once they were alone, Zella couldn't hold back her tears. Wyatt motioned her to a chair and sat behind his desk.

"Would you like some tea?" he asked.

When she nodded, he left and returned a few minutes later with a cup of hot tea and two shortbread cookies. By that time, her tears had stopped, and her mind was racing with ideas of what to do next.

"I'm sorry," Wyatt said and cleared his throat. "I need to know about the list you have. Where'd you get it? Who are those people?"

She pushed aside the desire to tell him about Pedro's journal and took a deep breath. Toby always said the truth was better than a lie, so she'd tell him as much of the truth as possible.

"Pedro works odd jobs to help his mother. None of them pays much, and they are part-time. We made a list of all his employers. We thought we could ask them if they'd seen Pedro or knew where he was."

"You've already told me that. I think there's more."

He looked at her. The seconds ticked by slowly. He didn't seem to mind the silence. She wiggled in her chair and tried to think of a way to answer him.

"We put everyone on the list who might be connected to the smuggling ring. Pedro told me he followed Mr. Hornsby, who met up with a couple of other people. And, no, it was dark, and he couldn't see them clearly. They put crates in a large boat. Officer Henderson came by, talked to them, and left after they gave him something in an envelope. But some of the people are just people he works for. We were being thorough."

"You and Pedro didn't think of telling me? Or some other officer?"

"We were investigating, not working a case." Zella hoped she sounded professional.

He let the comment pass. Opening his desk drawer, he took out a sheet of paper and read off the list of names on their list.

"Is this everyone?"

Garcia and Lee weren't on the list. For now, she wouldn't tell him about Garcia. She didn't think Pedro would want him to know.

"Mr. Lee. He has a Chinese herbal shop."

Wyatt wrote his name on the paper.

"I know that shop," he said. "What about Officer Henderson? Why's he on your list?"

Zella sat up straighter and glared at Wyatt.

"Like Toby said, Marie told him Pedro was missing, and he didn't report it. Pedro saw him take a bribe. He acted strange when we were here yesterday. Maria said Henderson hated Pedro." She paused and thought about what she was saying. "She didn't say hate. She said he didn't like him because he made things hard for Pedro."

Wyatt studied her for a moment.

"I talked to Pedro's mother and sister. You were right. She is very sick, and they couldn't tell me much. I asked them what happened to their home, but both of them refused to say anything. They are frightened about something. Do you know anything about that?"

Zella shook her head.

"No. They just suddenly moved, and Pedro wouldn't tell us why. Until yesterday I didn't know how bad things were."

Wyatt leaned back in his chair.

"As Doctor Stone pointed out, their situation doesn't make sense. Mrs. Hernandez had a nice home and ran a boarding-house. Can you think of anything that would explain their move."

"No. Maybe I can talk to Maria. She might tell me something she wouldn't tell you."

"No," Wyatt snapped. "You might make things worse for them. If they are frightened, they might be in danger. I have Officer Mason watching out for them. I don't want you in Sonora Town. Go home, and for the sake of my sanity, stay out of trouble. Tell Alroy and Toby the same."

Zella had no intention of sitting around and waiting, but she also didn't want to argue. She nodded. A nod didn't mean much in the long run. If she had to, she could explain it away.

At the door, she looked back at Wyatt.

"I just remembered something," she said. "About a year ago, Pedro said a copper, I mean policeman, was boarding with them. Maybe he could tell you what happened to the house."

Wyatt sat up straighter.

"What's the officer's name?"

Zella shrugged. "Don't know. Pedro just said his mother felt safer with him around."

He forced a grin and nodded, turning back to his list and forgetting her existence.

Out on the street, she rushed toward Dr. Stone's office. She'd start there with her investigation, find out how Mrs. Hernandez was doing, and make plans. She also wanted to get home and talk to Alroy and Toby and change out of her hot dress. She'd dressed up to go to the newspaper office. Now all she could think about was putting on a cotton dress and getting cooler.

Behind her, a man called her name.

"Miss Doyle."

She turned and watched Officer Henderson rushing toward her. If she were hot in her dress, he must have been roasting. He wore his helmet and the long knee-length coat of the police uniform. His face was red from jogging toward her, and beads of perspiration ran down his chubby face. His dark beard glistened with moisture.

Stepping into the shade of the building, she waited for him. By the time he reached her, he was out of breath. She couldn't muster any pity for him because she suspected that he didn't care about Pedro.

"Miss Doyle, I want to tell you how sorry I am Pedro is missing. We are doing everything we can to find the boy. He's a fine lad. Has your brother found any new information?"

The man's foul breath wafted toward her.

"Your sentiments are admirable. Thank you for your concern. Talk to my brother about his discoveries. He doesn't tell me very much. Perhaps if you'd reported Pedro missing when his sister informed you, the police could have acted more quickly."

He glared at her for a second. "She must be mistaken. I wasn't informed that he was missing."

"Well, since you know Sonora Town so well, perhaps you could do some investigating and help my brother."

His brown eyes shifted back and forth as if he were trying to decide what to say next.

She should have felt guilty for behaving so poorly. Her

mother taught her to be kind, even when she didn't feel the gentle emotion. But then her mother really didn't care about her, so she felt free to misbehave.

"I must be going," she said and walked away.

Officer Henderson whispered, "little bitch" as she walked away. She stopped, glared back at him, and raised her eyebrows. He quickly scurried away, rushing back to the police station. She made a mental note to tell Wyatt about the encounter.

By the time she arrived at Dr. Stone's office, she gladly accepted the glass of water his receptionist offered her.

"He's with a patient. He'll see you after he's finished."

Zella took a seat and fidgeted with her handbag. Waiting wasn't something she particularly enjoyed. Now that she knew Pedro was still missing, she wanted to get home, talk to Alroy and Toby, and make plans.

She also wanted to snoop around and find out what she could about Henderson. He seemed nervous when he was talking to her, and he was pumping her for information.

A mother and a young boy exited Dr. Stone's exam room. He came to the door, looked at her over his glasses, and nodded. She followed him.

"Sit down," he said. "Come to check on Mrs. Hernandez?"

"Yes."

"She's mighty sick. I gave her some medication. Hopefully, she'll be okay in a week or so. I had a chat with Wyatt. He came to see her, asking questions and upsetting her."

"She's going to be all right?"

"I can't promise that. She needs to get out of that horrible room. No one should have to live the way they do. It ain't right. I opened the windows. Don't know if that'll do much good. Mrs. Garcia brought her some soup and will look in on her. Anything else?"

"No."

"How's your ma?"

"Same."

"Don't give up hope. She could snap out of it any time."

"Or she could never snap out of it."

Dr. Stone chuckled.

"Girl, you always look at the underside of the rainbow. I'll come by and check on her. Have Liza make some of those gingersnap cookies."

Zella stood.

"The way you eat, I don't know how you stay so thin."

"Missy, you got a tongue like a viper."

His words stung. She was talking to him as if he were Henderson, not jolly Dr. Stone.

"I'm sorry. I shouldn't have said that."

"Come here," he said, opening his arms.

He hugged her and kissed her forehead. Then he held her at arm's length.

"My ma used to say that hard times, they come and they go. If we're lucky, they stay gone for a long time. When they come, endure them. When they go, enjoy every second they are away."

"What if they never go away?"

He clicked his tongue and shrugged.

"The good times will be all the better."

He followed her into the waiting room and motioned a tall man in work clothes into the room.

"I'll be there tomorrow. Don't forget about the gingersnaps," he said, disappearing into his exam room.

Good times. Right now, it seemed good times were far off in the distant future. She straightened her shoulders and held her head up. She'd do everything in her power to bring the good times back.

CHAPTER 29: ALROY

THE NEW PLAN

July 20, 1890
12:00 p.m.

Back in their workshop, Alroy and Zella watched Toby pace. Pacing was his way of thinking. They needed a super-amazing plan. Another day had passed, and they still weren't any closer to finding Pedro.

"Okay." Toby stopped and glanced from Alroy to Zella. "We have to do this smart. Start with Hornsby. Pedro thought he was the leader of the smugglers, right?"

"Yes. He writes about him a lot," Zella said.

"Let's go through all the notes we've made and try to list our suspects in order of suspicion," Toby said.

"I like that," Alroy said. "We can go visit them, starting with the most suspicious ones first."

"I agree," Zella said. "But what about giving the notebook to Wyatt? We need to."

"No," Alroy and Toby said at once.

Toby nodded to Alroy.

"Because," he said, "they can't read it. We keep going through it and noting everything we find. Then we can tell Wyatt what we've found."

"He's going to want to know how we got the information. He'll want Pedro's notebook," Zella said.

"Then we'll tell him we found things out by asking questions. If we give it to them, they can't read it. Do you want to give them our code?"

Alroy watched Zella's face. She scrunched her lips together and clinched her teeth.

"You know," she said. "When we give him Pedro's notebook, he's going to explode."

"I'll take the blame," Alroy said.

"We could drop anonymous notes at the police station. Address them to Wyatt, and he'll just think someone in Sonora Town is too afraid to come to the coppers, so they are leaving notes." Toby grinned studiedly.

Alroy groaned, and before he could tell Toby he was crazy, Zella said, "Okay. Good idea."

Toby's eyes grew wide, and he mouthed to Alroy, "I was joking." Then he shrugged.

It was a ridiculous plan, and Alroy hoped Zella would get sidetracked and forget all about it.

"We could call the station from here and leave the anonymous tips," Alroy suggested.

Toby rolled his eyes.

"You know Wyatt can ask the phone company who placed the call," Toby said.

"I don't think they can do that," Alroy said.

"Stop it," Zella shouted. "Let's get to work."

For several seconds, she glared at them.

"Put Hornsby at the top of the list," Toby said and pointed to Alroy. "Telephone the laundry and see if Hornsby's there. If he is, we go there first."

"Good." Zella nodded. "I'm leaving Garcia on the list for now."

"Yeah, put him, Doc, and Lee last," Alroy said as he moved to the phone.

A man answered on the second ring.

"Mr. Hornsby? How late are you open? I have laundry to drop off?" Alroy listened as the man rattled off their working hours and hung up. "He's there."

"Officer Henderson," Zella said. "He accosted me outside the station. He was digging for information about Wyatt's investigation."

Alroy reached over and put a check by Garcia's name and a question mark by Henderson.

"Zella's onto something," Toby said. "If he was trying to get information about Wyatt from Zella, then Wyatt isn't telling him about the investigation. Maybe he's already in trouble, or he's afraid he will get caught taking bribes."

"That," Alroy said, "is something we can tell Wyatt right away. Call him and tell him exactly what happened."

His sister smiled at him and grabbed the phone.

"There's one good thing about Wyatt," Alroy whispered to Toby. "He's Mr. Do-Right-or-Die."

He was sure Wyatt would be hard on any officer he thought was dirty. If Henderson knew something about Pedro, his brother would find out.

Zella hung up the phone and whirled around to face Alroy and Toby, who were eating the ginger snaps that Liza had made for Dr. Stone.

"I almost forgot." She grabbed two cookies. "Dr. Stone thinks something fishy is going on at Pedro's old house. Wyatt asked me about why they left their nice house. I think we should go over there and snoop around."

"That doesn't sound like it would lead us to Pedro," Alroy said.

"It might," Toby said, stuffing another cookie in his mouth.

"You're going to make yourself sick," Zella said, slapping his hand when he reached for another cookie.

"You're just worried we won't leave any for you."

"I think it's a dead end," Alroy said.

"I don't." Zella glared at him.

"I'll go over there and see what's up," Toby said. "We should explore all possibilities."

"What do you think you'll find out?" Alroy thought they were wasting time.

"What if we're looking at this all wrong? What if something happened about their house? Dr. Stone and Wyatt asked about it and seemed concerned. Maybe smuggling has nothing to do with his disappearance?"

"Toby's right," Zella said. "Let's get to work."

Alroy hated it when Zella took over, but he had to admit she was usually right.

"We've got three suspects: Mr. Lee, Doc Grimes, and the Hornsbys." Toby snapped his fingers. "There's something else." He grinned. "Yes, we have four suspects. Add Jonah Lopez at the Good Time Saloon."

Zella frowned and put Lopez's name on the list.

"Let's take Pedro's notebook apart. Each of us takes the section related to one or two suspects," she said.

"Pedro won't like us taking his book apart," Alroy said.

"I know. It feels strange to rip his book. But Zella's right, we can work faster that way," Toby said.

In a few minutes, they each had a section. Toby took Mr. Hornsby and Mr. Lee, Zella grabbed up Jonah Lopez, and Alroy took Doctor Grimes and Mrs. Hornsby. Alroy felt a little cheated. Doc was their friend, and what could a woman do to Pedro? He was pretty sure he'd gotten the easy stuff.

When they finished, they didn't know much more than before. It seemed like they'd piece almost everything together.

Hornsby was probably the leader of a smuggling ring. Lee, they haven't talked to yet, and Doc had a time machine and believed in eugenics.

"The eugenics stuff is something Pedro wouldn't like. Heck, I don't like it. They believe that intelligent, healthy people should breed, and they don't care about everyone else. According to the pamphlet, the inferior people don't matter."

Alroy didn't want to explain eugenics because he thought it was an awful way to look at people. It was like some people matter and others don't. That went against everything his father had taught him.

"That doesn't surprise me," Zella said. "Mr. Grimes looks down his nose at everyone."

He ignored her comment. He couldn't defend eugenics or Doc. The ideas repulsed him.

"Hornsby first, he seems like the most dangerous, and Lee and then Doc," Toby said, glancing at Alroy. "What about Jonah Lopez?"

"We already know what people say about the shanghai stuff. I think he's as dangerous or more dangerous than Hornsby? Pedro said he didn't have proof, but he also believes the rumors."

"Okay," Toby said. "We've got two potentially bad suspects. Then Mr. Lee and Doc."

"And we need to check out Pedro's old house." Alroy glanced at his sister.

"I say we start with Lopez. If he has people in his basement, Pedro might be there," Zella said.

"I say start with Hornsby," Alroy said. "We know he's at the laundry, and we can talk to him."

"Look. It's two o'clock," Toby said. "By the time we get to Lopez's, there will be a lot of customers. We'd be better off going there first thing in the morning. Two of us can keep him busy, and the other one can snoop. Hornsby first," Toby said.

"I agree," Zella said. "Hornsby's place today. Lopez in the morning."

"After Hornsby, we talk to Doc and Lee. Then go by Pedro's old place, if we have time," Alroy said.

Zella picked up her pencil and drew a little map.

"Look. The laundry, Lee's shop, Doc's workshop, and Pedro's old house."

She glanced at Toby and Alroy. They nodded their agreement.

"Let's go," Toby said.

Zella went to the wall they called their photograph wall and grabbed a picture of Pedro.

"To show to people," she said.

"Who do you think is the most likely suspect?" Alroy asked as they hurried down the stairs.

"Hornsby." Toby jumped down the last two steps.

"Lopez," Zella said.

"I'm scared," Alroy said. "That's all I'm going to say 'cause I don't want to say what I'm thinking."

"Pedro knows how bad Sonora Town is," Toby said. "He's trying to make things better."

"I get it," Alroy said.

"He's the nicest and smartest one of all of us. It's not fair," Zella added.

Toby nodded.

They rode as fast as they could toward the laundry. They didn't talk. Alroy tried not to think about the fact they headed toward a person they knew was dangerous. Unexpectedly, he thought that maybe they should listen to Wyatt. Instead of riding toward danger, they should just swing by the police station and talk to their brother. He glanced at Zella and Toby. They stared straight ahead, faces set with determined looks. He kept his thoughts to himself and pedaled toward possible peril.

CHAPTER 30: ALROY

HORNSBY

July 20, 1890
1:00 p.m.

Wong's Laundry was located north of the Plaza. Alroy spotted the large warehouse-shaped building first and pointed it out to Zella and Toby.

The outside didn't look like much, but the inside fascinated Alroy. He admired the metal beams that arched at what would typically be the roof's peak. The efficient layout told him that Mr. Wong, who designed the building, used architecture to create beauty from steel and wood. In the center of the building, enormous round vats lined up in neat rows. Half were used for washing and the others for rinsing the laundry. At the moment, the iron agitators were up out of the water. Below the vats, concentric circles of electric coils glowed red. At another time, he would have been curious to examine the electric coils to see how the electricity was being generated.

About a dozen women folded clothes at long tables that ran along both the west and east walls. Pushcarts full of clothes and other sundries overflowed. A large section at the back of the warehouse was walled off, creating a backroom. When Pedro first started working here, he'd told Alroy about the huge fans at each end of that room. The room worked like a wind tunnel that dried the clothes. Pedro had helped fix the gear system, and after that Mr. Hornsby hired him to come in once a week to do maintenance.

Zella poked Alroy. "Quit gaping."

She nodded to a staircase leading up to a glassed-in office. From there, a person could view the building and the workers. A man and a woman huddled at a large wooden desk, deep in conversation. Since they weren't paying attention, now was the perfect time to talk to the workers.

Handing Toby and Alroy a picture of Pedro, Zella motioned toward the women who had stopped working to watch them.

Alroy walked over to an older, heavy-set woman at the folding table. She pushed her gray hair back and smiled. She, like the other women, wore a long white apron over her house dress. Alroy couldn't help smiling. The lady had a soft, friendly face. She glanced up at the office behind him.

"Hi," he said.

"Hi, yourself, young man. You shouldn't be in here. The missus is going to be annoyed that you're interrupting work. She'll be flying down those steps as soon as she notices."

The woman's eyes had a rebellious gleam in them, and Alroy wouldn't be surprised if she liked the interruption. He guessed she didn't mind annoying the missus.

"Before she does that, have you seen this boy, Pedro?" He handed her the picture.

She squinted, studied the picture before handing it back.

"That's Sara's boy. He's a good boy. Sweeps up after we're done. Helped the old man fix the fans but didn't get a dime for his help. Gotta love a tightwad. Haven't seen him in a couple days. Why you asking?"

"He's my friend, and he's missing. This is the second day."

She frowned and shook her head.

"His ma is sick. Hasn't been to work. If he's gone, that'll be hard on her. She's a nice lady. Did he run off?"

"No. We're worried about him. We were wondering if you knew anything?"

She shook her head.

"Have you heard anything? We think maybe something happened to him at one of his jobs."

She raised her eyebrows and whistled softly.

"Don't know nothing, but . . ." She glanced up at the office. "She's flying down them stairs."

Alroy turned to see a small, wiry woman rushing down from the office. She also wore an apron and a white cap over her hair.

She waved her hands and shouted, "I'm not paying you to gab. Get to work."

"My name's Martha," the older lady said, picking up a large piece of cloth. "She's a thunderstorm, but all thunder and no lightning. Now, the mister, he's another matter. Careful there. Tread lightly."

Mrs. Hornsby stood next to Zella, pointing her finger at his sister.

"What in the name of hellfire are you three doing here?" the woman shouted.

Both Alroy and Toby sprinted toward Zella.

"Don't talk to my sister like that."

Up close, Mrs. Hornsby looked a lot worse than she had at a distance. Her face looked like a wrinkled prune. She looked Alroy up and down as if she were examining a fish at the market.

"And just who are you?"

"I'm Alroy Doyle, and this is my sister, Zella Doyle, and my friend, Toby Bailey."

She put her hands on her hips. "Doyle? Hmph."

Zella spoke up.

"Mrs. Hornsby, we didn't mean to disrupt your business. We are sorry for the inconvenience."

She sounded as sweet and contrite as any proper young lady, which annoyed Alroy. He had a feeling that the Hornsbys knew something about Pedro, and the last thing he wanted was to be kind.

Toby handed her the picture of Pedro, which she glanced at and flung back at him.

"You tell that little scamp that if he doesn't get back to work, both him and his ma will be without a job."

"Mrs. Hornsby," Zella placed a hand on the woman's arm. "I have bad news. Pedro is missing. He's been gone two days. He's our friend. We're trying to find him."

The woman looked surprised. Her anger seemed to vanish, and her voice softened.

"What? What happened?"

"That's why we are here," Alroy said. "Pedro thought something was going on here. That you're hiding something."

Zella glared at him.

"What Alroy means," Toby said, "is that we thought you could help us—"

Above them, a crackling noise and the sound of metal scraping echoed through the building. Just above the door of the office, Alroy noticed a brass speaking trumpet protruding outward and downward to address the entire warehouse. A deep male voice boomed from the trumpet.

"Mrs. Hornsby, quit yapping and get up here. Bring those delinquents with you."

The woman gazed up at the office and frowned. It was the worst frown Alroy had ever seen. Her face scrunched up with hatred. He hoped she didn't have children. If he were her child, he'd run away.

She shook her finger at them.

"You three stay right here."

She lifted her skirt and headed for the staircase.

In silent agreement, they ignored her command and followed her. At the landing, she turned to them, and Alroy thought she hissed.

"You brats don't know what's good for you. Now you're in deep."

A tall burly man with an unkempt gray beard flung the door open.

"What's going on here?"

Facing her husband, Mrs. Hornsby seemed to shrink. She scurried into the office.

"Nothing's going on. These young'uns are looking for Pedro." She watched her husband as she said, "Pedro's gone missing. Two days now."

He glared at his wife with his dark hard eyes. After a few seconds, he spat tobacco on the floor, just missing Zella's shoe.

"Sir, would you kindly direct your spittle away from me."

"Sir?" He laughed, a forced kind of donkey laugh, like nothing was funny. "I ain't no sir. And, Miss-high-and-mighty, I'll direct my spittle wherever I want. And I don't give a goddamn care about Pedro being missing. I hope he's dead and buried in someone's goddamn basement."

Toby looked like someone punched him in the face. He lunged for Mr. Hornsby. Alroy grabbed him and held him back.

Hornsby made a come-here motion with his hand, inviting a fight. The problem was Mr. Hornsby was bigger and stronger than both of them put together.

Mrs. Hornsby was almost crying.

"Eldo, don't be like that," she pleaded. "These young'uns are just tryin' to find their friend. Pedro's a good boy. We should—"

Hornsby raised his hand as if he were going to hit his wife. She cowered and covered her head with her arms. Alroy stepped in front of Mrs. Hornsby, and Zella pulled the woman close to her.

"Mr. Hornsby," Alroy said in what he hoped was a loud, forceful voice. "We came here to ask if you've seen Pedro or know where he might be. Last time you saw him, did he say anything about where he was going? Anything you know might help us find him."

The man chewed his tobacco and stared at Alroy. He turned his head and spat away from Zella. The glob of brown juice turned Alroy's stomach. He'd never seen anyone so crude and careless as this man. Mr. Hornsby poked Alroy in the chest with his finger. It hurt, but Alroy didn't flinch. He took a deep breath and exhaled, trying to push down his anger.

"Can you help us?" Toby said.

Turning his gaze upon Toby, the man said, "I don't know a goddamn thing about Pedro."

When he said Pedro's name, he sounded hard and mean.

"That boy is a plague, comin' in here and accusin' me of things I never done. Upsetting my missus, so she's lookin' sideways at me. Now get the hell out of my goddamn establishment." He flung the door open. "Get out."

Before the door closed, Alroy heard Mrs. Hornsby say, "Eldo, those two is Doyles."

Outside the warehouse, they stopped.

"That went well," Toby said.

"He spat at Zella," Alroy said. "He's a monster. I bet he beats his wife."

"Pedro accused him of something, and his wife believes Pedro," Zella said. "Did you see how she watched him? When he said basement, she sucked in her breath."

"There's no basement in there," Toby said.

"Exactly," Zella said.

"He said he didn't care if Pedro were dead and buried in a basement," Alroy said.

"He gave us a clue," Toby said.

"Phsss. Phsss." Behind them, someone hissed in a loud whisper, "Over here."

The older woman Alroy had talked to stood by the side of the building and motioned them over.

"I told you to be careful. He's a dangerous man. I could see you got him all riled up."

She motioned them closer.

"Pedro was here three nights ago. He came to tell the mister his ma was sick and couldn't come to work. I heard them talking. The mister said he was going to fire Pedro's ma for being sick. Pedro looked real angry when he said that. Then I heard Pedro say he knew about the Wongs. He said, 'I know about the Wongs' a couple times. I didn't hear what he knew, but the mister was mighty angry. It looked to me like he was going to hit Pedro, so I came up to him and asked him a question. Pedro left, but the mister, he hollered, 'Keep your mouth shut, or you'll be sorry.' When he left here, Pedro was okay. The missus, she heard the conversation, and her face looked all sad and grief-struck."

"Do you know what Pedro meant?" Toby asked.

She shook her head.

"No idea. Wong used to own the laundry, but he left years ago."

"Thank you. Would you be willing to tell my brother about this?" Zella asked.

She paused a moment.

"The detective?"

"Yes."

"Yeah, name's Martha Gonzalez. But tell him to come to my house, not here. I can't afford to lose this job. 206 Baker. I gotta get back. You kids should be more careful."

She rushed back inside.

They watched her scurry around to the back of the building.

Zella whipped out her notepad and wrote the lady's name and address.

"Well, that's interesting." Toby scratched his head. "What's next?"

"Wyatt," Zella said. "We go tell him everything that just happened."

"No." Alroy shook his head. "We'll stick to the plan. Let's go talk to the others. Then we'll tell Wyatt."

Zella crossed her arms in front of her chest.

"If that man's not guilty, then I don't know who is."

"Remember what happened this morning? We all thought Pedro was on one of the ships, but he wasn't. Let's get all the facts we can. I don't want another big police raid and nothing happens," Alroy said.

"Sorry, Zella, but I'm with Alroy on this one. Wyatt's probably not happy about what happened with the boats."

She stood like a statue for a few more seconds before she threw her arms up.

"Okay, but I'm doing this under protest."

They rode back toward town, heading to Lee's Herbal Shop. It was well past lunchtime, and Alroy was hungry and hot. It didn't help that their bicycles were stirring up dust, which stuck to his sweaty skin.

"I don't like that guy," Toby called out. "Even if he doesn't have anything to do with this, I say we bring him in."

"What are you, the sheriff of Los Angeles now?" Alroy shouted because a train was passing, and the clanking and clacking seemed to go on forever.

"No, but I could be."

Zella laughed, and the sour look that had been on her face since they left the laundry was gone.

Alroy wasn't sure what he thought. Hornsby was rotten to the core, and his wife was not only afraid of him, but she was suspicious of him as well. He saw the way she studied her husband when they asked him questions.

Of course, there was that whole innocent until proven guilty thing. They needed to find some evidence.

Alroy couldn't remember ever wanting to punch an adult in the face before. He grinned to himself when he thought of Toby, rushing in to fight the man.

He wondered how one man could be so vile and disgusting. He hoped Mr. Lee was nicer.

CHAPTER 31: PEDRO

HOPE DEFERRED

July 20, 1890

Pedro stared at the two lit candles atop one of the boxes. His plan and his bargaining skills had failed. The only concession he was able to get was the book he'd had in his jacket pocket, *Leaves of Grass* by Walt Whitman, and two candles so he could read aloud to Elijah and Jaime. As much as he hated to admit it, plan B was their one remaining option.

Elijah sat and leaned against the bars nearest the light and smiling as he leafed through Whitman's book. Zella had given it to Pedro for his birthday last year. She'd written an inscription on the inside cover, *May this book bring you hours of enjoyment and pleasure*. He carried it in his pocket because he found the words inspiring. Little did Zella realize this book would bring joy to him and his new friends in what might be their last hours or days on earth. He felt certain their fates were intertwined and headed in the wrong direction.

"My plan," Jaime said.

"Yes," Pedro agreed.

"Why do you have this underlined?" Elijah said and read the

passage. "'We don't read and write poetry because it's cute. We read and write poetry because we are members of the human race. And the human race is filled with passion. So medicine, law, business, engineering... these are noble pursuits and necessary to sustain life. But poetry, beauty, romance, love... these are what we stay alive for.'"

"Because he's a romantic," Jaime said. "Forget poetry. Let's try staying alive. The plan."

"I'm scared. I don't want to fight him," Elijah said.

"Keep the book in your pocket. The words will help you," Pedro said. "Jaime's plan is good. When he brings food, we'll pretend to eat. Jaime will take a bite or two so he doesn't get the shakes. Then we'll pretend to sleep. When he comes into the cage, Jaime and I will jump him. Elijah, you jump up and run out of the cage and keep the door closed so we can get the keys from him."

"I can help you fight," Elijah said, closing the book and slipping it into his trouser pocket.

"No," Jaime said. "You are the only one whose chains are long enough to get outside the cage. You have the most important job. If this works, he's locked in with us, and we can get his keys."

"That's right. We'll undo your chain, and you run for help," Pedro added.

"You're going to save us," Jaime said.

"I'll save us?"

Pedro nodded.

"I can do that. While we wait, I'll read to us."

Pedro half listened to Whitman's word. He played their simple plan over and over in his mind. He'd never attacked anyone before, and every scenario he imagined seemed fantastical.

Unexpectedly, the door to the basement opened earlier than they had planned. Sunlight spilled over the stairs, and the man descended, carrying a tray with three tin cups and a plate of rolls. This wasn't the evening meal, so the food was probably safe. They'd have to test it.

"I see you are already enjoying your book. Good. I brought you a snack." He glanced at Pedro. "I'm not heartless."

Pedro didn't regret calling him heartless, but hearing the man repeat his word in a syrupy-sweet voice angered him. He didn't reply.

"Back away from the door," the man commanded.

The boys moved back. He opened the door, placed the tray on the floor, and slammed the cage door shut, locking it.

"Enjoy."

Pedro watched him climb the steps. He stopped on the top and glanced back before exiting. The door swung closed, shutting out the sunlight. Pedro stared at the rolls and the tin cups.

"Does he bring rolls at lunchtime?" Pedro asked.

"No," Jaime said. "I think your speech to him caused this?"

"How do you know it's lunchtime? And can we eat this?" Elijah asked.

Jaime glanced at Pedro. "The sunlight, right?"

"The rolls are from the bakery. They're probably safe, but we should be careful." Pedro nodded toward Jaime. "Take a bite and wait a bit. See if you can tell."

"It'll take a few minutes," Jaime said, before biting into the roll.

The minutes seemed to drag by as they waited for a reaction.

"The water's safe, right?" Elijah asked.

"Probably," Jaime said and glanced at Pedro. "What do you think?"

Pedro nodded. If something were in the water, they would taste it. Jaime and Elijah grabbed a cup and guzzled the water. They waited.

"Do you feel anything yet?" Pedro asked after what he figured was around fifteen minutes.

"No."

Pedro sighed, took a roll, and the last cup of water, nodding to Elijah that it was safe. The roll tasted heavenly. He didn't know how long he'd gone without food, but it had to be at least a day, probably more. Wanting to savor the experience, he took a small sip of water. A bitter taste filled his mouth. He spat the water out.

"Don't drink," he said.

He was too late. Both boys had emptied their cups.

"The water always tastes bad. He said the pipes are rusty," Elijah said.

Jaime's eyes grew wide. "It's been the water all along."

Pedro tossed his water out. He grabbed the tray and moved it to the far side of the cage.

"We'll make this work. You two fall asleep near the tray. I'll pretend to sleep near the door. When he crosses the room to get the tray, I'll jump him from behind."

Elijah started crying. "It won't work. You can't get out the door. Your chains."

"Maybe I can get the keys from him," Pedro said, knowing he was grasping at anything.

"Elijah's right. We have to wait. Now that we know it's the water, we'll try again," Jaime said.

Within a few minutes, both Elijah and Jaime were sleeping soundly. A few minutes later, the basement door opened. Pedro had been leaning against the cage door. He threw himself down, lying with his back to the door, pretending to sleep.

"You sure they're sleepin'?" a deep male voice asked.

"Yes, I gave them an extra dose. Let's get this done."

"Dang, it smells bad in here. This place is nasty."

"Get your business done and get out of here."

"Sure thing, but we got a few things to discuss," another man said. His speech was lazy and precise as if he measured each word carefully.

Cigar smoke filled the room.

"You're hired help. I don't have discussions with underlings."

"There you go, making assumptions," the lazy voice said.

Pedro wished he were facing toward them. If he saw the men, he'd be able to identify them later. There were at least three, their captor and two others.

"Mr. Stanbury, he likes throwing his money at you. He can be a little . . . What's the word, Frank?"

"Naive."

Someone snapped a finger. "Naive. But we ain't. You took that Pedro kid, and you got a bunch of people searching for him. That big fancy detective and his coppers are asking all kinds of questions."

Pedro grinned. He should have known that The League of the Daring would be looking for him. They probably got Wyatt involved.

"We can take him off your hands and disappear him."

"No. I got plans for the boys. Mr. Stanbury and I have plans for them. If you were more than hired help, you'd know that."

"You're starting to annoy me. Which of these boxes are we taking?

"These. There's nine. I sent a list of boxes and contents to your boss. I'll have you sign for them."

"Frank, I get the impression that he don't trust us."

"You're unsavory at best. I don't know the extent of your criminal activities, but I suspect they are legion. I don't understand why an upstanding citizen would hire the likes of you."

The deep voiced man laughed.

"You're quite the joker. We don't kidnap children. Seems to me that's worse than anything we ever done. The police would be mighty interested in you. Ain't that right, Frank?"

"Are you threatening me?"

A long pause followed the question.

"Get the boxes and get out of here."

After those words, the only sounds were of the men carrying boxes up the stairs. After three trips, the door to the basement closed. Pedro waited another few minutes before sitting up. He moved to the tray and examined the tin cups. The metal was too wide and flimsy to help loosen the gap on the chain link. He tried anyway.

He was no better off than he was when he first arrived. He looked at his two companions who slept soundly. Their only option was to wait and try again. No matter from what angle he viewed his situation, he couldn't find much hope. The League was looking for him. That was something, but was it enough?

CHAPTER 32: ZELLA

MR. LEE'S SHOP

July 20, 1890
1:45 p.m.

Lee's Herbal Shop was small and unremarkable. A wooden roof shaded the sidewalk and the front of the shop where Zella, Alroy, and Toby parked their bicycles.

"Come on. Let's get this over with so we can go see Wyatt," Zella said.

"Before we go in," Toby whispered, "let's make a pact to be cautious." He looked at Alroy. "No direct threats. Finesse."

"This from the boy who wanted to arrest him," Alroy said.

"I'm talking about all of us." Toby glanced around. "You two talk to him, and I'll look around. I'm thinking we should check out basements and cellars. See if there's one here. Hornsby said he didn't care if Pedro was dead and buried in a basement. Could mean something."

Zella frowned at Toby. She hated the words *Pedro* and *dead* being said in the same sentence.

"Which is why we should have gone to Wyatt first," she said.

"There wasn't a basement in the laundry. We'll have to go to his house. We need proof," Toby said.

Zella shrugged. With two against one, she'd never get her way.

"Toby, you think Hornsby is in cahoots with Lee?" Alroy said, ignoring Zella.

"Hornsby seems like the kind of man who would shoot Lee for being Chinese."

Zella stepped between them.

"You two stop it. We're wasting time. Toby's idea is good, except he and I will talk to Lee while you look around." She glared at Alroy. "That should at least keep you quiet."

"Hey, it wasn't all my fault."

"You didn't exactly make things calmer." Zella looked to Toby for support.

Alroy threw his hands up.

"You two go at it and waste a little more time," Toby said.

"Shut up." Zella scowled.

"Nag," Alroy whispered.

Zella took a deep breath and reminded herself they were trying to find Pedro.

Inside the herbal shop, she had to keep herself from exclaiming in wonder. She didn't think Alroy would have trouble looking around. She hoped he'd keep his mind on looking for clues.

The floor-to-ceiling shelves and cubby holes overflowed with boxes, tins, and bottles with Chinese characters. Unlike the mercantile store in town, which also had shelves up to the ceiling with a wide open expanse in the middle, this shop had tables with displays of various goods. Walking toward the back where Mr. Lee sat in an ornate chair was like wandering through a maze.

She gazed up at big colorful lanterns hanging from the ceiling. There were red, green, and gold with long gold tassels dangling from the center.

Toby nudged Alroy and pointed out the middle display of Red Dot cigars, Duck Soup with a white duck painted on the side of the box, Royal Baking Soda, and the Red Granite Candles. Alroy picked up a stick of dynamite, examined the red casing, and smelled it before putting it back in the box.

"It's definitely dynamite," he said, grinning at Zella.

Inwardly she sighed. Now they knew where to come if they wanted to blow something up. Great. She could only imagine what crazy schemes they'd concoct. Across the room, a large workbench took up one wall. She didn't recognize the items on the table, but Alroy began examining the boxes and gadgets. She was confident she'd eventually hear all about it.

Toby followed her as she moved toward Mr. Lee.

"Hello," she said.

He bowed his head slightly and greeted her in a soft, melodious voice.

He was dressed in baggy pants, a long shirt that looked like a dress with floppy sleeves, and an apron a little like her mother wore. Everything about him was foreign and exotic. She made a mental note to research Chinese clothes and styles.

Toby handed Pedro's picture to Mr. Lee.

"Pedro is missing. Have you seen him or know where he might be?" Zella asked.

He shook his head as he stared at Pedro's picture

"Bad news," Mr. Lee said. "He was here three days ago to make deliveries. He's fast on bicycle."

"Did he say where he was going when he left here?" Toby asked.

Keeping an eye on Alroy, Zella watched him walk to the padlocked door to their right. Maybe it was a basement or a storage room.

"When he leave, I don't see him again," Mr. Lee said.

The front door opened. Charlie from the newspaper stood in the doorway. He grinned at Zella.

"My son," Mr. Lee said. He waited until Charlie stood next to him before adding, "Friends of Pedro."

"I know them from school, Father. And Zella from work," he said, grinning at Zella.

Embarrassed, she lowered her eyes and felt her cheeks flush.

"How can we help you?" Charlie asked.

"We were just telling your father that Pedro is missing. We're worried about him and helping his mother look for him," Toby said.

"I heard about that today. He was here doing deliveries a few days ago."

"Do you know where he went when he left here? Or can you tell us anything that might help us?" Zella asked.

Toby stepped a little closer to her, crowding them so that Charlie had to step back.

"Yeah, anything might help us," Toby said a little too eagerly.

He shrugged and shook his head.

"No, can't think of anything. I just assumed he went home when he left here."

Zella glanced around the shop, trying to think of a way to ask about the locked door.

"Nice shop. Do you work here too?"

"Sure. We all do. My father was a boy when he came here with his father." He laughed. "My grandfather thought he was going to be a rich man and go back to China wealthy. He didn't find any gold, worked on the railroad, and finally came here and started selling herbs." He waved his hand toward the middle of the store. "And other things."

"Nice." Alroy joined them and nodded to Charlie.

Zella squinted her eyes at him and motioned with her head toward the front door.

"I notice the padlocked door. Do you have to lock some stuff away?" Alroy asked.

"The basement. Sure." He leaned in and whispered. "Opium and the cigars. Things people will steal. My father doesn't like the opium dens. Says they were bad for China and bad for here."

"But you sell it?" Toby asked.

"Yes, in small doses in herbal formulas. We sell it to doctors. They use it for patients."

"That's smart to keep it locked up," Toby said.

"If you think of anything that might help, let us know," Zella said.

When he didn't say anything, she pointed, "Our bicycles are out front."

She groaned inwardly. That was a dumb thing to say.

"Bicycle," Mr. Lee said, he pointed to the back of the store and nodded to his son.

"I forgot," Charlie said. "My father found Pedro's bicycle on New High Street. He brought it back here."

"Where on New High? How far away?" Toby sounded excited as if they finally had a real clue.

Charlie said something to his father in Chinese. The old man rubbed his chin. After a few seconds, he answered in English.

"Waters. New High and Waters. Not far," the old man said.

Charlie motioned them to follow him. He led them behind one of the shelves into a hallway, which took them through the Lee's home. The spacious room looked similar to the Doyle's parlor. Two overstuffed chairs and a small sofa circled the fire-place. A dark lacquered mahogany table sat in front of a window overlooking the small yard. Except for another smaller table with a Buddha statue and burning incense, this room seemed ordinary.

"It's out here," Charlie said as they stepped into the small grassy area. Scattered around were at least fifty potted plants.

Pedro's bicycle with a backpack strapped to the back frame

leaned against the wall. Toby grabbed the pack and opened it. Inside he found a pair of Pedro's night-vision goggles, another map with notes on the back, some hard bread wrapped in paper, navy gloves, and another notebook. Zella grabbed the gloves from Toby.

"Was he dressed all in navy?" She asked. "When you last saw him?"

"Well, if he was, then we know he was—"

"An assassin," Charlie said. "Ninjutsu—Japanese warrior assassin."

Charlie grinned. Zella blushed as his eyes met hers.

"Investigating," Alroy said in a cold voice.

Charlie's smile vanished.

"I was making a joke," he said.

"Our friend is missing and may be in danger. Not something to joke about."

Charlie bowed his head.

"Of course, my deepest apologies. I was insensitive."

"May we leave the bicycle here?" Toby asked. "We'll come back for it when one of us can ride it to his house."

"No problem." Looking at Zella, Charlie said, "My comment was in poor taste."

"Don't worry. I'm always making wisecracks at the wrong time," Toby said.

Zella tried desperately to think of something to say, something to make her seem smart, but her mind was blank. As they left, she glanced back. Charlie was watching her. When their eyes met, she glanced away.

They rode to the Plaza and found an empty bench. Toby took Pedro's belongings out.

"He had food," Alroy said. "He was on a stakeout."

"Don't forget the goggles and the gloves. Maria said she heard him sneak out when he thought they were asleep. He needed to see at night. He was watching someone," Toby said.

"Or several people," Zella added. "Maybe whoever he was spying on caught him."

"If his bike was at New High and Waters, he wasn't near the laundry," Toby said.

"True, but maybe he followed Hornsby. He's followed him before," Zella added.

"Maybe," Toby said.

"What are we going to do?" Alroy said.

"Wyatt. Go tell Wyatt. He can search Lee's basement, and go look around where Lee found the bicycle," Toby said.

"What? Why would he search Lee's basement? They told us about the bike. They didn't act suspicious," Zella said.

"Well, I didn't like the way Charlie was looking at you. That was suspicious. Right, Alroy?"

"Zella's right. We stick to the original plan and finish our investigation. Then, we go talk to Wyatt," Alroy said.

As much as she wanted to tell Wyatt everything, they hadn't learned anything. The store was interesting, but a locked door wasn't a clue. She was sure Charlie had been telling the truth about keeping supplies behind a locked door. But maybe she was thinking that because he was cute, and she felt all squishy whenever she saw him.

The only odd thing was they didn't mention Pedro's bicycle right away. But if they were trying to hide anything, they wouldn't have said anything about the bicycle. They didn't seem nervous about answering questions or telling them about the basement. They also weren't angry and rude.

Each hour that passed made it harder to find Pedro. That much, at least, she'd learned from listening to Wyatt. They had to work faster. She had a premonition they should go back and follow Hornsby.

CHAPTER 33: ALROY

REGROUPING

July 20, 1890
2:00 p.m.

They cycled to the Plaza to regroup and look over Pedro's notes. Alroy was getting antsy as he watched Zella flip through the notebook, and Toby read over her shoulder.

Pedro always used codes, and they wouldn't be able to read all of his notes until they got back to the attic. The map was a different story and might have a clue. So, while Toby and Zella searched through the notebook, he grabbed the map and spread it across his lap.

The map showed the Plaza, part of downtown, the Los Angeles River, and a residential section southeast of downtown. Alroy immediately recognized Doc's office, which was circled. Over the roof, Pedro had written "ethics?" in lower case letters. Around the circle FG/TM.

In Sonora Town, he had circled a building on the same street he and Toby had been on last night when they talked to Juan. Lettered in Pedro's neat handwriting on the outside of the circle was JL/GTS and in lower case letters "smug."

The next circled building was Garcia's Farm Supplies, closer to the Plaza and downtown. Alroy followed the thin black line that led to Garcia's house in Sonora Town. That circle had a large X through it. Alroy could still make out the lettering CG/AK, and in smaller letters "no."

Alroy went back to the JL/GTS shorthand and noticed a faint black line that pointed to a house several blocks from Pedro's home. Again more letters "JL," and in smaller letters "RLS-K" and in lowercase "smug??"

Pedro had also circled and labeled Lee's shop, Hornsby's Laundry, Hornsby's home, the police station, and Pedro's old house. Maybe there was something in the notebook.

Alroy glanced at Toby and Zella.

"You find anything?" he asked

"Zella shook her head. Code. We need to go home to read it."

"Look at this," Alroy said.

Toby moved to the other side of Alroy and spread the map out over their laps. He showed them that Pedro had marked Garcia's business and home on the map.

"We know CG/AK means Clyde Garcia and Arizona Kid. I'm pretty sure "no" means either not him or not guilty. Now, look at Hornsby. The laundry is circled and so is their house." He tapped the circled house on the map.

"So we need to check out the house too. HL is for the Laundry. And 'smug??' What does that mean?" Toby asked.

"That's Pedro being nice. I wouldn't call him smug. I can think of stronger words to describe him," Alroy said.

"Look," Zella said, tapping all the places on the map that were labeled 'smug.'

She pointed out a faint gray line that Alroy had missed. All three buildings had a line that went from the building to the river.

"Smug or S.M.U.G.?" Alroy repeated, hoping that some meaning would come to him.

Toby shook his head.

"Pedro's meticulous. He puts names in uppercase. Lowercase has to mean something else. All three of these businesses have lines connected to the river," Alroy said.

"There's four." Zella pointed to Pedro's old house in the nicer part of town.

"Smuggling, smugglers," Toby said.

"Who in their right mind would be in cahoots with Mr. Hornsby?" Zella said.

"Greedy fools," Toby said.

"But we don't know if Lee was," Zella said. "In the journal, Pedro said he saw them together, but he has question marks by Lee's name in the journal and on the map. Maybe he wasn't sure if Lee was involved. Henderson and Hornsby have exclamation marks."

Alroy really wished Pedro had just stated his thoughts in plain English that would make everything easier.

"Why didn't Pedro tell us about this stuff?" he asked.

"I've already told you. Quit asking the same question."

Alroy sat up straighter, and Toby raised his eyebrows as he stared at Zella.

"You two stop looking at me like that," she said. "I didn't know what he was doing. He said he'd check his facts and then we would—"

"You would what?"

"Good grief, Alroy, let me finish."

"No," Alroy said, "I'm not going to let you finish. You and Pedro were hiding this from me and Toby and Lavinia if she were here."

Toby put his hand up as if to ward off Alroy's words.

"Leave me out of this."

"Both of you just shut up and listen," Zella said.

When her voice sounded as if she were ten feet tall, Alroy always did what she said. Not because he was afraid of her but because he knew that tone meant she would relentlessly pursue her objective until she got her way. Instead of answering her, he tried to fold the map, but kept making a mess of it. Toby grabbed it from him and opened it back up.

"We didn't tell you because you would have fought the idea and put up such a fuss. Just like you are doing now, harping, and harping, and harping."

"Well, you should have told me."

"Why? So you can act like Wyatt and boss and bully me into doing what you want?"

That was a low blow, but she hit the mark with her answer. She was right. The last thing he wanted was to be like Wyatt.

Alroy couldn't look at her. Instead, he watched three pigeons fight over a piece of bread someone had dropped. Somehow he was angry at Pedro, and he shouldn't be. Also, he felt just as disagreeable toward Zella and her stupid idea of being an investigative reporter.

What was he supposed to do? Follow her around his whole life and make sure she didn't get into trouble?

He sighed.

Of course, she was right. Come rain, shine, hail, or earthquake, he wasn't going to let her run off and do something stupid. Unexpectedly, he found his thoughts ridiculous. Zella would do whatever she wanted, and he knew he'd never be able to stop her. He unfolded his arms and turned to her.

"You're right. I don't like the idea, but we are getting sidetracked," Alroy said. "Our first priority is finding Pedro. The second priority is, when we find him, I'm going to punch him in the nose. Not because he was helping you, but because it's a really stupid idea to get mixed up with smugglers."

"If you two are finished with your . . . arguing. I figured something out." Toby spread the map out so they could all see it.

"Look," Toby said, pointing to JL/GTS on the map. "GTS, Good Time Saloon. Remember Jonah Lopez owns and runs it?

Well, Pedro marked it here, and Lopez's house here. So we can go there and snoop around. Look at this."

Toby tapped the GTS circle. RLS. He looked at Alroy and grinned.

Alroy shrugged and shook his head.

"Robert Louis Stevenson—"

"Kidnapped," Zella said.

Toby nodded. "Aha, shanghaied. Wyatt didn't find him on the boat. Maybe they hold them somewhere else. The saloon or his house."

Alroy lowered his voice.

"What if he hasn't taken Pedro out to the ships yet? What if he heard about the police searching the boats? What if he's waiting to take him to the boats?"

"I always said you're smarter than you look," Toby said. "Let's make a plan before we head over there."

They finally had some clear-cut direction. Since they were so close to Doc's workshop, they decided to make a quick stop there. Then they could head over to the saloon. If there was a cellar or basement, either would be an excellent place to hide people before taking them to the boats.

Alroy wasn't comfortable taking Zella to a saloon with a reputation for kidnapping people. He wasn't comfortable taking himself there. He wondered if this was how Daniel felt before he walked into the lion's den.

CHAPTER 34: ALROY

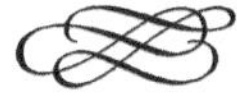

DOC'S PLACE

July 20, 1890
2:30 p.m.

They rode the short distance down Main Street, took a left onto Waters, and then a right onto Buena Vista Street. Alroy knocked once on Doc's door. Not waiting for an answer, they walked inside. Doc wasn't there.

"Strange," Toby remarked. "I know it's Sunday, but Doc is usually here seven days a week."

Zella picked up one of the eugenics pamphlets, glanced at it, and tossed it aside. She scanned a pamphlet supporting combustion engines.

Toby examined the various diagrams Doc had hung on the wall.

Alroy went to the rat table. Yesterday there had been four rats, but today there were three. He guessed the rat they sent to the future died.

He heard footsteps and looked toward the door that led to what Alroy had assumed was a storage room. Doc opened the door and started. He blinked a couple of times before smiling.

"Hello," he said, putting the padlock on the door before turning toward them. "To what do I owe the pleasure of this visit?" He looked at Alroy as he asked the question. "I'm not experimenting today."

"Oh, no, that's not why we're here," Toby said. "I was disappointed to miss the test yesterday." He glanced at Alroy with an accusing gaze. "How did it go?"

Doc shrugged and frowned, which made his beard do a strange wiggly thing.

"About the same as always. Maybe a little better." Doc grinned at Toby and noticed Zella walking around the room, looking things over, and examining his books.

She picked up *The Time Machine* and said, "We are reading this, too."

"No, I'm not reading that trash." Doc sounded annoyed. "Someone left it here. Take it."

He pushed his glasses up higher on his nose.

Zella grabbed the book and slipped it into her bag.

Toby plopped on one of the stools at the long table.

"Actually, we are looking for Pedro."

"Pedro?" he sounded confused. "Well, when you see him, tell him my laboratory needs to be swept."

"Doc," Alroy said. "Pedro is missing. He's been gone for two days. We are looking for him. We are afraid something might have happened to him."

The scientist sat down at his desk. He didn't go out into the sun much, so he was paler than most people who lived in Los Angeles. Now he looked like someone had drained all the color from his face.

"Tragic. I thought his mother was overreacting. What happened?"

"We don't know," Toby said. "He's missing. Something might have happened to him, or he's hurt, or . . . we don't know, which is the point. We were wondering if you could tell us anything."

Again he pushed his glasses up. "Umm, let me think. His sister brought me that note. The last time he was here, he seemed his usual self."

Alroy thought he might as well take a stab at annoying Doc.

"You know I read your pamphlet on eugenics. I don't think Pedro would have liked the ideas in that pamphlet. Did he discuss that with you?"

Doc laughed. Alroy always liked his laugh because it sounded like a chuckle somewhere between Santa Claus and an actor he'd seen play *Richard III*. Sometimes it came out comfortable and sometimes tense. Today his laugh was comfortable.

"Yes, indeed. We have had several lively discussions. He vigorously disagreed with the idea." He shook his head, looking rather jolly. "It is understandable. Pedro is quite brilliant, but he comes from a humble background, so, of course, it's natural for him to have this opinion. But I think he'll come to see the benefits of natural selection and breeding the best humans possible, producing a better human race. He'll be a fine father." He slapped his knee. "But we are on a tangent. I don't know what Pedro does in his free time. I'm not sure how to help."

"Mr. Grimes," Zella said.

She never called him Doc. She didn't like him and, more often than not, didn't want to be included in watching Doc's experiments.

"Where does that door lead, and why is it locked?"

He smiled condescendingly, which made Alroy realize part of the reason Zella and Lavinia didn't like him. He was about as progressive and concerned about women's rights as a bullfrog.

"Well, young lady. I'm a scientist, and . . ."

Alroy wanted to groan. He liked Doc and wished he didn't use that tone of voice.

Doc cleared his throat and spoke slowly. "Scientists have expensive equipment and gadgets, and, well, this isn't a very good neighborhood. I lock my valuables up so as not to tempt the needy."

"Or the inferior," Zella added.

Doc's face brightened.

"Yes, you're clever for a girl. You know, few women are intelligent and worthy of being part of eugenics." He shook his finger at her.

"If there aren't women, how do you expect to breed better humans?" Zella demanded.

"Exactly," Doc said. "Intelligent men must marry intelligent women. Women like you and your friend." He smiled at Zella, who glanced at Alroy and rolled her eyes.

"I see. I'll have to keep my eyes out for a worthy man," Zella said.

Alroy was sure Doc missed the sarcasm in her tone.

"Excellent. You come from good stock. Don't be surprised if you receive an invitation to join us."

"Thank you." Zella's voice sounded sweet and gentle, but Alroy knew she wanted to say a lot more. Her eyes seemed alive with anger that Doc obviously didn't see.

"It's funny you should mention the door. Pedro was also interested in the basement." Doc looked at Toby and then at Alroy.

"I don't want you boys to be jealous," he said, "but I did take Pedro down there. He wanted to see, and, well, I wanted to show off my time machine. I work with prototypes up here. Downstairs is my masterpiece. He was impressed. Of course, we couldn't test it. That will come later."

Doc's eyes sparkled as he talked as if the memory of showing off his machine made him happy.

"We aren't jealous," Toby said. "When was that?"

"Let's see."

Doc went to his desk and flipped through his journal.

"It was his last day here, in the afternoon, before he left for home."

He glanced at Alroy.

"The day before we tested the time machine. Oh, dear." He glanced at them and added, "You will let me know when you find him. How is his mother?"

Zella's face softened. "She's not well."

"Do let me know how I can help. Perhaps I can send Pedro's wages to her. And a little extra."

He didn't wait for a response. He took two bills from his wallet and handed them to Zella.

"I'll ask around the neighborhood. Perhaps someone knows something or saw him," Doc added.

"Thanks," Alroy said.

"Miss Doyle, since Pedro hasn't been here to clean, perhaps you would consider part-time employment. Dusting, sweeping up here and in the basement. I'll pay the same wages as Pedro."

Alroy could see from the look on Zella's face that she wasn't about to agree. His first thought was she could look in the basement, which tempted him to urge her to take the job.

"First," Zella said. "We will find Pedro. Second, I have part-time employment. I'm a reporter. Why didn't you offer one of the boys that job? Or do you only hire poor boys?"

Her hands were on her hips, and she glared at Doc.

Doc stared at her for a moment.

"Well," he said. "I have no doubt Pedro will turn up. As for the other part of your argument, I meant no slight." He stammered for a few more seconds as if trying desperately to say something soothing. Apparently nothing came to mind.

Zella stood her ground and waited for him to continue.

"We've gotta go," Toby said, moving toward Zella. "We have a couple more places to check before it gets late."

He touched Zella's arm.

"Right?"

As they got onto their bicycles, Zella glanced back at Doc's office building.

"He is a Neanderthal. We need to get into his basement. I'm going to ask him to show us."

She got off her bicycle.

"Hold on," Alroy said. "I think you scared him. Did you see his eyes? They were popping out of his head."

He was trying to lighten the mood and make Zella smile. She glared at him, looking every bit as frightening as Liza on a bad day.

"Let's go look in his basement window," Toby suggested.

Zella nodded. They rode around to the back of the building.

There were four small windows too small for a child to crawl through. They were painted over with black paint. Zella cupped her hands over her eyes and stared into one of the windows.

"I can't see anything. That's suspicious."

"Come on. Of course, the windows are covered. His time machine is there," Alroy said.

"Yeah," Toby said. "That machine is like his baby. I think he cares more about it than he does about people. It makes sense he's locked it up."

"I still want to get into the basement."

"Then go back in there and tell him you'll take the job," Alroy said, knowing she wouldn't do any such thing.

"Don't be ridiculous," she said. "You're probably right. I'm being unreasonable. But, for the record, I despise that man."

"We know. Let's go." Alroy wished he could tell her about the time machine. Then she would understand why Doc was so protective of his invention.

They cycled away from Doc's place and headed for the Good Time Saloon.

As anxious as Alroy was to find Pedro, he wasn't enthusiastic about going to a place where they might be kidnapping people.

He glanced at Zella. Maybe he should insist she go home and wait for them there. No sooner had the thought entered his mind than he realized it was a terrible idea. His thoughts sounded like Doc. He could see how Doc's attitude was demeaning. His better angel told him to trust his instincts. He certainly didn't want to be a Neanderthal.

CHAPTER 35: TOBY

THE GOOD TIME SALOON

July 20, 1890
3:15 p.m.

Toby took the lead as they rode toward the Good Time Saloon. Catching up to him and riding beside him, Zella glared straight ahead. Toby sure wasn't dumb enough to talk to her when she was angry.

When they reached Sonora Town, he slowed. It was afternoon, and the streets weren't packed. A few people here and there were walking on the sidewalks, but there was no music or painted women or loud drunks. In the daytime, this place seemed like the sleepy, rundown part of Los Angeles. Quiet streets and crumbling adobe buildings hid the nightlife behind a barrier of simplicity.

Last spring, he'd gone to the Camero farm with Alroy and Zella. The main house was an adobe, which didn't look like the buildings in this part of town because the Camero adobe was clean, painted white, and would look good in any neighborhood.

Sometimes he thought the buildings in Sonora Town looked

sick. It wasn't fair to the people who lived here. He thought of Pedro's family. They'd gone from middle class to poverty, and he didn't know why. If Toby knew anything, he knew that life wasn't fair.

He'd been thinking so much about life that he missed the street. They turned around and rode back another block. He slowed and glanced down the street. The building was long and narrow with a faded sign on top of the building that read Good Time Saloon. If this was a place where people were kidnapped and sold, the owner had a deranged sense of humor.

The door was locked, and the place looked deserted.

"Last night this place was overflowing," Alroy said. "They must not open until evening."

"I bet they're closed," Toby said, pointing to the Closed on Sundays sign.

"Let's go around back." Zella didn't wait for an answer. She pedaled around the building.

They leaned their bicycles against the wall. There were four steps leading up to the back door, and three windows that spread across the side of the building. There weren't any windows in the front, so it seemed weird to have them here. It was like the building was facing the wrong way. Below each window was a small basement window at ground level.

Toby squatted, cupped his hands around his eyes, and peered into the room. The dirty glass made it impossible to see. He took his sleeve and tried to wipe the grime from the window and peeked in again.

"I can't see much. Lots of boxes. Looks big."

Alroy tried looking through another window.

"Same here," he said.

Zella grabbed three pairs of night-vision goggles from the leather bag strapped to the back of her bicycle and handed Alroy and Toby each a pair.

"What are these for?" Toby asked.

"For inside, the basement will be dark."

She pushed on the largest upper window, trying to open it. It jiggled but held fast.

Toby watched as she searched the area and picked up a large gray stone. He grinned and thought she was going to make one great investigator.

"Have you lost your mind?" Alroy whispered, looking around. "You can't."

Zella threw the rock.

The window shattered. A large piece of glass hung at the top of the window frame for a few seconds before falling inside the building. Toby took his jacket off and used it to shield his hand as he knocked the rest of the glass out. He carefully picked away the jagged glass, making sure there were no shards sticking up. After shaking out his jacket, he folded it and laid it over the window sill. Using his hand for leverage on the window frame, he jumped and hoisted himself through the window.

Zella followed Toby's example. She sat on the jacket and reached out her arms so he could help her through. Alroy grabbed her shoulder.

"You can't do this. Wait out here. If we get caught, you can say you tried to stop us."

Zella pushed him aside.

"Careful of the glass when you get inside." Toby grabbed her waist and lifted her up and forward.

"Thanks," she said and signaled Alroy to follow.

"We're in this together," she said. "We can pay for the broken glass."

Toby's admiration for her skyrocketed. He didn't want to get into trouble, but time was running out. They had to do whatever they could, no matter the cost. He had a strong feeling that, before the day was over, they would be in deep trouble.

He reached out his hand and helped his friend through the

window. Alroy's momentum launched him inside, and Toby had to leap away to avoid getting hit.

"Good one," Toby said. "Are you cut?"

"Naw, I jumped over the glass. Not my most graceful moment."

Toby grabbed his jacket.

"My mom's going to have a hissy fit. Oh wait, she'll never know."

They were in a storage room. Floor to ceiling shovels lined the walls, which was strange and disturbing. Later he'd contemplate why a saloon might need so many shovels.

Toby glanced in the boxes and found liquor and a few canned goods. He tried to open the door he assumed led into the rest of the building. It was locked.

He and Alroy hit it with their shoulders. It didn't budge. They tried kicking it, first one at a time, then together on the count of three. Unlike the window, the door was solid.

"Give me your pocketknife, Alroy," Zella said.

Alroy always carried a pocketknife, string, and a nail with him, and Zella always teased him about the string and nail. He slapped the knife into her outstretched hand.

"Move out of my way," she said.

She opened the knife, began scraping the top of the pin on the door hinge.

As soon as Toby realized what she was doing, he took out his knife, found a box to stand on, and began slicing the grime away from the top hinge. When he saw the small space between the pin and the hinge clear, he wiggled his knife, pushing upward to loosen the pin. Pulling the pin out, he held it in place so Zella could finish hers.

Zella popped her pin out.

They laid the pins on the center shelf so they could put the door back together. Toby and Alroy pulled the door forward until there was about a three-inch crack. Then they yanked it forward, which ripped the lock out of its casing.

"We can pay for that too," Zella said.

"I have a feeling we'll pay double when Wyatt finds out," Toby said.

They leaned the door against a cabinet and stepped into the kitchen, which was small considering how many people the saloon served. The next door led into the main area. Pitch darkness met them, and they slipped on their goggles, and the room came into view.

To the right was a long bar. Tables with chairs sitting on the tabletops dotted most of the room. At the far end of the room was an open space, the dance floor.

Zella moved right, and Alroy left, so Toby walked forward.

A few seconds later, Alroy whistled and waved his hand.

"Over here."

A narrow door led into a short hallway. There were two doors on either side of the hall, one was open and had cleaning supplies, rag mops, a wooden bucket, and some brooms. They moved to the second door, which was padlocked. Alroy searched his pocket and pulled out a slender nail. He put it into the lock where a key would go and gently shook it, moving the nail around. He jiggled and worked with it, but nothing happened.

"Hurry," Zella said.

"It's not working."

"I guess a life of crime is out for you." Toby chuckled and went back to the closet.

He found two pipes. One was too big to fit through the small ring of the padlock, but the smaller one slipped right in.

"Give me a lever long enough and a fulcrum on which to place it, and I shall move the world," Alroy said, stepping aside for Toby.

Bracing the pipe against the door frame, Toby used his body

weight and pushed down, popping the lock open. They looked down into a dark basement. The rickety staircase didn't look inviting, but Toby stepped forward anyway.

"Make sure and hold the rail," he said.

Toby was thankful Zella had been insightful enough to bring the goggles. Without them they wouldn't be able to see anything. Once in the basement, they found boxes stacked up on the right and left. The boxes formed a wall and created a pathway, which they followed. Taking a right turn, they continued forward through the maze. He figured they were moving toward the front of the building.

Something smelled rotten like a neglected outhouse. The floor was dirt. As they moved forward, the aroma of body order and urine mingled with the damp soil. Behind him Zella coughed.

"Yuck," she said.

Toby stopped. Zella bumped into him and Alroy into her. He stared at the sight in front of him. His stomach knotted and the muscles in his neck tightened.

"Zella," Toby whispered, blocking her view. "Get out of here. Ride to the police station as fast as you can and get someone."

"I want to see."

"No, you don't. Alroy, get her out, and get back here as fast as you can."

"Is Pedro there?" Zella asked.

Alroy began dragging her away.

"Toby," she pleaded. "Tell me what's there. Is Pedro dead?"

He waited until Alroy and Zella were several feet away before turning around.

"I don't see Pedro," he called out. Bile rose in his throat. He ignored it.

"There are people locked in a cage." He couldn't stop the quivering in his voice as he continued speaking, "Two of them aren't moving. The other one is just staring."

He swallowed and took a breath before continuing.

"You need to go now. These people need help."

She shook her head as if she couldn't stop.

"All right. But check and make sure Pedro's not there."

"I'll check," he said. "But go to the top of the stairs. I'll call out and tell you."

She nodded, and he watched as she and Alroy moved back through the maze and up the stairs.

"I'm at the top. Check," she insisted. "Alroy's coming to help you."

Toby could feel the veins in his neck thumping hard and fast. He took a deep breath to calm himself and waited for Alroy. He tried to sound brave, but he was about five seconds from throwing up on the dirt floor. He didn't know if Pedro was in that cage, but he was afraid his friend was one of the ones not moving and possibly really hurt or dead.

What was taking Alroy so long?

Toby moved forward, one step at a time. As he got closer, he held his breath. He could see there were more people in the cage than he thought. They were lying on the ground still as corpses. Two were girls, and the other three were boys or men. It was hard to tell for sure.

Behind him, he heard footsteps. Alroy. At least he wasn't alone.

He knelt down and and moved his hand through the bars. He managed to reach one of the girls. He felt her pulse.

"Are they dead?" Alroy whispered.

"She's not, but her pulse is slow. Maybe they are drugged."

Even to himself, his voice sounded shaky and breathless.

"Pedro," Toby said and repeated, "Pedro, are you here?"

"No Pedro here," a man said. He sat up and stared at Toby. "Get help."

"Zella, Pedro's not here. Go get help," Toby shouted.

"Tell the coppers they'll need a doctor," Alroy added.

"Okay," Zella said.

Toby looked up at Alroy. "There has to be a light or lanterns. Look around."

"Sure--"

In that damp, dank, oppressive moment, Zella screamed, a loud, high-pitched sound.

Toby jumped.

"Zella," Alroy shouted.

They raced back through the maze of boxes. Zella's screams and shouts continued. Toby bumped his shins on a box. Ignoring the pain, he ran, limping forward. Alroy followed on his heels.

They took the stairs two at a time. When they burst into the saloon, Toby saw a large man struggling to keep his hold on Zella. She kicked at him, tried to punch him with her hands, and yelled as loud as she could. The man grabbed her around the waist. She bit his arm. He yelled and released her.

Toby raced forward and leaped on the man's back. He was big and broad. Grabbing Toby with one hand, he tossed him aside as if he were an annoying child. Toby remembered to cover his head and rolled. He jumped up. Raced forward.

Alroy hung onto the man's arm, kicking his shins. The man punched Alroy in the stomach. Before Toby reached them, his friend doubled up, lowered his head, and rushed toward the man.

"Run, Zella," Toby shouted. "Run."

A fraction of a second later, something hit Toby on the back of his head and everything went black.

CHAPTER 36: TOBY

ARRESTED?

July 20, 1890
4:00 p.m.

Pain drummed in Toby's head. He couldn't open his eyes. He managed a squint, but light forced him to squeeze his eyelids.

Nearby, people murmured. Their words sounded like gibberish. If the pain and the noise went away, he could sleep peacefully. That's what he wanted. Gradually the fog surrounding his mind cleared. He remembered someone was trying to hurt Zella. He opened his eyes, but the bright light hurt, and he quickly squeezed his eyelids together.

"Be still," Zella whispered. "I think we are arrested."

He slowly let his eyelids flutter open. Zella sat on the floor next to him. He didn't see Alroy, but standing in front of him was Officer Paul Mason, staring and frowning.

Someone stomped in through the front door.

"Gall dang, what's the fuss and the rush about?"

Doctor Stone stood inside the saloon, glancing around until he saw Toby on the floor.

"What happened to him?" Doctor Stone asked.

"Hit on the head," Officer Mason answered.

Toby moved to stand up, but the doctor pushed him back.

"Stay put until I examine you, boy." He winked at Toby. "You three manage to get into as much trouble as Wyatt used to."

The doctor felt the back of his head, told him to look up at the overhead gaslight. Toby obeyed. Doctor Stone squinted and stared at Toby's eyes.

"How bad does your head hurt?"

"Bad, but not too bad."

"Well, you're going to live. Just stay out of fights. Who hit you?"

"Don't know."

Zella, who hadn't left his side, scowled.

"Jonah Lopez hit him. Officer Mason has manhandled me." She glanced up at Mason, who looked away. "Toby was trying to stop Mason, when Jonah hit him on the back of the head. Alroy jumped on Jonah's back and wrestled him to the ground."

"Where's Alroy?" Toby asked.

"Downstairs with Wyatt."

That's all we need—Wyatt.

Toby wished he were allowed to say bad words aloud because knowing Wyatt was here made him want to say a lot of bad words. Instead, he looked up at Officer Mason.

"You brought Wyatt here?"

Mason found his voice.

"Laddie, would you rather be at the police station in a jail cell? Breaking and entering, property damage, assaulting a police officer. There's a lot of charges. I thought Detective Wyatt might come in handy."

Toby rubbed the back of his head. There was a marble-sized bump.

"Aww." He looked at his hand. There wasn't blood. "Why did you attack Zella?"

Zella looked like an angel sitting beside him, all innocent and helpless as if she were the victim. Mason clamped his lips together.

"Doctor Stone," Zella said. "There are some people downstairs who need looking after.

"Miss Doyle is correct," Mason said. "This way, Doc, I mean, Doctor."

Opening his black valise, the doctor pulled out a small pouch of powders. He gave the pouch to Zella but spoke to Toby.

"If your head continues to hurt, you can take some of this. Liza will know how to mix it for you. If you feel sleepy, don't go to sleep, send someone for me. What's down there?"

"Nothing good," Toby said.

Closing his bag, he stood to follow Mason.

"By the way, Mrs. Hernandez is doing better. Your ma and Liza took her some food. It was good to see your mother out and about. Lead the way, officer."

"What? My mother?"

"That's what I said, ain't it?"

Zella helped Toby stand. She was acting as if he were an invalid or something. He decided that it might not be a bad idea to play up the bang on the head. Sympathy never hurt.

When the doctor and Officer Mason disappeared into the hallway, he asked, "Is Wyatt angry?"

She grinned.

"He's angry-bear mad. For a couple seconds, he seemed worried about you. When Alroy told him there were people in a cage, he grabbed Jonah by the collar and marched him downstairs."

Zella looked at him and squinted.

"How bad is your head?" she asked, nodding to the officer standing by the door.

"It hurts, but not too bad, well, kind of bad," he whispered.

"Well, pretend you feel worse than you do."

She took a couple of chairs from one of the tables and motioned him to sit. He thought briefly that maybe they should take off, but they'd be leaving Alroy behind. That would only make things between Alroy and Wyatt worse. Now that the lights were on, the saloon didn't look so menacing or mysterious. It looked more like a disreputable bar with little to recommend it.

Zella glanced around and scooted her chair until her back faced the office.

"Wyatt didn't believe I broke the window," she whispered. "That annoyed me. He seems to think I'm a helpless female."

"Just shows that he doesn't know much. How long they been down there?"

"Ten minutes. Alroy went down to eavesdrop. He thinks maybe Jonah moved Pedro and is hiding him somewhere else."

They heard shouting coming from the basement. It sounded like Jonah because there were Spanish words peppered into the yelling.

"Wyatt found our map and took it," she whispered. "When things got a little chaotic, I slipped out and got my bag. It's hidden under my dress. I've got Pedro's second notebook."

He was surprised she didn't hand everything over to Wyatt.

"Don't look at me like that. I heard Mason tell Wyatt that it was too bad one Mexican running away was causing so much grief."

She leaned closer.

"Then Wyatt agreed with him. That made me so mad that I decided not to cooperate. I don't think the police are trying very hard."

This was new, Zella not taking Wyatt's part. He glanced out the window and saw it was still light. He fumbled in his pocket for his watch. It was almost five, which meant they had about four hours of daylight left. They had to get out of here and away from Wyatt.

The yelling stopped. Everyone but Doctor Stone came trooping into the room. Officer Mason had Jonah by the arm. Alroy looked as if he were bursting with information.

"Doctor says you're all right," Wyatt said. "Head hurt?"

Toby nodded.

"Do you thieves know where I could find some rope?" Wyatt asked.

Alroy rushed back into the hallway and came back with a coil of thick rope. He handed it to Wyatt, who passed it to Mason.

"Tie him up. I'll send some more men and a wagon around. If you can, help the doc. We're going to have to take those folks to the hospital. You're in charge when everyone gets here."

Mason stood up a little straighter.

"Yes, Detective Doyle. I'll take care of everything."

Wyatt turned to look at Alroy, Toby, and Zella and frowned.

"You've broken some laws here."

"Yes, sir," Toby said. "But we were only trying to—"

"No excuses. I'm fed up with you three and your antics."

Zella took a step closer to Wyatt.

"Are you going to arrest us?"

"No, you know I'm not going to arrest you, but no more snooping around, no more."

Toby saw what Wyatt couldn't. Zella had her hand behind her back and her fingers were crossed.

"Okay," she said.

"Is that a promise?"

She nodded.

Wyatt glanced at Officer Mason and Jonah, who seemed occupied with staring at the floor.

"You three, follow me."

The look on Wyatt's face was enough to tell Toby that any goodwill they may have had with Alroy's brother was spent to the point of bankruptcy. Whatever the detective had in mind for them, it wasn't going to be pleasant.

CHAPTER 37: TOBY

A FALLING-OUT

July 20, 1890
5:00 p.m.

Toby, Alroy, and Zella followed Wyatt. He walked through the Good Time Saloon's kitchen into the storage room where the broken window was. He looked at the door and shook his head.

"Too bad you don't put your resourcefulness to better use."

He examined the window, looked out at their bicycles, and motioned them to follow him. He used the back door, so they didn't have to crawl through a window or worry about broken glass. Outside, he searched first Alroy's bicycle pouch and then Toby's. He didn't find whatever he was looking for. He tossed each boy his bag.

"Tell me about the map," he said to no one in particular.

"May I point out that we led you to a kidnapper," Zella said. "I'm sure those girls weren't being sent to a ship. And we—"

"Stop," Wyatt said.

He pointed to Toby.

"You and my siblings are criminals. You can't take the law

into your own hands. I want some answers, and I want them now."

"I already told you. Pedro and I were investigating criminal activities in Sonora Town. That map is Pedro's. He marked out the businesses and suspects' homes on the map."

Wyatt looked a little less like a person about to explode.

"Thank you. Now, what do the notations mean?"

Zella glanced at Alroy and then Toby.

"Well, we only . . ."

She spoke slowly, and Toby knew she was stalling for time while she thought of what to say.

"We don't know everything," Toby said.

"Yeah, we figured out the CG was Mr. Garcia, but Pedro crossed him off, figured out he didn't know anything about the smuggling. Doc, um Dr. Grimes, is into science, not kidnapping or . . . um, trollops." Alroy said.

Zella stepped closer to Wyatt.

"We figured out that JL was Jonah Lopez and that GTS was Good Time Saloon. Smug is smuggling or, as it turned out, kidnapping. So we came to talk to Jonah, but when he wasn't here . . ." She shrugged. "We went in to investigate. The rest of it we haven't figured out."

He looked somewhat pacified with Zella's story. Toby doubted he knew she'd partly told the truth and partly lied. Toby was impressed with how easily she slipped right past some of the facts. It shouldn't take Wyatt too long to figure the map out. At least, he hoped he'd figure it out.

Wyatt stared at the ground while he rubbed his chin.

"I'm keeping the map. We'll talk about this when I get home. For now, you three go home and stay. I tried to get into your workroom and look at your notes, but that automaton wouldn't let me in."

"He is designed to keep people out," Alroy said.

Wyatt looked like someone had punched him in the face.

"Young man. A heap of metal should not keep a man from entering a room in his own home. This nonsense about you two having the run of the attic and doing whatever you want is over. Just because your mother has lost her mind doesn't mean you can do whatever you want. You've run wild for too long. I'll change all of that."

Alroy doubled his fists and stepped forward. Toby grabbed him by the back of his jacket, holding him back. It was Zella who got into Wyatt's face. She looked up at him and shook her finger in his face.

"You don't say anything about our mother. You hear me?"

She and Wyatt stared at each other. The seconds ticked by until the silence seemed heavy.

"Tell me," she said, her voice sounding hard. "Are you even looking for Pedro? Do you even care?"

He pressed his lips together.

"It's about time you grew up. Pedro ran away. Boys from this neighborhood do that. His father's gone, his mother's sick. He had the responsibility of a grown man. It was too much. He couldn't take it, so he left."

"Pedro would never do that," Alroy shouted.

"You have no idea what Pedro was going through. Face facts," Wyatt said. "Your friend deserted his family and took off to make a better life for himself. It happens. People can't deal with life, and they leave."

Alroy yanked away from Toby, who still held him by his jacket, and went to Zella, who stared up at Wyatt as if she were seeing him for the first time. Alroy put his arm around her and stepped away from Wyatt.

"We're leaving," Alroy said. "You go back in there and take credit for breaking up a kidnapping, smuggling ring."

He nudged Zella toward Toby, who put out his arms and hugged her.

"Pedro's not like you. You might desert your family, but

Pedro would never do that. He has integrity and honor. He's already more of a man than you'll ever be," Alroy said.

Wyatt clenched his jaws, and the veins in his neck stood out. Alroy stiffened as if waiting for a blow.

"Get home and stay out of trouble," Wyatt spoke as if he were spitting each word out like someone pounding nails into wood.

They jumped on their bicycles and rode away. Toby glanced back just before they pedaled into the street. Wyatt hadn't moved. He stood in place, stiff-backed, and looking like a friendless cowboy or a gunslinger.

One thought flittered through Toby's mind. *I could turn that image into a story.*

They cycled through Sonora Town with Alroy pedaling hard and riding ahead. Tears streamed down Zella's face. Toby rode next to her, glancing at her to make sure she was okay.

An awkwardness settled over Toby. Being an outsider, gave him insights an insider might now have. Sometimes he could see Zella's point of view about Wyatt, and sometimes he could see Alroy's. Right now, they were both disillusioned. From the look of their brother standing in that alley alone, he might be disgusted with himself. He sure didn't seem to care about Pedro. If Mr. Doyle were here, he'd be helping them look for Pedro. He was that kind of man.

Once Mr. Doyle had found Toby crying in the carriage house. He didn't scold him or judge him. He didn't even know why the neighbor kid was hiding in his building, but he guessed.

Toby remembered as if it were yesterday.

Mr. Doyle sat down on the old log and took his hand.

"The world can be mean to people who don't conform. Don't forget there is good inside those who are sometimes mean. They're blind or ignorant or both. There are good, accepting people, too. Find those people. You'll be okay," Mr. Doyle said.

Toby wiped his eyes with his sleeve, and Mr. Doyle handed

him a handkerchief to blow his nose. He felt weird blowing snot into the clean white material, but he did anyway. Then he looked up into the man's blue eyes.

"I'm a girl pretending to be a boy. I feel like a boy."

"No, you're a boy who happened to get the wrong body. Sometimes that happens. Don't let anyone tell you who you are. You know yourself better than anyone else."

"My ma and pa are embarrassed. They moved here so no one would know. They won't ever take me to visit family 'cause I'm not right. My pa tells me that all the time. I'm not right."

"Toby, here's a secret about parents. They don't know everything. They love you, but they don't know everything. People can change. They may not, but they might. If you can, find it in your heart to forgive their ignorance. Don't let their ignorance make you sad or angry. If you do, you're taking on their pain. There's already enough pain in the world."

"I'll try to find forgiveness, but I already got a lot of anger."

"I know, son. I know."

That speech changed his life. He wasn't always good at forgiving, but when he was, it worked. Maybe he'll tell Zella and Alroy about what their father told him. From where he stood, Wyatt was working with some big-time ignorance. Their brother might not change, but maybe they could.

It's funny how parents can be so different and how kids can be so different. Wyatt was like an old stallion with blinders, but Alroy and Zella were like colts with x-ray eyes.

All he knew was that Wyatt was dead wrong about Pedro. They'd show Wyatt he didn't know everything. Pedro wasn't a quitter. He was glad his friends weren't giving up because he'd hate to have to find Pedro on his own. No matter how it turned out, he was going to stick by his friends and hope that for once, the world would do something good.

CHAPTER 38: ZELLA

MRS. DOYLE

July 20, 1890
6:30 p.m.

When they got close to the Plaza, Zella signaled them to stop. She knew they needed to talk things out before they went any further. She found an empty bench, and they huddled together.

"Mom's awake," she said. "Doctor Stone said she and Liza were at Pedro's house, helping Mrs. Hernandez."

"Yeah, I know," Alroy said. "Are you still angry at her?"

"I don't know. I'll figure that out later."

Alroy nodded.

"You're right about Wyatt. I don't think the police are going to do anything, which means we have to find Pedro," she said.

"I agree," Toby said. "What's the plan?"

"We need to go get Pedro's bike and look through his bag. See if we missed any clues," Zella said.

"Good idea," Toby said. "You still have our map?"

Zella shook her head.

"We don't need it," Alroy said. "What do you need to know? I memorized it."

Toby jumped up and moved to the Plaza's edge, where some of the grass had died, and there was a patch of dirt. He broke a small twig off the nearest tree and began drawing lines. Zella recognized the streets.

Alroy knelt down and drew an X.

"Here's where Mr. Lee found his bicycle. Here's the laundry. It's too far away for Pedro to leave his bike and have walked there, but here."

He drew another X.

"That's Hornsby's house, close enough to walk to. Garcia's is way over here. Too far. Lee's shop is here. Closer but still pretty far. Pedro's old house is here. Some distance from the bike, but close enough if Pedro left the bicycle behind so he could hide. Here's Doc's shop. Also close enough."

Alroy glanced at Zella and then at Toby. Zella pointed to Hornsby's house.

"That's where we need to start. He's dangerous and might have taken Pedro."

What she didn't say was that now she was more worried than ever. She thought Hornsby was the kind of man who would use violence first and think about his actions later. Plus, he seemed to be very angry with Pedro, and his wife suspected him of something.

"Yeah, my bet is on Hornsby," Toby said. "When do we go?"

Zella made her decision quickly.

"I'm going to go to the newspaper office and see if they've gotten any word about Pedro. If they know something, that might change our plans. You two go home and make sandwiches. Be ready to go as soon as I get back."

"Part of that sounds good, but I think when you get back, Alroy and I should go to Hornsby's house," Toby said. "Hornsby spends a lot of time at the cantina drinking. I bet Mrs. Hornsby will be alone. We can talk to her. Convince her to show us the basement."

"And just what am I supposed to do?" Zella asked. "I can go with you."

"Keep going through Pedro's stuff," Toby said. "If we're wrong about Hornsby, we'll need you to have another plan ready."

Zella hated the idea of not going with them, but she saw Toby's point. If Hornsby wasn't the culprit, they'd need another strategy. They could get twice as much done if they split up.

She nodded.

"I think we should all go to the newspaper." Alroy held up his hand to stop Zella from disagreeing. "Listen. If someone has Pedro, then whoever they are, they know we are looking for them. His story is in the papers, and our break-in is probably town gossip. For safety, I don't think any of us should go places alone. At least two of us together at all times."

Zella glanced at Toby.

"Yeah," he said. "Good idea. Better safe than sorry."

Zella thought about Pedro going out alone. He'd been alone, and no one knew where he was or what he was doing. Her brother was right, which scared her a little because he was known for being careless.

"Let's go," Zella said.

They pedaled fast and didn't slow when they got into downtown. They leaned their bikes against the brick wall and rushed into the newspaper. Several men were readying the printing press.

Toby walked up to the closest man.

"You guys are working late," he said.

The man chuckled.

"Naw, lad, we're getting set up for the morning run. There's a lot of work to get the presses ready to go."

"Toby," Zella called out as she rushed toward the elevator.

Zella held the door, and as soon as he stepped in, she slid the door closed and pushed the up lever. Alroy watched the gears turn and studied the layout as they rode up, even glancing down to see how everything worked. She suppressed a grin. He couldn't turn off his curiosity no matter what was happening around him. Right now, she loved him for his consistency.

Only a few reporters were in the newsroom. Kate's desk was empty, and the editor's office was closed and dark.

Zella glanced around. She didn't recognize any of the reporters. Taking a deep breath, she walked up to the nearest man, who was busy at his typewriter and didn't glance up.

"Excuse me, I wanted to see Kate."

"Not here." He kept typing and glanced up at her. "You're the new girl."

She nodded.

"Ike's in the darkroom. If you want to wait, he should be out any minute."

"Thanks," she said as the man returned his attention to his work. "I guess we should wait," she whispered to Toby and Alroy.

"We don't have time to wait," Alroy said. "They're all busy. Look."

"Hey, everyone," Toby shouted.

A couple of men looked up. The rest kept typing.

"We got a deadline, kid," the man who'd spoken to Zella said.

"We were wondering if there's any news about Pedro Hernandez?" Toby shouted again.

As he spoke, a door on the far side of the room opened, and Ike St James walked into the room.

"Ike, they're your problem," one of the men said, and everyone went back to work, ignoring them.

He hurried over to them.

"Hi, Zella. Here about Pedro?"

"Yes."

Ike stretched his hand out to Toby and then to Alroy.

"Ike."

"Toby and Alroy," Zella said.

"My wife left a stack of messages for you. She thought you might come by. She didn't think there was much news. She sent copies over to the police department."

He moved to Kate's desk, opened the middle drawer, and took out a stack of notes tied with twine. He handed them to Zella.

"Thank you," she said. "We're in a hurry."

"Of course. Let us know how things turn out. Any good news?"

"No news at all," she said. "We're still investigating."

A couple of minutes later, they were on their bicycles and pedaling toward home. As they rode into the driveway, Zella saw her mother standing in the parlor window. Mrs. Doyle waved and watched as they leaned their bicycles against the wall.

Zella jumped off her bicycle and grabbed Alroy by his jacket, pulling him back.

"Hey," he said.

"I'm going to see her first, and you are going to wait until we are finished talking."

"But—"

"No."

Her brother pressed his lips together and stared at her.

"Okay," he finally said. "Be kind." He spoke quietly, begging her.

"I will," she said.

The truth was she didn't know exactly what she was going to do or say. She just knew that she had to be the first to talk to her mother before everyone else pretended everything was all right.

When they stepped through the front door, Toby grabbed

Alroy's arm. Zella waited until they disappeared into the kitchen before stepping into the parlor.

Mrs. Doyle smiled, rushed toward Zella, and threw her arms around her.

To Zella, her mother's arms seemed like a vise, squeezing the life out of her. She stood still and stiff as her mother hugged her. Slowly, the arms relaxed and released her.

Zella stepped back.

Now that she was face to face with a woman who looked at her with a questioning gaze and hurt eyes, she realized that Alroy had been right. She was angry to the point of rage. The only words she could think to say were mean and spiteful. Her brother had pleaded with her to be kind, but not one kind word came to mind. She stared at her mother and noted that she was thin and pale and sad. She could do nothing for her, say nothing to her, nor care that her silence caused pain. Tears slid down Mrs. Doyle's cheeks, and Zella could only make a mental note of the fact. She found no compassion in her heart.

Zella turned and walked toward the door.

"Please," her mother said. "Say something."

Looking back at a broken woman, she said, "I promised Alroy I would be kind, but I have no kind words."

"Then say what's in your heart. I will hear it."

Taking a deep breath, she considered her mother. She remembered a woman who had cared for her and brought joy to her life. This was a shell of that person.

"You deserted us when we needed you. I don't know if I can ever forgive you."

Mrs. Doyle looked down at the wool rug.

"I understand."

Zella took one step closer.

"For Alroy's sake, I hope you can learn to be a mother. Right now, all I see is a selfish woman who wants forgiveness she doesn't deserve. Alroy has stood by you. Liza has been a mother to us. Wyatt is trying to help us. Don't expect anything from me."

She walked away and heard a sob. She glanced back. Her mother sat in her chair, bending forward with her hands covering her face. Standing in the doorway, she waited for several seconds. When her mother stopped weeping and wiped the tears from her face, Zella turned away and made her way to the kitchen.

In the hall, she took the notes she'd gotten from Ike and began looking through them. Several people claimed they'd seen him, but the descriptions they gave were vague and useless. One person said they'd seen him sweeping in front of Doc's workshop. She tossed that in the worthless pile. They already knew where he'd been in the day. They needed to know where he'd gone that night. Nothing in the stack of papers proved noteworthy. She'd ask Toby and Alroy to go through them in case she missed anything.

She was stalling so that Alroy wouldn't go into the parlor and see his mother red-faced. Enough time had passed, and her mother hadn't come out of the room. She tiptoed back and glanced into the parlor. Her mother stood at the window. At least, she wasn't in her chair, nor was she weeping.

A nagging sense of guilt tugged at Zella for lashing out at her mother. She'd been angry for months. How many times had she played her mother's betrayal in her mind? She didn't know. What she did know was that her anger hadn't felt right. Part of her was so happy to see her mother snap out of her lethargy, but another part of her insisted she had a right to be angry.

If all that were true, why did she feel so ashamed? In her mind, one thought pulled against another until she wanted to scream. Plus, right now, she didn't recognize herself. She wondered what she was becoming, and if she wanted to be that person.

CHAPTER 39: ALROY

FINDING COMPASSION

July 20, 1890
6:30 p.m.

In the kitchen, Liza hummed to herself as she kneaded bread dough.

Without turning to face them, she asked, "You three hungry? There are oranges and some bread on the side table for you."

"Thanks," Toby said. "It's just me and Alroy."

She dusted the flour from her hands and faced them.

"Any word on Pedro? Never mind, I can tell by your faces there's not. Where's Zella?"

"With Ma," Alroy said.

"You already talk to her?"

"No, Zella wanted to see her first."

"Well, that's interesting."

"What happened?" Alroy asked.

Liza shrugged.

"Don't know. After you three left, she walked into the kitchen and asked about Pedro. She helped me make up a basket, and we went to Sonora Town. I didn't know what to do. So I did what she wanted."

While Liza spoke, Toby moved to the counter and began peeling an orange.

"So, she okay?" Alroy asked.

"Seems to be. Not sure Zella is the right person to be talking to her."

"I'm not either," Alroy said. "But she promised to be kind."

"That's something, I guess," Liza said.

The next ten minutes crawled by for Alroy. He and Toby ate the food Liza forced on them. Toby and Liza were unusually quiet. He didn't want to talk, so he was fine with the silence. The only thing was he wished he knew what was going on in the parlor. He didn't hear any shouting or anything breaking, which were both good things.

After what seemed like ages, Zella walked through the door. She looked normal, not like someone who had a fight. She glanced at him.

"Mama probably wants to see you," she said and rushed to Liza, who opened her arms and hugged her.

"There, there, girl. It's going to be all right." She glanced over Zella's head and mouthed the words, "Go on."

"Grab some food. I'll meet you in the attic," Alroy whispered to Toby.

They left Zella softly crying into Liza's shoulder. He watched as Toby took the stairs two at a time. Then he dusted his jacket and smoothed back his hair. Stopping at the parlor doorway, he watched his mother. She sat with her hands folded in her lap and a blank expression on her face. She stared out at the trees in their yard and the street beyond. He never knew what she saw or if she saw anything.

His chest muscles tightened, and tears threatened to explode from his eyes.

Had she gone away again?

"Hello, Mama," he said.

He hesitated before approaching her. He touched her shoulder.

"Mama?"

She turned her head and looked at him. For a moment, her eyes looked blank and far away. Then Alroy saw a spark of recognition.

"Alroy."

"Yes, Mama."

She patted the armchair next to her, signaling for him to sit. He hated to sit in that chair. It was his father's favorite chair, and he and Zella avoided it. He hesitated.

"It's all right, dear. Papa wouldn't mind."

Reluctantly, Alroy sat. He didn't lean back, but sat upright, not touching the arms of the chair. His mother reached out and touched his face with her open palm. Her hand felt warm and gentle. He didn't remember the last time she'd touched him. It felt nice, like the old days when she laughed and told funny stories.

At Lopez's place, Wyatt had called her crazy. She wasn't crazy, just sad. A broken heart overwhelmed her.

He pushed those thoughts out of his mind. All he wanted was to hug her and cry on her shoulder just the way Zella did with Liza, but he waited and prayed she'd keep talking.

"I saw Mrs. Hernandez today," she said. "She's very ill, but Doctor Stone was there. He said she's getting better."

Afraid to be happy and hesitant to believe she was okay again, he didn't move. If he did anything, the spell might break, and she'd step back away from him.

"Is Pedro home?" she asked.

He shook his head.

"Oh, dear." She patted his hand. "Don't worry, dear. Wyatt will find him."

He took a deep breath and let it out slowly.

"I don't think Wyatt wants to find Pedro," he managed to say.

She glanced out the window and sighed.

"Of course, he wants to find Pedro. Wyatt is a good man and works hard. Remember, he carries a burden. He does his police work, and he takes care of us. It's odd. I've been sitting here thinking about Wyatt and how good he is to us. I should help him, but I can't seem to move. I miss your father so much that I've forgotten how to live. I want to get back to living."

She looked at Alroy.

From the corner of his eye, he saw Wyatt standing in the doorway, holding his hat in his hand, listening. While his mother continued speaking, Alroy met Wyatt's gaze.

"Of course, you miss your father. We all do. Poor Wyatt must be heartbroken too." She wiped the tears off her cheeks. "Don't worry. Wyatt will find Pedro. He's the kind of man who always does the right thing. Like your father. Like you."

Alroy couldn't stop the tears that rolled silently down his cheeks. He watched Wyatt look down at the floor as if it were the most fascinating wood he'd ever seen. His brother put his hat on and walked away.

When he looked back at his mother, she was gone again, seeing things he couldn't see.

"Mama," he said.

She glanced up.

"Maybe you shouldn't sit here alone. Go to the kitchen and help Liza. I can't stay because we need to make a plan to find Pedro."

"Yes, you're right," she said.

Mrs. Doyle stood and took his hand. Together they walked to the kitchen, where his mother kissed his forehead.

"Go find your friend," she said.

He slipped away and went to the attic. Zella and Toby sat on the armchairs, eating oranges and bread.

"I thought Wyatt might be up here," Alroy said.

"He left," Zella said. "He didn't say anything to you?"

Alroy shook his head. He thought for sure Wyatt would lay into them for breaking into the saloon.

Toby jumped up and went for the door.

"Where you going?" Zella asked.

"To put Mr. Hyde to guard the door."

"If Wyatt comes back, he will be annoyed," Alroy said.

"Who cares?" Zella snapped.

After seeing his brother standing in the doorway looking like an outsider, Alroy realized he cared. His mother had been right. Wyatt was trying to take care of them, and he was trying to do the right thing. Maybe it wasn't his fault he didn't know how to be their father. Alroy knew he could never be as kind as his father had been. Maybe no one could live up to that image.

He remembered the letter Doc had given him. His father had raised Wyatt differently. Maybe his father treated Wyatt differently. Maybe his brother was trying to do what he thought was best. Even if those things were true, Alroy still didn't believe the police were going to make an effort to find Pedro.

Once they'd finished their snacks, they gathered around the worktable where they'd left their notes. Toby quickly drew Pedro's map from memory.

"I've been thinking," Toby said. "I think Alroy and I should go check out Lopez's house. See if there's a basement. And find out if there's someone home who will let us look around. Maybe a kid who doesn't know any better." He grinned at Zella. "If that doesn't work, we could always break a window."

Zella stuck her tongue out at him.

"Then you go to Hornsby's house. He's our man. I feel it. I'll stay here and read Pedro's journals," Zella said.

Alroy looked over their notes and the list of suspects. They'd checked off Garcia. Doc didn't seem to be hiding anything except his time machine. He was pretty sure Wyatt suspected Officer Henderson of something. Wyatt was a stickler for doing the right thing no matter what. So Henderson was probably in trouble. Lopez didn't have Pedro at the saloon, but he was definitely under arrest. He could have stashed Pedro at his home. If he didn't have their friend that left Lee and Hornsby.

"What about Mr. Lee?" Alroy asked.

"Umm, I don't know." Zella scrunched up her face. "He didn't act like he was hiding something."

"Zella's right," Toby said. "But let's leave him on the list for now. We'll look at him if all else fails," Toby said. "You think Lopez is a dead end?"

"Yes," Zella said. "The police will search his house. We'll get caught if we go there."

"I think we should check anyway," Alroy said. "If the police are there, we'll leave and go to Hornsby's house."

"Yeah." Toby looked about as happy as Alroy felt.

He wasn't sure he wanted to go near Lopez's house, but they had to start checking people off their list. When he and Toby stepped out the attic window, Zella ignored them as she read Pedro's notebook. They took the elevator down and sent it back up so Wyatt couldn't use it to get to the attic.

CHAPTER 40: ALROY

CASING HORNSBY'S HOUSE

July 20, 1890
7:15 p.m.

Alroy and Toby were about to cross New High Street when Old Elijah came running out of the alley and right into their path. Alroy swerved. His bicycle hit gravel and slid about five feet. Toby managed to stop just before hitting the old man.

Elijah rushed over to help Alroy up.

"I didn't mean to scare you. Are you hurt?"

Alroy dusted his clothes.

"Naw, but why you running in front of traffic like that?"

The old man's eyes were wide, and his bottom lip trembled.

"That vampire. He's back. I seen him when I was a boy. He's back."

He pointed toward the alley, and his finger trembled.

"You been drinking?" Toby asked.

"No, son, but I sure wish I had something. I saw him with my own eyes, as tall as a building and all dressed in black, swooping through the alley. He threw bones in that garbage. Bones, like he licked 'um clean."

Toby pressed a coin in the old man's palm and closed it.

"Go get some coffee. Coffee and a sandwich."

Old Elijah nodded and took off running about as fast as a toddler.

"Coffee," Toby called out and then turned to Alroy. "You know we gotta go look. Let's hurry."

In the alley, they checked the garbage. It was a stinky job, and Alroy held his nose and peeked in each barrel. After a couple minutes, Toby whistled and waved him over. Alroy peered at several large bones that didn't look like any animal he'd seen. He glanced at Toby.

"Are you thinking what—"

"Yeah," Alroy said, glancing around the empty alley. "What do we do?"

Toby always carried a small notebook and pencil to write down story ideas.

"Send a note to the police."

Toby scribbled a note, read it to Alroy, and tore the page out of his notebook. He folded it into fourths and scribbled Detective Doyle on the outside.

"A vampire didn't do that," Toby said, pointing to the bones. "They suck blood, not strip a body down to the bones. Come on."

"You know vampires aren't real," Alroy said.

"Sure."

"Just making sure that your brain wasn't getting addled from writing penny dreadfuls."

They rode to Main and went north until they spotted Jasper Levin sitting on the grocery store steps.

When they pulled up, Jasper nodded. His big rimmed hat shaded his eyes. His brown pants were covered in dirt, and his white shirt looked about as clean as someone who'd been rolling in cow manure.

"Hey, would you take this to the police station and give it to whoever's at the desk. It's important. I'll give you a quarter."

Until Toby mentioned the quarter, Jasper seemed uninterested in moving, much less walking a few blocks.

"Let's see the quarter."

Toby held the quarter out.

"The police don't like me much."

"Really?" Alroy said. "You know my brother's a detective."

Jasper nodded.

"If you take this to him and tell him it's from me, he'll thank you for helping the police department."

He grabbed the coin, took the note Toby held out, and grinned.

"Thanks."

"Make sure and deliver it," Toby said. "If you don't, bad things will happen."

They watched Jasper scurry down the street.

"Somehow I don't think that was the best idea we've ever had," Toby said as they were riding toward Sonora Town.

Alroy didn't care. He simply enjoyed the thought of Wyatt's face turning red. Jasper was a good-natured kid, so he hoped Wyatt wouldn't take his frustration out on an innocent bystander.

They'd been to Sonora Town so many times the streets were starting to look familiar to Alroy. Nothing hindered them from reaching Lopez's house, which was as run-down as the other neighborhood houses. A small boy squatted in the dirt, playing marbles.

"You live here?" Alroy pointed to Lopez's house.

The boy nodded.

"Your pa home?"

He shook his head.

"Your ma?"

He nodded.

A wrinkled, stooped-over woman answered the door. She had to turn her head up to look at them. Alroy was pretty sure she wasn't the boy's mother. Maybe grandmother.

"*Señora* Lopez?" Toby asked.

She chuckled, showing missing teeth.

"Margarita," she called. "*Dos jóvenes están* aquí."

A younger woman appeared in the doorway. She wiped her hands on her apron and looked at them inquisitively. "Yes?"

"Uh, we were wondering if you had a basement?" Alroy asked, knowing full well from the dirt floors he saw that the house didn't have a basement.

She laughed, and her face became radiant and pretty.

"No. Is this a joke? What do you boys want? I'm fixing dinner and don't have time for games."

Alroy held Pedro's picture out for her to see.

"We were wondering if you've seen this boy? He's our friend, and he's missing."

Those words echoed in his ears. He'd said them so many times in the last two days that they seemed to mock him.

She frowned and shook her head.

"No. I heard Pedro was missing. He hasn't turned up?"

"No."

"Go to the Good Time Saloon. Ask for Jonah, my husband. He knows a lot of people. He might be able to help you." She started to close the door but turned back. "We are praying his family will find him."

She closed the door.

Alroy glanced at Toby, who shrugged. Lopez's wife didn't know he was arrested. She seemed like a nice lady.

"Don't start feeling guilty," Toby said. "Her husband's the one doing illegal stuff."

"Yeah. I can still feel for her."

"Sure. Not her fault either."

They got back on their bicycles and rode toward Hornsby's house. Alroy dreaded seeing Hornsby again. At least, he lived in a better neighborhood, on a street similar to theirs. Wyatt couldn't yell at him for being in a dangerous area. About a block away from the house, they stopped.

"Strategy?" Toby said.

"Hope he's not home," Alroy said, "If he is home, hope he doesn't kill us."

"How about we see who's home. If it's Mrs. Hornsby, maybe she'll talk to us," Toby said. "If it's the mister, we could . . . offer an apology? Sorta check for a basement."

Toby grinned that easy way he did, which made people think he wasn't serious.

"Toby, I hate to say this, but I think it would be pretty stupid to walk up to Hornsby after what happened this morning. Let's snoop around and see if there's a basement, and . . ."

"Yeah, let's be safe. If there's a basement, we gotta tell Wyatt cause Hornsby's way out of our league," Toby said.

Alroy sighed.

"We can sneak around the house and see what we can find."

When they got closer to the house, they leaned their bicycles against a tree and approached the house. They saw the basement windows. Toby motioned to him, putting his hands up around his eyes as if he were peeking in. Alroy bent down and made his way to the windows as Toby went around the house. Lying on his stomach, he peered inside. Two electric lights hung in the center of the room about eight feet apart. He figured someone was in there because the lights were on. He couldn't see Hornsby or his wife. Shelves filled with canned fruit, vegetables, and other foodstuff lined the wall.

There were sundry boxes here and there. Something metal

caught his eye, and he scooted around so he could see in the other direction.

An automaton.

No, two.

They stood off to the side. They looked very similar to the ones in Robinsons' grocery store. He knew those were pretty advanced models. It was strange that Hornsby would have those in his basement. They were designed, like their Hyde/Jekyll, to guard something or to keep people out.

Toby rounded the corner. He was bent over and running. Plopping down beside Alroy, he breathed heavily.

"Mrs. Hornsby's on the other side," he whispered. "She crying and digging up the basement. She looks upset."

Alroy pointed toward the automatons, and Toby scooted closer to the window for a better look.

"I'd guess she's looking in the wrong place. If Pedro's in there, he's behind one of those."

"Let's go in," Alroy said.

Toby shook his head.

"When I think something's a bad idea, then it's a crazy idea," he said. "Let's get your brother. Hornsby could be in there."

If Pedro were in there, Alroy didn't want to leave him there a minute longer.

"I admit it's a crazy idea, but it's Pedro. He could be right there." Alroy pointed to the basement window.

"But if Hornsby's home, you leave and get Wyatt," Toby said. "I'll stay here and watch the house. If he's not there, we'll try to talk to Mrs. Hornsby."

"What are you going to be doing when I run off to get Wyatt?" Alroy asked.

"Hide and watch. If something happens, I'll improvise."

One thing that Alroy loved about Toby is he never backed away, even when it was a crazy idea. His eyes had a little twinkle of mischief in them.

"I don't like leaving you, but let's do it."

They stood and dusted the dirt off their clothes and headed for the door. Alroy's throat was dry as a desert. If Mr. Hornsby answered the door, they could be stepping into more trouble than they could handle.

CHAPTER 41: ZELLA

THE DISCOVERY

July 20, 1890
7:30 p.m.

After Alroy and Toby left for Hornsby's house, Zella went to work reading Pedro's notebook. At first, she didn't find anything they hadn't already discovered. But she kept reading and making notes, hoping that something in the journal might help the police.

Pedro kept meticulous notes about everything. There was a clear chronological line of his actions. At one point, she became so frustrated because she wanted to find something new she got up and walked around the room. She mentally went through everything she knew, hoping something would stick out. Back at the worktable, she looked over the map and the names. Unless Alroy and Toby found something, they'd reached a dead end.

When she heard the stairs creak, she stopped and waited. In the hallway, Wyatt cursed at Mr. Hyde.

"Zella, Alroy, get out here and get this thing out of my way. Now."

She didn't care that he shouted. He could yell all night, but he wasn't getting into this room. He'd taken the first notebook. She wasn't going to allow him to take the second one.

"Did you hear me?"

She didn't answer and went back to reading. After a few minutes, Wyatt stopped shouting and marched downstairs.

Minutes later, a rapping sound on the window startled her. Wyatt stood on the roof, leaning over, looking through the window, he motioned to her.

"Let me in."

She shook her head. His face was red, and she swore she could see the veins in his neck standing out. He cupped his hand around his eyes and peered into the attic.

"Where's Alroy and Toby?" he shouted.

She shrugged.

"Where are they?" he yelled.

"Go away," Zella shouted, turning back to Pedro's notebook.

"I'm trying to help you. I think you're hiding things from me. I know those boys are up to no good. They are going to get into trouble."

Zella thought about closing the curtains but decided that might be a little much. She stepped closer to the window.

"They are out looking for Pedro. I'm doing research. I don't know where they are."

She felt that if Wyatt were in the room with her he might explode in anger. He threw his arms up and paced in front of the window a few times. Then faster than Zella would have thought possible, he slipped and slid down toward their elevator, which stopped him from falling off the roof. She thought about opening the window but didn't.

Wyatt marched back to the window, taking cautious steps.

"You stay there. At least they were smart enough not to take you with them."

"You are not a progressive man," she shouted and put her hands on her hips. "I'm researching. I'm good at research."

She turned away from the window and went back to the worktable. After a few seconds, she glanced back at the window. Wyatt was gone.

Turning her full attention to Pedro's notebook, she continued reading. She was beginning to think she'd never find anything helpful. Then, she discovered something new. They'd been so wrong.

CHAPTER 42: ALROY

MRS. HORNSBY

July 20, 1890
7:45 p.m.

Alroy and Toby knocked several times on Hornsby's door. When no one answered, they checked the door. The handle turned, and the door swung open. Nodding to each other, they stepped inside.

"Mrs. Hornsby," Toby called.

Alroy felt strange sneaking through someone else's house, but they had to get to the basement. The house was neat and tidy. The place looked like Mrs. Hornsby didn't have anything to do but clean. In the entry, a staircase led up to the second floor. Two parlors framed either side of the entrance. They followed the narrow hall, which led to the kitchen, where they found the basement door standing open.

"Mrs. Hornsby," Alroy called.

When she didn't answer, he cupped his hands to his mouth and shouted, but she still didn't answer.

Toby stepped through the doorway. Alroy pulled him back.

"Is it safe?" Alroy whispered.

"He's not here," Toby said. "Listen."

Below Mrs. Hornsby cried as if someone had died. Alroy nodded, and they both descended the stairs.

In the basement, Mrs. Hornsby jammed her shovel into the dirt floor, hitting the hard packed dirt over and over. There were a few nicks and clods of dirt around the area where she stood. She wasn't making headway.

Her eyes were red from weeping. The dust she'd kicked up layered her face, and tear lines streaked her face like tiny rivers. She didn't notice them.

Alroy knew Pedro wasn't buried where she was trying to dig. The ground was hard packed and hadn't been touched in years.

Sometimes Toby surprised Alroy. He went right up to Mrs. Hornsby and gently took the shovel from her. She didn't protest. He dropped the shovel and put his arm around her shoulder. She kept looking at the ground like something was going to pop up out of the dirt.

"Mrs. Hornsby, are you all right?" Toby asked.

She looked at him and shook her head.

"They was my friends," she said.

"Who?"

She glanced up at Alroy, who still stood on the steps.

"You boys. You're looking for Pedro?"

Alroy nodded.

She sighed.

"I don't think he's here. No fresh grave. He said he didn't hurt Pedro."

"Mrs. Hornsby," Toby said. "Let's go upstairs. Alroy and I will look around down here."

She stood up straight.

"It's my place to find them. They was my friends."

If Wyatt wanted to see crazy, he should come down here and talk to Mrs. Hornsby. This lady reminded him of his mama when papa lay on the floor dying. Crying and saying things that didn't make sense, which made him think she was mourning. He couldn't believe he felt sorry for someone who had been so mean to them, but he did. Maybe she was miserable. He came down the stairs and took her hand.

"Ma'am, are you talking about the Wong family?" he asked.

Her eyes grew wide.

"Yes." She howled the word like a coyote calling out in the night.

Alroy looked at Toby for help. He wasn't so good with old women, not like Toby. He raised his eyebrows and nodded toward Mrs. Hornsby.

Toby finally got the hint.

"Tell us what happened. Maybe we can help you."

She glanced at Toby.

"When you left, I asked him. I felt goosebumps all over when he said *buried in the basement* about Pedro. Like he'd kill Pedro and bury him in our basement. We had a big fight, but I kept on asking about the Wongs. Even when he hit me, I kept on asking. He said he killed them 'cause he wanted the laundry. He didn't have the money to pay them. He killed them," she wailed.

When she looked at Alroy, he thought she had the saddest eyes he'd ever seen, sadder than his mother's eyes.

"They was my friends. He called them damn Chinese. Said it didn't matter that he killed them. Said they were like dogs or chickens. Heathens." She put her hands to her face. "They was nice. Kind folks. I loved them children. They was beautiful."

She wiped her face, streaking dirt across her face.

"They called me auntie and, when they spoke Chinese, it sounded like they was singing to me. I couldn't never have children. They was like my own. I used to tell them they was sweet angels in the City of Angels. Only this is the city of devils."

Alroy wished he could make her stop talking. He wondered what kind of lady she would have been if she had her friends, and if she were an aunt to children. He felt as if he were watching someone's heart breaking right in front of him.

She glanced around.

"They're in here somewhere."

"Mrs. Hornsby," Toby said.

"Don't call me that. You call me Georgia. My name is Georgia. It's a good Christian name. No more Mrs. Hornsby." Her voice sounded like it did when they were at the laundry, angry and hard.

"Georgia," Toby said. "Where's your husband?"

"He run off. I told him I was going to tell the police. He came at me with murder in his eyes. I grabbed the gun in the desk and . . ." She looked past them and up the stairs. "I shot him in the shoulder. I was aiming for his black heart. He ran off."

"Okay. That's good, so he won't be able to hurt you or anyone else," Toby said. "Let me take you upstairs. Do you have a telephone?"

Toby pointed back toward the automatons.

Alroy nodded, happy he wouldn't have to go upstairs and help comfort her.

"Yes. It's in the hallway," she said.

"I'll make you some tea and call the police. And Alroy will look around down here. Maybe he can find a clue."

She patted Toby's cheek.

"You're good boys. Pedro's a good boy, too."

Alroy waited until they were upstairs and out of sight before starting his search. He wasn't interested in digging up the basement, but he was curious about the automatons and seeing what they were guarding. He slipped around a stack of boxes. They were standing about five feet apart like giant metal guards. One was against the outside wall, so there couldn't be anything behind it.

He moved closer to examine the other one. Prospero was written on the side of the arm. He recognized the name from yesterday when he talked to the girl in the carriage. Her automaton was also labeled Prospero.

This beauty was his height, but the torso was wide, out of proportion with the rest of the shape. The legs, arms, waist, and neck had joints. What he couldn't find was a control box. The League had put their control boxes on the front and back of their automaton so they could control him from either direction. This one didn't appear to have a control mechanism. Alroy stacked two boxes and stood on them to examine the back.

Nothing. There was nothing behind it. The other automaton was against the wall. There couldn't be anything behind it. He examined the second automaton anyway.

He wondered why a man like Hornsby with no education and scientific background would have sophisticated machines. They were designed to move. Doc had shown him some of his automatons. These were of finer craftsmanship than Doc's. Alroy thought maybe Hornsby used them for transporting goods. If he were smuggling, these two could be used to pull wagons or carry heavy loads.

He stood back and looked at them, thinking and considering. He knew he was missing something. It was probably simple. It was easy to overlook the simple and make it complicated.

When he'd helped Grace work on the ladybug airship, she told him not to make things complicated. Look for the simple answers first.

What was he missing?

He stepped back and looked over the automatons. He reexamined each part. At the hand, he stopped. Each finger had a small hole in the tip.

He rushed forward trying to peer into the hole, but he couldn't see anything. He poked his finger inside and immediately met resistance. Each finger had something round and metal inside. That's when he followed the arm, to the shoulder, to the hip joint, to the knee and foot. The space above the foot was not proportional to the rest of the design. It was wider than necessary and looked as if one double joint were a box.

He felt around until he found a latch. He pulled the metal forward. Like two doors, the torso of the automaton opened outward. Inside, a shiny metal plate sat a little back from the legs. It was big enough for a small person to sit on as a seat.

A folded piece of paper lay on the seat. He grabbed it. In Pedro's neat handwriting, the note read:

Mr. Hornsby, this is a very dangerous machine. I have disabled the shooting mechanism on both machines so no one will come to harm.

Pedro had been here. Maybe Hornsby found this note and did something to him? This was proof, something he could give to Wyatt.

Alroy's momentary joy faded. Hornsby wouldn't have left the note here.

He slipped the note in his pocket and examined the automaton. Now that he knew what he was looking for, he quickly found the small bullets, each sitting in a metal sling that went up each leg, into the body, and then to the shoulder, where the bullets dropped down into the fingers. A simple gear system transported the bullets up. He'd need more time to examine everything, but a cursory look suggested the machine could move forward, backwards, and sideways. The person controlling it could shoot in all directions.

He moved back up to the belly of the machine, looking for anything that would tell him how it worked. Finally, his fingers slid over a round thumb-sized impression on the back of the neck. He stood on a box so he could see better. The impression was definitely a button. When he pressed the metal, the torso and the top of the head slid apart, revealing a seat where a man could sit and look out the eye slits. Two handles slid down, creating arms with control panels.

"Corker," he whispered.

Without hesitation, Alroy stepped into the seat. His head

was level with the empty space where the head of the automaton was. A burly person would have trouble fitting inside, but an average sized man or woman could run the machine. On the arm control panels, he tested the first knob, turning it left.

Immediately, the noise of gears turning filled the room, and the waist of the machine moved, rotating left until it stopped at a forty-five-degree angle. Turning the knob right had the opposite effect. He moved the chair to its original forward-facing position and flipped the switch below the first knob. Nothing happened, but when he pushed the next lever forward, the automaton stepped forward. When he used the controls on each side, the machine marched forward three steps and then back.

He'd seen enough. He wasn't sure what Hornsby was using the automatons for, but they could shoot, which meant these were killing machines. He hoped Mrs. Hornsby was over her crying. He'd like to get out of here before the police arrived. Of course, that wasn't exactly the right thing to do. If Mr. Hornsby did murder the entire Wong family and bury them here, then his wife probably shouldn't be left alone.

CHAPTER 43: ALROY

BAD NEWS

July 20, 1890
8:30 p.m.

Alroy's worries turned out to be moot. Before he reached the top of the stairs, he heard the police. He found Wyatt and two police officers in the kitchen, looking down at Toby and Mrs. Hornsby. When his brother saw him, he frowned and motioned him over to the table.

"One of you tell me exactly what happened."

Wyatt had a small notebook and pencil ready to take notes.

"Now," Wyatt said.

Toby rattled off the story. Mrs. Hornsby confirmed what he said. She wasn't crying now, and her voice had that harsh edge she'd had at the laundry.

Wyatt turned to Alroy.

"Want to add anything?"

"Yeah, I found this." He handed Wyatt Pedro's note. "There are two automatons in the basement. They are designed to be ridden by a medium-sized man. They march forward, back-wards, can turn, and, most importantly, they shoot bullets from their fingers. From the design, I'd guess a gear system pulls the bullet through the legs and body to the fingers. Theoretically, they could shoot pretty fast. There are hundreds of bullets in each one. Pedro took out the control system."

"And the note?"

"Pedro's handwriting. He was here and dismantled the trigger mechanism."

Toby looked as if he were going to snatch the note from Wyatt, and Alroy was hoping his friend wouldn't try. Wyatt noticed Toby's anxious movements and handed him the paper.

The detective looked at Mrs. Hornsby and then at Alroy.

"Did the boys have your permission to look around?" Wyatt asked.

She nodded.

Wyatt studied Alroy for a moment.

"You think Hornsby caught him? Could he be down there?"

He shook his head.

"I found the note inside the automaton, which probably means Hornsby hadn't found it yet. All I know for sure is Pedro's been here. He's not in the basement, but Mr. Hornsby might know something."

"He told me he didn't hurt Pedro or know where he was," Mrs. Hornsby said. "I threatened to shoot him again if he didn't tell the truth. He's a coward. He would have told me."

Wyatt rubbed his chin. His frown deepened.

"What do you two have to say for yourselves?"

Toby shrugged.

"Nothing. Except we aren't in Sonora Town," Alroy said.

He waited for Wyatt to get angry, but he didn't. His bother looked tired and resigned.

"Mrs. Hornsby, do you have someplace to go? Someone you can stay with for a couple of days? We're going to have to dig up the basement. This is a possible crime scene."

"I have a sister," Mrs. Hornsby said, "across the river on Maple Street. "

"Johnson, let her pack a few things, and take her over there. Lewis, you stay here. Rope this place off. I'll send some more officers over." He pointed to Alroy. "You two, come with me."

Wyatt walked outside, and they followed.

In the west, the setting sun painted the sky oranges and yellows with streaks of gray. It meant another day had gone by, and Pedro was still missing.

"Don't either of you say a word."

Wyatt waited for a response, so Alroy nodded.

"I apologize for my earlier words. I misspoke and was harsh. I'm sorry. It's important to find Pedro, and I shouldn't dismiss your concerns. It's apparent I can't stop you two or your sister from being involved in this, so at least try to work with me. Tell me what information you have. Agreed?"

Alroy glanced at Toby, who nodded. It didn't seem they had much choice. Everything they'd discovered hadn't led them to Pedro.

Alroy also nodded in agreement.

"Good," Wyatt said. "Here's what I know. We decoded the map. I've talked to Garcia, Doctor Grimes, Mr. Lee, and we found Hornsby. We arrested him for being drunk and disorderly. The doctor is taking care of his wound. Then we'll put him in a cell."

Wyatt shook his head and rubbed his chin as if thinking about what he would say next.

"The others don't seem to know anything about Pedro," he finally added. "Jonah Lopez's in jail for smuggling and human trafficking. If he knows about Pedro, he's not talking. Officer Henderson is being investigated. He kicked Pedro's family out of their home and took over their boardinghouse. All illegal. I went by the house and tried to talk to Zella, but she wouldn't let me in the attic and refused to talk to me. Unless you two know something you haven't told me, I'm at a loss."

Alroy didn't know he could feel so discouraged. For a brief moment, he hoped Pedro ran away and was safe someplace, but he knew that wasn't true. His friend would not run away. Their last hope was Zella. Maybe she found something in Pedro's second notebook.

"We need to go home. Zella's reading Pedro's second notebook. We found it on his bicycle at Mr. Lee's house. We think he was riding it the night he went missing. Mr. Lee found his bike," Alroy said, while Toby vigorously nodded.

Wyatt looked down the street.

"There's one more thing."

His voice sounded deep and hollow as if he were going to say something terrible. His eyes, which Alroy hardly ever noticed, looked sad. He had the same look their father had when he told Alroy his dog, Skeeters, had died.

"It's not good news. You're going to have to prepare for the worst."

Toby bit his lower lip.

"I don't know how things could be worse than what I've been imagining," Toby said.

Wyatt forced a half-hearted smile.

"I read your book. I'm guessing your mind is full of all kinds of horrible thoughts. But this is serious. I sent an officer to fetch the bones in the alley. Our doctor examined them. They are human."

Alroy swallowed.

"Human? Are they Pedro's bones?"

He and Toby figured the bones could be human, but, until this moment, he hadn't thought they might be Pedro's bones. His mind was screaming things at him, things that were ugly and horrible, and he just wanted to stop thinking.

"They are the bones of a small man or a younger man. I want

you to hang onto this thought. The alley is not close to any of the people Pedro was investigating. This might not have anything to do with Pedro."

Toby stepped closer to Alroy and gently nudged his shoulder.

"We will," Toby said. "But how can someone only have the bones of a person?"

Wyatt shook his head.

"I don't know. I've never seen anything like this before. The thing is I can't do my job tonight if I'm worried about you two and Zella getting into more trouble. Your mother seems to be doing a little better. If she figures out what you've been doing, she's going to start worrying. Please, can you go home and stay put for the night."

"Yes, we'll do that," Alroy said. "If you find out something tonight, will you tell us, even if we are asleep?"

"Yes. I'm not sure when I'll be home. I have a lot of work. I've called in two other detectives to help with the paperwork and follow-up. We'll find out what happened to Pedro."

"By the way, Old Elijah found the bones. He was pretty upset, saying that a vampire threw the bones away. Maybe he saw someone," Toby said.

Wyatt wrote in his notebook as Toby spoke.

"I'll send the men out to find him. Tomorrow, I'll search all the homes and businesses of the people on your list. You two get home."

As they walked toward their bicycles, Wyatt said, "Wait."

"Ernest wants to talk to Toby. Stop by his office. He phoned me before I came over here. It's late, but he's waiting for you."

"Where?" Toby asked.

"Main 231, second floor."

Wyatt nodded and waved them away.

"What does Ernest want?" Alroy asked as they walked toward their bikes.

"He's helping me with my father. Maybe he talked to him?"

"You want to talk to him alone?"

"Naw. You know my father. He's not going to make this easy."

They rode in silence the rest of the way.

Beside him, Toby stared straight ahead, his lips pressed together.

Alroy hoped with all his heart Ernest didn't have more bad news for his friend. With all their worrying about Pedro, he'd forgotten how bad life was for Toby. Knowing Mr. Bailey, Alroy figured the man was mean enough to make Toby wish he'd never been born.

CHAPTER 44: ZELLA

WHAT WOULD NELLIE BLY DO?

July 20, 1890
8:30 p.m.

Zella read as fast as she could. The new entry she'd found was about Dr. Grimes and his time machine.

Pedro talked about the experiments with rats and how none of the tests worked. Later, the rats would vanish for five or ten minutes, but then they reappeared dead. So whatever the time machine was doing to them or wherever it was sending them, the rats didn't survive. Pedro wrote about this as if he were excited. The boys believed the time machine was working.

Zella wasn't sure if any of this was important. They had all been reading *The Time Machine* by H. G. Wells. Toby finished it. Alroy was almost finished with his copy, which he was going to let Zella read. So she didn't know much about it except that her brother thought it was corker. She hated that crass word, but he used it all the time.

As she continued reading Pedro's notes, she noticed that the little marks on the side of the notebook were words written so small she couldn't make them out.

She rushed to the cabinet and took out their magnifying glass. Placing it over the scribbles, the words immediately were big enough to read. Ethics. He'd written ethics again and again beside his account of the time machine. She couldn't figure out why ethics would be significant, unless Pedro was concerned about using rats to experiment, but she doubted that. There had to be something else. She reread the passages looking for anything that might be a clue. She'd skimmed over the section that some of the rats came back from their time travel as bloody bodies.

As she puzzled over this, she remembered the copy of *The Time Machine* Dr. Grimes had told her to take from his office. She wasn't sure where she put it. It wasn't in her bag, or with the other papers on the worktable. She searched the room and found it on the floor beside one of the armchairs.

Plopping onto the chair, she took the piece of bread left on the plate. She took a bite, spat it out, and drank a glass of water to get rid of the stale taste. She turned her attention to *The Time Machine*. On the inside cover, Pedro's handwriting grabbed her attention.

Why would he leave his book at Dr. Grimes? He treasured his books and was very careful of them. Why did he write in the margins? He wouldn't do that unless it was important. She began flipping through the pages. On page fifty-two, she found a note.

"What if he used humans to experiment?"

Did Pedro mean the man in the book? Or Dr. Grimes? Why would he make a note about Doc in his book? That didn't make sense. In his notebook, he'd connected ethics to Doc's time machine experiments.

What if Doc were experimenting with people? No, she didn't like the man, but that would be beyond what she could imagine him doing. She returned to Pedro's notebook and read faster, skimming and looking only for entries about Doc. Then she found one that sent her heart racing.

Pedro found bones. He guessed they were dog bones. Doc put them into a bag and left. Later he returned without the bag.

On the back page, he wrote, "Doc was kicked out of college without earning his PhD. I wrote to his father. He replied, explaining Doc was kicked out of school for doing unethical experiments. He cautioned me against pursuing a friendship with him. Is Doc dangerous?"

She flipped through all the pages and held the notebook up and shook it, but there was no letter. Flipping back to where she left off, she began reading again.

"Today, when I was sweeping up Doc's work area, I heard something downstairs. It sounded like someone crying. I couldn't go down and check because the door was locked. When Doc got back, I told him about it, but he said it was nothing, just a stray cat that got in through the window. I wanted to believe him, but I'd heard other noises coming from the basement, but they were muffled scurries, mice or rats maybe. These noises weren't the same."

"On the way home, I went around back to peek in through the basement window. The windows were painted black and nailed closed. It would have been impossible for a stray cat to get inside the basement. I'm going back tonight after Doc has gone home to see what's in the basement. I've made a key. I'm worried about what's in the basement."

"Doc," she said to herself. "It's been Doc all along."

She raced downstairs and found Liza in the kitchen making tea.

"Where's Wyatt?" she asked.

"Went back to work."

She raced into the hall. Sitting down and taking deep breaths to calm her voice, she lifted the telephone receiver and asked for the police station.

"Sergeant Landry."

"I want to speak to Detective Doyle, please."

"Sorry, miss, the detective is out on a case. I can leave him a message."

"Yes, please. Tell him to look for Pedro Hernandez at Dr. Grimes' workshop. In the basement. Tell him Zella phoned."

She hung up and peeked in the parlor, where her mother sat sewing. From the window, she could see the tip of the sun descending. Oranges, yellows, and reds streaked the skyline. It would be dark soon. As if her mother sensed her presence, she turned her head toward the door.

"Do you need something, Zella?"

She wanted to say *yes* and tell her mother everything that had been happening, but she couldn't. Since her mother had come back to life, she seemed fragile and weak. Zella thought one more sad thing might destroy her.

"No, Mama. I just came to tell you I'm going over to Grace's for a while."

"That's fine, dear. It'll be dark in an hour or so. Ask Ernest to walk you home."

"Alroy will bring me home," she said and added, "I'll light the lamps for you."

She tried not to hurry as she lit the lamps. Her mother might notice her agitation. When she finished, she kissed her mother on the cheek.

Her mother touched her face and patted her cheek.

"My beautiful girl. I love you."

"Please don't go away again," Zella whispered.

"Of course not, dear."

Her mother turned back to her work.

Zella promised herself she would never be weak, never let sadness or disappointment or mourning overwhelm her.

She rode her bike to Grace's. If she could get Ernest to go with her, they could go to Doc's and see if Pedro was in the basement. Inez opened the door and told her that Grace and Ernest were out. She invited Zella to wait as they should be home soon. Zella declined but left them a brief note.

I believe Mr. Grimes is building a time machine and may be using humans as test subjects. I think Pedro found out and has been kidnapped or used as a test subject. I am on my way to his workshop. I've left word for Wyatt. I thought since you know of such matters, you might be able to help me retrieve Pedro, who is probably locked in Grimes' basement.

She handed the note to the maid.

"Please give this to them as soon as they return. It's very important."

"Of course, dear."

"One other thing, ah, do you have a hammer I could borrow?"

"Um, if there is one, it's in the shed around back. Make sure and return it," Inez said.

Parking her bicycle in front of the shed, she used the light to search for a hammer. The tools were arranged neatly on the wall. She grabbed one of the hammers and closed the shed. If the windows were nailed shut, she could pry the nails out or break the glass and crawl inside.

She knew her actions were reckless, but she pushed down her fear and rode as fast as she could. A growing urgency braced her nerves. As she neared Doc's workshop, her mind argued for caution, urging her to wait for help to arrive. It wasn't logical to charge in without knowing the circumstances. Her reasonable self lost. She couldn't sit, staring at the truth, and ignore Pedro's danger.

What would Nellie Bly do?

Bly was her hero. She was the best investigative reporter in the world. Zella didn't think Bly would stop pursuing a story simply because she was scared. She wouldn't either.

CHAPTER 45: ZELLA

DOC'S WORKSHOP

July 20, 1890
9:00 p.m.

Half a block from Doc's, she stopped. She could see his workshop. The light was on. She left her bicycle by Franklin's Bakery and crept closer to see if she could peer in the window. Doc sat at his desk, writing in his notebook. She returned to the spot where she'd left her bicycle and thought for a moment. She was small enough to fit through a basement window. But breaking the window would make noise. Maybe she could wait until Doc left and then go in through the window.

She just had to figure out how to break the window without making noise. Breaking glass was a major stumbling block. What she needed was noise, but the street was quiet and no one was in sight. The logical action would be to wait for Doc to leave, or wait for Wyatt and the police. She dismissed both ideas because Doc might be in there for hours, and Wyatt might not get her message.

When she thought she'd exhausted all her options, she thought of Morse code.

Racing to the back of the building, she found Doc's narrow basement window. She was small enough to squeeze through, but Pedro probably couldn't climb back out. It was getting darker, and there weren't lights in the alley. She wished she'd brought her night-vision goggles. Kneeling down, she examined the window.

Tugging on the lip of the windowsill, she tested to see if she could open it. It didn't budge. Although she couldn't see or feel nails on the window frame, she assumed Pedro was right, and the windows were nailed closed.

Behind her, something fell, and the sound echoed through the alley. Still kneeling, she kept still. After a few seconds, she slowly turned. Squinting, she scanned the area in both directions but saw nothing. Next to her were two large trash containers. A cat jumped from the fence to a container and ran past, screeching into the night.

The light at Doc's back door came on.

She rushed to the side and hid behind the trash. Peeking out through the small opening between the containers, she watched as Doc stepped into the alley and glanced around.

"Is anyone there?" he called.

He took a few steps and paused. Then he walked down the alley toward Zella. Glancing around, he noticed the lid off one of the trash cans and replaced it.

She held her breath and suppressed the urge to run.

Doc took a half turn. If he moved a step closer and looked to his right, he would see her. He paused for a few moments and walked back to his workshop, closing the door behind him. Zella waited for her racing heart to return to normal before moving back to the window.

She took the hammer out of her bag and placed it on the ground beside her. Very gently, using her index finger, she tapped out Pedro's name in Morse code. She waited. No response. She tried again. This time she heard a metallic clank as if chains were sliding along the ground. Then the sound of something hitting metal.

Dash-dot-dash-dash dot dot-dot-dot. Yes.

He was there! She grinned as she tapped out:

How do I get in? Zella.

The seconds ticked by as she waited.

Go to police.

Are you safe?

Yes. With other boys. Go now.

Before she could reply, someone yanked her upright, and a large hand covered her mouth.

"Who do we have here? Ah, Miss Doyle. You and your family are becoming an annoyance."

Doc's hot breath on her neck made her shudder.

She kicked at his shins and tried to hit him. She kept struggling hoping to get loose so she could grab the hammer. But he was strong. No matter how hard she struggled, he held her tight.

She bit his hand as hard as she could.

When he moved his hand, she yelled as loud as she could.

"Help. Help. Help."

He lifted her up. Holding her like a sack of potatoes, he carried her inside.

She yelled, screamed, and called for help.

"My dear, there is no one to hear you. At night, this street is deserted."

He sounded eerily normal.

She screamed, loud and long.

He clamped a hand over her mouth. Dragging her to his coat rack, he fumbled in the coat pocket. He shook out the white handkerchief he'd retrieved. He released her mouth. When she screamed, he stuffed the cloth into her mouth. She choked. The fabric caught on the back of her throat. She reached up to pull it out, but he yanked her arms down, pinning them to her side.

His face was inches from her. He smiled.

"No one can hear you, but your banshee screams annoy me. Did you think I wouldn't know Morse code?"

He lifted her, letting her kick her legs, and carried her down to the basement. Two dim overhead lights illuminated the stairs. Below, she saw Pedro staring up at her, another boy crouched in the corner, and a slack-jawed boy watched. Doc put her down, holding her tight with one arm pinning her arms down. Using his other hand, he fumbled with his keys.

She butted him with her head. He yelped and his arm relaxed. She darted away.

"Take your hands off her," Pedro yelled.

Doc laughed.

Zella's head throbbed, and little streaks of lightning pain shot through her forehead where she'd hit him. She made it up four steps when he grabbed her by the hair, yanking her head back and pulling her into his arms.

"Stop it. Let her go," Pedro yelled. "Stop."

Her head burned where he yanked her. He dragged her back toward the cage.

"Stop. You're hurting her," Pedro screamed.

The cloth in her mouth had sucked up all the moisture in her throat, and breathing hurt her throat.

"You two stand back," Doc said.

"No, don't put her in here," Pedro said.

She squirmed and tried to get out of his grip, but stopped fighting when he squeezed her so tight she couldn't breathe.

Chains rattled as Pedro stepped in front of the cage door.

"Let her go. Don't put her in here."

Doc shrugged.

"Suit yourself," he said, slamming the cage door closed.

He yanked her backward. Grabbing the rope on the wall in

front of them, he used it to tie her hands together. The course fibers scratched her wrists. He worked fast looping over and over. Dragging her back toward the stairs, he pushed her down and tied her wrists to the banister.

All the while, Pedro called out, begging him to stop.

He rushed back to the cell, unlocked it, and pulled one of the boys to his feet. He undid the lock that held the boy's chains in place and pushed him forward, slamming the cell door and locking it.

"Now, my boy, I have a surprise for you. I'm going to set you free."

Zella stared at the boy. She knew him. Elijah Rojas. He didn't speak. He stared at Doc and didn't try to fight or run. His mouth was slack and his face expressionless.

"What are you doing?" Pedro asked.

"Come, lad." Doc dragged the boy toward the large chair in the corner of the room.

Seeing the chair, the boy pushed against Doc, fighting to get away. His efforts were useless. The man held him tight. Realizing he couldn't win, he went limp and began to weep.

"Please, don't," he begged.

"Now, now, be brave, and all will be well."

Zella didn't know what was happening, but she knew that Elijah was frightened. Pedro rattled the bars of the cage. The boy who'd sat back in the cage silent and unmoving stood, walking forward until he stood next to Pedro. Together the boys watched, their faces twisted in pain, as Doc placed the boy in the chair and began strapping him down.

"Please, don't," Pedro said, his voice little more than a whisper.

Zella realized what was happening. The chair had to be the time machine. He was putting Elijah in the machine.

She watched as Doc took a small notebook from his jacket

pocket, scribbled a quick note, and placed it in the boy's trouser pocket.

"I'm going to send you back thirty-five years. When you get there, you'll have about five minutes before the machine comes back. I'm going to release your hand restraints, so you'll be free to get out. When you get out, take the note and place it in this pocket."

He pointed to a pouch on the side of the chair. He reached into his pocket and took out a couple of bills and a few coins. Again he placed those in the boy's pocket.

"These are to help you start your new life. When you land, put the note in the pouch, get out quickly, and step far away from the machine. If you return with the machine, I'll shoot you. When I release your restraints, hang on to the machine so you'll land safely. Do you understand?"

The boy nodded.

"Tell me what you are going to do?

"Hang on tight. Leave the note in the pocket. Get out and get far away from the machine."

"Good lad."

Doc went to the old desk in the corner and opened a drawer. He held up a gun for them all to see.

"If you try to leave the machine, I'll shoot you."

Elijah nodded, his head shaking rapidly.

Doc cranked the machine. The sound of turning gears filled the room. Then he untied the boy, pointing the gun at him.

"Everything will be fine," Doc said.

Elijah whimpered and looked pleadingly at Pedro and the other boy.

Zella wished she could cover her ears as the sound from the machine became louder and louder. She glanced at Pedro. Both he and the other boy stared at Elijah, who seemed frozen in place as he stared at the boys in the cage.

The machine whined and vanished, reappeared, and

vanished again. After a few seconds, the device disappeared completely. An eerie silence settled over the basement.

Doc took out his pocket watch and paced as he stared at the timepiece. Pedro stared at the spot where the machine had been, tears running down his face. The other boy moved back to his place in the corner.

If Pedro's notes were correct, Elijah was probably dead. He was a couple of years older than Zella. It wasn't his shabby clothes or his unkempt hair that people noticed but his smile and sweet attitude. He always smiled and laughed. Now he was gone. Pedro held the bars of his cage and stared at the spot where the time machine had been. The other boy wept openly.

Zella's mind felt numb with disbelief. She'd read Pedro's notes and knew the horror of what had happened to Elijah.

This was worse than any of Toby's stories.

CHAPTER 46: TOBY

THE BARGAIN

July 20, 1890
9:00 p.m.

Toby thought it was odd for Ernest to be working so late. He wondered if something was wrong or if his father had done something else to exile him from his sister.

The office building on Main with its arched windows and brick walls blended with all the other buildings. Inside, an aura of business-like efficiency and emptiness reigned. A wide stairway invited clients to the upper floors. On the wall, a sign listed occupants and office numbers.

Alroy pointed to the stairs, and Toby followed him up. The quiet halls echoed with their footsteps. Sudden laughter from a nearby office startled Toby and broke the creepy spell of impending ruin.

For a fleeting moment, he thought about writing a book about an invisible man cursed to walk the halls of a quiet building but doomed never to interact with the people who came in and out.

The thought of what Ernest had to say about his father made

his eyes twitch. Also, he felt as if he might throw up and be sick all over the shiny waxed floors.

He took a deep breath and tried to smile. He didn't want Alroy or Ernest to know that he was scared sick. He'd pretend everything was all right because he firmly believed life's problems had a way of working out, one way or another. Right now, he'd face whatever negative news came his way.

Three doors down the hall, Alroy stood, staring at Ernest Camero's name on the door. Toby noted his friend's pale face, which surprisingly helped his mood. He shrugged off the desire to run and, trying for a devil-may-care look, grinned. Might as well get the interview over.

Inside, a gorgeous black-haired girl with green eyes and a heart-shaped face sat at the reception desk. Lisa, the girl of every boy's dreams, glanced up and smiled. Her smile made him feel as if the sun would shine day and night. He stepped forward and sat on the edge of her desk.

"Lisa, I didn't know you worked here. I don't know if you remember me, I'm Toby Bailey. Here to see Mr. Camero."

"Mr. Bailey, he's expecting you. You're the reason we are working late," she chided. "Take a seat. I'll let him know you've arrived" She glanced at Alroy. "And you are?"

"Alroy Doyle. I'm with Toby."

Her smile widened.

"Are you related to Detective Wyatt Doyle?"

Alroy sighed.

"He's my brother."

"He's very brave."

Toby could have sworn he heard her sigh before she entered Ernest's office.

"You should have said, 'So am I.'" Toby winked.

"You know she was three or four years ahead of us at school. She's practically a grown woman."

"Does it matter?" Toby asked.

Alroy laughed and shook his head.

"No, it doesn't. She's—"

"Striking," Toby said.

"Yes."

The office door opened and the receptionist stepped out, leaving the door ajar.

"He's ready for you."

From the satisfied look on her face, Toby surmised she knew they'd been talking about her. She wasn't displeased. He smiled and nodded as he stepped through the door.

"Come on in," Ernest said. "Lisa, you may go home. Thanks for staying late."

Ernest's office was more impressive than the reception area. Bookcases filled with leather-bound books lined two walls. The man had more books in his office than Toby's father had in his library. Most of the titles were law books, but mixed in were books of all sorts, history, science, architecture, biographies, and even novels. Some of them Toby would like to borrow. He was so caught up in looking at the titles that Alroy poked him twice before he realized Ernest had told them to take a seat.

"Sorry. The books," Toby said.

"Books are a good thing to distract a man," Ernest said as he took a seat behind his desk.

Toby sat down and stared at the large painting of Los Angeles on the wall behind the desk. He wasn't sure what to say.

"I spoke to your father this afternoon," Ernest said. "He's not a cordial man."

"Uh, no, he's not. I take it I'm not going to get anything I asked for?"

Ernest grinned.

"I'm also not cordial when I need to be. We had an unpleasant exchange, in which he made many threats. After I explained I planned to file a suit against him and to send the details to the newspapers here and those in San Francisco, he hung up on me. A few hours later, he called back. We came to an agreement. If the terms are acceptable to you, we can proceed. I called you here this late because I believe we should settle this quickly."

Toby let out the breath he'd been holding. Alroy glanced at him and nodded.

"What are the details?" Toby asked.

"I did some investigating, and your family's holdings both here and in San Francisco are extensive. Your father's probably more wealthy than you imagine. He's kept a low profile here, but in the bay area, he's well-known and influential."

"Is that good?"

"Well, it gave me bargaining power I didn't think I'd have," Ernest said.

He leaned back in his chair and smiled at Toby.

"My sister? Can I see my sister?"

"Yes. He will allow you and her to correspond, and she can visit twice a year accompanied by a companion."

Toby nodded.

"There are conditions. You'll agree that you, as in Rebecca Bailey, died in a boating accident. Apparently, that's the story he's told everyone. Plus, you'll change your surname and never contact him or ask for money."

"Sure," Toby said.

"Wait until you hear everything before you agree. I think I've managed a good deal for you, but not everything is favorable."

"Okay. Tell me the bad stuff first," Toby said.

"Do you really want to change your name?" Alroy asked.

"Sure. It doesn't matter."

"Your sister's correspondence and the visits are conditional on your sister's willingness to interact with you."

Toby nodded again.

"Your mother doesn't want to see you. This is what your father says. I wasn't permitted to speak to her."

"She'll never go against his wishes," Toby said. "I understand."

"He's willing to give you a liberal settlement and a yearly income. However, he wants a guardian to control and manage the money and property until you are twenty-five."

Ernest watched him closely as if he were waiting for him to object.

"Who's the guardian? I'm sure he chose someone who won't allow me to have any liberty," Toby said.

"Well, he suggested me, but someone else volunteered."

Toby glanced at Alroy, who leaned forward, waiting for Ernest to continue.

"Wyatt volunteered, but only if you agree. He wants to talk to you before you decide. If you have strong objections, I can inform him."

Toby stared at the painting of Los Angeles. Wyatt? Wyatt didn't like him. Why would he want to do this? Wouldn't Ernest be better?

"I don't think that's a good idea," Alroy said. "What about you?"

Ernest shook his head.

"I'm not guardianship material. I'm more of a man-about-town man. Irresponsible and carefree." He shrugged.

"I guess I'm not opposed to Wyatt," Toby said. "But he doesn't seem to like me."

"Wyatt won't necessarily be easy. He will be fair, guide you, and help you. You'd be lucky to have him on your side. As far as not liking you, you'll have to talk to him about that."

"What if I say no to Wyatt? What happens?"

"The court will appoint someone. I'd imagine they'll ask for your father's input."

"Oh. That doesn't sound good."

A stranger would be a lot worse than having Wyatt watching over his finances. He could stay close to Zella and

Alroy, but he'd have to figure out if Wyatt would let him be himself.

"What kind of settlement are we talking about?" Toby finally asked.

Ernest shuffled through the papers on his desk until he found one that appeared to be a list.

"He will start a trust fund for you, which will include the house you have been living in and its furnishings, stocks in Standard Oil, Union Pacific Railroad, 100 shares of his company, and twenty thousand dollars."

Toby listened with a growing sense of disbelief. His father had never been generous with him, and this sounded like a fortune, the kind of settlement someone made on a beloved son.

"He came up with all these concessions?" Toby asked.

"Let's say, I nudged him into agreeing. Since everything will be held in trust, he will provide you with an annual income of two thousand a year to be distributed at your trustee's discretion. There are lots of details, which will be in the paperwork," Ernest said.

"My father talks as if he's on the brink of financial ruin. He has this much money?"

"He has more than enough, and he didn't make the agreement willingly. There's one more item, your mother. He steadfastly refused to allow you to see or communicate with her. He wants you to agree that you will never make any effort to see or communicate with her. I know from our previous talk that you weren't interested in seeing her. She is your mother, and you may regret that decision in the future. I would counsel you to reconsider."

Toby shook his head. He couldn't imagine he'd change his mind. Ernest drummed his fingers on his desk.

"I believe I could negotiate something. Such as, if she wishes to contact or see you, she would be allowed to do so. Think about it, and talk with Wyatt as soon as possible. I want to hurry this process. If we give him too much time, he may reconsider his generosity. Consider your options and what you might want in the future."

Ernest continued talking and explaining more details, but Toby couldn't concentrate. It was suddenly real that he was alone. He knew the money was important, but it didn't make up for the fact his father and mother didn't want him. Maybe even his sister would be embarrassed to know him. Once he changed his name, he'd no longer be himself. Maybe he didn't want to change his name. Maybe he didn't want to make it so easy for his father to walk away. Maybe his parents told his sister he was dead, and she'd never contact him.

Ernest held out an envelope with the papers Toby was supposed to read. Alroy was standing, looking at him, waiting for a response.

He grabbed the envelope.

"Thank you," Toby said.

"This is a lot to take in," Ernest said. "Think it over. Wyatt has a good head for these things. Take his advice and come and see me anytime to answer any questions you have."

"I feel lost," Toby whispered. "I've never been this alone."

"You're not alone," Alroy said.

Toby glanced at his friend. "I know. It's just. . . . I don't know."

"There's a hole inside you, and you don't know if it will ever fill up again," Alroy said.

"That's it. Is that how you feel without your father?"

"Yes. You're not alone. We'll get through this together."

Toby forced a wide grin.

"Let's go."

At the door, he turned back to meet Ernest's gaze.

"Make my father pay your legal fees," Toby said.

"I already added that into the deal."

"Excellent."

Outside, Toby looked around and shook his head.

"Everything is strange. Would you mind if I accept Wyatt's help?"

"No, but he's a jerk. You know that, right?"

"Yeah, but he's our jerk, and he's better on our side than not. And I might get someone who would be horrible."

Alroy put his arm around his shoulder, and they walked together.

He tried to look at the bright side. He wasn't penniless, and he had friends. If they could find Pedro, everything would be better. Maybe Zella already found something in the second journal. All he wanted to do was to get back to the attic and find out what Zella knew.

CHAPTER 47: ZELLA

TO THE FUTURE?

July 20, 1890
9:45 p.m.

Zella watched the villain pace.

A thin, whining sound broke the silence. She blinked her eyes because something like a shadow appeared and vanished and reappeared. By the third materialization, the empty machine sat in the same spot it had been in before it left.

Doc whooped and rushed to the machine. He reached into the leather pocket and pulled out the note he'd written, waving it in the air. He turned to the cage.

"There, my boy," he said, looking at Pedro. "We did it."

"*We* did not do anything." The hardness of Pedro's face matched the hatred in his voice.

"No matter. I thought you might want to share in my success."

The man rushed to Zella and began untying her. As soon as the rope was released, he grabbed her and dragged her across the room toward the chair. With her free hand, she yanked the rag out of her mouth.

"Help."

Her mouth was so dry the word came out as little more than a whimper.

He slung her into the large chair. As soon as he released her, she reached for her head. She wouldn't have been surprised if all her hair were gone, but it wasn't.

"Stop. Take me instead. I'll go." Pedro sounded desperate. He grabbed the bars with his hand and shook them. He repeated the words over and over.

Doc pushed her against the back of the chair and held her there. With his other hand, he placed her wrist inside the leather straps on the hand rest and pulled tight until the snap on the leather clicked into place.

She pushed and fought against him, but he was too strong. Both her arms were pinned down, and a belt around her waist strapped her into the chair.

Finally, he let her go.

"You can't get away with this." Zella had tried to yell, but her throat burned with each word she spoke.

Pedro, who had been saying *no* repeatedly, looked at her with tears rolling down his cheeks.

"Please. Take me. I'll go," Pedro pleaded.

The other boy sat on the cage floor watching them. He was thin and dirty with a hollow look of someone who hadn't eaten in a long time.

Doc bent down to strap her legs into the chair. Before he could touch her, she kicked, aiming for his head, but missed. She brought her knee up and knocked him in the chin. He fell back, cursing at her.

"Miss Doyle, if you don't stop fighting me . . ." He put his hand around her neck. "I will break your neck."

Pedro rattled the bars. "Stop, please. I'll go with you. Stop. Use me instead. Use me."

The hand around Zella's neck tightened. Her throat felt as if it were caving in and all her bones were breaking. She glanced over at Pedro, who moved back and forth like a wild animal, shouting and pleading. The boy sitting on the floor watched her. He shook his head very slowly, warning her not to fight. Black spots danced in her eyes, and darkness rushed toward her.

"Doc," the quiet boy said. "She's not fighting."

Her captor looked down and grinned.

"Even the shrewd boy speaks for you."

He let go of her.

Holding her throat, she gasped, sucking in as much air as she could.

"It would have been better for you to go into the cage. I'm reluctant to put a girl in this chair." He shrugged. "But it seems necessary."

"Let her go," Pedro said, pronouncing each word as if it were a weapon. "Let her go. I'll take her place."

Doc already had one of her ankles strapped into the chair. He worked on the other one without speaking to Pedro.

"Please," Pedro said. "I won't fight you. I'll cooperate. I'll be your assistant."

Zella's gaze met Pedro's. He still held the bars as if he were going to shake them. His head rested against the metal. She realized they were all trapped. Pedro didn't think she'd survive whatever Doc had planned.

The boy in the cage with him stared at her. He reminded her of her mother before she woke up. Doc muttered to himself, writing something in the notebook.

It was in that quiet moment that the smell overwhelmed her. The odor reminded her of an outhouse, a damp, rotting toilet that should have been replaced years ago.

The boy in the cage put his head on his knees as if he couldn't watch what was about to happen. Pedro kept pleading with Doc, and Zella realized that she was about to be hurtled through time to die. Strapped into the chair with a pounding headache, she tried to look calm.

"Pedro, don't worry, I phoned Wyatt before I came," she said. "He'll be here any second."

"Young lady, we'll be long gone before the police get here," Doc said.

"We?"

"Of course, I have to leave. I can't go to jail. Science demands I keep learning."

He grinned.

Zella saw a madman.

Trying to make her voice sound calm, she said, "Let me go. I promise I won't stop you. There's no reason to take me."

The man considered her for a moment.

"Perhaps you're right. Do I have your word? I would much rather not take an inferior person with me."

Zella waited for him to realize her idea would work.

"On the other hand, you are intelligent for a girl. You could help me with my experiments."

"Doc, take me. I'll go and be your assistant," Pedro said. "I'll help you. I know more about your work than she does."

The man glanced from Pedro to Zella.

"Yes, you make a good point. I'd much rather have your help, Pedro. Will you promise to help me without trying to escape?"

Pedro stared at Zella and nodded.

CHAPTER 48: ALROY

THE CAVALRY

July 20, 1890
9:45 p.m.

Alroy glanced at Toby as they rode back home. He wasn't sure about Wyatt being a guardian. His friend didn't think his brother was as bad as he did. The trouble was Toby had never really experienced Wyatt the way he had.

He also thought about how Wyatt acted at Mrs. Hornsby's house. He replayed their encounter over and over in his mind. His brother seemed to be trying to understand them and to keep his frustrations in check. He's changing tactics.

Should he be relieved? Was Wyatt changing? Or was it something else?

Alroy knew they were making Wyatt's job more difficult. Sometimes he felt a twinge of guilt, but mostly he didn't. No matter how hard he tried, he couldn't forget that Wyatt abandoned them.

When they reached home, they found the elevator in its bottom position rather than up by the attic window as they had left it. They took it up. The window was open a crack, just enough to get a hold and push it up. Zella wasn't there. The attic door was wide open. Pedro's second notebook, a copy of *The Time Machine*, and her notes were on the workbench.

Alroy rushed to the map.

Zella had written DOC!! in huge letters defacing the map.

His throat tightened. A slow, creeping fear swept over him. He couldn't believe Doc would have anything to do with Pedro's disappearance. He was their friend.

Alroy and Toby grabbed Zella's notes and began reading as fast as they could. According to Pedro's notes, Doc could be the one who knew where Pedro was.

He shook with rage. He grabbed the rock Zella used for a paperweight. Yelling out his frustration, he threw it at the wall.

"She's gone after Doc," Alroy yelled.

"Yeah," Toby said. He tapped the copy of *The Time Machine*. "This is Pedro's. He left it at Doc's."

"Listen to this," Alroy said, reading from Zella's notes, "Pedro heard something in Doc's basement. Doc wouldn't let him investigate and sent him home early. On his way home, Pedro checked Doc's basement windows. They were painted black and nailed closed." Alroy pointed to the notes. "Doc, underlined three times."

"Let's go. Now," Toby said.

"The time machine," Alroy said. "It worked. He brought the rat back alive. He told me he'd eventually have to test it on a human."

"The bones in the alley . . . like the rat that came back as a skeleton."

Toby's words felt like a punch in the stomach.

They were wasting time trying to convince themselves Zella was right. They couldn't stand here working things out when they didn't know where Zella was. He glanced at Toby and nodded.

He and Toby raced for the stairs.

They left the door open. Alroy figured if Wyatt came, he could get into the attic. For the first time in his life, he wanted Wyatt to come to the rescue. The boys marched downstairs, sounding like an invading army. They stopped when they saw Liza, standing at the foot of the stairs, arms crossed and frowning.

"What in the devil do you two think you're doing?"

"Where's Zella?" Alroy shouted. "It's important."

Liza looked perplexed for a moment.

"She told your ma she was going to see Grace."

Toby stood in front of Liza, who was blocking their way.

"Please move. We've gotta find her. She might be in danger," Toby said.

"Telephone Wyatt," Alroy said. "Tell him to get to Doc's as fast as he can. We think Zella went there to find Pedro."

Liza squinted at them but stepped aside.

"You children are going to be the death of your ma, and my nerves are stretched like a rubber band."

"Thanks," Alroy said as he rushed past her.

He stopped.

"Do you think she really went to Grace's?"

Liza's brows came together, and she glanced up at the ceiling.

"I pray to the Good Lord that she did. I heard her say she needed help 'cause Grace knows about time machines."

In seconds, the boys were out the door, on their bicycles, and headed toward Grace's house. Alroy pedaled faster than Toby. When he reached the Camero's yard, he hopped off his still moving bike, dropped it, and raced toward the house. The door opened as he raised his hand to knock. Grace started to find Alroy's hand inches from her face.

She recovered quickly.

"Good, you're here."

"Zella—"

"Yes, come with me." Grace moved toward the driveway as Ernest, driving an open carriage pulled by two automaton horses, stopped at the edge of the walkway.

Ernest jumped down and helped Grace into the back. His jacket opened just wide enough for Alroy to see the pistol strapped to his side. He signaled the boys to get in. Before they were seated, Ernest was back in the carriage. The horses jolted forward, slamming Alroy back into his seat. The automatons moved faster than real horses and were an indestructible force with gears pushing them forward and metal bodies armored against attack. Alroy made a mental note—someday he'd build one or more metal horses for himself.

Ernest sat in front with a rifle on the seat beside him. Alroy approved of his precautions. Grace held a crumpled-up note in her hand.

"We are on our way to Dr. Grimes' workshop," she said. "We have a general idea of its location. Since you boys know, please direct Ernest if he goes astray."

Toby nodded, climbed over the leather seat, and sat in front with Ernest.

Alroy leaned forward, "Where's Zella? We hoped she was with you."

Grace shook her head.

"Ernest and I were out. When we got home a few minutes ago, this note was waiting for us. Zella suspects Dr. Grimes of Pedro's disappearance and has left to find him. She telephoned the police and asked them to apprise Wyatt, but when we called, your brother was out on a case. Zella's message hadn't reached him. We asked the sergeant to send some officers."

For a moment or two, Alroy's head spun, and everything seemed foggy as if he were in a dream. He took several breaths to clear his head. What he wanted to do was to punch someone, but not the people in the carriage. He forced himself to think. Right now, the most important thing was to get to Zella and keep her safe. If it took every ounce of his self-control, he would be cool-headed.

He surprised himself when he growled, like some kind of feral animal. He glanced at Grace.

"Well done," she said. "My sentiments exactly."

"Zella went alone." He knew it was a dumb thing to say, but he said it anyway.

"She thinks Grimes is experimenting with human subjects, using them to test his time machine."

He nodded. He never thought Doc would use other people. The thought made him feel sick and disgusted. He realized that after all the years he'd known Doc, he didn't really know him. What kind of person could do that when he'd seen rats come back dead or with only their bones as remains? That the last rat had come back alive was a slight positive.

"We're almost there," Toby shouted.

"Quickly, tell me everything you can about the time machine," Grace said.

Alroy closed his eyes and pictured the machine. Then he began describing it in detail.

When he finished his description, Toby shouted, "The jewels or stones. He moves them when he experiments, testing the right position."

Grace leaned forward and took Alroy's hand.

"Picture the experiment with the rat that came back alive. Now imagine the jewels. What order were they jewels in?"

He closed his eyes, but he couldn't picture anything. Taking a deep breath, he tried again.

"Breathe, and let your shoulders relax," Grace said.

"Red, clear like a diamond, blue," he said.

"Both of you listen. Whatever happens, whatever we find, I want you to remove the clear stone."

As she spoke, she leaned over and felt under her seat. She pulled out a short crowbar and a screwdriver, handing one to each boy. The tools were small enough to slip into their belts. Grace continued searching and pulled out a wooden club.

"Crystals conduct electricity. It doesn't matter if you break it, just get it out of the chair."

"Why?" Alroy felt confused and didn't understand why she sounded so confident.

"Listen to her," Ernest said. "She knows more about time travel than Grimes could learn in a lifetime."

Alroy and Toby stared at Grace. Although she'd told him, he was marked as a time traveler, he'd forgotten all about the tattoos. He and Toby had discussed her and time traveling, but it was different when her brother flat out stated it. She didn't exactly look like the kind of person who would be a time traveler, but then he didn't know any other time travelers.

"How do you do it?" Toby asked.

"I move between dimensions. It's like opening a door to another place and walking through. What Grimes is doing is like driving an automaton through the door and taking out the entire wall or the entire building, which would tend to annoy the people or animals in that space. More importantly, he's broken dozens of traveling rules. He'll be hunted. I'm surprised I haven't already heard an outcry. We'll talk about all this at a more appropriate time. Right now, do what I say."

"There," Toby shouted. "The third building with the lights on."

Ernest pulled up in front of Doc's workshop.

CHAPTER 49: ALROY

THE SCIENTISTS

July 20, 1890
10:15 p.m.

"I'll go first," Ernest said, grabbing the rifle. "Stay behind me. No heroics."

He looked at Alroy.

"Don't charge in. That won't help your sister. Listen to Grace. We don't know what or who is in there. Let's not let anyone get hurt."

Alroy and Toby nodded. The boys and Grace stood behind Ernest as he tried the front door. It was locked.

Ernest shouted, "Grimes, open up."

There was no answer, which didn't surprise Alroy, who could hear a lot of noise coming from the basement. Alroy looked in the window and glanced around.

"Room's empty," he said. "The door to the basement is open."

"What's down there?" Ernest asked.

"He's never let us down there, but we're sure it's the time machine."

Grace stepped forward with a ring of four keys. Alroy

assumed they were skeleton keys like the ones Wyatt carried. She tried one key at a time.

"The time machine is down there," she said. "What the boy's described is a prototype."

The third key opened the door.

"Behind me," Ernest said.

The basement door stood open about four inches. Ernest nudged it little by little until it fully opened. Noises like gears turning and something metal moving mixed with shouting voices.

Alroy couldn't make out what was being said, but he knew the sound of a time machine and the voices of Doc and Pedro.

"Time machine, Pedro, Zella," he whispered, pointing down.

Ernest nodded and put his index finger to his lips. He stood against the wall on the open side of the door. Cautiously, he glanced around the door.

"Damn." He looked at Grace and whispered, "Zella is strapped in the machine."

"Did he see you?" Grace asked.

"No, he and Pedro are having a shouting match."

"Let me talk to him," Grace said.

Ernest looked at his sister the same way Wyatt looked at Alroy when he disapproved of his brother's request. She handed him her club and stepped into the doorway.

"Dr. Grimes," she shouted and walked down the steps as if she were making a social call.

Doc turned around. He stared at her, his face flushed and contorted in anger.

"What in the blazes are you doing here? And how did you get in?"

"The door was open."

Alroy couldn't believe how cheerful she sounded. She took two more steps.

"Stay right there, Miss Camero."

"Whyever for?" She took two more steps.

"I said *stay*." Doc's voice sounded hard, the cheerful camaraderie Alroy knew had vanished. "You see, I am about to send this young lady on a little journey."

"Nonsense." Grace kept walking down the steps.

Alroy stared at Ernest, expecting him to do something. But he waited.

"Stop her," Alroy whispered.

Toby nodded in agreement.

"Never underestimate an intelligent woman, especially when she's your sister," he whispered.

"Your time machine won't work," Grace shouted. "You have several things wrong, and if you send Zella in that contraption, I will be compelled to carry you into Hades."

"Madam, you are obviously deranged."

"Alroy, come down here," Grace called.

Ernest motioned him forward. He stood in the doorway, checking to make sure the crowbar was secure on his belt. He came down the steps.

"Stop right there." Doc grabbed Zella by the hair and yanked her head back.

Zella grimaced but didn't scream.

Alroy clenched his jaw. He wanted to fling himself at Doc, but he forced himself to stay calm.

"I'll send her away." Doc glared at Alroy. "You know what that means."

Alroy nodded.

He was two steps from the bottom. He didn't know what Grace planned to do, but whatever it was, he didn't think it was working. While Alroy and Doc had been exchanging unpleasantries, Grace had inched closer and closer to the machine.

"If you need a test rat, use me. Let Zella ago," Alroy said.

"He won't listen. I've been arguing with him to take me, but he's not a gentleman," Pedro said. "He'll send a helpless woman rather than do what he cannot."

The young man in the cage with Pedro clapped his hands, "Bravo, Pedro."

"I am not helpless," Zella said, her voice husky and taut.

Alroy stared at Pedro, who stood in a cage, chained, and holding onto the bars. His face and clothes were dirty. His appearance startled Alroy. The terror of the situation outweighed the joy of finding his friend.

"Pedro."

His friend was alive. They'd found him, and all he managed to say was *Pedro*. He should have been happy and thrilled, but all he could think about was Zella.

"Coward," Pedro shouted. "Hiding behind a woman like a cowering toddler."

"You whining little Mexican brat, shut up," Doc shouted.

He pulled harder on Zella's hair. She grimaced but didn't cry out.

"Get back, all of you." Doc's face contorted into a grotesque shape.

He reached toward the front panel of the machine and pulled a lever up. Gears began to turn.

"He's started the machine," Alroy shouted.

"Stop it." Pedro shook the bars of his cage.

Doc shouted incoherently, shaking his fist at Pedro.

While Doc shouted, Grace took two more steps toward the time machine. Moving faster than Alroy could believe, she reached over and grabbed a brass handle. Something sparked, and the gears slowed, grinding to a stop.

"Now," Grace said.

"What have you done?" Doc shouted, releasing Zella's hair.

Toby raced down the stairs. He and Alroy ran to Zella. Alroy began untying his sister, while Toby lodged his screwdriver into the crystal. Doc grabbed Toby's arm, yanked him away from the machine, and bent his arm behind his back, holding him close.

Ernest fired his rifle from the top of the stairs.

"That was a warning shot," Ernest said. "Raise your hands and step away from the machine."

Doc released Toby and raised his hands. Alroy finished unbuckling Zella's hands, while Toby undid the straps holding her legs. Once freed, she hugged Alroy as if she hadn't seen him in years.

His heart thumped and pounded in his chest. He pulled her close and hugged her tight.

"You're hurting me," she whispered.

He released her.

"Sorry. You scared the daylights right out of me."

"Pedro," she pointed to the cage and grinned. "I found Pedro."

Ernest was already down the steps, demanding a key to the cage.

"May I lower my hands?" Doc's voice sounded normal again, but never again would Alroy think of it as friendly.

Ernest had the rifle pointed at Doc's chest. "Yes. Slow movements. Hand the key to Grace."

"I refuse to touch that woman. She has something concealed in her hand. She will likely electrocute me."

"She has more power in her hand than you have in your entire brain."

Ernest grinned as if he'd made a joke. Whatever he meant, it wasn't funny.

"I'm going to reach into my pocket," Doc said. "I'll do it slowly. I don't like guns pointed at me. I will give the key to Miss Doyle."

"No, you won't," Alroy said.

Zella stepped forward. "I'll get it. I'm not afraid of him."

Doc's eyes narrowed as he glared at her.

"Your words are meaningless tripe." He held out the key. "Here."

When Zella reached out and grabbed the key, Doc yanked her hand, pulling her toward him. His left arm wrapped around her, pinning her arms to her side. He'd managed to pull a knife out of his pocket when he reached for the key. He held the blade to her throat.

CHAPTER 50: ALROY

DESTINATION UNKNOWN

July 20, 1890
10:30 p.m.

Alroy balled his fists.

"Stay calm. Stay calm," he whispered to himself.

When Toby moved toward Doc, Alroy grabbed his arm and pulled him back.

"I will slit her throat," Doc said.

Toby lifted his hands, signaling his assent. "I'm not moving."

Zella looked too passive as she tossed the key down and kicked it toward Grace.

The madman pressed the knife to her skin. Alroy saw the slight indentation and raised his hands as a signal of surrender.

"Miss Doyle, that feeble attempt to get the key to your friend is the last movement you'll make without my permission. I would hate to scar your pretty little throat. Sir," he continued, nodding toward Ernest. "Kindly lower your rifle and place it against the wall."

Ernest did as he was instructed.

Doc pulled Zella back a few paces. Grace had put her foot on the key and inched her way toward Alroy, dragging the key with her.

"Miss Camero, stop moving," Doc said.

"Sir, I'm moving toward Alroy because he looks very much like he's going to do something stupid. You are holding a knife to his sister's throat."

Alroy probably did look the part. As much as he wanted to hurl himself at Doc and beat him senseless, he wouldn't take a chance of putting Zella in jeopardy.

Doc grinned.

"Yes, I see you are correct. Alroy, my boy, I do like you, but I will not hesitate to do what I have to do to protect my science. One little girl is nothing in the universal scheme of things. So don't do anything foolish."

"You're a monster," Alroy said, stepping on the key when Grace lifted her foot.

Grace reached out and grabbed Alroy. He pretended to push her aside and kicked the key toward the cage. Unfortunately, it landed a couple inches short of the bars. The boy in the cage who had been still and silent stood up and came to the bars.

"The kid's right, Doc, you're a monster." The boy's voice sounded singsong, soft and menacing. "I've seen him put boys in that chair and send them to their deaths. They all came back mangled or dead or just a stack of bones. Or they don't come back. What are you going to do, Doc? Put us all in that machine? There are too many of us."

Alroy noticed that while the boy talked, Doc's face grew angrier, and his gaze moved from one part of the basement to another as if he were formulating a plan.

"Move your foot away from the key," Doc said.

The boy didn't move. Doc put a little pressure on the knife, and a thin red line appeared on Zella's neck. The boy immediately stepped back and raised his hands.

Doc relaxed.

"You're at an impasse," Alroy said.

"You fail to see the big picture."

Alroy couldn't understand how Zella could be so calm, which worried him. She looked very much like he felt when he was about to do something incredibly stupid, which he would do now, if Doc didn't have a knife to her throat. The only option he had was to pray she would be her usual cautious self.

"Now, you will all move to the staircase," Doc said.

Grace tapped him on the shoulder. "Alroy, back up."

Reluctantly he retreated with the others. Ernest stood on the bottom step, Grace, Toby, and Alroy gathered around him. The boy in the cage had sat back down, but Pedro held the bars of his cage as if he were trying to bend them apart.

"Doc," Zella's voice seemed too loud as if she'd meant to speak but had yelled. Everyone looked at Zella. "You have a time traveler right here, and instead of pursuing science and learning from her, you are acting like a fool."

"Your tricks aren't going to work, girl. My science is more advanced than anything Miss Camero knows. I am the only one who can see the future and understand what time travel means."

"That's not quite accurate," Grace said. "I have been time traveling since I was a child. There are many travelers." She pointed to his machine. "This is very primitive. If you allow me, I could give you pointers."

"That's enough," Doc said. "The girl and I are going to get into the machine. If anyone interferes before the machine is ready, I will kill her. Is that clear?"

He stepped backwards to the machine, forcing Zella to move with him. He sat in the leather chair and forced her to sit. He flipped the first switch.

"Doc," Pedro shouted. "I volunteer. Let her go. I'll get everyone upstairs. I promise no tricks. I'll be your hostage and go with you."

"No," Alroy chimed in. "She's my sister. I'll go."

"Sir," Doc said to Ernest. "I see you moving toward the rifle."

Ernest straightened up.

"Alroy," Doc said. "Show your good faith, and perhaps I'll substitute you for your sister. I do dislike the thought of taking a female into the future. I'd probably have to abandon her. You, on the other hand, might prove helpful. Go to the panel behind you."

Hope worked like a stimulant surging through Alroy's body. He nodded, deciding he'd do whatever it took to get this madman to release his sister.

Alroy turned around. At first, he didn't see the panel. When he looked closer, he saw a faint outline.

"Push to open it," Doc said.

He opened the panel door. Inside were two rows of switches, three on the top and three on the bottom.

"Flip the top right and bottom right switches up."

Alroy flipped the top. Nothing happened. He flipped the bottom, and a sound of gears rotating filled the room.

"What is that?" Ernest asked.

From the ceiling, two platforms, one on each west corner of the basement, began lowering to the floor. A large metal spherical object about two feet in diameter sat on the stand.

"Now, the two on the left," Doc said.

When he flipped the switches, identical platforms lowered from the east corners.

"The middle switches."

"Stop, Alroy." Ernest pointed his finger at Doc. "This will go no further until you explain yourself, sir."

"Gladly, but I believe Miss Camero knows what these objects are. Unless, of course, her skills in the sciences have been exaggerated."

"I lose my patience with you," Ernest hissed.

"They're bombs," Grace said. "From the looks of them, they are big enough to blow the block up."

"Several blocks." Doc smiled. "Now, here is what is going to happen. You, sir, are going to take everyone, except for Alroy and Pedro upstairs. Don't try to deceive me. My hearing and deductive skills are excellent. When I hear you have all left the building, I will send the girl up. I suggest you run as fast as you can to get away from this building. The boys and I are going to take a little trip in my machine."

"I will not leave these boys in your hands." Ernest took a step down.

Doc put pressure on the knife.

Zella squealed.

Ernest put his hands up in the air.

Footsteps sounded upstairs. It sounded as if a herd of cattle stampeded through Doc's workshop.

"Police. Police," Wyatt shouted.

Doc pushed the last two switches on the time machine. The gears began to turn. Grinding and humming sounds filled the air.

Wyatt burst through the basement door.

"Police. Pol—"

He stopped and stared at Zella before glancing around the room. He focused on the cage and then the bombs.

"Stop. Or the girl dies," Doc said.

The lights on the time machine flashed on and off.

Wyatt motioned his men back.

Alroy's heart raced, and his pulse pounded in his neck. Logic told him to stay put, but he couldn't let Zella go in that machine.

Something snapped inside him. He lunged forward and jumped into the air. As if someone else moved his body, he glided forward and grabbed Doc's hand. He felt the knife cutting his skin, but he yanked anyway. The knife flew out of Doc's hand.

Zella bit the man's arm. When he released her, she shoved him.

"Run," Alroy shouted.

Before he finished speaking, Zella raced toward Grace. Doc shouted something and grabbed Alroy by the arm. He jerked him into the machine's chair.

Alroy's whole body burned with a fury he'd never felt before. He punched Doc, who held him tighter. As Alroy fought, Doc held him by one hand, and with his other, he clung to the seat of the time machine. The mad scientist might have been bigger and stronger, but Alroy's unbridled rage gave him strength he didn't know he had.

The machine shook violently. Alroy knew they would disappear at any moment. His opponent must have had the same thought because, in their struggle, Doc reached out as if he were going to adjust the time gauge. In that second when Doc's hold on him was weaker, Alroy reached past Doc and twisted the gauge as hard as he could. He hoped his mentor would release him to adjust the settings.

"No, no, no," Doc shouted.

People shouted and yelled, but he couldn't understand the words.

He heard the bars rattle. Pedro screamed.

The movement around them slowed. Alroy watched people moving in slow motion.

Doc reached forward to readjust the settings. Doc's knife had wedged on the floor of the machine. Alroy grabbed it and pushed the blade under the clear stone. Using the knife as a lever, he popped the gem out of its casing.

He'd lost precious time going for the gem. The machine bounced and jerked. It was too late for him to jump away. He felt the big jolt that comes seconds before the device vanishes.

A peacefulness rolled over Alroy. He relaxed, falling toward his fate. Wherever Doc's time machine was going, he was going, too. The journey might take him to a new destiny or to his death.

Either way, it didn't matter. His sister was safe, and they'd found Pedro.

He glanced toward where he thought Zella would be but couldn't see her. He saw Grace, Toby, Ernest. Slowly, they turned toward him. Their mouths opened as they shouted. Toby reached out toward him.

Beside him Doc laughed hysterically, cackling like a crone in a storybook.

Alroy knew no one could help him.

CHAPTER 51: ALROY

BOMBS AWAY

July 20, 1890
10:15 p.m.

The thought he should be frightened passed through Alroy's mind. In seconds, he would disappear and leave everyone he knew behind. Beside him, a mad scientist laughed like a villain from one of Toby's books.

His only feeling was sadness. He tried to wave to Zella, but he couldn't move his hands.

One moment he watched all the people in the basement, and the next moment, a hand grabbed his shoulder and yanked him sideways.

At first, he thought a traveler had touched him again. But the slow speed he'd been experiencing shifted back to normal-life speed. One second, he sat next to Doc, and the next, he flew through the air, landing on top of someone. The impact knocked the breath out of his lungs. He sucked in air and slowly breathed in and out.

Less than four feet from him, Doc frantically adjusted the gauges. A moment later, the machine vanished.

Relief swept through Alroy's body. He lay back. All he could think of was that they were safe.

He turned his head to look at the person who had rescued him. He expected to see Toby, but Wyatt was already getting up. He held out his hand to Alroy, who took it. Wyatt pulled him into his arms. Without thinking about anything but that he was glad to see his brother, Alroy hugged him back. His brother's arms held him tight, held him safe.

Alroy rested his head against Wyatt's duster. He could smell the leather and hear Wyatt breathing as if he'd run a race. Wyatt kissed the top of his head and released him. Then, his brother grabbed Zella and Toby and scooped them up in his arms.

Ernest was inside the cage, undoing the chains that bound Pedro and the other boy. When Wyatt released Toby and Zella, they raced to Pedro. Alroy flung himself into the huddle around Pedro. The other boy stood back as if he didn't belong until Toby and Pedro reached out and pulled him into their circle.

Zella was the first to step back.

"You two smell like an outhouse," she said.

Pedro laughed, nodding in agreement.

Alroy felt like shouting for joy. He was sure he'd never been so happy. All he could do was stand there and watch everyone.

"The bombs," Grace said in her serene authoritative voice.

Grace stood by the bomb closest to Alroy. She directed Toby, who was already unscrewing the casing.

"Everyone, outside. I have a carriage." Ernest grabbed the boy who had been caged with Pedro. "You, too. Now."

As Ernest, the caged boy, Zella, and the Police marched up the stairs, Police whistles sounded. Pedro rushed to the bomb nearest the cage. Toby lifted the top casing.

"What should I do?" Alroy asked Grace.

She placed the screwdriver into his hand. "Help Pedro."

"No, get out of here," Wyatt shouted. "All of you."

Alroy ignored Wyatt and began unscrewing the casing.

"You know how to dismantle this thing?" he asked Pedro.

Pedro grinned.

"We'll find out."

"Goddamnit, get out." Wyatt took Grace's arm. "Out."

She jerked away from him.

"For the love of God, stop playing the knight in shining armor. Make sure those people are safe."

"I'm not letting you blow up."

"I have no intention of blowing up. I'll look after the boys. You know I can get them out of here in a flash. You evacuate everyone," Grace said.

From Alroy's point of view, Wyatt looked very much like a man who wanted to strangle a woman. But it only took him a second to concede. Alroy wondered how Grace was going to look after them, and what made Wyatt think she could. Maybe they would all hold hands as the building blew up?

Pedro grabbed the screwdriver from Alroy. Unconcerned with the drama going on around them, he quickly removed the casing. He studied the bomb, looking very perplexed.

"These are dummies," Pedro said. "He was bluffing."

Grace grinned at Wyatt.

"You knew that," Wyatt said to Grace.

"I was ninety-nine percent sure." Grace grinned and patted Wyatt's cheek. "Don't be annoyed. I have to have some fun too."

Alroy noticed the look that passed between them. For the first time, he wondered if his brother might be in love with Grace. He glanced away and winked at Pedro. The thought of his conventional brother in love with an eccentric scientist amused him. Pedro nudged him, and they shared the moment.

Now that they were safe, Alroy glanced around.

"Where do you think he went? Is he alive?" he asked Grace.

"If he is alive, wherever he went, travelers will notice and hunt him down. You can't go blasting holes in dimensions without repercussions," Grace said. "No questions, we'll discuss all this later."

"Right now," Wyatt said. "The story is that Grimes escaped."

His brother glanced at each in turn until they all agreed.

"Good. I'll handle the police department," Wyatt said.

"Come along." Grace headed for the staircase. "It's altogether vile down here. A petri dish of bacteria and disease."

As they trooped up the basement stairs, Alroy whispered to Pedro, "How are you?"

"I don't know. The last couple of days I was sure I was going to die, now I'm not. Strange. I feel strange."

"What do you think happened to Doc? You got a theory?" Toby asked.

"No. But I hope he went to Hell." Pedro's face looked as hard as his voice sounded.

"He could be in a worse place than Hell," Grace said matter-of-factly.

Ernest had moved everyone else several blocks away. He'd sent two policemen to get the fire department, just in case. They encountered Ernest a block away from Doc's, walking toward them.

"You boys okay?" Ernest asked.

Ernest lifted his brows when he glanced at his sister. She nodded. Alroy wasn't sure what exactly passed between them, but they had communicated something to each other.

"I've volunteered to take Pedro and his friend home. We'll drop these three off on our way back," Ernest said.

"Make sure and bathe before going to bed. With soap," Grace said as she marched past Wyatt, who looked at her as if he had a million questions.

For the second time, Alroy wondered how well his brother knew Grace. The time travel and the machine he accepted as if such things were part of life. He knew. He'd known for a long time. For a moment, he wondered if Wyatt kept time traveling events secret by using his position as a detective. That was a question for another time.

Ernest dropped Jaime and Pedro off in Sonora Town. Pedro whispered that Jaime didn't have anyone and would stay with him. Grace and Ernest waited in the carriage while Alroy, Zella, and Toby escorted them inside. Maria began crying and hugging Pedro as soon as she saw him. His mother came from behind the curtain, looking healthier than the last time Alroy had seen her.

"*Gracias,*" Mrs. Hernandez said as she pulled Pedro and Maria into her embrace.

Toby nudged Alroy and motioned his head toward the door where Zella waited, holding the door open for them. Alroy took one last look at his friend, who had one arm around his sister as he pulled his mother closer and kissed her on the cheek.

At home, Wyatt insisted on a bath before bed, and Doctor Stone checked them for injuries. After he bandaged Zella's neck, he examined Alroy's hand.

"Would you three do me a favor?" he asked as he wrapped Alroy's hand.

"Sure," Alroy said.

"Stay out of trouble for a week. I'd like to have a break from fixin' folks up. Most of all I'd like a hot dinner at home."

When everything settled down, Alroy stopped by Zella's room to say good night. Her door stood ajar. Through the crack, he could see their mother sitting by her bed. When his mother reached out and took her hand, she didn't pull away.

"I'm sorry," Zella said.

"For what?"

"For hating you. I didn't understand. I still don't, but I'm glad you are back with us. I missed you. Please don't leave."

Alroy quietly turned away and returned to his room. Toby had made himself a bed on the floor and was already settled in.

He opened his eyes and glanced at Alroy.

"I think I should let Pedro's family stay in my house. I'm not sure where I'm going to live yet. Wyatt said to plan on staying here."

"Good idea," Alroy said, climbing into bed.

"I decided to take Wyatt up on his offer." Toby closed his eyes and turned on his side.

"Good." Alroy wasn't sure it was a good idea, but he would respect his friend's decision.

After the lights were out and Alroy was just slipping into dreamland, Toby said, "He's not so bad. Think about it."

"Yeah, he saved me. That was corker."

CHAPTER 52: ALROY

A DOYLE FAMILY BREAKFAST

July 21, 1890
8:30 a.m.

The next morning, Alroy stumbled into the kitchen. His mother was pouring coffee for Toby and Wyatt. Liza sat at the table holding a steaming cup of coffee. Toby's mouth was full of pancakes.

"Smells good," Alroy said.

"Grab some food and sit down," his mother said as she slipped into the chair next to Liza.

"Where's Zella?" he asked, putting four fluffy pancakes on his plate and reaching for the scrambled eggs in the cast-iron skillet.

The back door opened, and Zella rushed into the room. She wore a summer cotton dress with a high collar that covered her neck. Her smile was so big it looked as if it were trying to stretch off her face. She held a newspaper in her hand. She opened the front page and held it up for them to see.

The words "Pedro Hernandez Found" spread across the entire front of the paper.

She pulled out a chair and plopped down.

"They put out a special edition." She glanced at Wyatt, who sipped his coffee and smiled at her. "Wyatt took me to the paper early this morning. I got to help get the paper out. I helped edit the articles for accuracy. They want me to write a series explaining what happened to Pedro.

"Look," she added, pointing to a headline halfway down the page. "Detective Doyle Cracks a Smuggling Ring and Rescues Pedro."

"Are we mentioned in there?" Toby asked.

"Yes," Zella grinned.

Wyatt cleared his throat.

"I don't want any of you getting the idea you can become investigators. You made my job a hundred times harder."

"Yes, we did," said Toby as he shook his fork in Wyatt's direction. "But we solved crimes and saved Pedro and Jaime. Plus, now you're famous. You might become mayor or governor. Maybe a state senator. Also, I have a hundred story ideas."

"God help us all," Wyatt said.

Everyone laughed while Alroy stuffed his face with pancakes and gulped his glass of milk. He didn't know when he'd been so hungry or when breakfast food started tasting delicious.

"One thing," Toby said. "Make sure that the newspaper puts something in about my books when you write your article. Free advertising. You can call me a budding entrepreneur. A young author with big plans."

"I'm not in the business of giving out free advertising," Zella said.

"Okay, before things get out of hand, I have a few things I want to say," Wyatt said.

His words stopped the banter. Alroy wanted to groan and hoped there wasn't a lecture or something worse coming.

"First, as much trouble as you three caused, you also helped. I'm thankful."

"Next time we'll do better," Toby said.

Mrs. Doyle giggled and mussed up Toby's hair.

"Let's hope there isn't a next time," Wyatt said with a hint of a smile. "You'll be happy to hear that Officer Henderson has been dismissed and charged with extortion. He intimidated Pedro's mother and forced her out of her home and took over her boardinghouse. It's unfortunate they didn't report him. We could have taken care of this much earlier, but he threatened to harm her and her children."

"Can't blame her," Liza said.

"You're right," Wyatt agreed. "They can go back home, and Ernest is making sure Henderson pays for repairs. Your friend will soon be out of Sonora Town."

"That's good, but there are still a lot of people living in terrible conditions," Zella said.

"Well, maybe that's something for a reporter to investigate," Wyatt said. "I've done what I can."

"How's Pedro?" Alroy asked to change the subject before Wyatt and Zella ruined the moment with an argument.

"Doctor Stone said he'd examine both boys, make sure they're healthy. I'll bring them in this afternoon to question them. If you promise not to cause trouble, you three can come along."

"We promise," Alroy said. "Just what did you tell the police and the newspaper? You can't very well say Doc took off in his time machine."

Zella grabbed the newspaper and read aloud.

"Detective Doyle stated that Dr. Finch Grimes, who held the boys prisoner, escaped and is at large. He's also wanted for questioning in the case of two other missing boys."

"We'll have to get our story straight. If we start telling people about time travel, we might be sent to a sanitarium for the mentally insane," Toby said.

"Then Nellie Bly can rescue us," Alroy teased.

"Or better yet, Charlie Lee," Toby added, grinning at Zella.

"Who's Charlie Lee?" Wyatt asked.

"No one," Zella said, glaring at Toby.

"A boy," Alroy said. "We think she has a crush on him, and he works at the newspaper."

"I do not," she said.

"Look, she's blushing," Toby said. "Her cheeks turn pink when she sees him. She sort of bats her eyelashes when she talks to him. Plus, she looks at him like he's a cute puppy."

Zella folded her arms across her chest and glared.

"I can't help it. I observe people." Toby snatched a piece of bacon off Alroy's plate.

"Sounds like Toby might be right," Liza said.

"Is he nice?" Ma asked.

"Of course, he's nice," Zella snapped.

Everyone laughed, and Zella covered her face.

Wyatt excused himself and left to get ready for work. Alroy followed him, patting his pocket to make sure the letter was still there. He cleared his throat.

"Wyatt?"

His brother stopped and looked at him with those blue-gray eyes that reminded Alroy of his father.

"Um, I have a letter. Doc gave it to me a few days ago. Our father wrote him, and the letter talks about us. I thought you might want to read it."

Alroy pulled the letter from his pocket and held it out to Wyatt.

His brother stared at the letter in his hand as if it were dangerous.

"You might want to read it when you're alone. It made me cry. Zella, too."

"Thank you. I'll do that."

Alroy watched Wyatt climb the stairs before rushing back to join in the laughter coming from the kitchen.

* * *

Thank you for reading *Finding Pedro. Saving Elijah Is the next book it the series.* (books2read.com/b/Saving-Elijah)

Do you want to know what happened to Doc Grimes? Get a free bonus ebook chapter and sign up for Cora's newsletter. Or use this URL books.corafoerstner.com/84d4koene1

Where's Doc Grimes? He's not a nice man. What does the future have in store for him?

NEWSLETTER SIGN-UP

Get notices and updates from Cora Foerstner about new stories, sales, events, and more.

Use the link:

Sign up for Cora's Newsletter

Use the URL for the Sign-up Page:

https://woodsorrelstudios.com/pages/join-our-mailing-list

ALSO BY CORA FOERSTNER

If you enjoyed this short story, check out Cora's other short stories and short story collections.

Swords of Aroc:

A fantasy adventure series set in Cora's Dragon Speakers' World. These books take place seventy years after *Defying the King.*

Dragon Thieves (Swords of Aroc #1)

Results Unknown (Swords of Aroc #2)

Results Hazy (Swords of Aroc #3)

Results Pending (Swords of Aroc #4)

Results Baffling (Swords of Aroc #5)

Results Resolved (Swords of Aroc #6)

The Dragon Speakers: an epic fantasy duology.

Dragon Speakers (Dragon Speakers #1)

Defying the King (Dragon Speakers #2)

The League of the Daring: an alternate history, time travel, mystery series.

Finding Pedro (League of the Daring Book 1)

Saving Elijah (League of the Daring Book 2)

Miranda's Mystery (League of the Daring Book 3)

Short story Collections:

Mostly Friendly Spooks: Six Spooky Short Stories

Christmas Magic: 5 Original Holiday Shorts Stories

Have Portal. Will Travel: 5 Original Short Stories set in the League of the Daring World.

Short Stories

Buy directly from Cora at corafoerstner.com or woodsorrelstudios.com. Her books are available in major online retailers; use this link to find her books at your preferred retail store: https://books2read.com/corafoerstner/

NOTE FROM THE AUTHOR

Information about Lost in Los Angeles

This story is an alternate history that takes place in 1890 Los Angeles. I uses as many historical facts as possible, but I also took liberties with some facts, which is apparent in the steam technology in the story.

For example, Sonora Town was part of Los Angeles. It was located where China Town is today. Nellie Bly (Elizabeth Jane Cochran—her legal name) did write "Ten Days in a Mad-House" in 1887. The Los Angeles Daily Herald was popular with the public because it had a steam printing press, and people could watch the press in action through its large windows.

However, *The Time Machine* by H. G. Wells wasn't published until 1895, five years before this story. Ike and Kate St. James are inspired by Ike and Adela St Johns, who were reporters for the herald in the 1920s.

History buffs, if you found discrepancies between historical fact in this novel, please forgive my literary licenses. I took liberties for the sake of the story.

Los Angeles was originally named *El Pueblo de Nuestra Señora la Reina de los Ángeles de Porciúncula* (The Town of Our Lady the Queen of the Angels of Porciúncula).

I was born in LA at the Queen of Angels Hospital. I've always love the rich heritage of Southern California. Before and after California became a state, LA had a diverse population.

The first forty-eight Mexican settlers established the *pueblo* in 1781. They represented that diversity: Europeans, Mexicans, African Americans, and Indigenous People. The names of counties, cities, and streets still retain the surnames of those first settlers and the Spanish names early settlers gave them. I tried to capture that diversity as I imagined what the city might look like if stream technology became part of the world.

On the other hand, I didn't want to look at the past through a nostalgic lens. The United States has a long history of racial tension and inequality. LA is no exception. Although those issues are not the emphasis of this story, I didn't sidestep the implications when they played a role in this story.

ABOUT THE AUTHOR

Cora Foerstner wanted to be a spy when she was a young teenager. Since that didn't pan out, she figured the next best thing would be to tell stories about mysteries, awesome places, and people she wished were real.

When Cora isn't writing science fiction and fantasy stories, she plays drinks lots of coffee and tea green, and researches things like dragons, climate change, the end of the world, and other unsavory subjects. She likes video games, is a super fangirl of the Expanse (TV series & Books), and never misses a super-hero movie.

instagram.com/CoraFoerstner

www.ingramcontent.com/pod-product-compliance
Lightning Source LLC
Chambersburg PA
CBHW051203190726
48288CB00006B/1785